NEW YORK REVIEW BOOKS
CLASSICS

T0113081

THE LILY IN THE VALLEY

HONORÉ DE BALZAC (1799–1850), one of the greatest and most influential of novelists, was born in Tours and educated at the Collège Vendôme and the Sorbonne. He began his career as a pseudonymous writer of sensational potboilers before achieving success with a historical novel, *The Chouans*. Balzac then conceived his great work, *La Comédie humaine*, an ongoing series of novels in which he set out to offer a complete picture of contemporary society and manners. Always working under an extraordinary burden of debt, Balzac wrote some eighty-five novels in the course of his last twenty years, including such masterpieces as *Père Goriot*, *Eugénie Grandet*, *Lost Illusions*, and *Cousin Bette*. In 1850, he married Eveline Hańska, a rich Polish woman with whom he had long conducted an intimate correspondence. Three months later he died.

PETER BUSH has translated, among other books, Josep Pla's *The Gray Notebook*, which was awarded the 2014 Ramon Llull Prize for Literary Translation; Joan Sales's *Uncertain Glory*; and Ramón del Valle-Inclán's *Tyrant Banderas* (all available as NYRB Classics). He lives in Bristol.

GEOFFREY O'BRIEN is the author of ten collections of poetry and twelve volumes of criticism, memoir, and cultural history, including *The Phantom Empire*, *The Browser's Ecstasy*, *Castaways of the Image Planet*, *Sonata for Jukebox*, *Where Did Poetry Come From*, and *Arabian Nights of 1934*.

THE LILY IN THE VALLEY

HONORÉ DE BALZAC

Translated from the French by
PETER BUSH

Introduction by
GEOFFREY O'BRIEN

NEW YORK REVIEW BOOKS

New York

THIS IS A NEW YORK REVIEW BOOK
PUBLISHED BY THE NEW YORK REVIEW OF BOOKS
207 East 32nd Street, New York, NY 10016
www.nyrb.com

Translation copyright © 2024 by Peter Bush
Introduction copyright © 2024 by Geoffrey O'Brien

Library of Congress Cataloging-in-Publication Data
Names: Balzac, Honoré de, 1799–1850, author. | Bush, Peter R., 1946– translator.
Title: The lily in the valley / by Honoré de Balzac; translation by Peter Bush.
Other titles: Lys dans la vallée. English
Description: New York: New York Review Books, 2024. | Series: New York
Review Books classics |
Identifiers: LCCN 2023050120 | ISBN 9781681377988 (paperback) |
ISBN 9781681377995 (ebook)
Subjects: LCGFT: Romance fiction. | Novels.
Classification: LCC PQ2167.L8 E5 2024 | DDC 843/.7—dc23/eng/20231026
LC record available at https://lccn.loc.gov/2023050120

ISBN 978-1-68137-798-8
Available as an electronic book; ISBN 978-1-68137-799-5

Printed in the United States of America on acid-free paper.
10 9 8 7 6 5 4 3 2 1

CONTENTS

INTRODUCTION

"NEVER will any mind have existed in so many spheres," writes Honoré de Balzac to his longtime correspondent (and later wife) Madame Hańska, "I am forced to be ten men at the same time, with several spare brains, never sleeping, always being happily inspired and refusing to be sidetracked." He is referring to the period in the mid-1830s when he was producing in a steady stream such diverse novels as *The Quest of the Absolute*, *Père Goriot*, *The Marriage Contract*, *Louis Lambert*, *Seraphita*, and *The Lily in the Valley*—elements of the prose epic which he had not yet titled *The Human Comedy*—although the word "steady" suggests a tranquility that hardly describes how Balzac went about his work.

From the time he announced in early 1835 that he had begun *The Lily in the Valley* until its publication in June 1836, Balzac also finished the novellas *The Girl with the Golden Eyes* and *The Cursed Child*, completed under great stress his spiritualist fantasia *Séraphita*, made revisions to the already published *Louis Lambert* and to the novella *Gobseck*, composed the short novel *The Marriage Contract*, and (in a characteristically disastrous business move) became the majority owner of the weekly paper *Chronique de Paris*, for which he was obliged to furnish an enormous quantity of political journalism. The first installments of *The Lily in the Valley* were serialized in *Revue de Paris* in November, at which point Balzac—enraged at learning that an early draft of the novel had appeared in a Russian periodical—balked at giving the *Revue*'s publisher the rest of the book. A lawsuit and trial ensued, on which Balzac, who won the case, wrote a long report (some 20,000 words), drafted by his account in a single night.

(He also, in April 1836, spent a week in jail for failing to show up for mandatory National Guard duty.) As for *The Lily in the Valley* itself, it took shape as was usual with Balzac through a series of extensively revised printer's proofs, with major elements added at each stage and further significant changes made in the second edition of 1838.

Such were the conditions that produced a novel that stands apart in *The Human Comedy*: It is perhaps the most lyrical of his works, a seeming refuge for the most private and painful experiences. The machinations of intrigue and meticulously detailed profit-seeking that so often dominate his novels recede to the background. He focuses relentlessly on two individuals, an inexperienced young man barely emerged from adolescence and a married woman ten years older, as they enact a singular love story that is also a study in fixation and frustration. Told (aside from a few interpolated letters) in the first person, it reenacts an impasse caught between a union that cannot quite be and a separation that cannot quite be, a constant wavering on the brink that, for the survivor, will not be resolved even by death.

That at least is one way of looking at it. Balzac had publicized his intention to portray a completely virtuous woman—"an image of perfection on Earth"—in a forthcoming novel, as if to atone for the dubious morals of women like Delphine de Nucingen in *Père Goriot*. He also privately acknowledged being struck by *Volupté*, a novel by Sainte-Beuve (the renowned critic who had notably denigrated Balzac's artistry), which in theme, broad outline, and a good many incidental details paralleled what would become *The Lily in the Valley*. But for Balzac, Sainte-Beuve's work crucially lacked the awareness of passion necessary for such a subject: "It is a puritanical book. [Sainte-Beuve's heroine] is not enough of a woman, and there is no danger." The virtue Balzac would seek to embody in Henriette de Mortsauf would be meaningful only if it were sustained despite overpowering temptation—mutual temptation whose force, resisted by Henriette and alternately urged and repressed by her suitor Félix de Vandenesse, courses jaggedly through the book, sweeping everything else to the periphery and turning erotic indecisiveness literally into a matter of life and death.

In its final form, arrived at through successive recastings, the novel consists of a letter written by Félix to a woman he is courting, Natalie de Manerville, who has insisted he tell her of his past as a means of explaining his persistent moodiness and distraction. At the outset he announces: "Yes, a ghost dominates my life ..." His long monologue, a reconstruction of every stage in his relationship with Henriette, is at once a failed resurrection and a failed exorcism. He is addressing himself to another woman, and his account is punctuated with rationalizations, explanations, self-justification, self-mockery; but as he wades deeper into his story, his true intended listener seems to be Henriette herself, as if he could make contact with her through language alone. Balzac's narration drives forward without pause but finds room at every turn for minute specifics—the obscure tokens and hints shared between lovers—that assume nearly sacral importance.

Félix begins with his early years, a story that starts bitterly with the memory of maternal neglect and rejection, evoking "the sorrow of a babe whose lips suck on a sour tit." So many of the details correspond to Balzac's own experience—as he recounts how he was sent to be nursed by a peasant woman and only restored to his loveless family three years later—that these pages have often been taken for overt autobiography. Likewise the figure of Henriette drew comparisons to his early great love Laure de Berny, to whom he read the just-completed novel on their last occasion together. Mme de Berny was, like Henriette, an older woman (twenty-two years Balzac's senior), married with children, and an aristocrat to whom he attributed his most important moral and worldly education; like Henriette, for a long while she firmly resisted his advances. He described her as "more than a friend, more than a sister, almost a mother and even more than that a sort of visible divinity"—it could be Félix de Vandenesse speaking. Balzac, for what it is worth, in a preface to the first edition of *The Lily in the Valley* ridiculed readers who mistook employment of the first person for authorial confession, and insisted that he had "at no point put himself on stage." "I have a horror," he remarked elsewhere, "of prostituting my private emotions to the public."

Indeed, Félix could never be more than a sliver of the complete

Balzac, a self-portrait as unformed adolescent. Félix is just twenty—but perhaps on account of his social awkwardness strikes others as much younger—when he attends a ball in Tours (Balzac's native city) in honor of the Duc d'Angoulême, returning from exile following the Bourbon Restoration of 1814. What follows not only instigates all that comes after but marks the moment that Félix and Henriette can never get past, the decisive point for two destinies. Too shy to fully participate in the festivities, Félix retreats sullenly to a bench in the corner of the crowded ballroom; Henriette, mistaking him for a child, sits down next to him. Her presence imposes itself on Felix in a suite of fragmentary perceptions—by "a female perfume" somehow akin to Oriental poetry, and then, as he shifts his gaze toward her, by "white, rounded shoulders," glimpses of satin skin, breasts partly perceived through a layer of gauze, a neck seen through the parts in glinting hair, a cascade of impressions like newly opened pathways. Without thinking, Félix launches himself at her back "as an infant throws himself on his mother's bosom," kissing her shoulders as she shrieks and reprimands him sharply but with what he perceives as unspoken understanding. After she walks away, he is overwhelmed simultaneously by shame, confusion, and newly awakened desire. From this spontaneous childish assault, in a matter of a few seconds, an association forms that is more indissoluble than either can imagine.

The book begins to sound its epic dimension after Félix's mother, perturbed by his dazed demeanor, sends him off to stay with a family friend in the Touraine countryside. Traveling on foot, as he pauses to look down into a valley bathed by the Indre River, Félix spots a glint of white amid the grounds of the château Clochegourde. It is, as he will soon learn, his unknown idol, standing in a white muslin dress under an apricot tree. The glimpse unfurls an extended evocation of the scene before him—of "the long ribbon of sunny water flowing between two green banks, past the lines of poplars," of the valley where "birds sang, cicadas chattered, it was one great melody"—the first of many such exultant passages. No matter what is happening to the humans in its midst, the landscape will continue to speak in a language of fecundity, enchanting and troubling in equal measure. The valley—its terrain, vegetation, and waterways, its odors and colors—becomes in Balzac's rhapsodies an ecstatic permeating presence, often in stark contrast to the miseries of its inhabitants. When Félix goes hunting for flowers to make bouquets for Henriette, they become elaborate carnal visions, "tousled and unruly, flames and triple darts; jagged, spear-shaped leaves; stalks as tortuous as the desires writhing in the depths of your soul." The natural images that interpenetrate the book's sentences—metaphors for emotions and imaginings that cannot otherwise be articulated—function as an embedded poem tracing the novel's central neural pathways.

Introduced as a guest at Clochegourde, Félix at first senses his heart electrified in the assurance of "secret acts that would change it forever, the way animals cheer up when they sense fine weather is coming." Given the opportunity to bask in Henriette's presence, he unfolds in extraordinary detail his fetishistic attachment to all her aspects, imagining himself "wallowing in the ringlets of her hair," and finding a distinct pleasure in her voicing of each separate vowel and consonant: "the *ch*, on her lips, was like a caress." But his expectations of voluptuous fulfillment are quickly entangled in the reclusive and dreary circumstances of Henriette and her family. Her husband, the Comte de Mortsauf, an émigré during the Revolution, has been prematurely "aged by the great shipwreck that brought the eighteenth century to a close"; he is ill-tempered, prone to gratuitous cruelty, his mind increasingly disordered. Her two children are sickly, an inheritance from the count's "loves of a low order" during his years of exile. Raised like Félix by an unloving mother, she found sympathy only from an aunt, now dead, who initiated her into mystical Christian doctrines. Henriette has now resigned herself, as a stoic obligation, to the silent sufferings of her marriage.

In the world beyond the château, history is happening. The Bourbons are restored; Napoleon escapes from Elba; Félix, having run secret messages for the newly exiled king, finds prolonged refuge at Clochegourde; after Waterloo the Second Restoration reestablishes the fortunes of Henriette's family. "This revolution," Félix testifies, "meant nothing to me. Mme de Mortsauf's least word or gesture were the only acts I deemed important." The two now inhabit a secret world they have created for themselves, like children seeking a haven from the adult realm. They recognize themselves as soul mates: "We felt we were twins from the same breast." It is a world with its own rules and rituals arrived at through a series of advances and repulses. For the first time Henriette feels entirely understood: "How can one so young know such things? Were you a woman once?" Félix still hopes to be her lover, but learns to accept the privilege of calling her Henriette, the special name her beloved late aunt gave her (to her husband she is Blanche, a name white like her muslin dress), and the only rarely accorded pleasure of kissing her hand—"the back of which was all she ever offered—never the palm—the boundary beyond which sensual pleasure perhaps began for her." He persuades himself that he feels hallowed, ordained like a priest into an order of worship.

Felix and Henriette speak to each other at a level of heightened consciousness somewhere between Romantic poetry and mystical explication. But the world they inhabit is altogether palpable, and its pressures (as always with Balzac) inexorable. The demands of protocol and caste and efficient property management are not to be denied, any more than the demands of the body. Even if Félix wants to experience the ethereal as carnal, to merge with another soul somehow "visible and tangible," he is soon enough caught up in mundane practicalities—urged on by Henriette, who turns out to have a firmly pragmatic side and who if she is not to be his lover will be his worldly mentor. Summoned to Paris by Louis XVIII, he finds his role as a government functionary and habitué of fashionable society; in due time he meets with a reckless Englishwoman prepared to cater lavishly to his long-suppressed desires.

Nothing, however, liberates him from Henriette's sway, and when the knowledge of his affair triggers her catastrophic physical decline, he will remain at her side. This last paroxysm is stretched to agonizing length, as Henriette reveals layer upon layer of hidden selves, doubts and desires never before admitted. She dies, as it were, a succession of deaths before a final ostensible redemptive triumph, expiring amid what feels like a religious tableau. A doctor administers opium to calm her "mad outpourings," a cleric absolves her, and appearances are preserved: a modern reader finds it easy to detect irony in the scene. Balzac intended, he asserted, a very different reading. He wrote to Madame Hańska after the book's publication: "There are know-nothings who fail to understand the beauty of Madame de Mortsauf's death, and who do not perceive the struggle between matter and spirit which is the basis of Christianity. They see only the imprecations hurled by the disappointed flesh ... and refuse to do justice to the sublime calm of the soul, when the Countess has made her confession and dies in sanctity."

Henriette had already told Félix, "There are lots of different *me*s in me." The same of course goes for Félix, who in his conversation with himself tries out different roles, different self-images, different interpretations of what has already happened. As he persists in revisiting the ground of a passionate standoff, the effect is not of repetition but of constant reframing, evoking Balzac's own impulse toward continual revision. His first version of *The Lily in the Valley* gave franker expression to Henriette's crisis of regret; it was at the urging of Laure de Berny—her own death approaching as Henriette's was read to her—that he deleted the more extreme details. There are lots of different Balzacs in Balzac. Not only are his books filled with characters; his characters are filled with characters, overflowing with what they might have been, were once but no longer are, or can imagine themselves becoming for better or worse. Félix and Henriette constantly shift identities, becoming mother and son, brother and sister, and at length an androgynous fusion, "that wonderful creature dreamed of by Plato." Bedeviled by change and contradiction both within and without, Félix searches for a final fixed vision in which he can rest. A natural image that charms his eye early in the book has become by its end an omen of final disaster: a solitary flowering bush on a desolate heath.

Félix does not get the last word. His narrative is followed by a reply from its recipient, a sarcastic brush-off: "Do you know the woman I pity? The *fourth* woman you love ... I renounce the glorious task of loving you . . . No woman, I warn you, will ever want to enter your heart and rub shoulders with the dead woman you keep there." But there is no need to take Natalie de Manerville's letter as a final judgment. It is just another irrevocable boundary line, in the same way that Félix, departing Clochegourde, is left definitively alienated from "the poetry of balconies, borders, balustrades, terraces, trees, and every perspective": the map of a private world lost to all but memory.

—GEOFFREY O'BRIEN

THE LILY IN THE VALLEY

To Monsieur J.-B. Nacquart
Member of the Academy of Medicine

Dear Doctor, here is one of the most closely hewn stones in the second layer of a literary edifice that has been built slowly and laboriously. I want to inscribe your name here, both to thank the man of learning who once saved me and to celebrate someone who has been a friend day in and day out.

de Balzac

TO MADAME LA COMTESSE NATALIE DE MANNERVILLE

I will bow to your wishes. It is the privilege of the woman we love more than she loves us to make us forget the rules of common sense at every turn. Lest a scowl form on your brow or a sulky expression on your lips that are saddened by the slightest refusal, we travel prodigious distances, give our blood, and apportion our future. Today, you want my past, and here you have it. Although by obeying you, Natalie, you should be aware that I have had to revisit some hideous places. But why are you so suspicious of the long reveries that suddenly descend on me at moments of intense joy? Why must you, a woman who is loved, be so angry when I fall silent? Couldn't you speculate on the reasons for my moodiness without demanding to know what they are? Do you harbor secrets that require mine for their absolution? In the end, Natalie, you have intuited something, and perhaps it is for the best if you know everything: Yes, a ghost dominates my life; vague traces of it surface, provoked by the tiniest word, and often hover above my head. Startling secrets are buried deep in my soul like those marine outcroppings that break the surface in placid weather, fragments of which storm waves cast up on beaches. Although the effort required to express these ideas may have constrained old emotions that hurt when they flare up, if this confession strikes out and wounds, remember that you were the one who threatened me if I didn't obey; please don't punish me for doing just that. I can only hope my candor stokes your affection. Till this evening.

Félix

TWO CHILDHOODS

To WHAT tearful talent will we one day owe that most melancholy of elegies, the portrayal of the silent torture suffered by souls whose tender roots find only stone in the soil of home, whose first shoots are ravaged by hands of hate, whose flowers are blighted by frost the moment they blossom? What poet will sing of the sorrow of a babe whose lips suck on a sour breast, whose smiles are crushed by a harsh glint in a cruel eye? A fiction describing the misery of those oppressed by their nearest, who ought to have cherished their feelings, would be the true story of my early years. What pride could I, a newborn babe, possibly injure? What physical or moral defect warranted my mother's coldness? Was I a child spawned by duty, a chance birth, a life that was a constant reproach?

Sent to a wet nurse in the countryside, forgotten by my family for three years, when I returned to the parental hearth, I was so totally ignored that the servants felt sorry for me. I can't think what warmth or good fortune it was that saved me from that first disappointment: as a child, I was unaware, as a man, clueless. Rather than soothe me, my brother and two sisters enjoyed tormenting me. That pact by which children usually conceal each other's peccadillos, a first step in learning a sense of honor, was nonexistent. Indeed, I was often punished for my brother's mischief, and I was never allowed to appeal against such unfairness. Was it a growing knowledge of the ways of the world, flourishing in childhood, that drove them to intensify their persecution of me and ingratiate themselves with a mother they also feared? Or was it because they were eager to imitate her lead? Or needed to test out their own strength? Or lacked compassion? Perhaps

7

it was a combination of all those things that denied me the comfort of sibling affection. Deprived of tenderness so young, I found nothing to love, even though nature made me crave tenderness! Does an angel exist somewhere who collects the sighs of sensitive, constantly rejected souls? If spurned feelings turn to hate in some hearts, in mine they hardened into a crust through which they later erupted into my life. Depending on one's character, trembling fits may loosen the fibers, and engender fear, a fear that that impels one to cower and feeds a debilitating weakness that induces servility. However, in my case, relentless mental torture fired an energy that only expanded with use, and predisposed my soul to offer moral resistance. As I was always awaiting the next blow, like a martyr anticipating the next turn of the screw, my whole being was permeated by tight-lipped resignation that stifled any childlike spontaneity and fun, a stance interpreted as a sign of stupidity, which only bolstered my mother's dire premonitions. The stream of injustices aroused premature pride, which I struggled to comprehend, and which, naturally, nipped in the bud any inclination to malevolence such an upbringing might have nurtured.

Although my mother neglected me, I did sometimes irk her conscience, and she would talk about my education and indicate she wished to take it over herself, triggering horrible bouts of shaking as I imagined the misery daily contact with her would bring. I was grateful for my state of abandonment, and I was happy to linger in our garden playing with pebbles, observing insects, and gazing into the blue sky. Although solitude itself gives rise to reverie, my love of contemplation was sparked by an incident typical of my early trials. I was so left to my own devices that our governess often forgot to put me to bed. One evening I was peacefully crouched under a fig tree, gazing at a star with that curious rush of enthusiasm that captivates children, my own precocious melancholy adding to it a kind of emotional depth. My sisters were playing and shouting: I heard their distant din as an accompaniment to the flow of my ideas. The noise stopped; night fell. My mother suddenly noticed I wasn't indoors. To avoid criticism, our governess, the horrendous Mademoiselle Caroline, gave substance to my mother's misplaced fears by implying that I hated our home; that if she hadn't kept a wary eye on me, I'd have fled long ago: I was sly, not stupid, and that, of all the children committed to her care, she'd never once met a child whose attitude was as appalling as mine. She pretended to look for me, calling my name out: I replied; she walked to the fig tree, where she knew she would find me.

"And what do you think you were doing here?" she asked.

"I was stargazing"

"You were *not* stargazing" said my mother, listening to us from her balcony. "As if children your age knew anything about astronomy!"

"Oh, madame!" exclaimed Mademoiselle Caroline, "he's turned on the cistern tap and flooded the garden."

That caused a hue and cry. My sisters had been having fun turning on the tap and watching water stream out, but, surprised by a sudden gush that had drenched them, they'd panicked and scampered away without turning it off. I was cornered, found guilty of the prank, and, accused of lying when I protested my innocence: I was severely punished. And that *was* horrendous! My love of the stars was ridiculed and my mother banned me from the garden in the evenings. Such tyrannical decisions fan greater passion in children than in grown-ups; children can focus only on what they are being denied, which at a stroke becomes irresistibly attractive. I was often whipped because of my star. As I could confide in nobody, I recounted my sorrows to the star, in the delightful inner patter children employ when stammering out their first ideas, just as those children once stammered their first words. A twelve-year-old schoolboy, I still felt indescribable pleasure when gazing at my star: impressions from our first encounters in life stay deeply etched in our hearts.

Five years my senior, Charles was as handsome a child as he later was a man: favored by my father, doted on by my mother, the great hope of the family, he was king of our household. My brother, a well-built and robust child, had a private tutor. A sickly whelp myself, I was sent from the age of five to a prep school in town, as a day boy; my father's valet took me in the morning and brought me back at night. I was sent with a basket of meager provisions, while my classmates brought copious amounts of food. The contrast between my penury and their wealth spawned unimaginable grief. The famous rillettes and rillons of Tours were the main dishes for them in what was our midday meal, between the breakfast and the supper we ate the moment we arrived home. Those tasty delicacies, so prized by gourmands, were rarely served on aristocratic tables in Tours: though it was possible I might have heard of them before I became a day boy, I'd never had the good fortune to see the scrumptious brown stuff spread on a slice of bread. However, even if these dishes hadn't been in vogue at my school, my desire to try them wouldn't have been any the weaker; it had become an obsession, like the craving aroused in a most elegant Parisian duchess by the stew her concierge prepared, and that she, given her status, could soon satisfy. Children detect the envy in a look as easily as a person knows an amorous gaze: I thus became the chief target of their taunts. My classmates, who almost all came from lower-middle-class families, would walk over to show me their high-quality rillettes and ask whether I knew how they were cooked and where they were sold, and why it was that I never had any. They licked their lips as they paraded their rillons, scraps of pork offal sautéed in the pig's own lard, with the appearance of cooked truffles; they inspected my basket, found only cheeses from Olivet or dried fruit, and hurt me sorely with the murderous jibe "So is this beyond your means?" and for me, that summed up the different treatment my brother and I were receiving.

In my case, this contrast between my neglected state and the happiness of others blighted the roses of childhood and stunted the green shoots of youth. The first time I held out my hand to receive the tidbit I had so coveted, duped by the generous glance and disingenuous flourish of the practical joker who offered it to me, it was only for him to withdraw his slice of bread, to guffaws from his friends, who were in on the act. If even the finest minds are susceptible to vanity, mustn't we forgive a child who weeps to see himself scorned and jeered? Put to such a test, haven't many children become greedy, cringing, or beggarly? I fought back against my baiters. Courage, driven by despair, made me someone to be feared, though I continued to be an object of hatred, and I was ill equipped to deal with their treacherous stratagems. One evening, when returning home, I was hit in the back by a handkerchief full of pebbles. When the valet, who brutally beat my attacker, told my mother what had happened, she exclaimed: "This nasty child will bring us nothing but calamity!"

My self-esteem continued to dwindle when I saw that I bred as much repulsion at school as at home. I became deeply introspective. A second fall of snow withered the seeds scattered in my soul. Nonetheless, the children I saw being treated lovingly were out-and-out hellions, and that sustained my pride: I kept myself to myself. I found it impossible to find an outlet for the feelings swelling my heart. My teacher always saw me as lonely, frowning, and hated by the other students, and he confirmed to my family their erroneous suspicions as to my bad character. The moment I could read and write, my mother sent me to Pont-le-Voy, a boarding school run by Oratorian brothers, who received children my age in a class known as Latin Steps, for pupils whose backwardness made them struggle with the Latin primer.

I stayed eight years, receiving no visitors and leading the life of a pariah. And this is how and why. I was given a mere three francs for my monthly allowance, a sum that barely covered the cost of the pens, penknives, rulers, ink, and paper we had to supply ourselves. As I was in no position to buy stilts, skipping-ropes, or any of the items necessary for games at school, I was excluded from all play; to join in, I'd have been forced to toady to the wealthy or flatter the bullies in my house. I despised those options that many children are quick to take. I skulked under a tree, engrossed in mournful daydreams, and read books the librarian gave out every month. I felt so much bitterness in my wretched solitude! My lonely spirit suffered so! Just imagine what my sensitive soul must have felt on my first prize day, when I was to be awarded the most coveted prizes, those for composition and translation. The time came to go up on the stage and receive them, to applause and cheers, but neither my father nor my mother was there to celebrate, though the hall was packed with the parents of all my classmates. Instead of kissing the prize-giver, as was the custom, I threw myself at his chest and sobbed my heart out. That night, I burnt my certificates on the stove. Parents stayed in town in the week preceding the prize day; every morning my classmates cheerfully decamped with them, while I, whose parents were but a few miles away, stayed in school with the *outre-mers*, the name given to pupils whose parents lived in the colonies or foreign parts. In the evening, during prayers, the vindictive returning classmates boasted of the wonderful meals they had eaten with their parents. You will see my misery continue to deepen as the social spheres I enter widen.

I worked with might and main to overthrow the sentence condemning me to a life trapped inside of myself! I clung to many hopes at length, but they would soar only to be dashed in a day. To persuade my parents to visit me, I wrote emotional missives that were perhaps overly demonstrative, but should my mother really have reproached me for that, and carped ironically at my style? I didn't lose heart, and merely pledged to meet whatever conditions my parents set if they were to come: I begged my sisters to help, wrote them on their birthdays and saint's days, like a pathetic waif, but it was all to no avail. As the next prize day approached, I redoubled my supplications and mentioned my coming glories. Duped by my parents' silence, I waited for them in high spirits, and told my classmates that they were coming; then, when families started to arrive, the footsteps of the old porter who called out pupils' names rang out across the playground, and I shuddered and felt sick. The old fellow never uttered mine.

On the day I revealed to my confessor how I had led an accursed existence, he pointed to the skies, where the palm promised by our Savior's *Beati qui lugent* was growing! After my first communion, I threw myself deep into the mysteries of prayer, entranced by the religious ideas whose moral fairy tales so enchant youthful minds. Driven by my ardent faith, I prayed to God to rekindle on my behalf the fascinating miracles I'd read about in the Martyrology. At five, I flew off on a star; at twelve, I went knocking on sanctuary doors. Aroused by the flow of dreams in my imagination, spiritual ecstasy imbued my sensibility and heightened my capacity to think. I've often attributed those sublime visions to angels charged with readying my soul for a divine destiny. They endowed my eyes with the gift of seeing the inner spirit of things and prepared my heart for the magic that renders the poet unhappy when he is gripped by a fatal impulse to compare what he perceives with what exists, or his great aspirations with his puny achievements. They inscribed my mind with a book in which I read what I should say; they gifted my lips with the wit of a scribbler.

My father wasn't happy with what the Oratorian brothers taught, and he took me out of Pont-le-Voy and placed me in a Paris lycée, in the Marais. I was fifteen. When they assessed my ability, Pont-le-Voy's master of rhetoric was deemed worthy of joining the third-year students. I again felt the pain I had experienced at home, prep school, and the oratory, though it found a new guise in the Lepître establishment. My father had given me no money. When my parents discovered that the school would feed and dress me, stuff me with Latin, and cram me with Greek, they soon came to an arrangement. In the course of my school life, I've had over a thousand classmates, and I never found another subject to such indifference. A fanatical supporter of the Bourbons, M. Lepître had been in contact with my father on the occasion of the royalist attempt to rescue Queen Marie-Antoinette from the Temple Prison; they had now gotten back in touch and M. Lepître felt obliged to make up for my father's "oversight," but the monthly amount he gave me was a pittance, because he was unsure of my family's true intentions.

Boarding facilities had been established in the Joyeuse town house, which, like all former grandee residencies, had a porter's lodge. During the recess before the monitor took us to Lycée Charlemagne, well-heeled pupils ate breakfast there, served to them by Doisy, the porter. M. Lepître knew nothing about it, or he turned a blind eye to the little side business run by Doisy, a die-hard smuggler whom the pupils were keen to cultivate an association with: he secretly covered up for our misdeeds, said nothing when we got back late, and acted as an intermediary with people who rented out banned books. Breakfast with a cup of milky coffee was an aristocratic repast, explained by the excessive prices charged for colonial produce under Napoleon. If sugar and coffee were a luxury for our parents, we pupils saw them as a sign of arrant superiority that would have been enough to fire our passion, if inclination to imitate, greediness, and the contagiousness of fashion hadn't sufficed. Doisy gave us all credit, assuming we had sisters or aunts who would honor pupils' pledges and pay their debts. I resisted the lure of his refreshments for a long time. If those so quick to judge me had known the power of the temptation, the heroic way I stoically resisted its lure, and the rage I kept on a leash during my months of resistance, they would surely have stanched my tears rather than increased the flow. As a child, how could I possess the nobility of spirit to scorn the contempt of others? Besides, I was perhaps prey to a series of social vices whose strength was reinforced by my own covetous desires.

Towards the end of my second year, the parents came to Paris. My brother dropped by to tell me the day they would be arriving: he lived in Paris but had never paid me a visit. My sisters were included in the trip and we were to explore Paris together. On the first day we would dine in the Palais-Royal so as to be close to the Théâtre-Français. Despite the heady excitement aroused by the prospect of such unexpected festivity, my glee was soon doused by a stormy blast that individuals used to being unhappy are quick to anticipate. I was compelled to come clean about the hundred francs I owed Doisy, as he was threatening to ask my parents for the money himself. I contrived to make my brother my go-between with Doisy and the man, to voice my regret and mediate forgiveness. Father was inclined to be indulgent. Mother was pitiless, petrifying me with her piercing blue eyes as she hollered horrific prophecies. "What would I be like later in life if, at the age of seventeen, I committed such outrages? Was I really *her* son? Did I plan to ruin the family? Did I think I was the *only* child in the house? Did not the career my brother Charles was pursuing require a tidy investment that was truly merited by behavior that would bathe our family in glory, while I would only bring it shame? Was I going to force my two sisters to marry without dowries? Was I unaware of the value of money and what I cost? When did sugar and coffee ever contribute to a good education? Wasn't the life I led an apprenticeship in every known vice?" Marat was an angel in comparison. After being battered by that torrent which released a thousand terrors in my soul, my brother took me back to the boarding-house: I missed out on the meal at the Frères-Provençaux and was deprived of the sight of Talma acting in *Britannicus*. And that was the nature of the conversation with my mother, after I hadn't seen her for twelve years.

When I finished studying the humanities, my father left me under the tutelage of M. Lepître: I had to learn geometry and calculus, complete my first year in law, and begin my higher education. With a room and my daily board provided, and liberated from classes, I believed I had signed a truce with poverty. However, though I was now nineteen, or perhaps *because* I was now nineteen, my father continued with the system that had sent me to prep school without a bite to eat, to secondary school without proper pocket money, and put me in debt to Doisy. I had barely a sou. What can you hope to do in Paris if you are broke? Besides, my freedom was cleverly curtailed. M. Lepître charged a monitor with accompanying me to law school, delivering me to the teacher, and picking me up later. A girl would have faced less surveillance than what my mother's fears prescribed to keep me out of harm's way. Paris quite rightly terrified my parents. On the sly, students are also concerned by what preoccupies the young ladies in their boardinghouses; whatever precautions are taken, girls will always talk of lovers, and boys, of women. But in Paris at the time, conversations between friends focused on the oriental, exotic world that was the Palais-Royal. The Palais-Royal was an El Dorado of love where, any given evening, everything ran on a flow of cash. The most virginal doubts ended there, and burning curiosity could be soon satisfied! The Palais-Royal and I were two asymptotes that were pointed at one another, but never met. This is how fate thwarted all my attempts.

My father had introduced me to one of my aunts, who lived on the Île Saint-Louis, where I was to dine on Thursdays and Sundays, escorted by Mme or M. Lepître, who went out on those days and collected me in the evening on their way home. What curious entertainment! The Marquise de Listomère was a grand lady, fond of ceremony, who never thought of giving me a ducat. Old as a cathedral, her face painted like a cameo, sumptuously dressed, she lived in her town house as if Louis XV were still alive, welcoming only old women and gentlemen to gatherings of fossilized bodies where I felt I must be in a cemetery. Nobody addressed me, and I didn't feel confident enough to take the initiative. Their hostile or frosty glances made me ashamed of my youth, which seemed to rile everyone. I plotted my escape, benefiting from their indifference, and decided to slip off one day, the moment dinner was over, and rush to the Palais-Royal esplanade with its fashion shops and fashionable strollers. Once my aunt was engrossed in her game of whist, she ignored me completely. Her valet, Jean, wasn't concerned about M. Lepître, but those dire suppers were miserably protracted by their aged jaws and ill-fitting dentures. Finally, one evening, between eight and nine, I did make it to the staircase, shaking like Bianca Cappello,[1] on the day she made her escape, but when the porter opened the front door, I spotted M. Lepître's carriage in the street and heard the fine fellow wheezily summon me. Chance fatally intervened three times to stop the Palais-Royal hell from becoming the paradise of my youth. The day when, ashamed I was twenty and still so innocent, I resolved to confront all potential dangers and put an end to that, at the precise moment I was trying to part company with M. Lepître as he climbed into his carriage—a difficult operation, because he was as fat as Louis XVIII and club-footed!—my mother turned the corner in her post chaise! Her gaze halted me in my tracks and I was rooted there like a bird faced by a snake. What chance occurrence had led to that encounter? Nothing could have been more natural. Napoleon was making his last flourishes. Sensing the return of the Bourbons was nigh, my father had come to enlighten my brother, who was already employed as an imperial diplomat. He had come from Tours with my mother. My mother had taken it upon herself to remove me from the dangers that seemingly threatened the capital, in the eyes of those who cannily followed every step being taken by their enemies.

I was plucked from Paris the very moment my stay there might have proved lethal. A tormented imagination continuously rocked by repressed desires, the cares of a life made miserable by constant privation, had led me to plunge myself into my studies, as men tired of their fate used once to shut themselves inside a cloister. Study had become a passion that might have been fatal if it had incarcerated me at a moment when young people should be enjoying the enticements of the springtime of life.

This brief sketch of a youth, in which you can discover countless laments, was necessary to explain the influence it had on my future life. Afflicted by so many sickening measures, I was small, skinny, and pallid, even in my twenties. My impulsive soul struggled in a body that appeared to be frail, but which, according to an old doctor in Tours, was undergoing the final phase of its fusion with a temperament of iron. Childish in body and old in thought, I had read so much, meditated so much, that metaphysically I was acquainted with life's lofty heights by the time I was on the verge of experiencing the tortuous twists of the gullies and gravelly paths on its plains. The unexpected and random had brought me to that delectable stage when the soul first begins to ache, when it is aroused by voluptuous pleasure, when it discovers that everything is fresh and piquant. I found myself between a puberty prolonged by my woes and a manliness sprouting its green shoots late. No young man was ready to feel and to love more than I was. If you wish to understand my story, think back to that beautiful time when one's lips have yet to tell a lie; when one's gaze is sincere, though veiled by eyelids weighed down by timidity contested by desire; when one's mind resists worldly casuistry; and one's timorous heart quashes the generous spirit of first forays.

I won't describe in detail the journey from Paris to Tours with my mother. Her icy manner killed dead my outbursts of tenderness. As we left each new posting house, I promised myself I would speak, but a look or word would scare off the opening sentences I'd carefully conceived. In Orléans, at bedtime, my mother reproached me for being silent. I threw myself at her feet, embraced her knees, wept warm tears, and opened a heart to her that swelled with affection; craving tenderness, I tried to win her over with eloquent pleas, in a tone that would have stirred the cruelest stepmother. My mother responded by saying that I was playacting. I complained that she had abandoned me; she called me a hard-hearted son. I was so desperate I ran to the bridge in Blois, prepared to throw myself into the Loire. The height of the parapet foiled my suicide bid.

Upon my arrival, my sisters, who didn't know me at all, displayed astonishment rather than affection, though, later, comparatively, they came to seem very friendly. I was given a bedroom on the third floor. You will understand the extent of my wretchedness if I tell you that my mother left me, a twenty-year-old, with no linens beyond the miserable provision from my boardinghouse, and no wardrobe beyond what I had worn in Paris. If I rushed from one end of the sitting room to the other to retrieve her handkerchief, she only deigned to grant me the cold thank-you a woman grants her manservant. Forced to scrutinize her to detect any wavering moment when I might offer a bouquet of tenderness, I met only a dry, lean, grand lady, a gambler, and selfish and rude, like all the Listomères, whose contemptuousness is part of their dowry. All she saw in life were duties to be performed; all the cold women I have known have made a religion of duty as she did; she received our adoration as a priest receives incense at Mass; my brother seemed to have soaked up all the scant maternal feeling her heart possessed. She aimed endless barbs of cutting sarcasm at us, the weapon of the heartless, turning it against us, and we could say nothing in reply. Despite her prickly attitude, our instinctive feelings were so strong that they held fast, despite the religious terror inspired by a mother who extracted such a great price for disappointing her, and our love's sublimely misconceived expectations continued until the day that, later in life, she received her comeuppance. The moment children begin their reprisals, their indifference, spawned by past disappointments, swollen by the bitter wreckage, endures well beyond the grave. This arrant despotism killed off the voluptuous ideas I had so foolishly thought to satisfy in Tours. In my desperation I threw myself at my father's library and read all the books I'd never read. My lengthy study sessions spared me all contact with my mother, but also undermined my morale. Now and then, my elder sister, the one who married our cousin, the Marquis de Listomère, tried to console me, but she could never dim the fury I felt. I wanted to die.

Historic events, of which I had no knowledge, were on the horizon. The Duc d'Angoulême was making his way from Bordeaux to join Louis XVIII in Paris, and each town he visited welcomed him with ovations fanned by the enthusiasm old France felt for the restoration of the Bourbons. The Touraine hustled and bustled, rejoicing at the prospect of its legitimate princes: bunting in windows, locals in their Sunday best, and festive preparations; a mysteriously intoxicating *je ne sais quoi* in the air made me want to attend the ball to be held in the prince's honor. When I summoned up the courage to inform my mother of my wish—she was too ill to go herself—she flew into a rage. I was so ignorant I must surely have just arrived from the Congo! How could I ever think that our family would *not* be presented at this ball? Wasn't it my responsibility to go, given that my father and brother were absent? Didn't I have a mother who always thought of her children's happiness? At a stroke, a son she'd almost disowned was placed center stage.

I was as bewildered by my newfound importance as by the flood of sarcasm with which my mother greeted my request. I questioned my sisters, and learned that my mother, ever inclined to histrionic gestures, had expressed her concern about the state of my wardrobe. Shocked by her demands, no tailor in Tours had felt capable of taking on my outfitting. My mother had therefore given the task to her daily help, who, as was the custom in the provinces, knew how to cut every kind of cloth. A cornflower-blue suit was secretly assembled in a rough-and-ready manner. Silk stockings and new dancing shoes were easily purchased; men's waistcoats were worn short, so I could borrow one of my father's, and for the very first time I wore a frilly shirt, its flutes swelling my chest and tangling with the knot of my tie. When I was dressed, I looked so unlike myself that I needed flattery from my sisters before I could drum up the courage to appear before the great and good of Touraine. It was a formidable challenge! This august occasion had too many takers for the number of invitations issued. Thanks to my slender build, I was able to sneak under the tent erected in the grounds of the Papion mansion and approach the armchair where the prince was enthroned. I was instantly stifled by the heat and dazzled by the lights, the red drapes, the gilded decorations, and the costumes and diamonds on display at this, the first gala ball I'd ever attended. I was jostled by a host of men and women who rushed and collided in a cloud of dust. The blaring brass and thunder of Bourbon military music were drowned out by cries of "Vive le Duc d'Angoulême!" "Vive le Roi!" and "Vivent les Bourbons!" The gala was a riot of enthusiasm where everyone strove to outdo their neighbor in the furious race to approach the rising Bourbon sun, genuine self-serving egotism that left me cold and made me shrink back and retreat within myself.

Buffeted like straw in that gale, I felt a childish wish to *be* the Duc d'Angoulême and mingle with those princes parading before a gawping public. A man from Tours's ridiculous envy led ambition to flower that my character and circumstances ennobled. Who hasn't longed for that adoration, which I was to see repeated on a grandiose scale a few months later, when the whole of Paris rushed to the emperor on his return from the island of Elba? That power wielded over the masses, whose feelings and lifeblood flow to a single soul, suddenly summoned me dedicate myself to Glory, that high priestess who slaughters the French today, as a Druid priestess once sacrificed the Gauls.[2] Out of nowhere, I then chanced upon the woman who was never to stop encouraging my ambitious desires, and who fulfilled them by launching me into the heart of royalty.

Too shy to invite someone to dance, afraid anyway that I would make a mess of it if I did, I naturally became a wallflower with no idea what to do. I was still hurting from the bruises I'd received from the trampling throngs, when an officer stamped on my feet, which were already swollen, as much from the tight-fitting leather as from the heat. That final disaster put me off any idea of celebrating. Because I couldn't possibly leave, I took refuge in a corner and sat and skulked at the end of an empty bench.

Misled by my feeble appearance, a woman decided I must be a child dozing off while waiting for his mother to return at her convenience, and she sat down next to me, as a bird settles on its nest. I immediately smelled a female perfume that fired my soul like a poetic illumination from the Orient. I glanced at my neighbor: more dazzled by her than I'd been by any aspect of the festivities, I found in her my reason to celebrate. If you've understood my life before that time, you can imagine the feelings that welled in my heart. My eyes were bewitched by her white, rounded shoulders that I wanted to roll down like a hill, the pale pink shoulders now seeming to blush at their newfound nakedness, modest shoulders with a soul, satin skin gleaming like silk. Those shoulders were separated by a dip, that my eyes, much bolder than my hands, ran themselves down. I sat up straight, all atremble, to stare at her bodice, and I saw a beguiling, chastely veiled bosom, its perfect, azure globes nestling cozily in layers of lace. Every least aspect of her head was a lure that aroused infinite joy: glinting hair gathered above a neck velvety as a young child's, white lines a comb had drawn that my imagination ran along as if tracing virgin paths: everything made me feel faint. After I'd checked that nobody was watching, I threw myself at that back, as an infant throws himself on his mother's bosom. I kissed and nuzzled those shoulders. She shrieked—a cry the music drowned out—then she turned, saw me, and said: "Monsieur!"

Naturally, if she'd said: "My good little fellow, what *do* you think you are doing?" I'd probably have killed her, but that "Monsieur" brought warm tears to my eyes. I was riveted by a gaze that brimmed with saintly anger and a gorgeous head crowned by a tiara of silvery hair that perfectly matched her beautiful back. A purple flush of offended modesty smoldered on her cheeks, but it had already been disarmed by the forgiveness of a woman who had glimpsed the onset of furious passion and infinite adoration in my tears of regret. She departed regally. I felt then the ridiculousness of my situation and only then realized how absurd I looked in my suit. I was truly ashamed. I was in a daze, savoring the apple I'd just bitten, my lips cherishing the warmth of the blood I'd just sensed, as my eyes pursued that woman who'd descended from the heavens. Gripped by the first fleshly signs of heartfelt passion, I wandered through the ballroom, as if it were a desert, unable to find my stranger. I returned to that bench and stretched out in a state of metamorphosis.

A new soul, a soul with iridescent wings, had burst from its chrysalis. Fallen from the blue steppes where I had admired it, my precious star had turned into a woman, who retained its brightness, glitter, and freshness. Totally ignorant of love, I found that I was suddenly in love. Isn't the first eruption of man's fiercest sentiment the strangest thing? I'd met a number of pretty women in my aunt's salon, but none had made the least impression. Is there really a moment, a convergence of stars, a confluence of circumstances, a woman among the many, that shapes an exclusive passion, at a moment when passion embraces the entire sex? As I reflected that my chosen one lived in the Touraine, I delighted in the air I was breathing and in the blue of its sky discovered a color I'd seen nowhere else. If I was mentally ecstatic, I looked as if I were seriously ill, and my mother felt a mixture of fear and remorse. Like an animal sensing a coming danger, I crouched in a corner of the garden and dreamed of the kiss I had stolen.

A few days after that memorable ball, my mother attributed my neglect of my tasks, my indifference to her withering looks and her sarcasm, and my gloomy moods to the natural crises suffered by young people of my age. It was decided that the countryside, that eternal remedy for afflictions medicine cannot cure, was the best way to save me from apathy. My mother resolved I should spend time at Frapesle, a château situated on the Indre, between Montbazon and Azay-le-Rideau, the home of a friend of hers, to whom I expect she issued secret instructions.

The day when I received the key to rural life, I'd swum so vigorously in love's ocean I had already crossed to the other side. I didn't know that stranger's name: What could I call her? Where could I find her? Who could I mention her to? My shyness magnified the untold fears that overwhelm a young heart when love first flares, and it threw me into a melancholy state that can devastate a passion that has no hope. I craved nothing more than to be able to come and go, and to run across country fields. A child's undoubting courage fed my chivalric spirit, and I resolved to search the châteaux of the Touraine on walks and visits during which I would declare at the sight of every pretty turret: "She is there!"

On a Thursday morning, I left Tours via the Saint-Éloi gate, crossed the Saint-Sauveur bridges, arrived in Poncher, gazing starry-eyed at every house, before reaching the Chinon road. For the first time in my life I could stop under a tree, walk as slowly or as quickly as I wished, all without being interrogated by anybody. For a poor wretch previously crushed by the various despotic attitudes that more or less inhibit all young people, I found my first use of free will, even when applied to mere trifles, gave my soul a genuine sense of release. So many things converged to make that day a feast of enchantment. As a child, my walks had never taken me more than a few miles from town. My excursions around Pont-le-Voy or Paris hadn't spoiled my love of rural beauty. Besides, from my very first memories, I retained a feeling for the beauty that suffuses the familiar landscape around Tours. Although a complete novice as regards the poetry of place, I nevertheless spontaneously became exacting, like those who've never practiced an art, but have imagined its ideal form.

To reach the château in Frapesle, whether on foot or horseback, people take a shortcut through the so-called Charlemagne heathland, barren terrain at the top of the plateau separating the Cher from the Indre basin, and reached by a path you take in Champy. Those flat, sandy heaths sadden and depress you for about a league, and then past a thicket, meet the road to Saché, the name of the commune to which Frapesle belongs. This road joins the one to Chinon, well beyond Ballan, and runs along a gently undulating plain as far as the small area of Artanne. There one comes upon a valley that starts in Montbazon, finishes in the Loire, and seems to unfold beneath the châteaux on those twin hills: a magnificent emerald cup along the bottom of which the Indre River snakes and coils, the sight of which provoked shivers of sensuous pleasure the tedious heathland or my weariness had prepared the way for.

"If this woman, the flower of her sex, lives anywhere in this world, it has to be here."

When that thought entered my head, I leaned against the walnut tree I rest under whenever I return to my beloved valley. Beneath that tree with which I share my thoughts, I wonder how much I've changed in the time that has gone by since I left it last. And she did live *there*, my heart didn't deceive me; the first château I saw on a sloping heath was her home. When I sat beneath my walnut tree, the midday sun glinted on the tiles of her roof and the glass panes of her windows. Her muslin dress created the splash of white I spotted under an apricot tree among the vines. As you know already—though you know nothing yet—she was *the lily in this valley*, where she grew towards a sky that enjoyed the scent from her virtues. I'd discovered infinite love, nurtured solely by a glimpse that had filled my soul, now expressed in the long ribbon of sunny water flowing between two green banks, past the lines of poplars that adorn this valley of love with their rustling lace, past the oak woods that advance between the vineyards on hillsides the river rounds always differently, and past blurred horizons that turbulently recede. If you want to see natural beauty, pristine like first love, visit that spot on a spring day; if you want to soothe your bleeding heart, return at the end of autumn; in spring, love beats its wings center-sky; in autumn, one thinks of those who are no more. Sick lungs breathe in the healthy fresh air, eyes linger on gilded hills that suffuse your soul with their sweet serenity. At that moment, the mills located on the falls of the Indre gave voice to this shimmering valley, swaying poplars laughed, no gray clouded the sky; birds sang, cicadas chattered, it was one great melody. Don't ask me again why I love the Touraine; I don't love it as you love your cradle or an oasis in a desert, I love it as an artist loves his art; I love it less than I love you, but, perhaps, without the Touraine, I would perhaps no longer be alive. Unsure why, my eyes returned to that splash of white, to the woman resplendent in that vast garden, like the bell of a convolvulus exploding amid the green shrubs, and which would wither if touched.

My heart was on fire as I walked to the bottom of the hollow, and I saw a village that the poetry spilling out of me found uniquely beautiful. Imagine three mills set among elegantly contoured isles, garlanded with clumps of trees, amid a *prairie* of water; what other name could one give to that bright, colorful aquatic greenery that lines the river, rises above it, undulates with it, follows its whims, and bends to the crash of water whipped by mill wheels? Here and there mounds of gravel break the surface of the water and create pools that glitter in the sun. Rich tapestries of amaryllis, nenuphar, water lily, reed, and phlox drape the banks. A rickety bridge, its beams rotted, with flower-bedecked supports and parapets awash with sparkling vegetation and velvety moss, bends over the river, yet does not collapse; battered boats, a fisherman's nets, a shepherd's monotonous song, ducks roaming between isles or preening their feathers on the *jard*, the name locals give to the gravel banks built up by the Loire; millers' boys, caps tilted over their ears, busy loading their pack mules: each detail lent the scene a splendid simplicity. Imagine two or three farms beyond that bridge, a pigeon cote, turtledoves, thirty or so tumbledown cottages separated by gardens and hedges of honeysuckle, jasmine, and clematis; then pungent manure in front of every door, hens and cockerels on every path, and you have the village of Pont-de-Ruan, a pretty spot, overlooked by an old church, full of character, dating back to the Crusades, the kind painters seek for their canvases. Frame all that with ancient walnut trees, young poplars with pale golden leaves, add a few graceful mills amid long meadows where your eyes lose themselves under a warm, hazy sky, and you have some idea of one of the best prospects that this beautiful country has to offer.

I followed the Saché road to the left of the river, scrutinizing every aspect of the hills that lined the opposite bank. Finally, I came to a large stand of ancient trees that signaled to me that these were the grounds of the château of Frapesle. I arrived just as the bell was announcing lunch. After our meal, my host, not suspecting I'd walked from Tours, showed me his estate, where I saw the valley from every vantage point; sometimes a glimpse, sometimes an entire panorama; my eyes were often drawn to the horizon by the beautiful golden blade of the Loire, where sails drew phantasmagorical shapes blown about by the wind. As I climbed a ridge, I admired the château of Azay for the first time, a cut diamond set by the Indre, raised on pilings hidden by flowers. Then, in the distance, I saw the romantic outlines of the château in Saché, a melancholy place full of harmonies, too austere for frivolous folk but beloved by mournful poets. And later I came to love the silence, the tall, bleached trees, and the mysterious aura over their solitary vale! But whenever I looked back to the delightful castle on the neighboring slope, the one my eyes had first picked out, I gladly rested my gaze there.

"Ah!" said my host, seeing desire simmer in my eyes; at my age, still a quite innocent expression, "you scent a beautiful woman from afar, like a dog with a nose for game."

I found that last word distasteful, but asked him for the name of the castle and its owner.

"That is Clochegourde," he replied, "a lovely house belonging to the Comte de Mortsauf, scion of a historic Touraine family, whose good fortunes go back to Louis XI, and whose name indicates the deeds to which he owes his coat of arms and his distinction. He is the descendant of a man who survived the gallows. That's why the Mortsauf heraldry bears *gold, on a cross-potent and counter-potent sable, charged with a fleur-de-lis couped*, with God Save the King our Sire, as a motto. The count established himself in these domains after he returned from his time as an émigré. The property belongs to his wife, a Duchesse de Lenoncourt, of the house of Lenoncourt-Givry that will soon be no more: Mme de Mortsauf is an only child. Her family's lack of luck is in striking contrast to the distinction of its names, and out of pride, or perhaps necessity, they continue to live in Clochegourde, where they never see a soul. At present, their support for the Bourbons might be a reason for their isolation, though I suspect the king's return will not change their way of life. When I settled here last year, I paid them a courtesy visit; they returned the honor and invited us to dinner; winter kept us apart for a few months; then political events delayed our return, because I've not lived in Frapesle for very long. Mme de Mortsauf is a woman who could adorn the front rank anywhere."

"Does she often go to Tours?"

"Never. But," he resumed, "she did go there recently, when the Duc d'Angoulême passed through, who, by the way, has acted very favorably towards M. de Mortsauf."

"It is *she* then!"

"Who *she*?"

"A woman with the most beautiful shoulders."

"You will find many women with beautiful shoulders in the Touraine," he said, and laughed. "However, if you aren't too weary, we can cross the river, go up to Clochegourde, and you might even catch sight of those shoulders."

I agreed, not without blushing from a mixture of pleasure and embarrassment. We reached the small château I'd been eyeing for so long around four o'clock. It is in fact a quite modest mansion that fits its landscape beautifully. It has five front windows, each completing the south-facing facade and jutting out about two yards, an architectural effect that simulates two buildings and lends the house a graceful tone; the middle window acts as a door, and you walk down a double flight of steps into terraced gardens leading to a narrow meadow along the Indre. Although a communal path separates this meadow from a final terrace, shaded by an avenue of acacias and lacquer trees, it looks as if it is part of the gardens, because it is a sunken path, flanked on one side by the terrace and on the other by a Norman hedge. Well-tended slopes put enough distance between mansion and river to avoid the inconvenience of being close to water without diminishing its charm. Beneath the mansion stand coach houses, stables, sheds, and kitchens, the various entries to which create a series of arcades. Roofs are graciously shaped at the corners, adorned with iron-barred attic windows and lead flashing on the gables. No doubt neglected during the Revolution, the roof tiles are covered by the rust produced by flat, reddish moss that grows on south-facing houses. The French window onto the steps is topped by a campanile where the coat of arms of the Blamont-Chauvries is sculpted: Gules, a pale vair, flanked by two clasped hands of red and gold, and two lances in chevron sable. I was struck by the motto: *See, but touch not!* The supports, a griffon and a dragon with jaws chained in gold, were a pretty sight in relief. The Revolution had damaged the ducal coronet and crest comprising a vert palm tree with golden fruit. Senart, the secretary of the public-health committee, was the magistrate in Saché before 1781, and that explains the damage.

These features give the mansion an elegant appearance, fashioned like a flower, and almost levitating above the ground. Seen from the valley, the ground floor looks like a first floor, but on the courtyard side, it is level with a long sandy avenue overlooking a lawn adorned by several round flower beds. To the right and left, vineyards, orchards, and a few expanses of arable land planted with walnut trees rapidly descend, the trees enveloping the house with their trunks and reaching down to the Indre, the riverbank too adorned by clumps of trees, their shades of green painted by nature herself. As I walked up the path alongside Clochegourde, I admired the charming play of shapes, I breathed an air redolent with happiness. Does moral nature, like physical nature, possess its own electric messages and rapid changes of temperature? My heart throbbed in anticipation of secret acts that would change it forever, the way animals cheer up when they sense fine weather is coming. That day, so significant in my life, wasn't denied a single hallowing feature. Nature had dressed up like a woman going to meet her beloved; for the first time, my soul heard her voice and my eyes marveled at her exuberance, as variegated as my imagination had represented her in dreams at school, which I've said a few words to you about, but I can't hope to explain their influence. They were like an apocalypse that fleetingly foretold my life: each happy or unhappy event was locked there by strange images, by bonds only the soul could see.

We crossed a first courtyard of outbuildings dedicated to agricultural tasks, a barn, a press house, stables, and cowsheds. Alerted by the barking guard dog, a servant came out to meet us, and he told us the count had gone to Azay that morning and would no doubt be back soon, but the countess was at home. My host glanced at me. I was afraid he wouldn't want to see Mme de Mortsauf in her husband's absence, but he told the servant to tell her we were there. Like an impulsive, eager child, I rushed into the long antechamber that ran the length of the house.

"Do come in, gentleman!" said a voice of gold.

Although Mme de Mortsauf had said only one word at the ball, I immediately recognized her voice, and it entered my heart, filling it like a sunbeam flooding and gilding a prisoner's cell. Then I thought she might remember my face and I wanted to flee; I had no time to do that: she appeared on the doorstep and our eyes met. I don't know whether she or I blushed the brightest. Taken aback, she said nothing, and sat down in front of a tapestry frame, after her servant had pulled up two armchairs; she finished threading her needle as if to justify her silence, counted a few stitches, and looked up, warm and aloof, at M. de Chessel, and asked what happy chance led to our visit. Though curious to discover why I was there, she looked at neither of us; her gaze remained focused on the river, but the intense way she listened suggested that, like the blind, she sensed the tremors triggered in my heart by her words' imperceptible inflections. And that was so true.

M. de Chessel told her my name and sketched in my biography. I had come to Frapesle after spending several months in Tours, where my parents had brought me when war threatened Paris. She would find that I was a child of the Touraine, to whom the Touraine was unknown, and now, as a young man exhausted by overwork, I had been sent to Frapesle to relax. He had been showing me his estate, which I was visiting for the first time. At the foot of the hill, I'd just mentioned my long walk from Tours to Frapesle, and, fearing for my already fragile health, he'd decided to come to Clochegourde, thinking she might allow me to rest there awhile. M. de Chessel had told the truth, but such a happy coincidence seemed so unlikely that Mme de Mortsauf remained aloof; she gazed at me coldly and severely, forcing me to lower my eyelids, as much from a sense of humiliation as to hide the tears my lashes were holding back. That magnificent lady of the manor could see the beads of sweat on my brow, and perhaps she also suspected the tears, because she was quick to offer me whatever I needed, in kind, consoling words that encouraged me to speak up. I blushed like a girl caught out, and I replied, in the quavering voice of an old man, thanking her, but declining the offers.

"All I would wish," I looked up and told her, as our eyes met for the second time, as swift as lightning, "is not to be turned out; I'm so numbed by fatigue I couldn't walk another step."

"Why do you doubt the hospitality of our beautiful country?" she asked. "You will, of course, grant us the pleasure of your company at dinner tonight in Clochegourde?" she added, turning towards her neighbor.

I looked so imploringly at my host that he quickly accepted the invitation despite the wording that intended it to be a polite, but empty offer. If knowledge of society enabled M. de Chessel to distinguish such nuances, a raw young man believes so implicitly in the union of word and thought on a beautiful woman's lips that I was quite astounded when we were returning in the evening and he declared: "I accepted because you were clearly desperate that we do so, but, if you don't make amends for it, it might mean I'll be on bad terms with my neighbors."

That "if you don't make amends" gave me food for thought. If Mme de Mortsauf liked me, she would never harbor a grudge against the man who had brought me into her home. M. de Chessel earlier had surmised that I might be of interest to her, and, if given the opportunity, I could prove him right, and thus make amends. Such a conclusion reinforced my hopes at a moment when I was in need of assurance.

"I'm not sure," he replied to Mme de Mortsauf, "Mme de Chessel is expecting us."

"But she sees you every day," retorted the countess, "and we can inform her. Is she by herself?"

"No, the Abbé de Quélus is with her."

"That's all decided, then," she said, standing up to ring the bell, "you will dine with us."

At this point, M. de Chessel thought she meant it, and he gave me a congratulatory smile. That instant when I realized I would spend an evening under that roof felt like an eternity. For many unhappy individuals, *tomorrow* is a meaningless word, and, at the time, I included myself among those with no faith in the morrow, and when I did have a few hours to myself, I tried to squeeze in a lifetime of pleasure. Mme de Mortsauf launched forth on the locality, harvests, and vineyards in a conversation that felt alien to me.

When the lady of the house behaves like that, it betrays either a lack of good manners or her contempt for the individual she is thus placing on the periphery of her chatter, though it was in fact a sign of the countess's own embarrassment. If initially I thought she affected to treat me like a child, if I envied the privilege of a thirty-year-old man like M. de Chessel, who was permitted to consult his neighbor on serious subjects beyond my ken, if I took offence thinking that everything was directed at him, a few months later I realized how significant a woman's silence can be and how the vagaries of a conversation can conceal many a thought.

I first tried to relax in my armchair; then I recognized the advantages of my situation and simply let myself bathe in delight at hearing the countess's voice. She channeled the breath from her soul into the recesses of each syllable, as sound can be intuited beneath the keys of a flute; it vanished in waves into my ears and made my blood pound. Her way of saying the words ending in *i* brought to mind birdsong; the *ch*, on her lips, was like a caress; and the manner in which she attacked her *t*'s betrayed a despotic heart. Though quite unaware of it herself, this was her way of elaborating the meaning of words and enticing your soul into an otherworldly universe. I have so often allowed an argument to run on that I could have concluded! So often I unjustly reined myself in to listen to that concert of human sound, breathe in the soulful air from her lips, embrace that spoken light with the ardor I would have experienced if I had clasped her to my chest! Such a joyous swallow's chirping, when she essayed a smile, but what a swan's cry to summon her friends when she spoke of her sorrows! The countess's inattentiveness allowed me to observe her. My gaze rejoiced to glide over that beautiful conversationalist, squeezing her waist, kissing her feet, wallowing in the ringlets of her hair. Yet I was prey to a terror that will be familiar to those who have experienced the boundless bliss of true passion. I was afraid she might catch me staring at the place on her shoulders I had embraced so fondly. That fear only stoked temptation and I surrendered, gazed at them, and saw again the freckle marking the start of the pretty dip dividing her back, a beauty spot adrift in milk, that ever since the ball had always glowed at night in the shadows where young people appear to slumber, imaginations blazing, while their lives remain chaste.

I could pencil in the countess's main traits that people everywhere found arresting, but the most accurate sketch, the warmest coloring, could never capture them. Her face is such that a likeness would need the hand of that nonexistent artist adept at painting reflections of innermost fire and rendering the luminous haze science denies, that words cannot translate, but a lover sees. Her fine, silvery hair often made her suffer, and such pain was no doubt caused by sudden rushes of blood to her head. Her rounded forehead, as prominent as the Gioconda's, seemed full of unvoiced reflections and constrained feelings, flowers that languished in stagnant water. Her greenish, brown-speckled eyes were always pale, but, if it concerned her children, or she displayed a fervent outburst of joy or sorrow—rare in the lives of women resigned to their lot—her eyes radiated a subtle glow that seemed to flame in the wells of life and dry them out; a flash of lightning that brought tears to my eyes when she showed the icy disdain that made the most valiant look away. A Greek nose, as if sculpted by Phidias, matched by a double arc of elegantly sinuous lips, gave spirituality to her oval face the complexion of which, comparable to the petals of a white camellia, was tinged a pretty pink. The fullness of her figure didn't mar her graceful waist or the roundness necessary for her shape to retain its buxom beauty. You will understand the nature of her perfections if I say her dazzling treasures extended to her forearm, without a single unsightly crease. The lower part of her head bore none of the crevasses that can make almost a tree trunk out of some women's necks, her muscles created no unsightly bumps, and every contour softened into rounded forms that were a source of despair both to the eyes and to the paintbrush. Stray down died away on her cheeks and her neck was charged with silken light. Her small, delicate ears were, in her own words, the ears of a mother and a slave. Later, after I had won a place in her heart, she'd say: "M. de Mortsauf is here!" and she would be right, while I still perceived nothing, though I had the keenest sense of hearing. Her arms were beautiful, as were her hands, with their long, curved fingers, flesh brimming over the exquisite sides of her nails as on an ancient statue. I would irk you if I preferred flat waists to plump ones, if you weren't the exception to this. A plump waist is a sign of strength, but women built that way tend to be domineering, willful, and voluptuous, rather than tender. Conversely, flat-waisted women are devoted, refined, and inclined to melancholy; they are better women than the others. A flat waist is supple and soft; a plump waist ungiving and jealous. Now you know how she was built. She had a properly feminine foot, one that walks little, tires quickly, and is a delight to the eye when she wears a short dress. Though she was the mother of two children, I've never known anyone of her sex to be more youthful. Her demeanor breathed simplicity and hinted at forbidden reveries that drew one back to her, as a painter draws one back to a face his genius has translated into a world of feeling. Perhaps only comparisons can express such visual qualities. Remember the pure, wild scent of the heather we picked when we came back from Villa Diodati,[3] that flower whose black and pink you praised so highly, and you can imagine how elegant that woman is, away from the social whirl, how natural her expressions, and how complex in things that become her, at once pink and black. Her body had the freshness we admire in leaves that have just emerged, her mind, the keenness of the wild; she was childlike in her feelings, stoic in her sorrow, lady of the manor and yet a young girl. She brought pleasure without artifice in the way she sat, stood, was silent, or conversed. Usually self-engrossed, alert like the sentinel on whom everyone's safety depends, on the lookout for evil, she would sometimes smile and betray a cheerful nature buried under life's restraints. Her coquettish style was mysterious, she inspired dreams, didn't crave gallant attention like other women, allowed one to see her character's brightly burning flame and the first hints of happy daydreams, as one glimpses patches of blue through clearings in clouds. Such spontaneous revelations plunged anyone who didn't sense inner tears dried by the fire of desire into the profoundest meditation. Her scant gestures or gazes (she gazed solely at her children) endowed everything she did or said with incredible gravitas, with the air women assume the moment they compromise their dignity with a confession. That day, Mme de Mortsauf wore a pink dress with countless stripes, a broad-hemmed collar, a black belt, and black ankle boots. Coiled simply above her head, her hair was held in place by a tortoiseshell clasp.

That's the imperfect sketch I promised you. But the constant way her soul shone over her family, flowing in waves and as nourishing as sunlight, and her innermost nature, her demeanor at tranquil times and her resignation at moments of anxiety: every such shift in an individual's reactions to life depend, like the changing sky, on unexpected, transient circumstances that share nothing except for the backdrop against which they move, the depiction of which will necessarily merge with the events in my chronicle; a truly domestic epic, as grand in the eyes of the learned as tragedies are in the eyes of the crowd, the recounting of which will interest you, both because of the role I played and the similarity it bears to the fate of a great number of women.

Everything in Clochegourde bore the mark of a genuinely English property. The drawing room where the countess received visitors was entirely wood-paneled and painted in two shades of gray. The mantelpiece was home to a clock in mahogany surround crowned with a finial, and two large white, gold-striated porcelain vases filled with tall flowers of Cape heath. A lamp stood on the console. A backgammon board sat opposite the fireplace. Two long cotton tiebacks held the fringeless white percale curtains in place. The seats covered in green-trimmed gray fabric and the tapestry on the countess's frame sufficed to explain why the furniture was upholstered in that way.

It was a simplicity verging on the grand. No apartment I've seen since has offered me the rich, fruitful impressions I experienced in that Clochegourde drawing room, which was as quiet and inward-looking as the countess's life, a setting where one could imagine the monastic nature of her tasks. Most of my ideas, even the boldest in science or politics, were born there, like scents emanating from flowers, though it was an unknown plant that grew there and scattered its fertile pollen over my soul, in the warmth of a sun that nurtured the good and blighted the evil in me. From the window, one's eyes traced the hill where Pont-de-Ruan reaches as far as Azay-le-Rideau, then follows the sinuous slopes of the hills opposite, marked out by the Frapesle towers, and the church, town, and old manor of Saché, whose buildings overlook the meadow. In perfect accord with that restful life and the emotions only a family can provide, those places imbued the soul with serenity. If I had met her there for the first time, between the count and her two children, rather than having discovered her splendor in a ball gown, I would never have stolen the insane kiss that now brought me so much remorse, believing, as I did, that it would destroy any future my love might have! No, in the dark depths where unhappiness had thrust me, I would have knelt down, kissed her ankle boots, wept a few tears, and thrown myself into the Indre.

However, after nuzzling her fresh jasmine skin and drinking milk from that cup flowing over the brim with love, my soul watered at the expectation and taste of voluptuous pleasure; I wanted to live, and I hung on to that moment of ecstasy, like a savage relishes his coming moment of revenge; I wanted to hang from trees, crawl through vines, take cover in the Indre; I wanted the silence of night, the lethargy of life, and the heat of the sun to be my accomplices, so I could finish the delicious apple I had already bitten. If she'd asked for the flower that sings or the riches buried by the companions of Morgan, the buccaneer,[4] I'd have brought them to her in order to obtain the treasures and silent flower I desired! When the daydream where the long contemplation of my idol had taken me ended, and during which a servant had come to speak to her, I heard her mention the count. I could only think, obsessively, that a wife *must* belong to her husband, and that idea sent me into a spin. I felt a dark, raging curiosity to see the man who possessed that jewel. Two feelings overwhelmed me: hatred and fear, a hatred that brooked no obstacle and fearlessly took measure of them all, and a vague, real-enough fear, of a conflict, of the outcome, and, above all, of *her*. Falling prey to horrible premonitions, I lived in dread of embarrassing handshakes, and already anticipated prolonged confrontations where the rawest wills clash and are blunted; I feared the power of the inertia that nowadays empties social life of the conclusions craved by passionate souls.

"That must be M. de Mortsauf," she said.

I reared up like a frightened horse. Although my reaction didn't go unnoticed by M. de Chessel or by the countess, there was no response to it, because a young girl walked in and created a diversion; she was six or so, I thought, when she said: "My father's arrived."

"Madeleine, I beg you?" said her mother.

The child offered M. de Chessel the hand he sought, then she stared hard at me, after a little wave of her astonished hand.

"Are you happy with her present state of health"? M. de Chessel inquired.

"She's better," the countess replied, stroking the hair of the child who'd already sunk into her lap.

I learned that Madeleine was nine from something M. de Chessel then asked; I was surprised by how wrong I'd been, and my astonishment clouded her mother's brow. My host glared at me in the way that people acquainted with social graces do when having to educate someone for the second time. There, no doubt, was the source of the mother's pain, the signs of which I would have to carefully respect. A sickly child with pale eyes and skin white as translucent porcelain, Madeleine would probably never have survived in the dank environment of a town. The fresh country air, the loving care of her mother, the hen who kept her under the wing, preserved life in a body as delicate as a plant nurtured in a greenhouse against the rigors of a foreign climate. Although she looked nothing like her mother, Madeleine seemed to possess her soul, and that sustained her. Her sparse black hair, sunken eyes, hollow cheeks, skinny arms, and meager chest heralded a life-and-death struggle, a duel without truce, in which so far the countess had been victorious. She put on a lively front, no doubt to spare her mother's pain, because at times her concentration slipped and she was more like a weeping willow. You could have imagined her to be a starving Gypsy girl, come begging from her country, exhausted, but courageous and ready to perform for her audience.

"So where did you leave Jacques?" her mother asked, as she kissed the white part that divided her hair into halves, like the wings of a crow.

"He'll be along with Father."

The count walked in on cue, followed by his son, whose hand he was holding. A mirror image of his sister, Jacques betrayed the same signs of debility. When you saw those two frail children by the side of their mother, with her gorgeous beauty, you rapidly intuited the source of the sadness that softened the countess's demeanor and silenced the thoughts that were confided only to God, though they lined her anxious temples.

As he greeted me, M. de Mortsauf glanced my way awkwardly, fretful rather than observant, like a suspicious man incapable of shrewd analysis. After she had given him the picture and told him my name, his wife made way for him and departed. The children glued their eyes to their mother's as if they were their only source of light, and they wanted to leave too, but she said: "Stay here, dear angels!" and put a finger to her lips. They obeyed, though their eyes misted over. What wouldn't they have done to hear the word *dear* again? Like them, I felt less at ease when she was gone.

The resonances of my name altered the count's attitude toward me. From being cold and supercilious, he became at least politely engaged, if not warm, showed respect, and seemed happy to welcome me. Long ago, my father's conscience had led him to play an important, if obscure, role on behalf of our rulers; he had faced danger and been largely effective. When all was ruined by Napoleon's rise to power, he, like many clandestine conspirators, took refuge in the quiet pleasures of provincial life, and fended off accusations that were harsh and undeserved; the inevitable payoff for gamblers who stake everything on the top prize and subsequently fall, after having been kingpins in a political machine. I knew nothing of my family's fortunes, the antecedents or the future, and I was equally ignorant of the specific detail of that ill-fated outcome the Comte de Mortsauf had recalled. However, if my ancient name—in his eyes, a man's most valuable quality—justified a welcome that rather flummoxed me, I discovered why much later. For the moment, his sudden change settled me. When the two children saw the three of us deep in conversation, Madeleine slipped her head from her father's hands and slid out like an eel, followed by Jacques. Both joined their mother, and I could hear their voices and movements in the distance, like bees buzzing around the beloved hive.

I stared at the count and tried to intuit his character. I was sufficiently fascinated by his main features to want to review them in a quick survey of his face. Though forty-five, he seemed more like a man in his late fifties, suddenly aged by the great shipwreck that brought the eighteenth century to a close. Encircling the bald back of his head, his monkish tonsure faded by his ears and dotted his temples with salt-and-pepper tufts of hair. His face vaguely resembled a white wolf's, with a bloody snout, because his nose was inflamed, like that of a man whose life had been undermined by his principles, whose stomach had deteriorated, whose humors were plagued by ancient maladies. Too broad for a face that narrowed to a point, and crisscrossed by uneven wrinkles, his forehead spoke of an open-air life, though not of mental fatigue, the burden of constant misfortune, or any striving to overcome it. Brown cheeks protruding from the wan pallor suggested a frame solid enough to guarantee long life. His bright, yellow gaze fell harshly on you like a ray of wintry sun, luminous yet icy, restless yet unreflecting, and naturally distrustful. His mouth threatened imperiously; his chin was straight and long. He possessed the attitude of a tall, lean gentleman sustained by convention, who knows that birthright places him above others, and reality, below. The casual nature of country life had led him to neglect his appearance. He dressed like a farmer; the peasants and neighbors recognized him only because of the quantity of land he owned. His swarthy, gnarled hands revealed that he wore gloves only to ride his horse or to attend Sunday Mass. His footwear beggared belief. Although ten years as an émigré and another ten years as a farmer had changed his physical appearance, he retained traces of nobility. The most embittered liberal—a word yet to be coined—would have quickly recognized his chivalric loyalty and the incorruptible convictions of a lifetime subscriber to *La Quotidienne*. He would have found him a religious man, passionate about his cause, frank in his political dislikes, unable to serve his party personally, and quite capable of hastening its downfall, with no knowledge of the present state of France. Indeed, the count was one of those conservatives who never offer to do anything, but stubbornly oppose everything, who are ready to die, weapon on arm, in the post they may be assigned, but are miserly enough to surrender their lives rather than their money. During dinner, his hollow, flaccid cheeks, and the sharp glances he arrowed at his children, manifested traces of untimely thoughts, the thrust of which rapidly faded. Watching him, who would fail to understand? Who wouldn't have accused him of deliberately giving his children bodies that were so lacking in life? If he damned himself, he denied others the right to judge him. Like an embittered grandee who knows he is at fault but hasn't the character or charm to atone for the sorrow he has caused, his inner spirit must have been infused with the asperities signaled by his angular features and ever-restless eyes.

When his wife returned, followed by the two children clinging to her skirts, I immediately suspected something was amiss, as when you walk over cellar vaults and become aware of the depths below your feet. I observed those four individuals interact, scrutinizing them, switching from one to the other, studying their respective faces or expressions, and melancholy permeated my heart, as gray drizzle mists pretty countryside after a beautiful dawn. When we'd exhausted the subject of our conversation, the count focused on me to the exclusion of M. de Chessel, and informed his wife of various circumstances concerning my family that were quite unknown to me. He asked how old I was. When I told him, the countess was as surprised to hear it as I'd been by her daughter's age. Perhaps she thought I was fourteen. I later discovered that this was a second bond being strongly forged between us. I read into her soul. Her maternal feelings simmered, illuminated by a late ray of sun that hope bestowed. When she saw I had survived into my twenties, skinny and fragile yet sinewy, a voice perhaps cried out to her: "They too will live!" She gave me a curious look and I felt much of the ice between us had melted. She seemed to have a thousand questions to ask, though she kept them to herself.

"If study debilitated you," she said, "the fresh air in our valley will be invigorating."

"Modern education is lethal to children," continued the count. "We stuff them with mathematics, kill them with science, and wear them out before their time. You should rest here," he told me, "an avalanche of ideas has collapsed on you and it has crushed you. What a century awaits us now that this kind of education has been put within everyone's reach, if we don't forestall that evil and restore public education to the control of religious institutions!"

Those words heralded his quip on an election day when he refused to allow himself to vote for a man whose talents could have served the royalist cause: "I will always distrust intellectuals," he retorted to the man gathering the votes. He stood up now and suggested we go for a stroll around the gardens.

"Monsieur..." the countess said.

"Yes, my dear?" he replied, turning around sharply, revealing how much he longed to wield absolute power in his own home, but how little of it he actually enjoyed.

"Monsieur walked from Tours; M. de Chessel wasn't aware of that and had him walk here from Frapesle."

"Which was most unwise," he said, "although, at your age..."

He shook his head, expressing his regret.

We resumed our conversation. I soon noted what an intransigent royalist he was, and how adept one had to be to avoid clashes in those waters. The servant, who'd quickly donned his livery, announced that dinner was served. M. de Chessel gave his arm to Mme de Mortsauf and the count eagerly took mine, and we entered the dining room, which was adjacent to the drawing room in the design of their ground floor.

The floor was tiled in the white Touraine style, and the dining-rooms walls, wainscoted to elbow height, were papered in large shiny panels bordered with fruit and flowers; the windows had red-hemmed cotton cambric curtains; the sideboards were old Boule furnishings, and the carved oak chairs were upholstered in handmade tapestry. The table was laid in abundance, but the settings weren't at all sumptuous: family silverware from unmatched sets, Dresden china that had yet to come back into fashion, eight-sided carafes, agate-handled knives, laquered mats under the bottles, and flowers in polished, gilt buckets on wolf-tooth-edged lace mats. I liked those old things; I adored the

Réveillon paper and its marvelous flowery borders. The contentment billowing out my sails prevented me from seeing the unsurmountable hurdles the narrow life of rural solitude placed between her and me. I was near her, on her right, and I poured her drink. Yes, such unexpected bliss! I brushed against her dress, I ate her bread! It had taken only three hours for my life to intertwine with hers! After all, we were bound by that horrible kiss, a secret source of mutual shame.

I was gloriously amenable; I went out of my way to please the count, who was fooled by my obsequious fawning; I'd have stroked their dog, satisfied the children's slightest whims, bought them hoops and agate marbles, been their horse, I begrudged them for not using me as their toy. Like genius, love has its flashes of intuition, and I vaguely sensed that forcing my luck or acting peevishly or aggressively would only dash my hopes.

Dinner was one extended inner joy for me. Seeing myself in her home was enough; I ignored her actual coldness and the indifference hidden behind the count's politeness. Love, like life, experiences a puberty that is quite self-sufficient. I responded awkwardly, in keeping with my tumult of hidden passion, which nobody could divine, not even *she*, who knew nothing about love. The rest of the time passed like a dream. This beautiful dream came to an end when, in the moonlight, on a warm, scented night, I crossed the Indre through the white fantasia that bedecked meadows, riverbanks, and hills, listening to the bright chirrup, the single melancholic note a treefrog—whose scientific name I don't know—trills, whatever the weather, and which I've heard with infinite delight ever since. There, as elsewhere, I perceived after the fact the marble insensitivity that had blunted my feelings hitherto; I wondered whether it would always have to be like that; I thought I must be under an unlucky star; the sinister events in my past contrasting with the purely personal pleasures I had enjoyed. Before reaching Frapesle, I looked back at Clochegourde, and spotted a boat they call a toue in the Touraine, moored to an ash tree and swaying by the water. This toue belonged to M. de Chessel, who used it to go fishing.

"So," said M. de Chessel, when we were in no danger of being overheard, "I don't need to ask if you caught another sight of those beautiful shoulders; I must congratulate you on the welcome you received from M. de Mortsauf! By hell, you became the immediate center of attention."

That statement, followed by the one I've already mentioned, cheered my despondent heart. I hadn't said a word since leaving Clochegourde, and M. de Chessel had taken my silence as a sign of my happiness.

"How do you mean?" I replied in an ironic tone that could easily have seemed dictated by restrained passion.

"I have *never* seen him welcome anyone like that."

"I confess that I too found myself surprised by his welcome," I retorted, sensing the sourness lurking behind his last remark.

Although too inexperienced in the ways of society to understand what M. de Chessel was feeling, I was nonetheless struck by the way his words betrayed him. My host had the misfortune to be called Durand, and he had made himself look ridiculous by rejecting the name of his father, a distinguished manufacturer, who had made his huge fortune during the Revolution. His wife was the only heir of the Chessels, an old bourgeois parliamentary family under Henri IV, as were the families of most Parisian judges. Ambitious to scale the highest echelons, M. de Chessel decided he must kill off his Durand origins to attain the heights he craved. First he called himself Durand de Chessel, then D. de Chessel and then M. de Chessel. Under the Restoration, he established an entailed property that brought him the title of count, by virtue of the letters patent of nobility granted by Louis XVIII. His children will reap the fruit of his audacity and never knew the source of their grandeur. A barbed comment about him, making a play on the name "Durand," from a caustic prince often irked him: "M. de Chessel isn't generally a very durable fellow." That quip has amused the Touraine for a long time.

Upstarts are like monkeys, and share their agility: you see them up high, you admire their nimble climbing, but when they reach the top, you only see their dirty rumps. This aspect of my host is a small-mindedness swollen by envy. The peerage and he are like two tangents that can never meet. To have an exaggerated belief in oneself and justify it is an impertinence that brings strength, but acting beneath one's avowed superiority nurtures a constant source of ridicule that in turn animates the small-minded. M. de Chessel hadn't kept to the straight lines of a winner: twice a member of parliament, twice rejected in elections; yesterday a chief administrator, today nothing, not even a prefect, his successes or failures had marred his character and made him an embittered, thwarted parvenu. Although he was a witty, charming man capable of high achievements, perhaps the envy that drives existence in the Touraine, where locals use their wits to carp at everything, had led him to fare poorly in heady social spheres where success rarely comes to those who snarl at the success of others, or to sullen lips that readily spin an epigram but are slow to flatter. If he'd wanted less, he might have achieved more, but, unfortunately, he always felt sufficiently superior to want to walk on his own two feet.

At that time, M. de Chessel was facing the twilight of his ambitions, and the royalists looked favorably on him. He may have affected the grand manner, but he was perfect for me. Besides, I liked him for one simple reason: for the first time in my life, I'd been able to relax in a house. The possibly feeble interest he took in me struck me, an unhappy, rejected child, as a reflection of paternal love. His hospitable ways were such a contrast to the indifference I'd encountered so far that I displayed a childish gratitude at being able to live without chains, at feeling I was almost loved. For that reason, the owners of Frapesle are so much part of the dawn of my happiness that they always come to mind in the memories I like to relive. Later, and precisely in the matter of the letters patent, I had the pleasure of repaying some favors to my host. M. de Chessel enjoyed his fortune with an ostentation that caused some neighbors to take offense; he was always replacing his beautiful horses and elegant carriages; his wife never economized on her finery; he gave lavish parties; he had more servants than was customary in the region, and he gave himself princely airs. His Frapesle estate was enormous. In the presence of his neighbor, faced with all that luxury, the Comte de Mortsauf was limited to a family gig, which in Touraine is halfway between a rattletrap and post chaise. Forced by the poor state of his finances to make do with Clochegourde, he was merely a man of Touraine until the day royal largesse restored an unexpected shine to his family. The welcome he'd given a young man from a ruined family whose coat of arms dated from the Crusades had helped him humiliate new money, and diminish the woods, fields, and meadows of his neighbor, who wasn't a man of high birth. M. de Chessel had understood what the count intended. And they were always courteous to each other, but with none of the quotidian rapport, none of the pleasant intimacy that should have existed between Clochegourde and Frapesle, two estates separated by the Indre, where, from their respective windows, both ladies of the manor could wave to each other.

Jealousy wasn't the only reason for the solitude that was the Comte de Mortsauf's lot. His early education had been that of most members of grandee families, incomplete, superficial learning supplemented by the precepts of high society, the customs of the court, and the exercise of important responsibilities on behalf of the crown, or eminent posts. M. de Mortsauf had emigrated precisely at the time when the second stage of his education would have begun, and its absence showed. He was one who thought the monarchy would soon be reestablished in France, and, from that perspective, his exile had been a period of the most deplorable idling. When Condé's army was dispersed,[5] in which his courage had led him to enroll as one of the most devoted royalists, he expected to return promptly under the white standard, and didn't seek, like some émigrés, to embark on a life of industry. Perhaps he also didn't possess the moral fortitude to renounce his name and earn his living by sweat from labor he held in contempt. His expectations, ever looking to the future, and perhaps also his sense of honor, prevented him from putting himself at the disposition of foreign powers. Pain undermined his courage. Long journeys on foot without the requisite nutrition, trusting to hopes that were always dashed, had damaged his health and dispirited his soul. His poverty gradually became extreme. If many men take impoverishment as a spur, for others it is but a catalyst for degeneration, and he found himself in the ranks of the latter.

When I thought of this wretched, well-born gentleman from the

Touraine, walking and sleeping along the byways of Hungary, sharing a quarter of a sheep with Prince Esterhazy's shepherds, as a traveler who asked them for crust that, as a gentleman, he'd never have accepted from their master, and that he refused time and again from the enemies of France, I never felt any venom towards that émigré, even when I felt his pomp and circumstance to be ridiculous. M. de Mortsauf's white hair spoke to me of terrible suffering, and I felt too much sympathy for those who emigrated to stand in judgment over them.

Both the French and the Touraine sense of good cheer forsook the count; he became morose, fell ill, and received charitable care in a German hospice. His sickness was an inflammation of the intestine, frequently fatal, while the cure for it leads to moodiness and almost always causes hypochondria. His affections, buried in the deepest recesses of his soul, which only I have laid bare, were loves of a low order, which not only undermined his life, but ruined his future. After ten poverty-stricken years, he turned his eyes back to France, where Napoleon's decree had now allowed him to return. As he crossed the Rhine, our weary foot-slogger spotted the bell tower of Strasbourg on a beautiful evening, and fainted.

"La France! La France!" I shouted: "Voilà la France!" he told me, like a child crying out for his mother when he is hurt.

Born rich, now he was poor; made to command a regiment or govern the state, he had no authority now, no future; born healthy and sturdy, he returned sickly and worn out. Without a formal education, he found himself in the midst of a country where men and things had advanced; decidedly unable to wield any influence, he felt stripped of everything, even of physical and moral strength. His lack of wealth meant his name became a burden. His rigid opinions, his antecedents in Condé's army, his grief, his memories, his long-lost health, all gave him a natural susceptibility that is hard to endure in France, a country that likes to jeer.

Half dead, he reached the Maine, where, by chance, perhaps as a result of the civil war, the revolutionary government had forgotten to sell off an extensive farm his tenant had kept for him by convincing people that he himself was the owner. When the Lenoncourt family who lived in Givry, a château located close to that farm, learned of the Comte de Mortsauf's arrival, the Duc de Lenoncourt went to him to suggest he should live in Givry for however long he needed to organize an abode for himself. The Lenoncourt family acted with noble generosity towards the count, who stayed several months, and they made considerable effort to hide their own sorrow during that first resting period. The Lenoncourts had lost their vast wealth. By dint of his name, M. de Mortsauf was an eligible match for their daughter. Far from resisting marriage to an aged, infirm man of thirty-five, Mlle de Lenoncourt seemed delighted by the idea. Marriage would give her the right to live with her aunt, Duchesse de Verneuil, the Prince de Blamont-Chauvry's sister, who was her adopted mother, as far as she was concerned.

A close friend of the Duchesse de Bourbon, Mme de Verneuil belonged to a religious society at the center of which was M. de Saint-Martin, born in Touraine, and nicknamed the "Unknown Philosopher." This philosopher's disciples practiced the virtues recommended by the lofty speculation of mystical quietism. His doctrine provides the key to divine worlds, explains existence via the transformations by which man proceeds to a sublime destiny, releases duty from legal degradation, applies a Quaker's unflinching warmth to life's sorrows, dictates contempt for suffering, and inspires maternal affection in the angel we carry to heaven. It is stoicism with a future. Active prayer and pure love are the elements of a faith that abandons the Catholicism of Rome to return to the Christianity of the primitive church. However, Mlle de Lenoncourt remained within the apostolic church, to which her aunt was equally loyal. Harshly tested by the turmoil of revolution, the Duchesse de Verneuil had developed, in the last days of her life, a store of impassioned piety which she poured into the soul of her beloved child, "the light of celestial love and the oil of inner bliss," to use the expression of Saint-Martin himself. The countess welcomed this man of peace and virtuous wisdom in Clochegourde on several occasions after the death of her aunt, whom he had often visited. It was from Clochegourde that Saint-Martin organized the printing of his last books by Letourmy in Tours.

Motivated to do so by the wisdom of dowagers who have navigated the stormy straits of life, Mme de Verneuil gave the young wife Clochegourde, so she could make a home of her own. With the graciousness old people have, which is always perfect when they *are* gracious, the duchess gave her niece everything, and contented herself with a bedroom above the one she'd once occupied, which was now the countess's. Her almost immediate death veiled the joy of that marriage in mourning, and brought ineffable sadness to Clochegourde and to the young wife's superstitious soul. Those early days when she was settling down in the Touraine were the only time in the countess's life that she was, if not happy, at least untroubled.

After the vicissitudes of his sojourn in foreign parts, M. de Mortsauf was glad to look to a rosier future and feel his soul begin to convalesce; he scented the heady aromas of hope spurring his family on. Forced to concentrate on the state of his finances, he threw himself into establishing his agricultural business and began to enjoy a taste of success, though Jacques's birth was a thunderbolt that ruined the present and the future: the doctor pronounced the newborn babe incurable. The count carefully concealed that sentence of death, consulted further, and received despairing responses that Madeleine's birth only confirmed. Those two events and his resolute acceptance of the doctor's lethal diagnosis aggravated the old émigré's sickly disposition. His reputation was gone forever, but with a pure, irreproachable, unhappy wife at his side, who was dedicated to the anguish of motherhood without the enjoyment of any of its pleasures, the soil of his previous life was now sown with new suffering that put the seal on the destructive tendencies within his heart. The countess divined past from present and read into the future. Though nothing is so difficult as bringing happiness to a man who feels he has erred, the countess assumed that angelic task. In twenty-four hours, she became a stoic. After descending an abyss from which she still glimpsed the sky, she pledged herself, on behalf of one man, to the mission a Sister of Charity embraces on behalf of humanity, and, in helping him reconcile with himself, she forgave him what he couldn't forgive himself. The count became a miser; she accepted the privations he imposed; he feared he was being duped, as do all those who have only experienced worldly life in order to cling to its repellent aspects; she remained solitary and adapted to his suspicious character without demurring; she used her female guile to make him want what was right, and he thus valued his ideas and enjoyed a sense of superiority at home he would never have found elsewhere. Then, after she had advanced along the marital path, she decided she could never leave Clochegourde, because she recognized that the count's hysterical temperament and moods, in a country full of spite and gossip, could hurt her children. To ensure nobody suspected M. de Mortsauf's fault lines, she draped his ruins in a cloak of dense ivy. The count's irritability, rather than his discontent, together with his mercurial nature, were soothed by his wife; she provided a malleable terrain where he could lay himself down and feel her fresh balm applied to his inner grief.

This background is the clearest exposition of the insights I was able to drag from M. de Chessel by dint of his secret resentment. His knowledge of the ways of society had allowed him to see some of the mysteries buried in Clochegourde. But if Mme de Mortsauf's noble attitude fooled the world, it couldn't fool love's discerning intuitions. When I was in my small bedroom, my premonitions of the truth made me toss and turn; I couldn't bear to be in Frapesle when I could see her bedroom windows; I dressed, stealthily went downstairs, and left the château through the door of a tower with a winding staircase. The cold of night was refreshing. I crossed Red Mill bridge over the Indre, and I rowed the blessed toue to a position opposite Clochegourde, where a light shone in the last window on the Azay side. My old feelings flowed back, at peace now, but stirred by a cantor's roulades of amorous nights, the unique song of the nightingale over the water. Ideas surged within me like ghosts that stripped away the dark veils that had shrouded my beautiful future. My soul and senses were equally bewitched. My desire was focused violently on her! I wondered so often, like a fool, "Will I enjoy her?" If on previous days my universe had expanded, in a single night it now possessed a center. My hopes and ambitions were bound up with her; I wanted to be everything to her, to refashion and repair her tattered heart. I spent such a beautiful night beneath her windows, entranced by the water murmuring through the mill races, interrupted by the hourly chimes from the Saché belfry! On that luminous night where a starry flower had lit up my life, I pledged my soul to her with all the faith of the poor Castilian knight we mock in Cervantes, which is where we begin to love. At the first sign of dawn, at the first birdsong, I sped back to the grounds of Frapesle. No countryman saw me; nobody suspected my escapade, and I slept until the second when the bell announced breakfast.

Despite the heat, after breakfast, I walked back down to the meadow to see the Indre, its islands, valley, and hills, again, which I admired passionately, then, swift as a horse in full flight, I was reunited with my boat, my weeping willows, and my Clochegourde. Everything shimmered silently in the noontime countryside. Motionless foliage was silhouetted against the blue depths of the sky: insects that live on light, green damselflies and blister beetles, flitted to reeds and ash; flocks ruminated in the shade, the red earth of vineyards smoldered, and snakes slithered along slopes.

What a change in a landscape that had been so cool and flirtatious before I fell asleep! All of a sudden, I jumped from my boat and retraced my steps up the path around Clochegourde, where I thought I saw the count departing. I was right. He was walking by a hedge, no doubt heading to the gate to the Azay road, which runs alongside the river.

"How are you this morning, my dear count?"

He looked at me gratefully; he wasn't often addressed like that.

"I am well," he replied. "You must indeed love the countryside to go walking in this heat."

"You know, I was sent here to live in the open air."

"Would you like to come and see my rye being reaped?"

"I would be delighted to," I replied. "I am, I confess, incredibly ignorant. I can't tell the difference between rye and corn, a poplar and an aspen. I know nothing about cultivating crops or the different ways to exploit land."

"Come with me then," he said, gleefully retracing his steps. "Come in through the small gate at the top."

He made his way along the hedge on the inside; I went along the outside.

"You won't learn anything from M. de Chessel," he added, "he is too lordly to worry about anything except the balance sheets he receives from his administrator."

He showed me his yards and outbuildings, his ornamental gardens, orchards, and kitchen gardens. Finally, he led me towards the long path lined with acacias and Japanese varnish trees, that ran along the river, at the far end of which I spotted Mme de Mortsauf on a bench, busy with her children. She was so enchanting under those slender, rustling branches! Perhaps surprised by my ingenuous haste, she didn't budge, knowing full well we would go to her. The count had me admire the valley, which provides a variety of perspectives depending on the elevation of your vantage point. You would have thought it was a little corner of Switzerland. Divided by the streams pouring into the Indre, the meadow glories in its length and disappears into distant mists. Towards Montbazon, you see a huge expanse of green, and, on every other side, hills, masses of trees and rocky spurs. We strode along to greet Mme de Mortsauf, who dropped the book Madeleine was reading and lifted Jacques, who was in the middle of a coughing fit, onto her knee.

"What's wrong with him now?" rasped the count, turning wan.

"He has a sore throat," replied his mother, who appeared not to see me, "it's nothing serious."

She supported his head and his back, while two gleaming rays of light from her eyes poured life into the poor, weak child.

"You are so appallingly rash," retorted the count sourly, "you expose him to the cold from the river and then sit him on a stone bench."

"But, Father, that bench is burning," shouted Madeleine.

"It was stifling up there," said the countess.

"Women always think they are right!" he said, glancing at me.

To avoid giving him my approval or disapproval, I gazed at Jacques, who complained of a sore throat, and was taken off by his mother. Before they left, she heard her husband bellow: "When one produces such frail children, one should at least know how to look after them!"

Words that were deeply unfair, but his lack of self-esteem always drove him to justify himself at the expense of his wife. The countess raced up the slopes and terraces. I watched her disappear through the French windows. M. de Mortsauf sat on the bench, head bowed and pensive; my situation was intolerable; he neither looked at me nor spoke. I said goodbye to the stroll I'd hoped to use to give a favorable impression. I don't remember ever spending such a ghastly quarter of an hour. I sweated profusely, wondering: Should I go, or should I stay? What a wave of melancholy thoughts must he have experienced to make him forget to go to find out how Jacques was progressing! He stood up abruptly and walked over to me. We turned around and surveyed that happy valley.

"We must leave our stroll for another day, Monsieur le Comte," I said quietly.

"On the contrary, we should go!" he replied. "I'm unfortunate enough to see these attacks all the time, I, who would unhesitatingly give my life to save that child."

"Jacques is better, he's sleeping, my dear," said the voice of gold.

Mme de Mortsauf suddenly appeared at the end of the path; she came, showing no ill will or bitterness, and returned my greeting.

"I am pleased to see that you like Clochegourde so much."

"My love, would you like me to saddle my horse and fetch M. Deslandes?" he asked, seeking to make amends for his previous unfairness.

"Don't worry," she replied, "Jacques simply didn't get any sleep last night. He's a most restless child, he had a nightmare, and I spent the whole time telling him stories to coax him back to sleep. His is a purely nervous cough, which I've treated with a jujube, and he's finally dozed off."

"My poor wife," he continued, taking her hand, and giving her a watery glance, "I was quite unaware of any of that."

"Why should you worry about mere trifles? Go to your rye. You know that if you don't, the tenant farmer will let the gleaners from out of town into your fields before the sheaves are removed."

"Madame, I'm about to be given my first lesson in agriculture," I told her.

"You've come to a good school," she replied, pointing to the count, whose lips turned upward into that smile of satisfaction colloquially known as "turning the mouth into a heart."

Two months later I discovered she'd been horribly anxious that night, and feared her son had caught whooping cough. While I had been in that boat, cradling sweet thoughts of love, imagining she'd see me from her window, adoring the glow from a candle that was in fact illuminating a brow creased by lethal fear. A whooping-cough epidemic in Tours was causing devastation. As we walked towards the door, the count said, with high-pitched emotion: "Mme de Mortsauf is an angel!"

That word made me reel. I still knew the family only superficially, and the remorse that comes naturally to a young soul on such occasions exclaimed inwardly: "What right do *you* have to disturb this blissful peace?"

Pleased to find an impressionable young man to listen to his stories, the count told me of what future the return of the Bourbons heralded for France. We had a rambling conversation and I listened to infantile declarations I found strangely shocking. He was ignorant of the most blatant truths; he feared the educated; he denied superior talent; he mocked progress, perhaps rightly; in a word, I detected a raft of sensitive, sore places and was obliged to tread carefully to avoid upsetting him: our nonstop conversation demanded a degree of mental agility. When I had, as it were, touched a raw spot, I yielded the point, obliging him as readily as the countess would caress the raw spot. At another stage in my life, I'd surely have affronted him, but at that time, timid as a child, thinking I knew nothing, or that mature men knew it all, I was in awe of the miracles wrought in Clochegourde by that patient farmer. I listened admiringly to his plans. In an unconscious display of flattery that earned me the old gentleman's goodwill,

I ranked that lovely land, its location, that earthly paradise, well above Frapesle.

"Frapesle," I told him, "is a mass of silver-plating, whereas Cloche-gourde is a trove of precious stones!"

A sentence he would often repeat, mentioning who had said it.

"You know, before we came, this was all wasteland."

I was all ears when he spoke of his seeds and his cucumbers. New to agriculture, I bombarded him with questions about market prices, farming methods, and he seemed delighted to inform me in minute detail.

"What *do* they teach nowadays?" he asked in astonishment.

From that first day, the count told his wife on our return: "Monsieur Félix is such a charming young man!"

That evening, I wrote to my mother, asking her to send me clothes and linen, and informing her that I was going to stay in Frapesle. Quite unaware of the great revolution taking place, and not grasping how it would influence my future, I was intending to return to Paris to finish my law course, but law school didn't resume until early November. I had two and a half months before me.

From the first moments of my stay, I tried to cling closely to the count, and that was a period when I experienced his cruel outbursts. I discovered he tended to rage without reason and react immediately when he despaired, and I found that frightening. He suddenly recovered the courage of that gentleman in Condé's army, lightning strikes from the strong-willed, which, on momentous days, can wreak havoc in politics, and which, by a fortuitous union of right and courage, can also transform a man ordained to live as a gentleman into a d'Elbée, a Bonchamp, or a Charette.[6] When challenged by certain assumptions, his nose contracted, his forehead glinted, and lightning flashed in his eyes, though the thunder soon faded. I was afraid M. de Mortsauf might decipher the language of *my* eyes and kill me there and then. At the time, I was surprisingly even-tempered. The force of will, which can change men so strangely, had only just begun to show itself. Wild desires spawned rushes of feeling, as if I'd been terrified. I wasn't shaken by such turmoil, but neither did I want to lose my life before I'd tasted the happiness of requited love. Difficulty and desire grew in tandem. How could I broach my feelings? I was the victim of disturbing tensions. I waited for my opportunity; I watched; I got to know the children and they came to love me; and I tried to be in step with whatever was happening in that household.

The change occurring imperceptibly, the count became less defensive toward me. I became familiar with his rapid changes of mood, his moments of deep yet unwarranted depression, his abrupt bouts of aggression, his bitter, rasping complaints, his hateful aloofness, his outbursts of repressed lunacy, his childish whining, his manly cries of despair, and his compulsive rage. Moral nature differs from physical nature inasmuch as nothing is absolute: intensity of outcome is proportionate to strength of character or to the ideas we assemble around a particular act. My place at Clochegourde, my life's future, depended on his capricious temperament. I can't tell you the anguish that flowed into my soul, which was as ready to expand as to contract when I wondered, as I walked in: What kind of reception will I get today? Or how anxious I felt when a storm suddenly gathered on his snowy temples! I was constantly on edge. I was at the mercy of the man's despotic turns.

My own suffering made me suspect that of Mme de Mortsauf. We began to exchange knowing glances; my tears sometimes flowed when she held hers back. In that way the countess and I tested ourselves through sorrow. I discovered so much in those first forty days of bitter fruit and silent joy, of hopes dashed and hopes aroused! One evening, I found her religiously meditative before a sunset that sumptuously reddened peaks and sensuously revealed the long valley bed: it was impossible not to hear the voice of the eternal Song of Songs with which nature summons its creatures to love. Was the young woman cherishing hopes that had vanished? Was she suffering from some secret comparison? I thought I saw an abandon that invited first confessions, and said: "Some days can be so trying!"

"You've seen into my soul," she replied, "how *did* you do that?"

"We are so very alike!" I replied. "Don't we both belong to that small band of individuals who feel pain and pleasure intensely, whose sensory instruments are struck in unison, producing deep inner resonances, and whose nervous systems are in close harmony with the essence of things? Put them in a place where dissonance rules, and they suffer terribly, just as their pleasure heightens when they find ideas, sensations, or beings to their liking. However, for us, there exists a third state, whose trials are known only to souls troubled by the same infirmity, where they find intimate mutual understanding. Perhaps we are stirred neither for good nor for evil. Restless organ-pipes echo within us in a void, become impassioned without cause, make sounds but no melody, emit chords that are lost in silence: a horrible contradiction in a soul that rebels against the futility of the void; oppressive games in which our power slips away unnourished, like blood seeping from an unknown wound. Our feelings run amok, horrible fatigue ensues, and ineffable melancholy, to which the confessional turns deaf ears. Doesn't that express the pain we both feel?"

She gave a start, and, still gazing at the sunset, replied: "How can one so young know such things? Were you a woman once?"

"Oh!" I answered, enthralled, "my childhood was one long illness."

"I can hear Madeleine coughing," she replied, rushing off.

The countess saw how often I visited her but never took umbrage, for two reasons. Firstly, she was as innocent as a child, and her thoughts never strayed. Secondly, I entertained the count and was meat to that lion without claws or mane. I'd finally found an excuse to visit that everyone found plausible. I didn't know how to play backgammon. M. de Mortsauf offered to teach me, and I accepted. The moment we agreed on that, the countess couldn't help glancing pitifully my way, as if to say: Can't you see you are throwing yourself into the wolf's maw. I understood nothing initially, but by the third day I realized what was in store. My patience, which nothing can wear down, a product of my childhood, only deepened during that testing time. The count enjoyed mocking me cruelly when I didn't put into practice the principle or rule he'd just explained; if I pondered, he complained that slow games bored him; if I played quickly, he was irritated by my haste; if I blundered, he took advantage and told me I was in too much of a hurry. It was a schoolmasterly tyranny, despotism enforced by ferule, which I can only liken to Epictetus fallen under the thumb of a cruel child, just to give you some idea of what it was like. When we played for money, his constant wins led to petty, puerile displays of glee. A word from his wife consoled me and would abruptly restore his polite facade. I was soon plunged into the fires of a torture I hadn't anticipated. My money was vanishing in those games. Though the count always remained between his wife and myself until the moment I departed, sometimes at a very late hour, I fondly hoped I'd find a moment to enter her heart, but that meant waiting with a hunter's patience, and I was forced to continue those wretched games, which constantly battered my feelings and emptied my purse! We so often stayed silent, watching the play of sunlight on the meadow, the storm clouds in the gray sky, the hazy hills, or the moon glittering on pebbles in the river, saying only: "What a beautiful night!"

"Night is a woman, madame."

"It is so quiet!"

"Yes, one could hardly be entirely unhappy here."

At which, she would return to her tapestry. I had at last felt an inner response caused by the affection that was seeking its rightful place. But once I was without money, it was farewell to those evenings. I had written to Mother asking her to send some; Mother scolded me and sent none for a week. Who else could I turn to? My life was at stake! In the midst of that, my first true bliss, I was back to the anxieties that had plagued me everywhere else, but in Paris, at school, in the boardinghouse, my unhappiness had been passive; in Frapesle, it became an active torment; I felt the desire to steal, dreamed of profitable crimes, and fell into awful rages that sully the soul, ones that we must stifle if we don't wish to forfeit our own pride. Memories of the cruel thoughts and distress caused by my mother's parsimony inspired in me a sacrosanct indulgence for young people who, without ever erring, have teetered on the edge of the abyss, as if wanting to measure its depth. Although my integrity, nourished by cold sweat, strengthens at these moments when life opens out to reveal its gravel paths, when cruel human justice places its blade on a man's neck, I told myself: Penal laws were drawn up by people who have never been unhappy.

At that nerve-racking time, I discovered a backgammon manual in M. de Chessel's library and studied it hard; then my host decided to give me a few lessons; under his more lenient tutelage, I made progress, and I learned to apply the rules and calculations I'd memorized. Within days I was in a position to tame my master, though when I won, he flew into a fury, his eyes blazing like a tiger's, face contorting, and eyebrows contracting as I'd never seen anyone's contract before. He whined like a spoiled brat. He sometimes threw the dice around, fumed, stamped his feet, bit his ear trumpet. His violence was short-lived. When I had the better of him in a game, I conducted the battle at my own pace; I organized everything so that it came out almost even at the end, letting him win the first part of the game, and righting the balance in the second. The end of the world would have surprised the count less than the superior skills his pupil had rapidly attained, but he never acknowledged that. The repeated outcomes of our games opened up fresh pastures for his mind to exploit.

"Certainly," he would say, "my poor brain tires. You always win toward the end of our games, when my mind has grown quite exhausted."

The countess was familiar with the game and spotted my tactics from the start, and I intuited huge outpourings of tenderness. Such details can be appreciated only by those familiar with the immense difficulties of backgammon. It was no small thing! But love, like Bossuet's God, prizes the poor man's glass of water above the most decisive victory, or the efforts made by the lowliest soldier who dies unknown. The countess glanced at me silently and gratefully, enough to break a young man's heart: it was the glance she reserved for her children! After that blissful evening, she *always* looked at me when she spoke to me.

I couldn't describe to you the state I was in when I left. My soul had absorbed my body; I levitated; I didn't walk; I flew. I felt her gaze within me, flooding me with light, as if her "Adieu, monsieur" had aroused the "O filii, ô filiae!" of the Easter hymn in my soul. I was born into a new life. I meant something to her! I slept in purple swaddling clothes. Flames flickered past my closed eyes, chased each other in the shadows, like little red embers racing over ashes of burnt paper. In my dreams, her voice became tangible in some way, surrounding me in a haze of light and scent, in a melody that caressed my mind. The day after, her welcome communicated the fullness of the feelings she had bestowed, and thereafter I was initiated into her voice's secret ways. That was to be one of the most defining days of my life. After lunch, we walked the heights, we crossed barren heathland, over stony, parched soil without a blade of green, though there were a few oaks and hawthorn bushes, but rather than treading on weeds, our feet slid over a sunlit carpet of fawn, crinkled moss. I held Madeleine's hand to keep her steady, and Mme de Mortsauf's arm supported Jacques. Walking ahead of us, the count turned around, hit the ground with his stick, and addressed me grimly: "There is my life! Oh! I mean, before I met you," he added, looking apologetically at his wife.

His amends came too late; the countess had already blanched. What woman wouldn't have reeled when dealt such a blow?

"What exquisite scents! What beautiful plays of light!" I rhapsodized, "I would really like to own this moor. I expect I'd find treasure if I dug this soil, though the true riches would derive from being your neighbor. Who wouldn't pay a high price to contemplate such harmony and to look over that snaking river, where the soul bathes between the ash and the alder. That's the difference in our tastes! For you, this corner of the earth is barren heathland: for me, it is paradise!"

She glanced gratefully at me.

"Pastoral nonsense!" he retorted acrimoniously, "this is no place for a man bearing your name to live."

Then he broke off and said: "Can you hear the bells from Azay? I hear their loud chimes."

Mme de Mortsauf looked fearfully at me; Madeleine squeezed my hand.

"Would you like to go back and play backgammon?" I asked. "The clatter of dice will soon blot out the bells."

We returned to Clochegourde talking in fits and starts. The count complained of sharp pains but could never pinpoint one place in particular where they originated. When we entered the drawing room, I felt a vague awkwardness between us. The count sank into an armchair, absorbed in thoughts respected by his wife, who recognized the symptoms of his illness and anticipated an outburst. I replicated her silence. If she weren't begging me to leave, she was perhaps thinking that a game of backgammon would distract the count and ward off a lethal eruption of temper that was deadly to her.

Nothing was harder than persuading the count to play that game of backgammon, one he always wanted to play. Like a coquette, he craved to be implored, urged, so it wouldn't seem simply an obligation, maybe because that was actually the case. After a tentative exchange, if I forgot to bow and scrape, he turned sullen, prickly, and sarcastic, and, irritated by our conversation, contradicted everything I said. Forewarned by his vexed tone, I suggested we play a game, and he retorted, mischievously: "First of all, it is too late; secondly, it doesn't really appeal." In the end, he minced and flounced, like a woman who finally makes sure you don't know what she really wants. I went down on my knees, I beseeched him to indulge me, to allow me to exercise a skill I'd forget if I didn't practice. On this occasion, I was forced to go to outrageous lengths to convince him. He complained of dizzy spells that would prevent him from keeping score; his skull felt as if it were in the grip of a vice; he could hear a ringing in his ears; he stifled, then released, huge sighs. Finally, he agreed to come to the table.

Mme de Mortsauf left us to put the children to bed and to lead the house in prayers. All went well in her absence; I saw to it that M. de Mortsauf won, and he suddenly cheered up. His rapid progression from misery and morbid predictions about himself to a drunkard's glee, a lunatic's cackles of laughter, worried me, then froze the marrow in my bones. I'd never seen him take such a violent turn. Our close acquaintance had borne fruit; he never stood on ceremony with me. Every day, he tried to enfold me in his tyrannical grasp and gain a new object for his moodiness; there must be some truth to the idea that moral turpitude is a beast with its own hunger and instincts, which longs to expand its empire, just as a landowner strives to increase the size of his estate.

The countess came down, and she sat near our backgammon table, where she would have more light for her tapestry work, though she started sewing with an ill-disguised apprehension. A deadly blow in the game that I couldn't prevent transformed the count's face, which changed from jubilant to gloomy, from purple to yellow, while his eyes quivered. Then a final terrible eruption came that I could have neither foreseen nor forestalled. M. de Mortsauf made a calamitous throw of the dice and secured his own ruination. He stood up, threw the table at me, sending the lamp to the floor, banged his fist on the console, and leaped around the room—I could hardly describe it as walking. The torrent of insults and curses from his lips suggested he had been possessed by some medieval trance. Imagine how I felt!

"Go into the garden," she advised, squeezing my hand.

I left without the count noticing and made my way slowly to the terrace, where I could hear him bawling and moaning from his bedroom, adjacent to the dining room. During that storm, I also heard an angel's voice, which, now and then, soared like the song of a nightingale after the rain has stopped. I walked beneath the acacias on that wondrous night at the end of August, and waited for the countess to join me. She came; she had indicated she would.

A clearing of the air had been pursuing us for days, as if the first word to unleash the spring welling within our souls would generate it. What sense of tact delayed the moment we would find perfect accord? Perhaps she loved, as I did, that tingling emotion, like fear pummeling one's feelings, when one's life is about to spill over, when one hesitates to reveal one's innermost self, like the shyness seizing a young woman about to unveil herself to her beloved husband. Our hidden reservoirs of thought had been preparing such a long-overdue impulse. An hour went by. I was sitting on the brick balustrade when the echo of her footsteps and the swish of her flowing dress enlivened the evening calm: they are sounds that go straight to the heart.

"M. de Mortsauf is asleep," she told me. "When he's like that, I give him a poppy-head infusion, by which time his attacks are distant enough for that simple remedy to have an effect.

"Monsieur," she said, adopting a more persuasive tone, "a stroke of misfortune has revealed secrets to you that have been carefully concealed till now; you must promise to bury all memories of that scene in the deepest recesses of your mind. Please, do it for my sake. I don't ask for solemn pledges, and will be satisfied by the *yes* of a man of honor."

"Do I need to say that word?" I asked. "Have we never understood each other?"

"Don't judge M. de Mortsauf unfavorably when you witness the results of his suffering as an émigré," she went on. "Tomorrow he will have forgotten everything he said, and you will find him excellent, charming company."

"Madame," I replied, "please stop trying to justify the count, I will do everything you want. I'd throw myself into the Indre this minute, if by doing so I could reanimate M. de Mortsauf and restore you to a life of happiness. The only thing I cannot reshape are my beliefs; nothing is more strongly embedded within me. I'd give you my life, but I cannot give you my conscience; I can decide not to listen to it, but how can I prevent my conscience from speaking? In my opinion, M. Mortsauf is—"

"I understand," she said, interjecting, quite uncharacteristically, "you are right. The count is as skittish as a coquette"—she diluted any suggestion of lunacy by choosing her words carefully—"but he is only like that sporadically, at most once a year. Emigration has wrought so much evil! So many fine lives have been destroyed! He could, I am sure, have been a great warrior, an honor to his country."

"I know," I said, interrupting her in turn, hoping she would understand it was futile to try to fool me.

She stopped, put a hand on my forehead, and said: "Who brought you into our lives? Was it God sending me help, a stalwart friend and ally?" she continued, pressing her hand firmly down on mine. Because you are so good and generous..."

She lifted her eyes to the heavens, as if searching for visible proof to confirm her secret hopes, then focused her eyes on me. Electrified by that gaze, which etched her soul onto mine, I suffered, as social protocol would say, a lapse of tact; though some might call it selfless haste in the face of danger, a desire to forestall conflict, fear of a disaster that never comes, or, more often than not, a question suddenly directed at another's feelings, a blow dealt to see if it echoes in unison. Several lines of thought surfaced, glimmered in my mind, urging me to wash away the stain on my innocence, at a moment when I anticipated true initiation.

"Before we go any further," I said in a voice palpably shaking in that deep silence, "will you let me eradicate a memory from the past?"

"Shush," she admonished, lifting a finger rapidly to her lips, then removing it.

She looked at me proudly, as if she were too noble a woman to be hurt by that insult, and replied in a troubled tone: "I know what you are referring to. It was the first, last, and only outrage I have ever suffered! Never mention that ball again. This Christian woman may have forgiven you, but this wife still mourns."

"Don't be less forgiving than God," I replied, hiding the tears welling behind my lashes.

"I should be more severe, but I am merely weaker," she responded.

"Now," I retorted, in a fit of childish pique, "listen to me, even if it's for the first, last, and only time in your life."

"Very well," she said, "speak your mind! Otherwise you will think I'm afraid to hear you out."

Sensing that this was a unique moment in our lives, I told her, in a manner demanding her attention, that all the other women at that ball meant nothing to me, nor did any I'd seen previously, but the second I saw her, I, the young man who'd been so timorous and bookish, had been engulfed in a turmoil only those who had never experienced such emotion could criticize; never had a man's heart been so filled with a desire no creature could resist, a desire that conquers all, even death—

"And what about contempt?" she interrupted.

"Did you feel contempt for me?" I asked.

"We should forget all that," she replied.

"On the contrary!" I retorted desperately. "It affects my whole being, my hidden life, a secret you should know, or I will die of despair! And doesn't it also affect you, who, though unaware, have been the lady holding the glittering crown promised to the winners of the tournament?"

I told her of my childhood and youth, but not as I told it to you—making judgments with the benefit of hindsight—but with the passionate words of a young man whose wounds still bled. My voice echoed like a woodcutter's axe in the forest. Those dead years crashed around her with the endless sorrow that had hidden them under bare branches. My fevered words painted a multitude of terrible details that I have spared you. I set before her the treasure of my luminous vows, the virgin gold of my desire, a burning heart preserved beneath alpine ice, grown thick in a relentless winter. Then I bent under the weight of pain that I recounted with Isaiah's red-hot coals, I waited for a word from this woman who had listened, her head bowed, and a single glance lit up the darkness, as she stirred heaven and earth with a word: "We have endured the *same* childhood!" she declared, turning a face towards me that glowed with a martyr's halo.

After a lull when our souls were wedded by a single comforting thought: "I wasn't the only one to suffer!" spoken to me in a tone she reserved for her children, the countess told me how she had been unfortunate enough to be born a daughter after the demise of sons. She spelled out the differences between her grief as a girl permanently attached to her mother's skirts, and the grief of a child thrown into the world of boarding schools. My loneliness had been a paradise compared to the millstone that constantly crushed her soul, until the day her real mother, her good aunt, rescued her from that torture, the incessant pain that she had described to me. It was caused by her mother's dire captiousness, unbearable to a nervous disposition like hers, that didn't flinch before a dagger's thrust but would die under Damocles' sword; she faced expressions of generosity halted by icy orders, kisses received coldly, silences imposed and then reproached;

tears she swallowed that lingered in her heart; a thousand convent tyrannies, hidden from the eyes of strangers by a facade of much-vaunted motherliness. Her mother gloried in her and showed her off, but the day after she would pay dearly for the flattery her teacher had been forced to show her to achieve that glory. When she believed her obedience and charm had won her mother's heart, which had seemed to soften towards her, the tyrant reappeared, galvanized by her show of affection. A traitor couldn't have been more cowardly or treacherous. All her girlish pleasures and parties were sold to her at the highest price, because she would later be scolded for being happy, as if that were a sin.

Her lessons in refinement were never delivered lovingly, but with hurtful sarcasm. She bore her mother no grudges, and reproached herself for feeling terror rather than love in her mother's presence. Perhaps, thought this angel, her severity was necessary: Hadn't such lessons prepared her for her present life? Listening to her, I felt the Job's harp where I'd plucked such fierce chords, were now touched by Christian fingers, and responded by singing the Virgin's litanies from the foot of the cross.

"We lived in the same sphere before we ever met here; you set out from the east and I from the west."

She shook her head in despair: "The east is yours, the west mine! You will live happily while I die of sorrow! Men shape the events in their lives, while my life is ordained forever. No force can break the heavy chain a wife carries in her gold ring, that emblem of wifely purity."

Now that we felt we were twins from the same breast, she didn't grasp why revelations should only be half-hearted between siblings who had drunk from the same springs. After a sigh that comes naturally to the pure in heart when they begin to open up, she described the first days of their marriage, her first disappointments, and the *reiterated* anguish. Like myself, she had experienced the pettiness that is so damaging to beings whose brittle innocence is easily shattered, as a stone hurled into a lake stirs surface and depths alike. When she married, she possessed her savings, a handful of gold that represented hours of joy and the myriad desires of youth; on a turbulent day she had generously relinquished it, never explaining that they were memories, not mere coins of gold; her husband didn't take that into account, and had no idea what he owed her! In exchange for that treasure engulfed by oblivion's sleepy waters, she had never received in return a tearful look that can put the seal on everything, that generous spirits see as an eternal jewel whose fires glow at moments of crisis. She lurched from one upset to the next! M. de Mortsauf forgot to give her the money she needed for household expenses; he awoke as if from a dream, when she overcame her wifely reserve and asked him for some, and he never once spared her those cruel attacks! She was seized by such terror when that bankrupt's malevolence hit out at her! She'd been broken when his violent temper exploded for the first time. She had frantically racked her brain, often deciding her husband was both a nonentity and the towering figure who ruled her existence! Then came the calamities following her two confinements! The sudden seizures at the sight of two apparently stillborn children! And the courage to tell herself: "I will breathe life into them! I will give birth to them day after day!" Then despair followed when she met only obstacles in the heart and hands that should have helped her! She watched her appalling misfortunes unfold over thorny savannahs at every hurdle she overcame. After each rocky outcrop she scaled, she faced new deserts to cross, until the day she fathomed her husband's character, the way to organize her children and the land where she was to live; until the day when, like the child snatched by Napoleon from the tender cares of home, she had trained her feet to walk in mud and snow, accustomed her brow to every millstone, and her entire person to a soldier's passive obedience. My account for you is brief, but her story was full of horrible detail, a mass of harrowing incidents, marital squabbles, and futile confrontations.

"Finally," she told me, "you'd have to stay here for months to see how onerous it has been for me to bring improvements to Clochegourde, how exhausting it has been buttering him up so he would agree to do what best suited his own interests! Or how childishly spiteful he would become if something done on my say-so wasn't an immediate success! Or how quick he was to claim any breakthrough!

Or what patience I have to summon to listen to his every gripe when I am killing myself to free up his time, purify the air he breathes, bolster him, make paths flower where he had planted stones! My only reward is this terrible refrain: 'I will die! My life is such a burden!' When he's fortunate to have company at home, he is gracious and polite. Why isn't he like that with his own family? I can't explain such backstabbing from a man who can act with such chivalry. He is quite capable of riding at full gallop to Paris to find me a dress, as he did recently for the town ball. Miserly when it comes to household expenses, he can be lavish towards me, as if I have ever wanted that. It should be the reverse: I need nothing; it is his household that is demanding. In my desire to make him happy, never dreaming I'd be a mother, I have perhaps accustomed him to see me as his victim; if I wheedled and coaxed, I could lead him on like a child, that is, if I could stoop to playing such an odious role! But household interests require me to be serene and severe like a statue of justice, yet I too am a loving, generous soul!"

"Why" I asked, "don't you use your power to control him and tell him what to do?"

"If it were only about myself, I wouldn't tolerate his sullen silences, the hours spent resisting rational argument, or responding to his il- logical reasoning or infantile comments. I can find no reserves of courage to fight weakness or childishness; they hit me and I can't resist; perhaps I should oppose force with force, but I can find no energy to fight those I pity. If I had to compel Madeleine to do some- thing to save herself, I would die with her. Compassion loosens my every fiber and softens my nerve-ends. Ten years of his violent assaults have worn me down; my sensitivity, so often under attack, is sometimes threadbare and I find nothing to reinvigorate it; at times I lack the energy I once had to withstand these storms. Yes, at times I feel de- feated. Without rest and swims in the sea that might revive my nerves, I will perish. M. de Mortsauf will be *my* death, and my death will kill him."

"Why don't you leave Clochegourde for a few months? Why don't you and your children go the seaside?"

"First of all, if I traveled far, M. de Mortsauf would see that as his ruination. He refuses to confront his situation, though he *is* aware of it. He is a male and an invalid, two distinct states whose opposition explains many of these peculiar situations! And he'd be right to shudder at the notion. Everything here would go downhill. You have perhaps seen me as the family mother busy protecting her children against the hawk circling above. An exhausting task, exacerbated by the demanding needs of M. de Mortsauf, who never stops asking: 'Where is Madame?' That's the least of it. I am also Jacques's tutor and Madeleine's governess. And that's not all! I am steward and administrator. One day you will grasp the implications of what I am saying when you realize that farming land here is a the most time-consuming business. We receive little income in terms of money. Our land is only half farmed, in a system that requires constant surveillance. One must sell one's own grain, animals, and every harvest. We compete with our own tenant farmers, who do deals in taverns with buyers and agree prices after being the first to sell. And I would bore you if I started to explain the thousand difficulties we face tilling our land. However diligent I am, I cannot watch out to ensure our tenants don't nourish their own land with our manure; I can't even go to find out whether our gang-masters are reaching deals with them when they are sharing out the harvests, or know when it's the best time to sell. If you reflect on M.de Mortsauf's scant powers of recall, on the efforts you have seen me making to compel him to look after our estate, you will understand how heavy my burden is, and how I couldn't relinquish it for a single moment. If I weren't here, we would be bankrupted. Nobody would listen to him; most of the time, the orders he gives out are contradictory; besides, nobody likes him, he is always moaning, he is too high-handed, and, like all weak individuals, too quick to be led by his inferiors to inspire those around him with the affection that brings families together. If I were to leave, no domestic staff would stay here a week. You must appreciate that I am as stuck in Clochegourde as the lead flashing is to our roofs. I have held nothing back, monsieur. Nobody in the region knows the secrets of Clochegourde, and now you know them all. Say only good, complimentary things about this place, and you will enjoy my esteem and respect," she added still warmly. "That is the price you must pay to be always welcome in Clochegourde and find a kindred spirit here."

"But," I replied, "I've never really suffered! You alone..."

"No," she retorted, with a womanly smile of resignation that could split granite, "please don't be shocked by my revelations, they show life as it is, and not as your imagination led you to expect. We all have our faults and good qualities. If I had married a spendthrift, he would have ruined me. If I had been given to an ardent, sensuous young man, he might have been successful, perhaps I would have lost him, he would have left me, and I would be dying of jealousy! I am jealous!" she exclaimed loudly, like a thunderclap from a passing storm. "After all, M. de Mortsauf loves me as much as he is able; all the affection his heart holds, he pours at my feet, as Mary Magdalen poured the dregs of her perfume over the feet of our Savior. You must accept what I'm about to say! A life of love is a fatal exception to the laws of this earth; every flower will wither, great bliss augurs a sad tomorrow, when there is a tomorrow. Real life is anguish; its image is the nettle at the foot of the terrace, that, starved of sun, remains green on its stem. Here, as in northern climes, there are bright lights in our sky, however rare, that make up for much suffering. In any case, aren't women who are exclusively mothers bound more by sacrifice than by pleasure? In this place, I attract to myself the storms I see about to break over the servants or my children, and, as I divert them, I'm filled with a feeling that gives me unseen strength. The previous evening's resignation always prepares tomorrow's round. God never leaves me without a scrap of hope. If at first my children's health was a source of despair, the more they progress in life, the better they are. After all, our house has been modernized; our fortune is being rebuilt. Who knows whether M. de Mortsauf might not enjoy a happy old age because of me? One must cling to that! The individual entering the presence of the great judge on high, green palm in hand, leading back to Him those who cursed life and are now consoled, that individual has transformed His sorrows into delight. If my suffering serves to make my family happy, can one really call it suffering?"

"Yes," I said, "but they were as necessary as mine were to make me appreciate the flavor of the fruit ripened on our rocks; perhaps we will now enjoy them together, and admire their wonders, the affection flooding our souls, the sap reviving the yellowing leaves. Life is no longer a burden, is no longer ours. My God, dost thou not harken unto me?" I continued to employ the mystical language our religious education had accustomed us to. "Behold the paths along which we have walked to one another; what magnet has drawn us over the ocean's briny waters to a freshwater spring, flowing round the skirts of hills, and over the spangled sand between two green, flowering banks. Like the magi, did we not follow the same star? Here we are, before the crib where a holy child will wake up and fire his arrows at bare treetops, rekindling our world with his joyful cries, who, through infinite pleasure, will revive our lust for life, restore sleep to our nights, and bliss to our days. Year after year, who tied the new knots between us? Aren't we more than brother and sister? Never undo what the heavens have united. The suffering that you describe was seed cast by the sower's hand to help a harvest bloom that was already gilded by the most beautiful sun. Lo and behold! Won't we go forth and gather ear of corn after ear of corn together? What strength has infused me so I dare speak to you like this! Give me an answer me now! Or I will never cross the Indre again."

"You spared me the word *love*," she interrupted sternly, "but you've spoken of a feeling I don't recognize and that I'm not permitted. You are a child, I can forgive you again, but for one last time, monsieur, you should understand that my heart is inebriated by maternal affection. I don't love M. de Mortsauf out of social duty or the calculation of any eternal blessings I might earn, but out of an irresistible feeling that ties him to every fiber of my being. Was I browbeaten into marriage? No, it was decided by my compassion for the hapless. Isn't a woman tasked with compensating for the evils of her times and caring for those who ran the gauntlet and returned wounded? What more can I say? I experienced a kind of selfish satisfaction when I saw you keeping him amused: Wasn't that purely maternal feeling? Hasn't my confession shown you enough of the *three* children I can never fail, who I must soothe with my balm and warm from my soul, never diluting a single attention? Don't sour a mother's milk! Although the wife within me is invulnerable, don't talk to me like that again. If you can't respect my simple self-defenses, I must tell you that you will be forbidden entry into this house. I believed in a pure friendship, in voluntary fraternity truer than any that is imposed. What a mistake! I wanted a friend who wasn't a judge, a friend who would listen in moments of weakness when the voice that reprimands is the voice that kills, a hallowed friend who gave me no cause to fear. Youth is noble, doesn't lie, and is capable of sacrifice and disinterest: seeing how persistent you were, I believed, I confess, that it must be heaven's design; I thought I had found a soul for myself alone, as a priest is for everyone, a heart where I could pour my sorrows when they overflow, and cry out when my tears are relentless and threaten to choke me if I continue swallowing them down. That seemed a way, my life, so precious to my children, could have lasted until Jacques reached manhood. But wasn't I being too selfish? Can Petrarch's Laura start again? I was mistaken. It's not what God wants. I must die at my post, like a friendless soldier. My confessor is coarse, severe, and . . . my aunt is no more."

Two large tears lit by a moonbeam slipped from her eyes, rolled down her cheeks, teetered on the edge, where my hand was swift enough to catch them, and I drank them with the pious alacrity aroused by words marked out by ten years of secret tears, wasted feelings, constant worry and perpetual alarums, the most sublime heroism of your sex! She looked at me in a sweetly foolish fashion.

"You see there," I replied, "love's first holy communion. Yes, I've just joined you in your sorrow, been united with your soul, as we are united in Christ when we drink his divine substance. Love without hope is still happiness. After all, what other woman on this earth could bring me the joy I felt when I tasted your tears! I accept this pact that will make me suffer. I surrender with no ulterior motives and will be whatever you wish me to be."

She gestured to me to stop, and continued emphatically: "I agree to this pact, provided you never tighten the links that bind us."

"Yes," I replied, "but the less you grant, the more I will surely possess."

"Now you have struck a suspect note," she responded with the melancholy of doubt.

"No, it was a note of pure joy. Listen! I'd like to call you by a name that was mine alone, like this sentiment we pledge to each other."

"That is a lot to ask," she said, "I am not as young as you think I am. M. de Mortsauf calls me Blanche. A single person in this world, the one I most loved, my darling aunt, used to call me Henriette. Let me be Henriette once again—for you."

I took her hand and kissed it. She gave it to me with the trust that makes women so superior to us, a trust that overwhelms us. She leaned on the brick balustrade and looked out at the Indre.

"My friend," she asked, "I don't think it can be right to reach the end of the race with your first sprint? With your first wish, you have drained a cup offered in all innocence. But real feelings aren't shared, they must be whole, or they don't not exist." After a moment's silence, she continued, "M. de Mortsauf is essentially steadfast and proud. You will perhaps be tempted, for my sake, to forget what he said; if he doesn't remember, I will remind him tomorrow. Stay away from Clochegourde for a time, and he will hold you in higher regard. He will approach you when we leave church next Sunday; I know what he's like, he will put his bad behavior behind him and be grateful to you for treating him like a man who is responsible for his words and deeds."

"Five days without seeing you, without hearing your voice!"

"Never put that kind of warmth into the words you say to me," she warned.

We walked twice around the terrace—in silence. Then she announced, in a manner that told me she was taking possession of my soul.

"It is late and we must go our separate ways."

I wanted to kiss her hand, she hesitated, then gave it me, while imploring: "Take my hand only when I offer it, and leave that to my free will; otherwise, I would be yours, and that is quite impossible."

"Goodbye," I said.

I left through the small bottom-gate, that she opened for me. When she was about to close it, she opened it again, held out her hand and said: "You've been so kind tonight and brought consolation to my entire future; take it, my friend, take it!"

I kissed her hand repeatedly, and, when I looked up, I saw tears in her eyes. She retraced her steps up the terrace and looked at me for a moment across the meadow. When I was on the path to Frapesle, I saw her white dress lit by the moon; a few moments later, a light lit her bedroom.

"Oh, my Henriette!" I told myself, "my love for you is the purest that has ever graced this earth!"

I walked to Frapesle, looking back at every step I took. I felt ineffably blissful. A dazzling future had finally opened up for the devotion that fills youthful hearts and that had remained inert in mine so long. Like the priest who takes one step and moves on to a new life, I was hallowed, I was pledged. A mere "Yes, madame!" had sufficed to commit me to keeping an irresistible love to myself, within my heart, and to never misusing our friendship to entice her imperceptibly towards love. All the noble sentiments she'd aroused made their confused voices speak within me now.

Before shutting myself in my room, I decided to linger for a few voluptuous moments beneath the starry azure and listen to the ring-dove's wistful coos, the innocent melody of that ingenuous trust, and gather in the air everything flowing from that soul towards me. She was so noble in the profound way she dismissed her own ego, in her devotion to beings who were injured, frail or grieving, a dedication unfettered by legal chains! She was so serene on the pyre of a saint and martyr. I wondered at her face looming in the darkness, when suddenly I thought I discerned a meaning in her words, a mysterious significance that made her absolutely sublime in my eyes. Perhaps she wanted me to be for her what she represented in her own small world; perhaps she wanted to draw strength and consolation from me, and thus place me in her sphere, at her level or higher. Some bold constructors of worlds say that is how the stars share movement and light. That thought suddenly lifted me to ethereal heights. I was back in the skies of my old dreams and saw my childhood sorrows in the light of the immense happiness suffusing me now.

Geniuses washed away by tears, misunderstood hearts, saintly Clarissa Harlowes,[7] abandoned children, innocent pariahs, all who have entered life through its deserts, who have found only cold faces, closed hearts and ears, never complain! You alone can experience the infinite joy when a heart opens out to you, when an ear listens, and a gaze responds. A single day erases all those days of despondency. Past sorrow, introspection, despair, and melancholy, which are never forgotten, are so many bonds that tie our soul to that trusting soul. Embellished by our repressed desires, a woman now inherits our squandered sighs and love; she sighs, magnifies and restores our betrayed affection, and justifies previous suffering as the payment destiny demands for the eternal happiness it grants us on the day that we pledge our souls. Only angels can utter the new name by which this hallowed love must be known, as only you, dear martyrs, can understand what Mme de Mortsauf suddenly meant to me in my wretched solitude.

FIRST LOVES

THAT CONVERSATION took place on a Tuesday; on my strolls I didn't cross the Indre till the Sunday. They were five days when Clochegourde experienced notable developments. The count was given a field marshal's commission, the Croix de Saint-Louis, and a pension of four thousand francs. The Duc de Lenoncourt-Givry was named peer of the realm, recovered two forests, and resumed his duties at court, and his wife had restored to her some unsold property that had fallen under the domain of the imperial court. The Comtesse de Montsauf thus became one of the richest heiresses in Le Maine. Her mother arrived with a hundred thousand francs saved from Givry income, the balance of her dowry, which had never been paid, something the count had never disclosed, despite their financial straits. In matters of the outside world, his behavior displayed a defiant lack of self-interest. By adding that sum to his savings, the count was able to buy two neighboring estates worth around nine thousand pounds annually. As his son would succeed to his grandfather's peerage, he immediately decided to create an entailed property that would comprise the landholdings of both families, without detriment to Madeleine, who would of course find a fine match thanks to the Duc de Lenoncourt's influence. These changes and windfalls poured a little balm on the former exile's wounds.

The arrival of the Duchesse de Lenoncourt in Clochegourde was no small event in the life of the region. I painfully reflected that she was a grande dame and perceived the caste spirit in her daughter that in my eyes hid her nobility of feeling. What was I—a poor soul with no future beyond my courage and wits? I hadn't thought through the consequences of the Restoration as it regarded myself or others.

On Sunday, from the private chapel where I sat in church with M. and Mme de Chessel and Abbé Quélus, I glanced eagerly at another side chapel, occupied by the duchess and her daughter and the count and his children. The straw hat that hid my idol never wavered, and her willful ignoring of me seemed to bind me tighter to everything that had happened in the past. The noble Henriette of Lenoncourt, now my dear Henriette, whose life I wished to help flourish, was praying ardently; faith gave her demeanor a sense of rapt absorption, of prostration, the poise of a religious statue, and all of that went straight to my heart.

As is the custom with village priests, vespers were sung sometime after Mass. When we left church, as a matter of course, Mme de Chessel suggested to her neighbors that they spend those two hours in Frapesle, rather than cross the Indre and the meadow twice in that heat. Her offer was accepted. M. de Chessel gave his arm to the duchess, Mme de Chessel accepted the count's, I gave mine to the countess, and for the first time I felt that beautiful arm at my side. On the walk back from the church to Frapesle, on a path through the Saché woods, where the light filtering through the leaves created pretty plays on the sand like painted silks, I was struck by feelings of pride and by ideas that made me shudder violently.

"What *is* the matter?" she asked after we'd walked a few steps in a silence I dared not break. "Your heart beats too hard . . ."

"I've heard about the changes that bring you such good fortune," I said, "and like all who love dearly, they make me fearful. Won't your new exalted status damage your friendships?"

"Do you really think so? If you express such an idea again, I won't simply hold you in contempt, I shall forget you forever."

I looked at her, entranced, as she must have noticed.

"We are taking advantage of benefits from laws we neither prompted nor requested, but we will act neither like beggars nor misers, and, besides, as you know only too well, neither I nor M. de Mortsauf can leave Clochegourde. On my advice, he has refused the position in the

Maison Rouge[8] that was his by right. It suffices that my father bears that burden! Our enforced modesty," she said, smiling bitterly, "has already served our son well. The king, whom my father serves, has graciously announced that he will bestow the favor we declined upon Jacques. We are engaged in serious debate about Jacques's education that we must plan now: he's going to represent two dynasties, the Lenoncourts and the Mortsaufs. My ambitions have to focus on him alone and it makes me doubly anxious. Jacques must not only live his life, but become worthy of his name, two obligations that are in conflict. Until now I could look after his education and strike a balance between his studies and his physical energy, but where will I find a suitable tutor now? In due course, what friend will protect him from the horrors of Paris, where everything is a snare for the spirit and a peril to the body? My friend," she said excitedly, "looking at your own brow and eyes, who could fail to see that you are a bird destined to live among the high peaks? Take flight, and one day be our son's godfather. Go to Paris; if your brother or father can't finance you, our family, especially my mother, a genius when it comes to business, will bring her influence to bear; make the most of our patronage! You won't lack help or support, whichever career you chose! Channel all that excess energy into high-flying ambition."

"I understand what you are saying," I interrupted, "ambition will be my mistress, but I need none of that to be entirely yours. I don't wish my good behavior here to be rewarded by favors there. I will go, grow up alone, and accept anything you offer, but I want nothing from anyone else."

"Don't be so childish!" she muttered, striving to contain a smile of satisfaction.

"Besides, I've pledged myself," I reacted. "I've thought about our situation, and decided to be bound to you by ties that can never be severed."

She trembled, stopped, and looked at me.

"What do you mean?" she asked, allowing the two couples walking in front to proceed while she kept her children by her side.

"Well!" I replied, "be candid and tell me how you would prefer me to love you."

"Love me as my aunt did, whose rights I passed on to you when I authorized you to call me by the name she chose for me when she lived with my family."

"Then I shall love you without hope, but with total devotion. Indeed, I'll do for you what men do for God. Isn't that what you're asking? I will enter a seminary, come out a priest, and educate Jacques. Your Jacques will be another me; I will give him everything he needs: political ideas, thought, energy, and patience. That's how I will stay close to you, without my love, preserved in religion like a silver image in glass case, ever being suspected. You won't live in fear any of outbursts of manly ardor that seize men, like the one I once allowed to overwhelm me. I will be consumed by that flame and love you with a love thus purified."

She blanched and responded hurriedly: "Félix, don't become entangled in ties that one day will stand in the way of your happiness. I would die of sorrow if I were to be the cause of such suicide. My child, why must despair in love end in a vocation? Wait to experience life before you pass judgment; that's what I want and what I order you to do. Don't marry the Church or a woman, don't marry at all, I forbid you. Stay free. You are twenty-one. You hardly know what life holds in store. My God, can I have misjudged you? I thought two months would be enough to appreciate a certain sensibility."

"And what do *you* hope for?" I asked, my eyes glowering.

"My friend, accept my help, go forth and prosper, then you will know what I hope for. I mean," she said, as if letting a secret slip out, "never let go of Madeleine's hand that you're holding now."

She'd leaned over to whisper those words that showed the extent of her concern for my future.

"Madeleine?" I replied. "Never!"

Those two words plunged us back into fraught silence. Our souls were racked by the kind of turmoil that leaves eternal scars. A wooden gate came into view, an entrance to the Frapesle gardens, which I can see now with their two crumbling piers, overgrown by climbing plants and moss, weeds, and brambles. All of a sudden, an idea, the death of the count, shot across my brain like an arrow, and I said: "I understand."

"And that's just as well," she replied, in a tone that indicated I was imagining an idea that could never have entered her own head.

Her selflessness brought tears of admiration to my eyes but they were soon soured by selfish passion. I thought hard and concluded she didn't love me enough to crave her own freedom. Whenever love retreats from erring, we think it is limited, when love must be infinite. My heart thudded.

She doesn't love me! I thought.

I kissed Madeleine's hair, so she couldn't read my mind.

"I'm afraid of your mother," I told the countess, resuming our conversation.

"So am I," she replied, gesturing childishly, "and please don't forget to call her Madame la Duchesse and speak to her in the third person. The youth of today has lost the habit of polite forms, regain them; do that for me. Besides, it's only good taste to show respect for women, whatever their age, and to recognize social distinctions without question. The homage one pays to established authority is surely a guarantee of the respect owed to oneself? Everything is self-sustaining in society. Cardinal Rovère and Raphael from Urbino were once two powers in the land that were equally respected. In your high schools you have been suckled on the milk of the Revolution, and that has shaped your political thinking, but as you proceed through life, you will learn that vague principles of freedom are no help when people's happiness is at stake. As a Lenoncourt, before I ever consider what an aristocracy should be, my common sense as a country woman tells me that societies only exist thanks to their hierarchy. You are at a moment in life when you must make the right choices! Support your party. Especially," she laughed, "when it is triumphant."

I was deeply moved by her words, which hid profound political insight beneath warm affection, a combination that makes women hugely seductive; they can bring sense and sensibility to the most rebarbative arguments. In her desire to justify the count's actions, Henriette had anticipated the thoughts welling in my soul as I felt the impact of courtly habits for the first time. M. de Mortsauf, king of his castle, and enhanced by the halo of history, had assumed a grandiose stature in my eyes, and I confess I was shocked by the distance he placed between the duchess and himself, in comportment that was quite obsequious. A slave has his vanity and wishes to obey only the greatest despots; I felt humiliated to witness the abjection of a man who made me cringe as I felt forced to rein in my love. That insight enabled me to understand the torture suffered by generous women who are hewn to a man whose miserliness they conceal day after day. Respect is a barrier that protects great and small alike; on either side one can look ahead. I acted respectfully towards the duchess, because I was so young; but where others saw a duchess, I saw *my* Henriette's mother and that added a kind of sanctity to my reverence.

We entered the great courtyard in Frapesle where the entourage had assembled. The Comte de Mortsauf introduced me graciously to the duchess, who scrutinized me with icy reserve. At the time Mme de Lenoncourt was fifty-six, a woman in a perfect state of preservation, who acted in the grand manner. When I contemplated her stern blue eyes, wrinkled temples, thin, mortified face, haughty stance, peculiar movements, and the fawn pallor that had become so dazzling in her daughter, I identified the cold race from which my mother was descended, as swiftly as a mineralogist would recognize Swedish iron ore. Her language belonged to the old court, she pronounced *oit* as *ait* and said *frait* for *froid* and *porteux* instead of *porteurs*. I was neither obsequious nor stiff; I performed so well that on our way to vespers the countess whispered in my ear: "You are perfect!"

The count came over, took my hand, and said: "We aren't angry, are we, Félix? You must forgive your old companion for what he said in the heat of the moment. We will probably stay on here for supper, and invite you on Thursday, on the eve of the duchess's departure, when I have business to finish in Tours. Don't forget Clochegourde. My mother-in-law is an acquaintance I urge you to cultivate. Her salon will set the tone in the Faubourg Saint-Germain. She embodies the traditions of the highest society, is immensely learned, and knows the coats of arms of every single gentleman in Europe."

The count's good taste, perhaps on advice from his guardian spirit, now revealed itself in the new circumstances where the victory of his cause had thrust him. He was neither presumptuous nor obsequious; he acted with equanimity and the duchess was never patronizing. M. and Mme de Chessel were delighted to accept the invitation to lunch on the upcoming Thursday. The duchess looked favorably on me, and her demeanor told me she looked at me as a man whom her daughter had mentioned. When we were walking back from vespers, she questioned me about my family and asked if I was related to the Vandenesse who already held a diplomatic post.

"He's my brother," I replied.

Then she adopted an almost affectionate tone. She told me that my great-aunt, the old Marquise de Listomère, was a Grandlieu. Her manner became as polite as M. de Mortsauf's were the day he met me for the first time. Her eyes lost the haughtiness grandees of this earth use to indicate the distance separating you from them. I knew very little about my family. The duchess informed me that my great-uncle, an old abbot whose name I didn't even know, was a member of the Privy Council; my brother had been promoted, and, finally, as a result of a clause in an ancient deed I was also unaware of, my father was once more the Marquis de Vandenesse.

"I am only one thing, Clochegourde's serf," I whispered to the countess.

The wave of the Restoration wand worked so swiftly, it astonished children raised under the imperial regime. This revolution meant nothing to me. Mme de Mortsauf's least word or gesture were the only acts I deemed important. I didn't know what the Privy Council was; I knew nothing about politics or worldly things; my only ambition was to love Henriette better than Petrarch loved Laura. The duchess took my lack of worldliness for childishness.

Many guests attended the Frapesle lunch: thirty in all. It was intoxicating for a young man like myself to see that the woman he loved was the most beautiful one there, and to know her chaste eyes reserved their gleam for him alone, and to be familiar enough with her intonation to detect in every apparently frivolous or mocking word evidence of her constancy, even when my heart felt fiercely jealous of the distractions of the social round.

Pleased by the attention he was being paid, the count seemed almost rejuvenated, but his wife was anticipating a change in his mood. I laughed with Madeleine, who, like a child whose body reacts to the whim of the moment, made me laugh with her incisive comments that ridiculed, never maligned, but spared nobody. It was a marvelous day. A word, hope born in the morning, had flooded nature with light, and seeing I was radiant, Henriette was radiant too.

"He believed that good fortune in the gray fog of his life was a blessing," she told me next morning.

Naturally, I spent the day in Clochegourde; I'd been banished for five days; I ached for my life there. The count had left at six a.m. for Tours to draw up purchase contracts. A serious disagreement had arisen between mother and daughter. The duchess wanted the countess to follow her to Paris, where she would fulfill her duties at court, while the count would renege on his previous refusal and obtain a position of influence. Considered a happy wife, Henriette declined to reveal to anyone, even to her mother, the horrendous way she suffered at her husband's hands or his incompetence. She'd dispatched M. de Mortsauf to Tours, where he had issues to discuss with notaries, to avoid her mother catching a glimpse of their household secrets. As she'd said, I was the only one who knew what they were. After seeing how the valley's pure air and blue skies eased mental irritation and the bitter pain of sickness, and how benignly life at Clochegourde treated her children's health, she mounted strong arguments the domineering duchess fiercely rebuffed, less chagrined than humiliated by her daughter's poor marriage. Henriette realized her mother wasn't at all worried about Jacques and Madeleine, and that was a most disagreeable discovery! Like all women accustomed to extending their despotic control over their married daughter to their granddaughter, the duchess advanced arguments that brooked no rebuttals; now she affected capricious affability to coax her into agreeing with her views, and now frosty sourness, to achieve by fear what she couldn't by charm. When she saw her efforts were futile, she deployed the same sarcasm I'd seen my own mother use.

In the course of those ten days, Henriette suffered all the inner distress young women feel who have to rebel to establish their independence. You are fortunate to have the best of mothers, and could never understand such a state of mind. To form some idea of that struggle between a dry, calculating, ambitious mother, and her eternally innocent, good, spontaneous daughter, you must imagine the lily, which I have continually compared her to, entangled in the cogs of a machine made of polished steel. She was a mother who'd never understood her daughter or discerned the real difficulties that had forced her to pursue an isolated life rather than take advantage of the Restoration. She believed her daughter and I were having a fling. That word, which she used to voice her suspicions, opened up a chasm between the two women that nothing could subsequently bridge.

Although families are careful to bury intolerable disagreements, if you get close to them, you'll almost always detect festering sores that kill natural feelings dead or the real affection that individual susceptibility renders eternal, and that upon death lead to backlashes whose dark bruises never heal, or latent hatred that slowly freezes hearts and weeps dry tears on days of eternal farewell.

Tortured yesterday, tortured today, struck down by everyone, even by the two angels who weren't complicit either in the ills they endured or the ones they caused, how could that poor soul *not* love the man who never rebuffed her, who wanted to surround her with a triple hedge of hawthorns and defend her against all storms, contagion, and injury? If I suffered from those squabbles, they also pleased me at times when I sensed Henriette turning back to me to confide fresh pain. I learned to appreciate her serenity amid grief and the stoic patience she always displayed. Every day I better understood the meaning of her words: "Love me as my aunt loved me."

"Do you not have *any* ambition?" rasped the duchess over dinner.

"Madame," I replied, gazing at her intently, "I feel I'm strong enough to conquer the world, but I'm only twenty-one, and quite alone."

She glanced at her daughter in astonishment, convinced *she* had killed all ambition in me in order to keep me by her side. The time the Duchesse de Lenoncourt stayed in Clochegourde was a period of constant agonizing. The countess advised me to be courteous; she feared any word that was spoken too quietly, and, to please her, one had to wear a cloak of pretense. That momentous Thursday came and it was a day of tiresome ceremony, the kind hated by lovers used to the cajoling of everyday laissez-faire, seeing their chair in its rightful place and the lady of the house with time only for them. Love detests everything that isn't itself. The duchess departed to enjoy the pomp at court, and everything went back to its normal routine in Clochegourde.

My little contretemps with the count meant I could now go there more than ever: I visited whenever I wanted without sparking the slightest suspicion; the previous pain I'd experienced in life enabled me to spread like a climbing plant over that beautiful soul where an enchanting world of shared feelings opened up for me.

Hour after hour, second after second, our trusting, fraternal marriage coalesced: we reinforced our respective stances: the countess swathed me, like a wary wet nurse, in the white drapes of maternal love, while my love, angelic in her presence, glowered far from her, threatening and angry like a red-hot iron; I loved her with a double love that fired a thousand arrows of desire, that vanished into the sky and perished in the impenetrable ether.

If you were to ask me why I, a young man full of fiery urges, clung to an excessive belief in hurtful platonic love, I would have to confess I wasn't yet man enough to lay siege to a woman who always feared the worst for her children and always anticipated her husband's violent changes of mood. She was under attack from him, when she wasn't afflicted by Jacques's or Madeleine's illnesses, and seated at the bedside of one or the other when her subdued husband allowed her a little respite. Too sharp a word cut her to the quick; desire was offensive; for her sake, I had to veil my love, imbue it with tenderness, in a word, be everything she was for others. And I can tell you, a woman, that this situation brought a bewitching languor, moments of divine gentleness and the satisfaction that follows tacit self-sacrifice. Her awareness was infectious, her devotion that granted no earthly rewards vanquished through its very persistence; her energetic, secret compassion, linking other virtues, spread everywhere like spiritual incense. And, in any case, I was young! Young enough to channel my feelings into a kiss of her hand that was rarely permitted, the back of which was all she ever offered—never the palm— the boundary beyond which sensual pleasure perhaps began for her. If two spirits never embraced more ardently, the body was ever more audaciously, or more triumphantly, tamed, but later on, I understood the reason for that sense of fulsome joy. At my age, no self-interest shackled my heart, no ambition stopped that flow of feeling unleashed like a torrent that swept away all before it on the crest of a wave. Later in life, to be candid, we love all women in one woman, whereas we love every aspect of the first woman we love: her children are ours, her house is ours, her interests are ours, her misfortune is our greatest misfortune; we love her clothes and her furniture; we are angrier to see her capital squandered than our own money lost and are quick to bawl at any visitor who jumbles our keepsakes on the mantelpiece. That hallowed love makes us live in one another, whereas later, alas! we draw that other life into ourselves, expect the woman to enrich our impoverished faculties with her youthful feelings

I was soon part of the household, and for the first time experienced the infinite balm that soothes a tortured mind as a bath relaxes a weary body; one's soul is calmed and tranquil, and cherished in its innermost folds. You could never understand that, you are a *woman*, and this is happiness you give and never receive like in return. Only a man can know the sweet pleasure, in someone else's house, of being favored by the chatelaine, as the secret center of her affections; the dogs no longer bark at you, and, likewise, the servants recognize the secret emblems you wear. Children, who miss nothing, know their share will never shrink, and that you are nourishing the light of their lives; children with their gift of intuition, behave like cats towards you, employ the subtle, tyrannical ways they keep for adored and adoring beings; mentally discreet, these innocent accomplices tiptoe towards you, smile, then silently depart. Everything comes to you in a rush, loves you, and smiles at you. True passion is like a beautiful flower: all the more pleasurable to behold, the more inhospitable the land where it grows.

However, if I welcomed all the delightful advantages that accompanied acceptance in a family where I found the kin my heart had always sought, I was also saddled with the burdens. Hitherto, M. de Mortsauf had acted with restraint in my presence; I'd only experienced his deficiencies in general. Now I sensed them actively everywhere and realized how benevolently the countess had described her daily battles. I felt the intolerable fellow's sharp edges: I heard him gripe endlessly over trifles, complain about wrongs for which no evidence was ever found: I experienced his innate dissatisfaction that plagued life daily and revealed a tyrant's perpetual impulse to devour fresh victims every year. When we went for an evening stroll, he lead the way, but, wherever we went, he always found fault; when we walked back, he blamed his fatigue on others: his wife was to blame because *she* had led him where she wanted to go against his wishes; forgetting that *he* had been our guide, he complained that she decided every little detail of his life, that he could never harbor a wish or thought for himself, that he counted for zero in his own house. If his harsh words met only patient silence, he lost his temper over the way his status was being undermined; he asked bitterly whether religion didn't instruct wives to gratify their husband, or it was right to hold her children's father in contempt. In the end, he always struck a sensitive chord in his wife, and when it resounded, he derived immense pleasure from his petty maneuvers. Sometimes, he affected sullen silence and morose despondency, and his wife took fright and soothed him endearingly. Like a spoiled child who wields his power and doesn't worry about alarming his mother, he let himself be cosseted like Jacques and Madeleine, and was jealous of them. I eventually discovered that, in minor or major tantrums, the count acted towards his servants, children, and wife exactly as he did towards me when we played backgammon.

The day when I glimpsed the root and branch of the difficulties choking that family's movements and breathing—lianas with a thousand fine threads that cramped the functioning of the household and delayed improvement in its fortunes by obstructing vital change—I felt a terrible sense of awe that inhibited my love and put a brake on my heart. My God, what was I? The tears I'd swallowed were sublimely intoxicating and I found happiness marrying into that woman's suffering. Till then I'd yielded to the count's despotism like a smuggler who pays his fines; I now willingly offered to bear the brunt of that despot's blows, so as to be closer to Henriette. The countess sensed that, let me take a place beside her, and rewarded me by allowing me to share her pain, like the repentant apostate in bygone times, desperate to soar skywards with his brothers, granted the favor of death in the Circus.

"Without you, life would have overwhelmed me," Henriette told me one evening when the count had been harassing her like a cloud of flies on a sweltering summer's day, more biting, prickly, and moody than ever.

The count had retired to bed. Henriette and I stayed a while beneath the acacias; the children played around us, bathed in the rays of the setting sun. Our sparse, exclamatory words revealed shared thoughts that rescued us from our shared suffering. When words were lacking, silence loyally served our souls, which, in a manner of speaking, interpenetrated, without ever being invited in by a kiss: we savored the delights of meditative languor, swam in the waves of the same reverie, dove into the river together, emerged refreshed like two nymphs as perfectly joined as jealousy could want, but without earthly fetters. We plunged into a bottomless chasm, then surfaced, emptyhanded, our mutual glances asking: Will we ever have a single day to ourselves amid so many? When voluptuous pleasure picks for us from those flowers born without roots, why must the flesh complain?

Despite the enervating poetry of an evening that dyed the brick balustrade a pure, soothing orange, despite the religious atmosphere that wafted the children's cries gently towards us and left us in peace, desire surged through my veins like a warning signal from a rampaging fire. After three months, I started to feel I was unhappy with my lot and gently caressed Henriette's hand in an attempt to communicate the sensual pleasure burning within me. Henriette rapidly turned back into Mme de Mortsauf and removed her hand; a few tears welled in my eyes, she saw them, glanced warmly at me, and raised her hand to my lips.

"You ought to know," she said, "that this costs me tears too! Friendship that longs for such great favors is perilous."

I exploded, seethed with reproaches, spoke of my pain and the paltry relief needed to make it tolerable. I dared tell her, that at my age, if the senses were all soul, the soul also had a sex, that I could contemplate death, but not a death with lips sealed. Her haughty gaze silenced me and I thought I read there the "And am I on a bed of roses?" uttered by the last Aztec emperor.[9] Perhaps I too had erred. From the day in front of the door to Frapesle, when I misjudged the declaration that forged our sepulchral happiness, I felt ashamed to sully her soul with wild, passionate desire. She took the initiative, in honeyed tones murmuring she could never be entirely mine, which was something I had to accept. The moment she uttered those words, I knew that I'd dig an abyss between us, were I not to obey. I lowered my eyes. She went on to say it was her religious conviction she could love a brother without offending God or mankind, and that it was a benign challenge to make this devotion a true image of the divine love that, according to her good Saint-Martin, was the lifeblood of the world. If I couldn't be in her eyes like her old confessor, less than a lover, but more than a brother, we should never see each other again. She would meet death taking to God that excess of acute anguish, borne with tears and heartache.

"I have given," she concluded, "more than I should, I possess nothing more you can take and I have already been punished."

I could only soothe her, promise never to trouble her, and to love her at twenty as an elderly father loves his last child.

The next morning I came early. She had no flowers for the vases in her gray drawing room. I ran across fields and vineyards looking for flowers to make two bouquets, but, as I picked them one by one, admiring them as I cut the bottom of their stems, I discerned a harmony in their colors and foliage, a poetry born in the mind as it delighted the eyes, like musical phrases that inspire a thousand memories in hearts that love and are loved. If color is organized light, it surely has a meaning like combinations of air? Helped by Jacques and Madeleine, the three of us happy to plot a surprise for the one we cherished, I began the two bouquets that were my attempt to depict a feeling on the last terrace steps where we established the headquarters for our flowers. Imagine flowers bubbling out of two vases like a spring, vaguely forming two surrounds, from the center of which my wishes surged as white roses, as lilies to the silver cup. Cornflower, forget-me-nots, and viper's bugloss, blue flowers all with sky-tinted hues, shone against this luminous backcloth, that go so well with white: Are they not two kinds of innocence, one that knows nothing and one that knows all, a child's thought and a martyr's?

Love has its blazon which the countess secretly interpreted. She glanced in my direction, a sharp glance that hurt like the cry of an invalid when her sores are touched: she was embarrassed and delighted. What a rewarding glance! I was so gratified that I was making her happy and replenishing her reservoir of feelings! I'd reinvented Father Castel's theory of love[10] and rediscovered for her knowledge that had disappeared in a Europe where flowers on a bureau have taken the place of pages written in the Orient with colored scents. I was so delighted to express her feelings through those daughters of the sun, sisters to flowers opened by rays of love! I soon possessed a fund of knowledge about countryside flowers, like a man I later met in Grandlieu who knew all there was to know about bees.

Twice a week, during the remainder of my stay in Frapesle, I resumed the long task of an unfinished poetic work that required all kinds of woodland plants and grasses, that I studied in depth, more as a poet than as a botanist, studying their spirit rather than their form: to find a flower where *she* was to be found, I often walked huge distances, to the water's edge, down valleys, to the top of crags, across heaths, gathering thoughts amid woods and heather.

On my promenades, I initiated myself into pleasures unknown to learned men engrossed in meditation, to farmers busy with their crops, to artisans locked in towns, to traders chained to their counters, but familiar to a few forest rangers, woodcutters, and dreamers. The effects of nature hold boundless meanings that emulate the greatest moral ideas. Whether blossoming heather, with its glittering diamond droplets of dew, infinitely decked out for a single gaze deliberately cast there. Or a corner of a forest enclosed by crumbling rocks, criss-crossed by sandy paths, moss lined, through dense junipers, which astound you with their jagged, terrifying wildness, all of it pierced by the cry of the osprey. Or a shimmering, stony heath, barren expanses with a desert's horizons, where I discovered a sublime, solitary flower, a pasqueflower, its purple flag of silk spread with golden stamens: the tender image of my white idol, alone in her valley! Or great pools of water where nature draws patches with green, midway between plant and animal, where life appears within days, afloat with plants and insects, like a planet in the ether! Or a thatched cottage and its garden of cabbages, vines, and trellises, suspended above a dell, framed by a few sparse fields of rye, the image of so many modest existences! Or a long path through a forest, like a cathedral nave with trees for its columns, branches for the vault's arches, and at the end a distant clearing looms through foliage streaked with black or red from the sun, like a stained-glass window of a chancel that holds a songbird choir. As you leave those cool, thick woods, you meet chalky fallow land, where sated snakes slither back to their lairs, raising their sleek, sinuous heads above the rustling, smoldering moss. Imagine rays of sun streaming like benignly lapping waves or masses of gray cloud, wrinkled like an old man's forehead, or cold tints from an orangey sky, flecked with pale blue; then listen, and hear ineffable harmonies amid a stunning silence.

In the months of September and October I never gathered a single bouquet that didn't take at least three hours of searching. Gifted with a poet's gentle abandon, I so admired those transient allegories painting the most contrary sides of human life, sumptuous scenes where my memory will now forage. Often, now, I find I'm still wed to those magnificent vistas, as I remember a soul that was opening itself to nature. I still walk there with my sovereign, her white dress gleaming in the depths of woods, floating over lawns, thoughts of whom arise, like the promise of a fruit, from each chalice filled with loving stamens.

No declaration, no proof of ecstatic passion was so violently infectious as those symphonies of flowers, where my frustrated desire drew on the emotions Beethoven expressed in his scores: those profound incursions into his inner self, those wondrous skyward surges. Mme de Mortsauf was always Henriette in the presence of these flowers. She kept returning, thrived on them, detected every thought I had placed there; when she accepted them, she would look up from her tapestry frame and exclaim: "Heavens, that is so beautiful!"

You will understand this precious interchange via the ingredients of a bouquet, as you'd understand Saadi from a fragment of his poetry.[11] Have you ever smelled a meadow in May, with its scents that invoke a universal mood of intoxicating fertility and fruitfulness, that makes you dip your hands in the water over the side of a boat, allow your hair to blow in the wind, and you feel your thoughts revive, like the bare branches budding in the forest. A small herb, a yellow vernal grass, is one of the most powerful signals of the beginning of that hidden harmony. Nobody can be in its presence and remain unmoved. Place its striped, gleaming blades in a bouquet, like a white-and-green-threaded dress, and a flood of perfumes will awaken rosebuds in your heart that modesty had been stifling. Imagine around the porcelain vase's bell-mouthed neck a dazzling fringe of the white tufts of the stonecrop one finds in the vineyards of Touraine; vaguely suggesting an image of the forms you desire, enrapt like a submissive slave. White-belled convolvulus spirals out, sprigs of pink cammock, fern, and young shoots of cork oak, their leaves bright, colorful, and glistening; all advance humbly, bowing like weeping willows, imploring timidly, as if in prayer. Above them, blossoming, shimmering spikelets of pale crimson quaking grass spilling out yellowish anthers; snowy pyramids of bluegrass and sweetgrass from meadows and streams, green tresses of barren bromegrass, slender plumes of bentgrass also known as wind spike; the purplish expectations that garland first dreams and stand out against a gray backdrop of flax, light bending around its flowering ears. Yet taller still, a scattering of Bengal roses, amid the crazy lace of wild carrot; feathery cotton grass; meadowsweet, with its marabou; wild chervil's umbrellas; fair-haired, fruiting clematis; luscious milk-white crosswort; clusters of yarrow; smoke-of-the-earth's gray spikes and black and pink flowers; tendrils of the grapevines; twisting, entangling honeysuckle; in a word, everything these simple creatures possess that is most tousled and unruly, flames and triple darts; jagged, spear-shaped leaves; stalks as tortuous as the desires writhing in the depths of your soul. Out of that exuberant, overflowing torrent of love rises a magnificent double red poppy, its bud ready to open and spread the sparks from its flames above starry jasmine, soaring above a nonstop drizzle of pollen, a beautiful cloud hovering in the air, a thousand glinting shards reflecting the light of day! What woman, inebriated by Aphrodite's scent hiding in the vernal grass, could fail to understand that treasure trove of suppressed feeling, that amorous pallor disturbed by untamed movements, the red desire of love pleading for the happiness denied to the eternal, conflicted passion that is reborn hundredfold. Place that lyre in the light of a casement window, display fresh detail, subtle contrasts, and arabesques, and your sovereign will be moved to see a flower open, and she will shed a tear; on the point of surrender, it will take an angel or her child's voice to bring her back from the edge of the abyss. What do we give to God? Scent, light, and song, the most ethereal expressions of our nature. Now isn't everything we offer to Him offered to love in that poem of luminous flowers that constantly plays its melodies to her heart, caressing hidden voluptuous pleasures and undeclared expectations, hopes that flame and then die like gossamer threads on a hot summer's night?

Those oblique delights were a great boon helping us delude natures frustrated by long contemplation of the beloved, in gazes that exult when shining into the depths of the forms they penetrate. That was my situation—I dare not speak for her—like those cracks in a once impenetrable dam where water pours through, often preventing disaster by partly surrendering to necessity. Abstinence leads to a lethal exhaustion that could be assuaged by the few crumbs falling singly from the sky, which from Dan to the Sahara provide manna to the traveler. However, I often caught Henriette looking at those bouquets, with her arms by her side, in those tempestuous reveries when thoughts swell the bosom, excite the brow, surge in roiling, ominous waves, then leave enervating exhaustion. I have never again made a bouquet for anyone! Once we had created that language that so suited our purpose, we felt as contented as a slave tricking his master.

The rest of the month, when I strolled in the gardens, I sometimes saw her press her face against the windowpanes, and, when I entered the drawing room, I found her at work on her tapestry. If I didn't come at the agreed time, even though we'd never agreed to one, her white figure was sometimes meandering on the terrace, and when I caught her by surprise, she'd say: "I came here to meet you. Isn't one allowed to be coy with one's last child?"

The count's and my cruel games of backgammon had been called off. His recent purchases obliged him to pursue a large number of deals, searches, surveys, measuring, and staking out; he was too busy issuing orders, rural tasks that required the master's eye and that he and his wife made decisions about together. The countess and I often went with their two children to seek him out on his new estates and, along the way, they'd run after insects, stag beetles and carabids, and make their own bouquets or, to be more exact, bunches of flowers. Walking with the woman you love, giving her your arm, choosing your path! Those boundless joys sustained life! Conversation became so trusting! We went alone, and we returned with the General, the mildly mocking title we gave the count when he was in a good mood. Those two ways of walking were opposites that gave nuance to our pleasure, a secret known only to hearts ill at ease in their union. On our way back, the same felicitous acts, a gaze, a squeeze of the hand, now mingled with anxiety. Words, so free when we were going there, assumed a mysterious significance on our return, when, one of us, after a lengthy pause, found an answer to an insidious question, or when a debate begun was pursued in the enigmatic guises that our language lends itself to so readily, and that women create so ingeniously. Who hasn't enjoyed the pleasure of such mutual understanding, as if you had found yourself in an unknown zone where minds separate out from the crowd and come together by foiling the rules of convention?

One day, I was embracing an absurd hope that was swiftly dashed when, at the request of the count, who wanted to know the subject of our conversation, Henriette replied with a sentence full of double entendres and he teased her for it. The innocent jesting amused Madeleine and then made her mother blush: her stern glance indicated she could withdraw her soul, as she had once withdrawn her hand, because she wished to remain a wife beyond reproach. But our purely spiritual union had so many attractions, and we resumed it the following day.

The hours, days, and weeks sped by like that, full of repeated bliss. We reached the grape-harvest time, always a festive season in the Touraine. Towards the end of September, the sun is cooler than when the wheat is harvested, and you can stay in the fields without fear of sunburn or fatigue. Picking grapes is easier than scything corn. All the fruit is ripe. The harvest done, bread becomes cheaper, and this abundance make for a happier life. Finally the fears that hang on the results from the toil in the fields, which consumes as much money as it does sweat, disappear, now that the barn is full and the cellars are about to be. The grape harvest comes as a tasty dessert after the banquet has been cleared away, and the sun always smiles in the Touraine, where the autumns are magnificent. In this hospitable country, grape pickers are fed in farmsteads, and these are the only times when those poor people eat substantial meals of well-cooked food; they celebrate like children enjoying a birthday party given in their family home. They run around the farmsteads in gangs and are treated by their masters without evident meanness. Houses are full of people and food. Winepresses are always open. Everything is animated by that throng of wet coopers, carts pulled by laughing girls, people who, being paid better wages now than at any other time of year, burst into song at the least excuse. This is yet another source of pleasure, that all classes and ranks may mingle: women and children, masters and workers, everyone joins in the glorious gathering of the grape.

Such a variety of factors explains the mirthfulness that is passed down from generation to generation, which surges in the last fine days of the year, and the memories of which inspired Rabelais long ago to give bacchanalian form to his masterpiece. The children, Jacques and Madeleine, always ill, had never picked grapes; I was like them; they enjoyed such great childish pleasure to see their excitement shared. Along with their mother, we had gone to Villaines, where they make baskets, and purchased some handsome items; we four were to pick grapes from ten-meter rows of vines reserved for us, and it was agreed we shouldn't eat too many. Eating the fat Touraine côt grape, so black and juicy, straight from the vine, was such a delight that we scorned the more beautiful bunches on the table. Jacques made me swear never to grape-pick anywhere else, and to hold myself in reserve for Clochegourde's vineyards. Those two little ones, always so pale and miserable, were never more eager or in the pink, as nimble and energetic, as they were that morning. They babbled on for babble's sake, ran to and fro, for no apparent reason, but now, like other children, seemed to possess a surfeit of life they wanted to set free; M. and Mme de Mortsauf had never seen them act like that. I became a child with them, because I too was looking forward to my harvest. We went to the vines in the best of weather and stayed half a day. We argued over who would pick the finest bunches, who would fill their basket first! They went back and forth to their mother with their grapes, and not one grape was picked that wasn't shown to her. She burst into laughter, was full of youthful spirit, when I brought my pannier after her daughter and said, like Madeleine: "And what about mine, Mama?"

She replied: "My dear child, don't get too hot!"

Then she ran her hand around my neck and through my hair, patted my cheek, adding: "Tu es en nage!"

That was the only time I'd heard the caress in her voice, the "*tu*" of lovers, as she remarked on my perspiration. I looked at the pretty hedges bedecked with red fruit, hawthorns and blackberries; I listened to the children's shouting, I watched the gang of women pickers, the cart laden with barrels of grapes, the men with their burden of baskets . . . ! I etched everything into my memory, even the young almond tree beneath which she stood, so cool, her cheeks radiant, laughing under her open parasol! Then I began to pick grapes, fill my pannier, and empty it into the harvest barrels in a silent exercise of sustained, physical diligence, and at a slow, measured pace that liberated my soul. I relished the ineffable pleasures of open-air toil that drives life forward and puts a brake on a rush of passion that, without such mechanical movements, teeters on the verge of destroying everything. I grasped the wisdom of routine tasks and the raison d'être of monastic rules.

For the first times in ages, the count was neither crusty nor cruel. His well-behaved son, the future Duc de Lenoncourt-Mortsauf, pinkish-white grape juice dripping down his chin, made his heart rejoice. It was the last day of the harvest and the General had promised to organize a dance in front of Clochegourde to honor the return of the Bourbons: an almost perfect end to the party for everyone. As we walked back, the countess took my arm, leaning on me so I felt the whole weight of her heart next to mine, the movement of a mother wanting to share her joy who whispered in my ear: "You bring us such happiness!"

Of course, I was aware of her sleepless nights, her alarums, and a previous existence in which she was sustained by the hand of God and everything was barren and wearisome, and that sentence, underlined by her rich voice, inspired pleasure as the words of no other woman in the world could.

"My life's wretched monotony is at an end, life is beautiful and full of hope again," she said, after pausing. "Don't leave me! Don't ever betray my innocent illusions! Be the elder brother who brings good fortune to his siblings!"

Natalie, I have invented none of this: to discover the infinite nature of deep feelings, one must have plumbed the depths of the great lakes near home in one's youth.

If many see passion as a torrent of lava flowing between parched banks, aren't there souls for whom passion, constrained by unsurmountable difficulties, fills a volcano's crater with the purest water?

We still had more festive bliss in store. Mme de Mortsauf wanted to accustom her children to life's practicalities, and to give them the experience of the exhausting labor required to earn money; thus she provided them with a source of income dependent on the capricious nature of agriculture: Jacques owned the produce of the walnut trees and Madeleine, of the sweet chestnuts. The harvest of walnuts and chestnuts came a few days later. Beating Madeleine's chestnut trees, hearing the fruits fall, and their husks rebound on the dry, matte velvet of the stony ground where the sweet chestnut trees grow, seeing the young girl's serious expression as she examined the heaps and estimated their value, brought her untrammeled joy, and congratulations from Manette, the housekeeper and the only person who helped the countess with her children; the lessons taught by the demonstration of the hard work needed to collect the smallest reward, so often imperiled by changes in the weather, all this was part of a scene in which childhood's simple pleasures seemed full of charm amid the gloomy tints of early autumn. Madeleine had her own small barn, where I went to see her store her brown wealth and share in her excitement. To this day I still give a start when I remember the noise each basket of chestnuts made as the nuts rolled on the yellowish chaff mixed with earth that served as a floor. The count took some for the house; the tenant-farmers and the people living around Clochegourde also tried to find buyers for the Mignonne, a friendly epithet that peasants readily granted even to strangers, but which they seemed to keep exclusively for Madeleine.

Jacques was less fortunate when it came to harvesting his walnuts, as it rained for several days, but I consoled him by advising him to keep his walnuts to sell later. M. de Chessel had told me that the walnut trees in Brehément, the area of Amboise, and Vouvray had brought forth no harvest that year. Walnut oil is much used in the Touraine. Jacques could earn at least forty sous from each tree, and he had two hundred, so that came to a tidy sum! He wanted to purchase horse appointments so he could ride. His ambition led to a public debate in which his father made him reflect on the instability of his income, the need to save for years when the trees bore no fruit, in order to maintain an average income. I intuited the countess's feelings in her silence: she was happy to see Jacques listening to his father and his father recovering some of that good standing he lacked, thanks to the wondrous scheme she'd put in motion. When I described this woman to you, didn't I remark that the language of this earth could never capture the extent of her brilliance!

When you witness that kind of scene, you relish in the delights of it without resorting to analysis, and such things stand out strikingly against the dour backcloth of hectic life! Like diamonds, they sparkle, set within thoughts full of dull alloys and regrets that have dissolved into memories of a happiness that has vanished! Why do the names of the two recently purchased estates, where M. and Mme de Mortsauf were now so busy, La Cassine and La Rhétorière, move me much more than the most beautiful place-names in the Holy Land or ancient Greece? *Whoever loves, says it is so!* La Fontaine proclaimed. Those names possess the virtues of talismans, are words that constantly enliven my reveries, speak to me of magic, awaken dormant figures who sit up and talk to me, return me to that happy valley, re-creating those skies and landscapes: Haven't reveries always existed in the world of the mind? Please don't be upset to see me entertaining you with such intimate family scenes. The smallest detail in this simple, almost commonplace life has been one of the many apparently fragile links binding me to the countess.

The interests of her children brought Mme de Mortsauf as much sorrow as their poor health. I soon saw the truth of what she'd told me about her secret role in household business matters, to which I was slowly initiated, as I learned the facts about the locality a man of state must know. After ten years of continual effort, the countess had changed the way her land was cultivated; she had "divided them by four," an expression used in the area to explain the consequence of the new method by which farmers sow corn only every four years to ensure an annual crop from the land. In order to overcome the peasants' stubborn resistance, she'd had to renew leases, split her estates into four large farms where the farmers paid rent in kind, and retained 50 percent, the *cheptel* form of leasing specific to the Touraine and

its neighboring areas. The owner gives dwellings, outbuildings, implements, and seed to tenants of good will and shares the cost of farming
and production with them. This form of sharing, overseen by a *mé-
tivier*, the man charged with dealing with the half due to the owner,
was a costly system additionally complicated by accounts that were
always changing the nature of the distribution of land. The countess
had organized things so that M. de Mortsauf farmed a fifth farm,
comprising land held back for them around Clochegourde, as much
to keep him busy as to show her half-share farmers the excellence of
the new methods *in practice*. Skilled in organizing farmwork, with
female persistence, she'd slowly won over two of her métaires to the
new rotation schedule for the Artois and Flandre farms.

It was easy to see what she had in mind. After the 50-percent leases
expired, the countess wanted to create two excellent farms from the
four halves, and rent them out for money to energetic, intelligent
farmers, thus simplifying Clochegourde's finances. Afraid she might
be the first to die, she was trying to leave the count with income that
was easy to collect and her children with property that incompetence
couldn't ruin. For the moment, the fruit trees planted ten years ago
were at their peak in terms of production. The hedges that guaranteed
the estates from all future challenges were put in place. Poplars and
elms were planted, everything was welcome. With the new acquisitions and the introduction of the new farming system everywhere,
the Clochegourde estate, divided into four big farms, two of which
were yet to be built, was likely to accrue sixteen thousand francs annually, in a ratio of four thousand per farm, not counting the vineyard
and the two hundred acres of adjoining woodlands, or the model
farm. The roads from its four farms could all converge on a large
avenue that would go straight from Clochegourde to the road to
Chinon. As it was only fourteen miles from this avenue to Tours, the
farmers would be using it, especially when everyone was talking about
the improvements introduced by the count, their success, and the
improvements to the land. The countess wanted to invest some fifteen
thousand francs in each of the two newly purchased estates to convert
the main farmhouses on the two large farms, and therefore to be able

to rent them out for a better price after cultivating them for one or two years, assigning as administrator one Martineau, the best, most honest of her tenant farmers, who would find himself without a job, because the half-share leases of those four farms were coming to their end, and the time to turn them into two farms and rent them out for cash had arrived.

Her clear-sighted ideas, tested by the thirty-thousand-odd francs that needed to be spent, became the source of lengthy arguments between her and the count: horrific quarrels, in which she was sustained only by the need to protect the interests of her two children. The thought, "What happens if I die tomorrow?" gave her palpitations.

Only gentle, tranquil spirits who abhor anger and want to project their own profound inner peace around them know what strength of mind is needed in such strife, what amount of blood rushes to the heart before combat is engaged, and what lethargy descends when nothing has been gained after all the conflict. Now her children were less wilting and more active, after the season of mellow fruitfulness had animated them, she watched them play their games with moist eyes, with a satisfaction that renewed her own energy and refreshed her spirits, though she only faced more hurtful cavils and rancorous attacks from her bitter adversary. Frightened by all the changes, the count stubbornly denied their advantages and potential. When presented with conclusive arguments, he responded with the objections of a child who would contest the sun's influence in summer. The countess won out. The victory of good sense over folly was a balm to her, and she soon forgot her wounds.

That day, she walked to La Cassine and La Rhétorière, to decide on the new buildings. The count went ahead by himself, the children followed, and we brought up the rear, in slow pursuit, as she spoke to me in that quiet, soft tone that made her sentences seem like wavelets plashing over fine sand.

She was sure of success, she told me. There would be competition for the Tours-to-Chinon service, led by an active fellow and courier, the cousin of Manette, who wanted to have a big farm on the route. He had a large family: the eldest son would drive the carriages; the second would see to maintenance; the father, based on the road at La Rabalaye, one of the farms to be rented out and located in the center, could look after the staging post and enrich the land with the manure that would come from his stables. As for the second farm, La Baude, the one around the corner from Clochegourde, one of the four tenant farmers, an honest, intelligent, hardworking man who grasped the advantages of the new agricultural methods, was already offering to take on the lease. La Cassine and La Rhétorière had the best land in the region; once the farm buildings were ready and the crops reached their peak value, it would be enough to advertise them in Tours. Within two years, Clochegourde should thus be worth around eighty thousand francs' rent; Gravelotte, the farm in Maine recovered by M. de Mortsauf, had just been leased out for seven thousand francs for nine years; the field marshal's pension came to four thousand, and even if all that income didn't amount to a fortune, it would sustain a comfortable standard of life; other, later improvements might perhaps allow her to go to Paris one day to oversee Jacques's education—in two years, when the future heir's health was stronger.

Her voice shook when she pronounced the word *Paris*! I lay in the back of her mind; she wanted the least time possible away from her friend. When I heard that word, I reacted furiously and told her she really didn't know me, that I hadn't told her, but I was planning to finish my education by working night and day so I could become Jacques's tutor; I couldn't bear the idea of some young man living in her household.

When I said that, she looked serious: "That would be like taking holy orders. If a single word from you touched the depths of a mother's heart, as a woman, she loves you too sincerely to allow you to become the victim of your allegiance. The price of such devotion would be an irrevocable slight and I would be powerless. I can't hurt you in any way! You, the Vicomte de Vandenesse, a tutor! You, whose family bears the noble motto 'Is never sold'! Even if you were a Richelieu, that would destroy your prospects. You would cause your family the deepest sorrow. My friend, you don't know how scathing a woman like my mother can be, with her withering glances, or how she can put you down with a single word and infuse her greetings with contempt."

"But if you love me, why would I worry about what society thinks?"

"My father is very well disposed and prepared to grant me whatever I ask, but he wouldn't forgive you if you did take yourself down in society and he would refuse to protect you there. I do not want you to see you as the dauphin's teacher! Accept society for what it is, and don't take any disastrous decisions. My friend, that lunatic suggestion prompted by . . ."

"Love," I whispered.

"No, by charity," she replied, holding back her tears, "this madcap idea reveals so much about your character; your feelings will bring you only harm. I demand the right to teach you a few things; let my woman's eyes be yours now and then. Yes, from the depths of Clochegourde, I want to witness your success, and silently revel in it. And don't you worry about a teacher, we'll find a good old abbot, a retired Jesuit, and my father will gratefully supply money for the education of the child who will bear his name. Jacques is my pride and joy. He is, however, eleven years old," she continued after pausing. "But he's so like you: when I first saw you, I'd have said you were thirteen."

We'd reached La Cassine, where Jacques, Madeleine, and I trailed behind her like small children following their mother and getting in her way; I left her for a moment and entered the orchard, where the elder Martineau, her gamekeeper, along with the younger Martineau, her tenant farmer, were assessing whether to cut down the trees; they were arguing the matter as heatedly as if it was their own property. I then realized how much the countess was loved. I said as much to a poor day-laborer who, foot on spade and elbow on handle, was listening to the two doctors in pomology.

"Oh, certainly, monsieur," he replied, "she is a good woman, and not arrogant, like all the nasty women in Azay, who would rather see us die like dogs than give us a sou towards a grave! The day when that lady leaves here, the Holy Virgin will weep, and so will we. She knows what she is due, but she also knows how we struggle and helps out."

It was such a pleasure to give that man all the money I had on me!

A few days later, a pony arrived for Jacques, whom his father, an excellent rider, wanted to slowly ease into the physical challenges of horsemanship. The child had a beautiful riding outfit he'd bought with the proceeds from his walnuts. The morning he took his first lesson, accompanied by his father, and cheered on by an astonished Madeleine, who jumped up and down on the turf where Jacques was hurtling around, was the first great, festive moment in the countess's life as a mother. Jacques wore a muslin collar embroidered by his mother, a small, sky-blue riding coat cinched by a shiny leather belt, white jodhpurs, and a tam-o'-shanter over his unruly blond curls. He was a ravishing sight. The entire household staff had gathered outside to share in that display of domestic bliss. The young heir smiled at his mother as he cantered by, fearlessly seated on his mount. It was a fine reward to see that first manly deed performed by a child whose death had so often seemed imminent, and the expectations of a beautiful future for him, assured by a canter that showed him to be so handsome, poised, and open to new experiences! Then there was the joy of his father, who seemed rejuvenated, smiling for the first time in ages, the happiness reflected in the eyes of all the domestic staff, and the cry of an old Lenoncourt groom returning from Tours, who saw how the child handled the reins and cried: "Bravo, Monsieur le Vicomte!"

It was all too much; Mme de Mortsauf dissolved into tears. She'd been so calm when he was ill, and now felt too weak to hold back her happiness as she admired her child trotting on sand where she'd often wept in sad anticipation while taking him for a walk in the sun. She leaned on my arm, without remorse and said: "I don't think I ever suffered. Don't leave us today."

When his lesson was over, Jacques threw himself into the arms of his mother, who held him tight with the energy an excess of delight brings, and a stream of kisses and caresses followed. I went off with Madeleine to prepare two magnificent bouquets to adorn the table in the cavalier's honor. When we returned to the dining room, the countess told me: "The fifteenth of October will go down in history! Jacques had his first horse-riding lesson and I have added the last stitch to my tapestry."

"Very good, Blanche," said the count, with a laugh, "I would like to pay you for it."

He offered his arm and walked her into the first courtyard, where she saw a calash her father was giving her, for which the count had purchased two English horses that had been transported along with steeds destined for the Duc de Lenoncourt. The old groom had prepared everything in the first courtyard during the lesson. We inaugurated the carriage with a ride to see the layout of the new approach road that would lead directly from Clochegourde to the Chinon road, and that the recent land acquisitions had made possible. As we rode back, the countess told me in a most melancholy vein: "I'm too happy, and happiness affects me like a sickness. I find it overwhelming, and fear it will fade like a dream."

I was too passionately in love not to be jealous, and I was in no position to give her anything! In my fury, I sought a way to die for her. She asked what thoughts were veiling my eyes, and naively I told her; she was much more moved by this than by the other presents, and soothed my feelings by walking with me to the terrace and whispering: "Love me as my aunt loved me—wouldn't *that* be the way to give your life to me, and if I accept it in that way, wouldn't that place me under an obligation to you at all times?"

"It was time to finish my tapestry," she continued as we returned to the drawing room, where I kissed her hand as if renewing my pledge. "Félix, you probably don't understand why I gave myself this lengthy task? Men find the resources to fight their woes in everyday occupations; business activity distracts them, but we women find no support within our realm against our grief. To be able to smile at my children and husband when I was beset by gloomy anticipation, I needed to control my suffering through regular physical movement. It was my way of avoiding the depression that follows from a great expenditure of energy or peaks of exhilaration. The act of raising my arm at regular intervals lulled my thoughts and brought to my heart, where a storm raged, a peaceful ebb and flow that calmed my spirit. Each stitch responded to a secret, do you see? And, you know, when I was making this last armchair, you were far too much in my thoughts!

Yes, far too much, my friend. What you put into your bouquets, I placed in my patterns."

Dinner was a cheerful affair. Like all children who see how they are cherished, Jacques leapt up around my neck when he saw the flowers I'd picked for his garland. His mother pretended to sulk because of my act of infidelity; a source of jealousy, but you can imagine how gracefully that dear child offered that nosegay to her! That evening M. and Mme de Mortsauf and I played backgammon as a threesome, I pitted alone against them, and the count was charming. At the end of the day, they accompanied me to the path to Frapesle, on a quiet evening, whose harmonies bring a depth to one's feelings that compensated for any liveliness lost. It was a unique day in that poor woman's life, luminous hours, and the memory of it often returned to her at more testing times. And, naturally, the horse-riding lessons soon became a source of discord. The countess feared, with good reason, the harsh way the father cajoled his son. Jacques was already losing weight, and his beautiful blue eyes had rings under them; he preferred to suffer in silence than to cause his mother any pain. When the count flew into a temper, I suggested that a way out of Jacques's troubles might be for him to tell his father how tired he was, but that wasn't enough: the old groom was obliged to replace his father, who didn't give up his pupil without railing. Shouting matches and arguments were the order of the day again; the count found excuses to gripe continually about a woman's lack of gratitude: twenty times a day he threw the calash, the horses, and their livery in her face.

Finally, one of those incidents occurred that was both meat and drink to him and his malaise: expenditure came out 50 percent above the estimates in the work at La Cassine and La Rhétorière, where some walls and ceilings had collapsed. A worker foolishly broke the news to M. de Mortsauf, rather than telling the countess. It became the subject of a quarrel that started quietly enough, but then became gradually more poisonous, and the count's hypochondria, which had been quiet for a few days, demanded poor Henriette repay him with interest.

That day I had left Frapesle at half past ten, after breakfast to take a bouquet to Clochegourde with Madeleine. She had put two vases on the terrace balustrade, and I gathered flowers in the nearby gardens, looking for rare, but beautiful, autumn blooms. After my last foray, I lost sight of my little pink-waisted lieutenant in her serrated edged cape, but I could hear her shouting in Clochegourde.

"The General," said a tearful Madeleine, and she used that name to underline her hatred of her father, "the General is scolding our mother, please go and defend her."

I flew up the steps and into the drawing room unnoticed by the count or his wife. I listened to the madman shrieking, as I went around shutting all the doors before returning: I'd seen that Henriette was as white as her dress.

"Félix, never marry," said the count, "women seek advice from the devil, the most virtuous would invent evil if it didn't exist. They are all nasty brutes."

Arguments followed that made no sense at all. Drawing on his previous snipes, M. de Mortsauf echoed the silly reasoning of the peasants who refused to adapt to the new ways. He asserted that, had he been in charge of Clochegourde, he'd be twice as rich as he was. He cursed, insulted, swore, jumped from one piece of furniture to another, shoving and kicking them; then, midsentence, broke off to complain about the marrow burning in his bones, or the gray matter he was leaking in waves, like his money. His wife was ruining him. The wretched fellow already owed over twenty thousand of his thirty-one thousand pounds of earnings to his wife. The property of the duke and the duchess was worth over fifty thousand francs in income set aside for Jacques. The countess smiled haughtily and looked at the sky.

"Yes, Blanche," he screamed, "you are my executioner, and you are murdering me: I'm a dead weight in your eyes and you are a terrible hypocrite. She's laughing! Do you know why she is laughing, Félix?"

I said nothing and looked down.

"This woman," he resumed, answering his own question, "denies me all happiness, she's as much yours as she is mine, though she pretends to be my wife! She bears my name but fulfills none of the duties ordained by human and divine law, and thus lies both to man and to God. She piles work on me, tiring me out so I leave her alone; she doesn't like me, in fact, she hates me, and uses all her guile to stay a maiden; she drives me mad by the way she rejects me, and it all rushes to my head: she's slowly killing me, yet she thinks she is a saint, and even takes Communion every month!"

The countess was by now in a flood of warm tears, humiliated by those despicable attacks, and could only respond: "Monsieur...! Monsieur...! Monsieur!"

Although the count's outburst should have made me blush as much for him as for Henriette, it stirred violent emotions in me, because he referred to a delicate sense of chastity that is, in a way, the stuff of which first loves are made.

"She is a virgin to spite me," said the count.

When she heard that word, the countess screamed: "Monsieur...!"

"What's that imperious *monsieur* of yours? Am I not the master here? Must I teach you a lesson?"

He walked toward her, like a white wolf wagging his hideous, head, with his yellow eyes giving him the look of a famished animal running out of the woods. Henriette slipped from her chair to the floor to receive a blow that never came, and she was sprawled unconscious on the parquet floor. The count was like an assassin who can feel his victim's blood spurting into his face; he gawped vacantly. I took the poor woman in my arms, which the count allowed me to do, as if he felt unworthy to carry her, but he walked ahead and opened the bedroom door adjacent to the drawing room, a hallowed bedroom where I'd never set foot. I kept the countess upright with one hand, while I placed the other around her waist, as M. de Mortsauf pulled back the eiderdown and bedclothes; then we lifted her and laid her down fully clothed. As she regained consciousness, Henriette gestured for us to loosen her belt. M. de Mortsauf found some scissors and snipped through everything; I made her smell salts, and she opened her eyes. The count walked out, shamefaced but not sorrowful. Two hours passed in complete silence. Henriette's hand was in mine, pressing mine, though she couldn't speak. Now and then she looked up, as if to say she wanted only peace and quiet; then there was a moment of truce, when she pulled herself up onto an elbow and whispered in my ear: "That unhappy fellow, if only you knew...!"

She rested her head back on the pillow. Memories of past troubles, joined by her present grief, led to nervous convulsions I could only calm by applying love's magnetic power; a force I still don't recognize but which I brought to bear instinctively. I supported her with the tenderest use of strength, and during her last attack, she glanced at me in a way that made me weep. When her nervous shuddering stopped, I tidied her disheveled hair I was touching for the first and only time in my life; then I took her hand again and contemplated her brown and gray bedroom, the simple bed with Persian curtains, the table covered with old-fashioned toiletries, and the shabby quilted couch. What a poetic place! What a dearth of luxury for her! Her luxury was to relish the spartan and the spotless! It was the noble cell of a religious wife full of saintly resignation, where the only ornament was the crucifix above her bed, under a portrait of her aunt; on either side of the holy water stoup, her pencil drawings of her two children, and locks of hair from when they were small. What a sanctuary for a woman whose appearance in high society would have made the most beautiful turn pale! This was the boudoir where the daughter of an illustrious family always wept: in that bitter moment despondent, and rejecting love that would have brought her consolation. A secret, inviolable grief! A victim's tears for the executioner, and an executioner's for the victim. When her children and maid walked in, I walked out. The count was waiting for me, because he now accepted me as a mediator between his wife and himself; he seized my hands and exclaimed: "Stay, Félix, stay!"

"Unfortunately," I replied, "M. de Chessel has guests, and it wouldn't be at all seemly for his visitors to inquire after the reasons for my absence, but I will come back after lunch."

He accompanied me out of the house and down to the lower gate without saying a word, and then as far as Frapesle, really quite unaware of what he was doing. I finally told him: "For God's sake, Monsieur le Comte, let her manage your household, if that is what she wants, and don't torture her anymore."

"I don't have long to live," he retorted solemnly, "she won't suffer much longer because of me. I feel my head will explode any minute."

And he left me with that parting shot that was pure spontaneous selfishness.

After lunch, I came back for news of Mme de Mortsauf, who already looked better. How could she live if that was the joy in her marriage, if such scenes were common? A slow murder that went unpunished! That evening I understood the intolerable torture the count was inflicting on his wife to undermine her. But what court of law would ever hear her case? Those reflections numbed me; I could find no words to say to Henriette, but spent the night writing to her. Of the three or four letters I wrote, I've kept only these initial pages that I disliked, because I decided they said nothing or spoke too much of myself when I should have spoken only of her, but they will at least show you my state of mind:

TO MADAME DE MORTSAUF

There were so many things I wanted to say to you when I arrived, thoughts that had come to me as I was walking, but that I forgot as soon as I saw you! Yes, the moment I see you, dear Henriette, I no longer find that my words are equal to the reflections from your soul, which enhance your beauty. I experience at your side such infinite happiness my feelings in the present erase any from my previous life. Each time, I'm reborn into a more expansive life, like the traveler who climbs rocky crags and discovers a new horizon at every step. Doesn't each new conversation add new treasure to my trove? There lies, I believe, the key to long, indefatigable relationships. I cannot speak of you when I am far from you. In your presence, I'm too dazzled to see, and too happy to question my happiness, too full of you to be myself and too eloquent before you to speak, too ardent to seize the present moment to recall the past. Please understand my constant inebriation and forgive my waywardness. By your side, I only feel. Nonetheless, I dare tell you, dear Henriette, that, never, among the many joys you've given me, have I felt such bliss as the ecstasy that overcame my soul yesterday when, after that horrendous onslaught when you had to fight evil with superhuman courage, you regained consciousness alone with me, in the half light of your bedroom, where that wretched scene had led me. I alone saw the glorious splendor of a woman returning from the gates of death to the gates of life, and the dawn of rebirth gilding her brow. Your voice was so full of harmony! Words seem trifling—even yours—vague resentment at past sorrows lingering on in the tone of your adored voice, mixed with the divine consolation you assured me, when you told me of your first thoughts. I already knew all human light shone in you, but yesterday I glimpsed another Henriette who would be entirely mine, God willing. Yesterday, I glimpsed a different being released from the bodily trammels that prevent us from fanning the fires of the soul. You were so beautiful in your dejection, so majestic in your frailty! Yesterday I discovered something more beautiful than your beauty, something sweeter than your voice, lights that glowed more than the light in your eyes, scents no words can describe: yesterday your soul became visible and tangible. I suffered so much because I couldn't open my heart to you and revive you there and then. Finally, yesterday, I lost that respectful terror you inspired in me: Didn't your fainting fit bring us closer together? I experienced the gift of breathing in step with you, when a nervous attack lets you breathe *our* air. I sent so many prayers heavenwards in a second! If I didn't expire crossing the spaces I climbed in order to ask God to leave you to me, it is proof that one cannot die from joy or sorrow. That moment buried memories deep in my soul that will never surface without floods of tears; each joy will increase the furrow, each sorrow will deepen them. The fear that shook my soul yesterday will truly act as a point of comparison for all future sorrows, like the joys you've bestowed on me, dear eternal inspiration of my life, which will rise above all the joys God ever deigned to give me. You've allowed me to understand a divine love, a secure love that, confident in its own strength and longevity, conceives of neither suspicion nor jealousy.

Deep melancholy ate into my soul, the sight of that inner life had been chastening for a young man, new to society's impact on the emotions: the discovery of that chasm on the threshold of that wider world, a bottomless chasm, a dead sea. That horrible exhibition of misery encouraged me to meditate endlessly, and, when taking my first steps in the social round, I had a huge benchmark to measure by, against which other scenes I've described could only seem lesser. My sadness led M. and Mme de Chessel to conclude I was unhappy in my loves; I was blessed by a passion that brought no harm to my superb Henriette.

The following morning she was alone when I entered the drawing room; she stared at me for a second as she offered me her hand, and said: "Will my friend always be too demonstrative?"

Her eyes moistened, she got up, then desperately implored: "Never write to me like that again!"

M. de Mortsauf was well disposed. The countess had regained her spirits and seemed tranquil enough, but her complexion betrayed her suffering from the previous night; it had ebbed but not died. That evening as we walked over dry autumn leaves that crackled under our feet, she told me: "Sorrow is infinite; joy has its boundaries."

A declaration that revealed her suffering, through the comparison she made to fleeting happiness.

"Don't decry life, I beg you: you don't know what love is, or its pleasures, that shine even in heaven."

"Shush," she snapped, "I don't want to know. A Greenlander would die in Italy! I feel calm and content by your side, I can tell you everything I think; don't destroy my trust. Why can't you possess the virtue of a priest and the charms of a free man?"

"You'd have me swallow cups of hemlock," I answered, putting her hand on my thudding heart.

"You're being like that again!" she exclaimed, removing her hand as if she'd felt a sharp pain. "Do you really want to deprive me of the pleasure I find in a friendly hand that stanches the blood from my wounds? Don't add to sorrows of which you only know the half! The most hidden are the hardest to bear. If you were a woman, you'd understand the mixture of melancholy and loathing a proud spirit feels when she sees she is the object of attentions that redress nothing and with which *one* thinks all is redressed. For a few days, I will be courted, *one* will wish to be forgiven for the wrong *one* has inflicted. Then I could find *one's* consent to the most outrageous wishes. I feel humiliated by this abasement, by these caresses that stop the day *one* believes I have forgotten everything. Only encountering the master's good graces as a result of his errors . . ."

"His crimes!" I retorted.

"Isn't this a horrendous way to live?" she asked, smiling wanly. "In any case, I am unable to wield power that is transient. At such times, I am like those knights who didn't finish off their fallen adversary. Seeing the person we should honor on the ground, pulling him back to his feet only to receive more blows, suffering more from his fall than he suffers himself, and feeling it dishonorable if you make the most of momentary advantages, even if the goal is beneficial; consuming your energies, exhausting your mental reserves on petty squabbles, reigning only after you've been mortally wounded! I would prefer death. If I didn't have children, I'd let life take its toll, but what would become of them without my fortitude behind the scenes? However painful life is, I have to live on for them. And you speak to me of love? My friend, imagine the hell I'd find myself consigned to, were I to give this pitiless fellow, like all weak minds, the right to hold me in contempt. I couldn't bear the slightest suspicion. My strength derives from my faultless behavior. Dear child, virtue has its holy water, where you dip and emerge renewed by God's love!"

"Listen, Henriette, I only have one more week left here, I want you to— "

"So you are abandoning us?" she interjected.

"Don't you think I should find out what my father is planning for me? I've been here a good three months..."

"I have never counted the days," she replied, with the lack of composure of a woman in a state of shock.

She recovered and said: "Let's walk. Let's go to Frapesle."

She summoned the count, her children, and asked for her shawl; then, when everything was ready, she, who was usually so slow and calm, hustled and bustled like a Parisienne, and we left en masse for Frapesle to pay a visit that wasn't due. She kept herself busy speaking to Mme de Chessel, who, fortunately, answered at length.

The count and M. de Chessel talked about business matters. I was afraid M. de Mortsauf would boast about his carriage and its harnessing, but he acted in perfect good taste. His neighbor asked about the work he was having done at La Cassine and la Rhétorière. As I heard the question, I watched the count and thought he would avoid a subject of conversation that brought back bad memories with a cruel, bitter aftertaste, but he argued how urgent it was to improve the state of agriculture in the canton and build the best of farms where locals could be fit and healthy; in short, he embraced his wife's ideas for his own glory. I looked at the countess and blushed. I was appalled by that lack of tact in a man who could on occasion show so much, the way he could forget such a recent frenzied scene, and adopted ideas he'd so violently shot down, by his incredible self-belief.

When M. de Chessel asked: "Do you think you will recoup your expenditure?"

"And more besides!" he yelped.

You could understand such flights only from the perspective of his lunacy. Henriette, that heavenly soul, was radiant. Didn't the count appear to be sensible, a good manager and excellent agronomist? She stroked Jacques's hair in delight, happy for herself, and happy for her son! What a playactor he was, what a farce it all was! I was shocked. Later, when the curtain was lifted on the social scene, I came to see there were many Mortsaufs, often without even the flashes of loyalty, or religion! What strange, acerbic power exists that perpetually throws

angels to madmen, a scheming woman to a sincere, poetic, affectionate man, a noble woman to an abject tyrant, and this sublime, beautiful creature to that ape; to every noble Juana, a Captain Diard, whose
story you learned in Bordeaux; a d'Ajuda to Mme de Beauséant, that
husband to Mme d'Aiglemont, and that wife to the Marquis d'Espard.[12]
I can tell you I've often sought answers to this riddle. I've investigated
a number of enigmas, I have discovered the reasons for several natural laws, the meanings of a few divine hieroglyphs, but I fail to understand this particular one at all; I still study it like the face of an
Indian totem whose symbolism is known only to Brahmins. In this
case, the evil genie is too visibly in charge and I dare not accuse God.
Who enjoys weaving misfortunes that have no cure? Could Henriette
and her Unknown Philosopher be right? Could their mystical beliefs
contain a general meaning for humanity?

The last days I spent in that region belonged to an autumn that
had shed its leaves, and cloud-filled days that sometimes hid the skies
of Touraine, usually so clear and warm in this fine season. On the
eve of my departure, Mme de Mortsauf led me onto the terrace, before
lunch.

"My dear Félix," she said, after we'd walked in silence beneath the
bare trees, "you are about to enter society, and I would like to accompany you there in thought. We who have suffered a lot, have lived
a lot; don't think solitary souls know nothing of that social whirl: we
judge it. If I must live through my friend, I don't wish him to be
uneasy in heart or conscience; in the midst of the melee it can be hard
to remember the rules, so let me fill in some background, like a mother
to her son. Dear child, the day you depart I'll give you a long letter
where you will find all my womanly thoughts about that social world,
about men, and the way to tackle difficulties in that maelstrom of
self-interest; promise you will read it only once you are in Paris. My
plea expresses an emotional fantasy that is our secret as women; I
don't think you can possibly understand, and we would probably be
upset if you did; indulge these small byways where a woman likes to
walk alone."

"I promise," I answered, kissing her hand.

"By the way!" she continued, "I have one more plea, and you must agree to accept it in advance."

"Of course," I replied, thinking she referred to issues of fidelity.

"It's not about me," she responded, with a bitter smile. "Félix, never gamble, in whatever salon you find yourself; there is no exception."

"I will never gamble."

"Good. I have a much better way for you to spend your time; you'll see how you can always win, whereas others will lose everything, sooner or later."

"How?"

"It will all be in my letter," she replied brightly, thus sparing her recommendations the solemn tone that accompanies grandparental advice.

The countess spoke for nearly an hour and showed me the depths of her affection by revealing how intensely she'd studied me over the last three months; she penetrated the recesses of my heart trying to apply her own inner wisdom; her emphasis changed, she was persuasive, her words fell from motherly lips, indicating, in their tone and substance, the numerous bonds that already joined us.

"If you only knew," she said finally, "how nervously I shall follow your progress, how happy I shall be to see you keep to the straight and narrow path and what tears I shall shed if you hit any sharp corners! Believe me, my affection is unparalleled: it is both spontaneous and premeditated. I so want to see you happy, powerful, and held in high esteem: you will be like a living dream for me."

She made me weep. She was at once charming and forbidding; she bared her true feelings too boldly, yet was too pure to allow a young man riding high with pleasure the slightest hope. In return for the flesh left in shreds in her heart, she poured out the incessant, incorruptible light of a divine love that could satisfy only the soul. She rose to summits where love's dappled wings that had led me to nuzzle her shoulders could never take me; to reach the peak where she had settled, you needed the white wings of a seraph.

"At every moment, I will think: 'What would Henriette say?'"

"Good, I want to be your star and your sanctuary," she replied, alluding to my childhood dreams and seeking to offer me a way to fulfill them that would deflect my desires.

"You will be my religion and light! You will be everything to me!" I exclaimed.

"No, I can never be the source of your pleasure."

She sighed, with a smile inspired by secret sorrow, the smile of a slave who rebelled momentarily. From that day on, she wasn't simply my beloved, but my greatest love; she didn't inhabit my heart like a woman who wanted to find a place there, who etched herself there via her devotion or excessive pleasure; no, she possessed my entire heart, and was essential to the play of its tissues; she was transformed into what Beatrice represented for the poet from Florence; the purest Laura, to the poet from Venice; the mother of my every thought, the unconscious prompt for my every cautious decision; the foundation sustaining my future; the light shining like a lily amid the darkest foliage. Yes, she dictated key resolves that doused the fire, that rescued the object in danger; she granted me a Coligny kind of firmness that allowed me to defeat conquerors, to be reborn after defeats, and to exhaust the fiercest fighters.[13]

The following morning, after breakfasting in Frapesle and bidding farewell to my hosts, who were so tolerant in respect to my selfish love, I visited Clochegourde. M. and Mme de Mortsauf had planned to take me to Tours, where I was to leave that night for Paris. On the journey, the countess was quietly affectionate: at first she pretended to have a migraine; then she blushed at her deceit and made up for it by saying she was sorry to see me depart. The count invited me to stay with him, should I ever want to see the Indre Valley when the Chessels were away. We went our separate ways, heroically, without tears, but, like the sickly child he once had been, Jacques felt a wave of emotion that did bring a few tears, and the now womanly Madeleine gripped her mother's hand.

"My dear baby!" said the countess, fervently kissing Jacques.

When I was by myself in Tours, I was struck after lunch by one of those strange and furious whims that only young men experience. I hired a horse and covered the distance from Tours to Pont-de-Ruan in an hour and a quarter. Ashamed to reveal my folly, I ran stealthily along the path to reach the area beneath the terrace, like a spy. The countess wasn't there. I imagined she must be feeling sad; I'd kept the key to the side gate, and I went in; at that very moment she was coming down the steps with her children, wanting to absorb, wistfully and slowly, the gentle melancholy of the landscape at sunset.

"Look, mother, it's Félix!" said Madeleine.

"Yes, it is I," I whispered in her ear. "I wondered why I was still in Tours when it was so easy to come and see you. Why shouldn't I fulfill a desire, something that will be impossible in a week's time?"

"He's not leaving us, Mother!" shouted Jacques, jumping up and down.

"Shush, you," said Madeleine, "you'll alert the General."

"This isn't sensible," muttered Henriette, "it's madness!"

Such a reaction, so tearfully expressed, was a fine reward for what you might call love's miserly calculations!

"I'd forgotten to return this key," I replied with a smile.

"You won't be coming back?"

"Are we abandoning each other, then?" I asked with a glance that made her lower her eyelids and veil her silent response.

I left after enjoying a few seconds in that happy stupor a soul feels when excitement ends and lunacy begins. I walked slowly away, looking back all the time. When I reached the top of the plateau, I surveyed the valley one last time, and thought how different it was now than it had been when I first arrived there: Didn't it bud and blossom back then just as my hopes and desires first budded and blossomed? Now I had been initiated into a family's somber, melancholy mysteries, sharing the anguish of a Christian Niobe, as sad as her, my soul in a dark place, the valley now matched the bent of my ideas.[14] Fields were bare, leaves were falling from the poplars, and those that hadn't fallen were a rusty color; vines were burnt, treetops displayed that austere dun kings used to adopt for their garments, thus hiding the purple of power beneath the brown of sorrow. In harmony with my thoughts, the valley, seen by the dying rays of a tepid sun, precisely reflected the state of my soul.

Leaving a woman you love can be a straightforward step or an anxious one, depending on your character. I suddenly felt I was in a foreign country whose language I didn't know; there was nothing I could hang on to, seeing these objects to which my soul was no longer attached. Then, my expansive love reacted and dear Henriette surged in that desert where I lived only on memories of her. She was a figure I adored so religiously I resolved to remain pristine in the presence of my secret deity, and mentally I wore the white garb of the Levites, imitating Petrarch, who only appeared before Laura de Noves dressed entirely in white.

How impatiently I looked forward to the first night when, at my parents' house, I could read the letter which I'd touched on my journey like a miser fingering a wad of money he is forced to carry on his person. At night, I kissed the paper where Henriette had written down her wishes, where I would grasp the mysterious stream that had flowed from her hand, where her voice's intonation would hurtle through my settled mind. I always read her letters as I read that first one, in bed and in total silence; I know of no other way of reading letters written by the one you love, though men do exist who are unworthy of being loved, who like to mix reading those letters with their prosaic worries, putting them down and picking them up with contemptible ease.

Here, Natalie, is the adorable voice that suddenly reverberated in the silence of night, here is the sublime figure who stood up and pointed me in the right direction when I stood at a crossroads:

I am so happy, my friend, to gather the motley fruits of my experience and show them to you, equipping you thus against the dangers of a world where you must act shrewdly! I have felt all the legitimate pleasures of maternal love as I thought of you these past few nights. While I was writing this letter, sentence by sentence, anticipating the life you will lead, I sometimes went to my window, observed the moonlit towers of Frapesle, and said: "He is asleep and I'm watching over him." Delightful feelings that reminded me of the first blissful moments in my life when I gazed at Jacques sleeping in his cradle, while I waited for him to wake up so I could give him my milk. Aren't you a man-child whose spirit now needs to be strengthened by instructions that you were not brought up with in those dreadful schools where you suffered so much, but which we, as women, can have the privilege of introducing you to? These trifles will foment your success, prepare and solidify your path. Could this not be a kind of spiritual motherliness that creates a system by which a man determines his actions, a motherliness that a child will understand? Dear Félix, allow me, even when I make the occasional mistake, to imprint on our friendship a disinterest that will bless it: Am I not renouncing you by surrendering you to the world? Well, my love is strong enough to sacrifice my joy to assure your fine future. For almost four months, you have led me to reflect anew on the laws and customs that rule our era. The conversations with my aunt, the substance of which pertains to you, who are her replacement!; the incidents in M. de Mortsauf's life as he has recounted them to me; the words of my father, who was familiar with life at court; circumstances, big and small, have rushed to my memory on behalf of the adoptive child I see poised to launch himself into that social whirl, almost alone, about to head off uncounseled into territory where some perish because of the good qualities they recklessly squander and others succeed because of evil qualities they exercise with cunning.

Above all, consider this spare expression of my opinion of society seen as a whole, because I know you need only a few words. I am unsure whether societies have divine origins or are invented by men, I am equally unsure how they function; what I do know for certain is that they exist; as soon as you accept that, rather than living on the margins, you must endorse their constituent elements as being good and tomorrow sign a contract with society. Does today's society extract more from a man than it gives back? I am sure it does, but whether a man finds more burdens than benefits, or pays over the odds for the advantages he accrues, is an issue that concerns the legislator rather than the individual. In my opinion, you must obey the general law in every respect, without quarrel, whether it is to your detriment or it serves your interests. This principle may seem sensible, but it is difficult to apply; it is like a sap that must filter through the smallest capillary tubes to give a tree life, sustain its greenery, nurture its flowers, and richly feed the fruit that will win admiration everywhere. My dear, laws aren't all written in books, custom also makes its laws, the most important ones being the least known; there are no teachers, no treatises, no school for its laws that govern your actions, your speeches, your external life, the way you present yourself to society, or face your destiny. If you fail to obey these secret laws, you will remain at the bottom of the social ladder rather than rise to dominate it. Even though this letter may often seem superfluous in terms of what you are thinking, let me confide my womanly politics.

To explain society through a theory of individual happiness expressly sought at the expense of others is a lethal doctrine, the harsh connotations of which drive man to believe everything he secretly gains, without the legal system, society, or individuals perceiving the damage done, is properly and duly acquired. According to this charter, the cunning thief is absolved, the woman who fails in her duty without anyone noticing is good and happy; kill a man without the law detecting any evidence, you will win some bauble, in the manner of Macbeth, and will have acted correctly; your own self-interest becomes the supreme law, the challenge is to turn to your own advantage, without witness or proof, the obstacles that custom and law place between you and your goals. For anyone who views society in this way, the conundrum of making one's fortune, my friend, is reduced to playing a game where the stakes are a million pounds or jail, political advancement or dishonor. Besides, is there enough green beige to go round to accommodate all the gamblers, and does it require the wit of a genius to devise a trick? I don't speak of religious beliefs or sentiment; what is at stake here are the cogs in machinery generating gold and iron, the immediate results men pursue. My dear, dear child, if you share my loathing of this justification of criminals, society can be explained to you, as to all healthy, intelligent minds, by a theory of duty. Yes, you owe each other in a thousand different ways. As I see it, the duke and the peer owe much more to the artisan or poor man than the latter owe the duke and the peer. The obligations contracted increase in ratio to the benefits society affords a man, and, according to this principle, as true in commerce as in politics, the burden of care to offer is in proportion to the profit recorded. Everyone pays their debt in their own way. Don't you think our poor man in La Rhétorière has done his duty when he reaches his bed, exhausted by his labors? He has certainly fulfilled it far better than many of much higher rank. Thus when you think about the social world where you want to take a position in line with your intelligence and abilities, you must consider this maxim as your guiding light: never allow yourself to do anything against your conscience or the public's. Although you may find I insist too much, I beg you, yes, your Henriette begs you, to think about those two words carefully. Though simple in appearance, my dear, they mean that legality, honor, loyalty, and politeness are the most secure, efficient instruments to ensure your good fortune. In this selfish world, a host of people will tell you one can't make one's way in life by depending on sentiment, that moral considerations, when overly respected, delay one's progress; you will see both ill-brought-up individuals and educated ones incapable of mastering their future, hurting a child, being guilty of rudeness towards an old woman, refusing to help an upstanding elderly man on the excuse that they aren't at all useful, later you will see individuals caught on thorns they haven't blunted, ruining their future over a trifle; while those who committed early to the theory of duty will encounter no such obstacles; perhaps they will reach the top more slowly, but their fortune will be solid and will resist when that of others crumbles!

If I tell you that the application of this doctrine requires, above all, knowledge of good manners, you may find my jurisprudence owes a little to the court and the teaching I received in the Lenoncourt household. My friend, I do attach much importance to those lessons, that seem to amount to very little! The ways of well-bred society will be as necessary to you as the extensive, varied knowledge you already possess: in effect, certain ignoramuses, endowed with natural wit, accustomed to following their ideas through, have reached a high station that escaped worthier folk. I have watched you closely, Félix, and know that the education you experienced overall in schools hasn't harmed you at all. God alone knows how pleased I was to see the quick way you made up for the little you lacked! Many people raised in these traditions display manners that are purely for show; fine courtesy and manners must come from the heart and express a profound sense of personal dignity, which is why, despite their upbringing, some nobles are unruly and some individuals of bourgeois stock have natural good taste and no need of lessons to act with excellent manners or to be a poor imitation. Believe this poor woman who is never going to leave her valley, that noble demeanor, that gracious simplicity in word and gesture, in dress and even in household, constitutes a kind of physical poetry whose charm is irresistible; make the most of that power flowing from the heart! Civil behavior, dear child, consists in forgetting oneself on behalf of others; for many people, it is a social flourish belied the moment self-interest is threatened, and shows its uglier side, namely, when a noble becomes ignoble. Yet, and this is how I would like you, Félix, to see it, true civility implies Christian thought; it is like the flower of true charity, and involves genuinely forgetting oneself. In remembrance of Henriette, don't be a spring without water, be form *and* spirit! Don't be afraid of being the victim of such social virtue, sooner or later you will reap the fruit from all those seeds seemingly thrown to the wind. My father once observed that one of the most harmful ways of misconstruing civility is to promise too much. When asked to do something you cannot deliver, say so loud and clear and don't nurture false expectations; consent to what you can readily grant: that way, you acquire good grace from a rebuttal and good grace from what is well done, a double boon that is a wonderful strengthener of character. I don't know if one bears a grudge more for a hope dashed than a favor given. Above all, my friend, and these trifles fall within my purview, and I am stressing what I think I know well: don't be overtrusting, vulgar, or hurried, three dangerous reefs! Excessive trust diminishes respect, vulgarity earns contempt, and zealousness opens the way for base exploitation. And, by the by, my child, you will have only two or three friends in the course of your existence, your trust in them is their capital; if you offer it to too many, won't you be betraying them? If you develop closer links to some men than to others, be cautious in respect of yourself, always keep yourself in reserve in case one day you discover they are your rivals, opponents, or enemies; life's randomness demands that. Maintain an attitude that is neither cold nor warm, learn how to find that median line a man can straddle without committing himself in any way. Yes, you must believe that a gentleman is as far from Philinte's cowardly laxity as from Alceste's grating self-righteousness.[15] The genius of the poet playactor shines through when he displays the true middle ground that noble spectators can grasp; no doubt, all will incline towards self-righteous nonsense rather than the preening contempt that conceals itself beneath selfish bluster, but they will know how to save themselves from both. As for the vulgar, if that means some fools say you are delightful, individuals expert in plumbing depths when assessing human qualities will detect your weakness and promptly send you packing, because vulgarity is the resort of the weak-willed; besides, the weak-willed are unfortunately scorned by a society that sees each of its members only as a limb; it may be right, nature condemns to death beings that are imperfect. Perhaps women's touching caveats are bred by the pleasure they find in fighting blind might and ensuring heartfelt compassion triumphs over brute matter. But society, more stepmother than mother, adores children who flatter her vanity. As for zeal, the first, sublime error of youth that finds true pleasure in deploying its energies and starting to be duped by itself before it becomes the dupe of others, keep that for feelings you share, for your wife and for your God. Don't bring treasure to the world's marketplace or political speculation in exchange for which they will give you glass trinkets. You must believe in the voice that insists on nobility in everything, as it also begs you not to spread yourself too thinly, because, alas, men value you in terms of your usefulness rather than your true worth. To employ an image that can be etched on your poetic spirit, whether the figure is excessively huge, drawn in gold, or traced in pencil, it will never be more than a figure. As a man of our times once said: "Never be zealous!"

Zeal verges on stupidity, and leads to disappointment; you will never find enthusiasm above you that matches yours: kings, like women, believe everything is their due. However dismal that principle may seem, it is true and doesn't demean the soul. Place your pure sentiments in inaccessible places, where their flowers are a source of passionate wonder, where the artist dreams almost amorously of his masterpiece. Duties, my friend, are not sentiments. Doing what one must is not to do as one pleases. A man must go and die coldly for his country, and happily give his life to a woman. One of the most important rules in the science of manners is to keep absolute silence with respect to yourself. Someday allow yourself the folly of talking about yourself to mere acquaintances; amuse them with news of your sorrows, your pleasures, and your business deals; you will soon see indifference set in where interest was once shown; then, when boredom is in the air, the mistress of the house will politely shut you up, and everyone will find a ready excuse to abandon your company. But if you want to win everyone's sympathy, act as the smart fellow, both companionable and steadfast; ask after them, find the way to put them center stage, even raise issues that might seem unsuitable: their faces will lighten, their lips smile, and when you've gone, they will all praise you. Your conscience and heart must indicate the boundary where obsequious flattery commences and graceful conversation ends. Just one more suggestion on the subject of social intercourse. My friend, youth always tends to make rapid judgments, which honor it, but then render a disservice; that is why young people were once taught to be silent when they spent time with their elders to learn about life; because, once, Nobility, like Art, had its apprentices, its pages devoted to the masters that fed them. Today, youth receives its knowledge from the hothouse, with a sour aftertaste that leads it to judge harshly the thoughts and writing of others: it cuts with the edge of a blade that has yet to be tested. Avoid such bad habits. Your pronouncements would be criticism that wounds many around you, and everyone will perhaps be more forgiving of a secret wound than a wrong raised publicly. Young people are trenchant, because they know nothing of life and its rigors. The old criticize with a light touch, the young are implacable; the latter know nothing, the former know everything. Besides, the base of all human acts rests on a labyrinth of crucial motives, and God has reserved for himself the definitive judgment on all of those. Be harsh only towards yourself. Your fortune lies before you, but nobody in this world can make theirs without help; so frequent my father's house, the relationships you form there will serve you a thousandfold, but don't yield an inch of terrain to my mother, who crushes anyone who yields and admires the pride of any who resist; she is like iron, that, if broken, can be joined back to iron, but breaks everything else it touches that isn't equally resilient. Please cultivate my mother: if she takes to you, she will find you entrance to salons, where you will acquire the sharpest knowledge of the social round, the art of listening, speaking, replying, presenting yourself, and making your mark; the exact language, that je ne sais quoi which is not in itself superior, for custom doesn't constitute genius, but without which the finest talent will never find acceptance. I know you well enough to be sure I don't deceive myself when I anticipate that you are what I want you to be: straightforward in manner, gently spoken, proud but not fatuous, respectful to the old, cautious without being servile, and above all tactful. Use your intellect, but don't let it be a source of ridicule to others; you should know that if your superior ways hurt a mediocre man, he will be silent, then say of you: "He is such a comedian!," an indication of contempt. Let your superiority always be seigneurial. Don't go out of your way to please. I recommend you be aloof with others to the point of impertinence and even anger some; everyone respects the person who shows them disdain, and that will also win you the good will of women, who will show you more esteem in ratio to the little regard you show other men. Never cultivate men of ill repute, even when their notoriety is undeserved, because society takes our friendships and our hates into account; in this matter, make sure you weigh your judgments maturely, and never go back on them. When men you spurn justify your rejection, people will seek out your esteem; that way, you inspire the tacit respect that enhances one man in the eyes of others. This will equip you with pleasing youthfulness, seductive grace, and wisdom that preserves its gains. An old saying sums up everything I have just said: Noblesse oblige!

Now apply these precepts to the conduct of your business. You will hear several people say that cunning is the key to success, that the way to make your way in the crowd is to divide men in order to rule. My friend, those principles were good in the Middle Ages, when princes had rival forces that destroyed each other, but, today, everything is out in the open, and such an approach would serve you extremely poorly. Indeed, you will find that you face either a loyal, true man, or a hostile traitor, a man who will use slander, calumny, and guile. You must learn that the latter is your best ally, and that man's worst enemy is himself; you can fight him by using tried and trusted weapons, sooner or later he will be sidelined. As for the first category, your frankness will earn his esteem; and once your interests are reconciled (for one can manage everything) he will serve you. Don't be afraid of making enemies, woe the man who doesn't have any in the world you are about to enter, but try not to give rise to ridicule or foul gossip; and I say *try*, because in Paris one is never fully in control, one is subject to fatal circumstance; you won't be able to avoid being splattered in mud or being hit by a falling tile. Morality has its streams from which dishonored individuals will try to spatter noble people with the mud in which they are drowning. But you can win respect wherever you are by showing yourself to be implacable in the way you implement your decisions. Where ambitions conflict, in the midst of entangled complexities, always go straight to the point, stride resolutely to your goal, and only ever fight on one front with all your might. You know how much M. de Mortsauf hated Napoleon; he held him up for execration, watched him as men of the law pursue criminals, every evening he asked after the Duke of Enghien, the only misfortune, the only death that led him to shed tears; well, you know, he admired him as the boldest of captains, and often explained his tactics to me. Can't we apply that strategy to the war of self-interest? It would save a lot of time, as the other saved men and territory; think about it, for a woman can often be wrong in things we judge instinctively or emotionally. I should insist on one point: all guile and trickery will be found out and will do harm, while I believe all situations are less dangerous when a man takes the high ground of truth. If I might put myself forward as an example, I could tell you that in Clochegourde, forced by M. de Mortsauf's character to anticipate anything litigious and to immediately arbitrate contested ground that would have turned into a quicksand for him that he would have relished, but ultimately succumbed to, I always had to cut things dead, by going to the crux and telling my adversary: "Either we do a deal, or we forget it!" You will often find you are being useful to others by helping them and will receive little recompense, but don't be the sort to complain about others and boast that everyone is ungrateful. Is that putting oneself on a pedestal? But isn't it also rather foolish to reveal your lack of knowledge of society? But will you do good like a usurer lending his money? Or will you do good for its own sake? Noblesse oblige! Besides, if you don't offer such help, you will force people to be ungrateful, and they will become your bitterest enemies: there is despair in duty, like despair in disaster, that can mobilize incalculable gains. As for yourself, accept the least possible from others. Be nobody's vassal, depend only on yourself. My friend, I am only advising you about the small things in life. In the world of politics, everything changes, the rules ruling your person pale before much grander interests. But if you reach the sphere where the great and the good operate, you will be like God, the sole judge of what you decide. You will no longer be a man, you will be the law incarnate. But if you deliver judgments, you yourself will be judged. Later, you will appear before future centuries, and you know enough about history to appreciate the sentiments and deeds that engender true greatness.

I will now broach a serious issue: your comportment with women. In the salons you visit, on principle beware of frittering yourself away in the petty habit of flattery. One of the most successful men of the last century was accustomed to dealing only with one person per night, and to taking an interest in those women who seemed neglected. That man, dear child, dominated his era. He had wisely foreseen that, after a while, everyone would praise him. Most young people squander their most precious capital, the time needed to establish relationships, which comprise half of social life; as they are appealing in themselves, and must do very little to win over people to support their interests, but this springtime is short, be sure to use it well. Cultivate influential women. They are older women and will teach you connections, every family's secrets, and the byways that can lead you quickly to your goal. They will cherish you from their hearts; the protection they offer is their last love, that is, when they aren't pious; they will give you fantastic help, promote you, and make you a man who is in demand. Avoid young women! And don't think there is any self-interest in my saying that. A fifty-year-old woman will do everything for you, and a twenty-year-old, nothing: the latter will want your whole life, the former will only crave a moment of your attention. Make fun of young women, take everything they offer in jest, they are incapable of serious thought. Young women, my friend, are selfish, petty, offer no true friendship, love only themselves, and will sacrifice you to their own success. Besides, they will expect you to be devoted, and your situation requires that for yourself, and those two aims cannot be reconciled. None will worry about your self-interest, they will all think of themselves and never of you; their vanity will harm you much more than their attachment will ever bring you; they will unscrupulously take up your time, ensure you miss golden opportunities, and destroy you with the best grace possible. If you complain, the most foolish will declare her glove is worth the world, that nothing could be more glorious than serving her. They will all say they bring happiness, and will make you forget your true destiny: their happiness is fickle, your success is guaranteed. You can have no idea of the treacherous skills they employ to achieve their fantasies, to transform a passing fancy into a love that begins on earth and must continue in heaven. The day when they leave you, they will utter the words "I no longer love you" to justify their departure, as the words "I love" excused their love, because love cannot be willed. A ridiculous idea, my dear! Believe me, true love is eternal, infinite, and always a mirror unto itself; it is tempered and pure, without violent eruptions; it is always young in heart, even when hair turns gray. You will find nothing like it in those mundane women; they are all playacting. One

will attract you with her woes, she will seem the sweetest, least demanding of women, but when she has become a necessity in your life,
she will slowly come to dominate you and make you do as she wishes;
you want to be a diplomat, to travel, study mankind, countries, and
the interests at play! No, you must stay in Paris or on her territory,
she will slyly sew you to her skirt, and the more devoted you are, the
more ungrateful she will be. Another will try to win you by being
submissive, she will become your page, follow you romantically to
the end of the world, will commit to protecting you, yet be a stone
around your neck. You will drown one day and she will swim ashore.
The least wily set endless traps; the stupidest will triumph because
she arouses so little suspicion; the least perilous would be a seductress
who would love but not know why, who would leave you without
cause and scold you out of vanity. But all will harm you in the present
or the future. Every young woman who enjoys the social whirl, who
lives for pleasure and vain satisfaction, is half-corrupt and will corrupt
you. She will be no chaste, reserved creature in whose soul you will
reign forever. Ah! The woman who loves you will be a solitary soul:
her best parties will be your looks; she will hang on your every word.
Let this woman be your whole world, for you will be everything to
her: love her dearly, don't give her cause for sorrow, or rivals, don't
arouse her jealousy. To be loved, my dear, to be understood, is the
greatest good fortune I could wish you to experience, but don't commit the flower of your soul rashly, be sure of the heart where you lodge
your affection. This woman will never be herself, must never think
of herself, but only of you; she will never argue, she will never flaunt
her own interests and will have a nose for danger where you see none,
and will forget the risks to herself; if she suffers, she will never complain, she won't vaunt herself, but will respect what you love in her.
Respond to this love by exceeding it. If you are fortunate enough to
find what your poor friend here will always lack, a love that is equally
inspired, equally felt, always remember, however perfect that love
may be, that a mother lives for you in a valley, her heart so laden with
the love you have poured there that you will never plumb its depths.
Yes, I feel an affection for you, the extent of which you will never

know; for her to show you what it is like, you would have to abandon your fine intellect, and even then you wouldn't know how far my devotion can go. Am I suspect when I insist you avoid women who are all more or less preening, vain, vapid, scoffing, and spendthrift, and bind yourself instead to women of influence, to domineering dowagers, as full of good sense as my aunt, and who will serve you so well, who will defend you against secret recriminations by belying them, who will say of you what you yourself can never say? Finally, is it not generous of me to bid you to keep your adoration for the angel with the pure heart? If this phrase, Noblesse oblige, contains most of my recommendations, my views on your relationships with women are to be found in the chivalric motto: *Serve all, love only one.*

You have a wealth of knowledge; your heart, preserved by suffering, has remained pure; everything is beautiful and good in you, *please let it be so*!

Your future now depends on those words, the words of great men. My child, won't you obey your Henriette and allow her to continue to tell you what she thinks of you and your relationships in society? My soul has an eye that sees the future for you, as it does for my children; allow me then to use this ability to benefit you, a mysterious gift that has brought peace to my life and that, far from weakening, holds firm in solitude and silence. In return I ask you to give me this great happiness: I want to see you make your way among men without a single success furrowing my brow; I want you to place your fortunes quickly at the elevated level of your name, and tell me that I, rather than desire, have contributed to your lofty status. This secret collaboration is all I can allow myself. I will wait. I am not bidding farewell. We are separated, you cannot feel my hand beneath your lips, but you have surely glimpsed the place you occupy in the heart of

Your Henriette

When I finished reading this letter, my fingers felt a maternal heartbeat at a moment when I was still weathering the chill of my own mother's icy welcome. I guessed why the countess had forbidden me to read it in the Touraine; she must have feared I would fall to the ground and drench her feet in tears.

I finally made the acquaintance of my brother, Charles, who'd been a stranger to me up to then, but there was a standoffishness in that most fragile relationship that distanced us too greatly from each other for any sense of brotherly love to exist; warmth of feeling depends on an equality of outlook, and ours found no point of contact. He pedantically lectured me on trifles the mind or heart intuit; on every front, he seemed suspicious of me; if my love hadn't sustained me, he'd have made me feel awkward and stupid by affecting to think I was an ignoramus.

Nevertheless, he did introduce me into circles where he meant for my gaucheness to accentuate his own worldliness. Were it not for my unhappy childhood, I might have seen his vanity as a protective mechanism of fraternal love, but moral solitude achieves the same results as the earthly kind: silence allows one to appreciate the least nuance, and the habit of seeking refuge in oneself nurtures a sensibility that exposes the finest gradations in love. Before I met Mme de Mortsauf, a severe glance hurt me, I found a sharp emphasis given to a word devastating; I suffered, but knew nothing of a life that could offer tenderness, whereas on my return from Clochegourde, I could draw comparisons that rounded out my stunted knowledge. Observations that stem from one's own pain are limited. Happiness enlightens too. I let myself be more readily crushed by the superiority an elder brother's status grants now that I was no longer overawed by Charles.

I went alone to the Duchesse de Lenoncourt's, where I heard little mention of Henriette; nobody, except for the old duke, simplicity itself, spoke to me of her, but the nature of his welcome suggested his daughter had secretly vouched for me. At a time when I was beginning to shed the naive awe felt by any debutant in high society, when I felt pleasure at the prospect of the opportunities it offered my ambition, I was delighted to try out some of Henriette's maxims and

wonder at their profound truth, the events of March 20 occurred.
Napoleon returned from Elba. My brother followed the court to
Ghent; following the countess's advice, from correspondence in which
I was the only active partner, I accompanied the Duc de Lenoncourt
there. The duke's usual affable ways changed to benevolent tutelage
when he saw I was wedded completely to the Bourbon cause: he introduced me to His Majesty. In times of trouble, courtiers are few in
number; youth has its ingenuous admiration and disinterested loyal-
ties, and the king was a fine judge of men; what would have gone
unnoticed in the Tuileries was soon appreciated in Ghent, and I was
fortunate to please the Louis XVIII. A letter from Mme de Mortsauf
to her father, brought with dispatches by a messenger from La Vendée
and containing a note for me, informed me that Jacques was ill.
Despairing to see his son in ill health and the second emigration
starting without him, M. de Mortsauf had appended a few comments
that conjured up my beloved's situation. No doubt tormented by him
for spending her every moment by Jacques's bedside, unable to rest
day or night, but able to withstand his taunts, though without the
strength to brush them aside, given that she was bound to put every
effort into caring for her child, Henriette must have longed for the
help of a friend who could make her life less unbearable, if it was only
by distracting M. de Mortsauf. More than once I'd taken the count
outside when he threatened to torment her; an innocent ruse the
success of which won me glances of passionate recognition, which
love saw as promises. Although impatient to follow in the footsteps
of Charles, who'd just been sent to the Congress of Vienna, and although I wanted, even if it meant risking my life, to abide by Henriette's foresight and free myself of my brother's yoke, and give free rein
to my ambition, my desire for independence and to protect my own
interests by not leaving the king, all that paled before the mournful
figure of Mme de Mortsauf. I decided to leave the court in Ghent
and go to serve my true sovereign. The messenger sent from La Vendée couldn't return to France, and the king needed a man to pledge
to take his instructions back. The Duc de Lenoncourt knew the king

would never forget the man who agreed to assume that perilous task; he had me appointed without even consulting me and I accepted, happy both to return to Clochegourde and to serve the good cause.

After an audience with the king, at the age of twenty-one, I returned to France, where I was fortunate to accomplish what the king had ordered in Paris and La Vendée. Towards the end of May, pursued by the Bonapartist authorities, to whom I'd been betrayed, I was forced to flee in the guise of a man returning to his manor house, walking from one estate to another, from one wood to another, across the Upper Vendée, Bocage, and Poitou, switching routes whenever necessary. I reached Saumur, from Saumur I went to Chinon, and from Chinon I reached the Nueil woods in a single night. There I was met on a sandy heath by the count, on horseback; I mounted behind him and he rode home. We saw no one who might recognize me.

"Jacques is better!" were his first words.

I told him of my present status as a diplomatic foot soldier hunted like a wild beast, and that fine fellow brandished his royalist credentials to deprive M. de Chessel of the dangers of hosting me. The second I saw Clochegourde, the eight months that had slipped by seemed like a dream. When the count told his wife as he preceded me: "Guess whom I have brought . . . ? Félix."

"Is that possible?" she asked, hands by her side, looking astonished.

I walked in, we both stayed still, she was riveted to her armchair, I was on the doorstep, eagerly eying each other like two lovers keen to make up for lost time with a single glance, but, wary of a spontaneous gesture that might expose her feelings, she stood up and walked over.

"I have prayed so much for you," she said, offering her hand to be kissed.

She inquired after her father, then, realizing I must be exhausted, went off to prepare my bedroom while the count fed me; I was starving. My bedroom was the one above hers, her aunt's; she told the count to accompany me there, after putting her foot on the first step of the stairs, no doubt pondering whether she herself could do that;

I turned around, she blushed, wished me a good night's sleep, and hurriedly withdrew.

When I came down for breakfast, I was informed of the disasters in Waterloo, Napoleon's flight, the alliance's march on Paris, and the probable return of the Bourbons. These events meant everything to the count, but nothing to us. Can you imagine what the biggest piece of news was after I'd hugged the children—I'm not referring to my alarm when I saw how thin and pale the countess was; I knew the pain any hint of dismay might cause, and only expressed pleasure at seeing her. *Our* big news was: "You shall have ice!" Last year she'd often been upset by the lack of water sufficiently cold for me, because when there was nothing else to drink, I preferred iced water. God knows what efforts she must have expended to have an ice pit constructed! You know better than anyone that loves needs only a word, a look, an inflection of the voice, the slightest flicker; its finest privilege is to prove itself through itself. Well, her words, her looks, her delight revealed to me the depths of her feelings, as my backgammon endeavors had once revealed mine to her. But there were many ingenuous signs of her affection; a week after my return, she was vivacious again; she sparkled with health, joy, and youthfulness; I rediscovered my dear lily embellished and flowering more finely, and felt the treasure trove in my heart had increased. Don't only small-minded, vulgar hearts feel that absence diminishes feeling, erases love's traces in the soul, and lessens the beloved's beauty? Ardent imaginations, beings whose thrills enter the bloodstream, rendering it a deeper purple, whose passion throbs constantly, feel absence like the torture that strengthened the faith of the first Christians and made their God visible. Doesn't a heart brimming with love feel a flow of longing that exalts the object of desire by allowing sight of the beloved to be enriched by the fire of dreams? Doesn't perception of ideal beauty irk only when the features of the beloved are belabored by thought? The past revisited, memory after memory, expands; the future is furnished with hope. When two hearts overflow, that meeting of electric clouds, that first exchange, is like a welcome storm reviving and fertilizing the earth with sudden lightning strikes. I enjoyed such subtle pleasure when I saw our thoughts and feelings were mutual. My eyes glowed to watch Henriette's happiness bloom! A woman reviving under her beloved's gaze perhaps gives greater testament to her sentiments than the woman dying, shot down by doubt, withered on the stem by lack of sap: I don't know which is the more moving.

Mme de Mortsauf's resurgence was natural, like a meadow awakening in the month of May, like wilting flowers bathed by sun and water. Like our valley of love, Henriette had survived her winter and been reborn in spring.

Before lunch we went down to our dear terrace. She told me of the nights spent by the side of her son's sickbed, as she now caressed his head, Jacques weaker now than I'd ever seen him, walking silently by his mother's skirts, apparently incubating another illness. In those three months, she recounted, she'd lived a self-absorbed life, inhabiting what seemed to be a gloomy palace, afraid to enter luxurious rooms with dazzling lights or forbidden festivities, on the threshold of which she kept one eye on her child and the other on a hazy figure, one ear listening out for cries of pain, the other, for a voice. She recited poems inspired by her solitude, the like of which no poet had ever invented, but naively, not knowing the slightest vestige of love or hint of sensual thought existed: orientally gentle poetry, like a rose from the land of Frangistan.[16] When the count joined us, she continued in that tone of the self-confident woman who can look her husband proudly in the eye and kiss her son's forehead without blushing. She had prayed a lot, clasping her joined hands over Jacques night after night, wishing him not to die.

"I would go," she said, "to the doors of the chapel and ask God to let him live."

She had seen visions, which she described to me, but the moment her angelic voice uttered these wonderful words: "When I slept, my ear watched!" the count interrupted: "What you mean is that you practically went mad."

She went quiet, riven by pain, as if it were the first time he'd wounded her, as if she'd forgotten that over the last thirteen years this man had never missed a chance to fire a bolt into her heart. A soaring bird downed in full flight by that gross lump of lead, she fell into stunned dejection.

"So, monsieur," she replied after a pause, "will a word uttered by me never find favor before the tribunal of your mind? Will you never feel compassion for my frailty, or understand my womanly ideas?" She stopped. My angel was already regretting the words she had uttered, and was measuring her past and future in a glance: Would she ever be understood? Was she going to let fly a violent outburst? Her blue veins throbbed violently across her temples, she didn't sob, but her green eyes turned pale; she looked down at the ground so as not to see her grief magnified in my gaze, her feelings divined, her soul cherished in my soul, and above all, the fervid compassion of young love ready, like a faithful dog, to devour the man hurting its mistress, never considering the assailant's strength or status. In those cruel moments, you ought to have seen the count's air of superiority; he believed he was triumphing over his wife, and unleashed a verbal tirade saying as much, like blows from an axe that rang out monotonously.

"Is he always like that?" I asked when the count had to leave, summoned by his groom.

"Always!" replied Jacques.

"Always excellent, my son," she told Jacques, trying to prevent her children from passing judgment on M. de Mortsauf. "You see the present and don't know the past, you can't criticize your father without being unjust, and even if you were unfortunate enough to see your father err, family honor requires you shroud such secrets in deepest silence."

"How are the changes in La Cassine and La Rhétorière working out?" I asked, wanting to stop her from dwelling on such bitter thoughts.

"Much better than I ever expected," she replied. "The buildings are finished and we have found two first-rate farmers who have taken one at four thousand, one hundred francs, after tax, and the other at five thousand, on leases agreed for fifteen years. We've already planted three thousand trees on the two new farms. Manette's relative is delighted to have La Rabelaye. Martineau has La Baude. Our four farmers' properties comprise fields and woods, where they never take manure destined for our own fields, as some rather unscrupulous farmers like to do. O*ur* efforts are being crowned with the greatest success. Clochegourde, without the home farm we set aside, with its woods and fields, earns nineteen thousand francs, and the plantations, a good anticipated annual return. I am now fighting to give the land we set aside to Martineau, our gamekeeper, whose son can take his position. He is offering three thousand francs if M. de Mortsauf will build a farmhouse at La Commanderie. Then we could free up the access routes to Clochegourde, construct the planned avenue as far as the Chinon road, and only have our woods and vineyards to look after. If the king returns, *our* pension will resume; *we* will agree, after opposing *our* wife's sound arguments for days on end. Then Jacques's fortune will be indestructible. Once these last gains are achieved, I will allow M. de Mortsauf to put away money for Madeleine, who will, in any case, receive a dowry from the king, as is the custom. My conscience is clear; my task accomplished … Now, will you tell me about yourself?" she asked.

I spoke about my mission, and explained how wise and fruitful her counsel had been. Was she endowed with a second sense that allowed her to anticipate events so accurately?

"Didn't I write to you about that?" she asked. "For you alone, I possess surprising abilities that I've only mentioned to M. de la Berge, my confessor, and he puts them down to divine intervention. After periods of deep meditation, provoked by fears for the state of my children, my eyes were often closed to things of this earth and only saw into another realm: when I saw a luminous Jacques and Madeleine there, they would enjoy good health for a while; if I found them wrapped in fog, they soon fell ill. As for you, I don't just see your radiant self, but I hear a gentle voice that tells me, without words, communicating mentally, what you must do. What law determined that I can use this wonderful gift only for my children and for you?" she wondered, falling into a reverie. Does God want to act as their father?" she asked, after a pause.

"Let me believe," I replied, "that I am beholden only to you!"

Then she smiled so graciously at me that my bewitched heart wouldn't have felt a fatal thrust.

"The moment the king returns to Paris, go there, leave Cloche-gourde," she continued. "It is as demeaning to chase after positions and favors as it is foolish not to be in the right place to accept them. Big changes are in the offing. The king needs capable men he can trust; be there for him. You will enter the affairs of state as a young man and do well, because, for men of state as for actors there are aspects of the trade that genius doesn't reveal, and must instead be learned. My father heard this news from the Duc de Choiseul. Think of me," she said a few seconds later, "let me taste the pleasures of high rank in a soul that wholly belongs to me. You are my son, aren't you?"

"Your son?" I retorted sulkily.

"Merely my son," she replied, ribbing me, "doesn't that give you a fine enough place in my heart?"

The bell rang for dinner; she took my arm and leaned on it fondly.

"You have really grown," she said, as we went up the steps.

When we were on the stairway, she shook my arm, as if my gaze had been too keen. She looked down, but she knew very well I had eyes only for her, and then added coquettishly, pretending to be impatient: "Come on, let's take a little look at our valley!"

She turned round, held her white silk umbrella over our heads, and pulled Jacques to her side; the flick of her head directed me to the Indre, the toue, and the meadows, implying that, after my stay and our many walks, she'd reached an entente with those hazy horizons and their meandering mists. Nature was the cloak beneath which she sheltered her thoughts. She now knew what the nightingale sighs at night, and what the cantor of the marshes repeats in its mournful chant.

At eight o'clock that evening I witnessed a deeply moving scene I'd been unable to see before, because I had always stayed back to play with M. de Mortsauf, while she went into the dining room at her children's bedtime. The bell rang twice and the whole household appeared.

"You are our host, submit to the rules of the convent!" she cried out, pulling my hand with the innocent glee that is the mark of a truly pious woman.

The count followed her. Master and mistress, children, servants, everyone kneeled, heads bared, in their usual places. It was Madeleine's turn to say the prayers; the dear little thing spoke childishly, her ingenuous tone echoing clearly in the silent harmony of the countryside, endowing the words with a candid, saintly innocence, an angelic grace. It was the most heartrending prayer I had ever heard. Nature replied to the child's words with a thousand small sounds, the accompaniment of an organ's gentle lowing. Madeleine was on the countess's right and Jacques on her left. The delightful tufts on the two heads between their mother's braided hair were completely overshadowed by M. de Mortsauf's white hair and yellowed skull, creating a tableau whose colors echoed in my mind with the ideas aroused by the rhythms of the prayer; finally, to achieve the unity of features that distinguishes the sublime, that tranquil gathering was suffused by the gentle light of sunset, bringing reddish hues into the room, allowing souls to believe, whether they were poetic or superstitious, that heavenly fire visited those faithful servants of God kneeling there without distinction of rank, in the equal standing ordained by the Church. My thoughts took me back to the days of patriarchal life and magnified a scene already grandiose in its simplicity. The children said good night to their father, the servants bid farewell, the countess left, giving a hand to each child, and I accompanied the count back to the drawing room.

"That way we give you salvation, and this way hell," he declared, pointing to the backgammon board.

The countess joined us half an hour later and brought her handicraft closer to our table.

"This is for you," she said, unrolling her canvas, "though my embroidery has quite languished over the last three months. My poor child has suffered so much between this red carnation and that rose."

"Come, come," said M. de Mortsauf, "let's not talk about that. Six-five, Monsieur le Roi's envoy."

When I was in bed, I lay quietly so I could hear her coming and going in her bedroom. If she was perhaps able to stay calm and pure, I was hounded by lunatic ideas, driven by unbearable desire.

"Why couldn't she be mine?" I asked myself. "Perhaps she too is prey to the same emotional turmoil?"

I went downstairs at one o'clock, I tiptoed without making a sound, reached her door, and lay down: my ear, next to the chink, heard her regular, gentle, childlike breathing. When I felt cold, I went back upstairs, got back into bed, and slept peacefully until morning. I can't think what destiny, what natural cause, derives pleasure from my fondness for the edges of precipices, for sounding out the abyss of evil, interrogating its depths, feeling its icy chill, and withdrawing overwrought. I'd spent an hour in the night by her door and wept uncontrollably, but the next morning she never sensed she'd walked over my tears and kisses, over her virtue that I had in turn destroyed and respected, cursed and worshipped; that hour, foolish in most people's eyes, inspires the strange feeling that pushes soldiers, so some have told me, into risking their lives, throwing themselves in front of a battery of guns to find out whether they'd escape the bullets raining down, and be happy like that, riding astride a chasm of probabilities, smoking on a barrel of gunpowder like Jean Bart.[17] In the morning I gathered and made two bouquets; the count admired them, a man never moved by that kind of thing, and for whom Champcenetz's quip seemed ready-made: "He builds dungeons in Spain."[18]

I spent a few days at Clochegourde, paying only quick visits to Frapesle, where I dined three times. The French army occupied Tours. Although I was clearly what gave Mme de Mortsauf her life and health, she urged me to head for Châteauroux, and back to Paris as soon as possible, via Issoudun and Orléans. I tried to resist, but she ordered me, claiming the voice she heard had spoken to her; I acquiesced. On this occasion, our farewells were tearful; she feared I would be sucked into the social whirl I was about to enter. Wouldn't I be forced to engage seriously with the dizzy round of self-interest, passion, and pleasure that make Paris a perilous sea for chaste loves and pure consciences? I promised to write every evening and tell her the day's events and thoughts, even the most frivolous. When I pledged to do that, she leaned her head languidly on my shoulder and said: "Leave nothing out, everything will be of interest to me."

She gave me letters for the duke and duchess, whom I visited on the second day after my arrival.

"I've good news for you," said the duke, "have lunch here and accompany me to the château this evening; your fortune is assured. The king said of you this morning: 'He is young, capable, and loyal!' And the king was sorry he didn't know whether you were dead or alive, where events had left you, after you carried out your mission so successfully."

That evening, I was appointed master of appeals in the Council of State, and was given a secret post with King Louis XVIII that would last as long as his reign, a position of trust, without astounding favors but with no possible disgrace, which put me at the center of government and became the source of my prospering. Mme de Mortsauf had been so clear-sighted, I owed everything to her; she'd guided and encouraged me, cleansed my heart, and given my ambitions a focus, without which youthful energy is futilely squandered. Later I was given a colleague. Each of us was on duty for six months. We could substitute for each other when necessary; we were given a bedroom in the château, our own carriage, and considerable expenses when called on to travel. A remarkable situation! To be the secret disciple of a monarch whose policies were subsequently recognized as right, even by his enemies, to hear him pass judgment on domestic and foreign policy, to have no obvious influence, but to be consulted occasionally, like Laforêt, Molière's servant, and sense the king's hesitation, from long experience, being aided by a youthful awareness. Our future was subsequently decided in a way meant to satisfy our ambitions. Apart from my income as master of appeals, paid from the Council of State budget, the king gave me a thousand francs a month out of his privy purse, and often added a few bonuses. Although the king believed a twenty-three-year-old wouldn't stand the workload he gave me for long, my colleague, now a peer of the realm, was only appointed in August 1817. It was difficult to know whom to choose, as the role demanded so many different qualities, and the king took a long time to decide. He honored me by asking me which of the men he was considering I would work best with. One was a friend of mine from the Lepître boardinghouse days, but I didn't select him: His Majesty wanted to know why.

"The king," I told him, "has chosen men who are equally loyal, but have different abilities; I have named the one I think best equipped, and with whom I am sure I will always work well."

My judgment coincided with the king's, and he was always grateful for the sacrifice I made on that occasion. He said: "You will always be Monsieur le Premier."

He informed my colleague of the situation, who, in return for the favor I'd done him, pledged his friendship. The Duc de Lenoncourt's high opinion of me was reflected in the society I frequented. The words "The king takes a keen interest in him; that young man will do well, the king likes him" might have obviated the role of talent, but they enhanced the gracious welcome given to young people with the veneer of respect granted to the powerful. Whether at the home of the Duc de Lenoncourt, or that of my sister, who had recently married her cousin the Marquis de Listomère, the son of the old relative I used to visit on the Île Saint-Louis, I gradually became acquainted with the most influential people in the Faubourg Saint-Germain.

Henriette soon introduced me into the heart of so-called Petit-Château society[19] through the aegis of the Princesse de Blamont-Chavry, whose great-niece she was by marriage; she wrote to her so warmly about me, that the princess immediately invited me to visit; I cultivated her, fell into her good books, and she became not simply my guardian angel, but also a friend, who acted quite maternally towards me. The old princess was most generous and presented me to her daughter, Madame d'Espard, as well as to the Duchesse de Langeais, the Vicomtesse de Beauséant, and the Duchesse de Maufrigneuse, women who by turns led the fashionable world, and who were all the more gracious when they discovered I was undemanding and always pleasant company. Far from rejecting me, my brother Charles now leaned on me, though my rapid success aroused a secret jealousy in him that later brought me sorrow. Surprised by my unexpected good fortune, my parents found that it flattered their vanity and they finally adopted me as their son, but, as their feelings were somewhat false, if not totally simulated, their return had little effect on my wounded heart; besides, affection tinged with selfishness merits little sympathy; the heart hates every kind of calculated self-serving.

I faithfully wrote my Henriette, who replied once or twice a month. Her spirit glided over me, her thoughts traveled long distances, enveloping me in an atmosphere of purity. No woman could tempt me. The king learned of my diffidence: in this respect, he belonged to the school of Louis XV and would laugh and call me "Mademoiselle de Vandenesse," but my good behavior delighted him. I'm convinced that the patience I'd become accustomed to as a child and, above all, in Clochegourde were key to my winning the good grace of a king who always treated me excellently. He was no doubt keen to read my letters, because it didn't take him long to see through my young, ladylike attitudes. One day the duke was carrying out a duty, and I was writing down a text dictated by the king, who, upon seeing the Duc de Lenoncourt had returned, glanced slyly at both of us and said: "So is that devil Mortsauf still clinging to life?" in the beautiful silvery tone he used to ensure his quips were all the more stinging.

"Absolutely," replied the duke.

"The Comtesse de Mortsauf is, however, an angel I'd much enjoy seeing here," the king continued, "but as I cannot make that happen, my chancellor," he said, turning towards me, "you will now be happier. You have six months' leave. I have decided to appoint as your colleague that young man we spoke of yesterday. Have a splendid time at Clochegourde, Monsieur Cato!" And he was wheeled, smiling, out of his office.

I flew like a swallow to the Touraine. For the very first time I was going to appear to the woman I loved in a less awkward form, and with all the panache of an elegant young man whose manners had been shaped in the most refined salons, whose education had been completed by the most sophisticated women, who'd finally earned the reward for all his suffering and put into practice the lessons from the most beautiful angel the heavens had ever entrusted a child to.

You know the state I had been in during the three months of my first stay in Frapesle.

When I'd returned to Frapesle at the time of my mission in La Vendée, I was dressed like a hunter. I wore a green jacket, with red and white buttons, striped trousers, and leather gaiters and shoes. The long march and the thickets had tattered my things so that the count was obliged to lend me clothes. This time, after two years in Paris, used to accompanying the king, accustomed to the ways of the wealthy, and having matured physically, with my young face burnished by an ineffable peace of mind, magnetically joined to the pure soul that shone on me from Clochegourde, I had been transformed. I was confident but never fatuous, and inwardly was contented to find myself at the political summit so young; I was aware I was secretly supported by the most adorable woman on earth, and was her unconfessed hope in life. I probably felt a flicker of self-pride when the whip of the postilions cracked on the new approach to Clochegourde from the Chinon road, where a new wrought-iron gate opened in the middle of a newly built circular fence. I hadn't written to the countess about my visit. I wanted to give her a surprise, and that was a mistake on two measures: firstly, she experienced a seizure caused by a long-anticipated pleasure she had deemed impossible, and secondly, as she pointed out, all such premeditated surprises were in bad taste.

When Henriette saw a young man whom she had only ever seen before as a child, she lowered her eyes slowly and tragically; she let the young man take her hand and kiss it, but never betrayed the inner pleasure her frisson had alerted me to, and when she looked up and gazed at me again, I saw how she had blanched.

"Ah, so you haven't forgotten your old friends?" said M. de Mortsauf, who hadn't changed or aged at all.

The two children jumped up around my neck. I saw the stern figure of Jacques's tutor, Abbé de Dominis, in the doorway.

"No," I told the count, "from now on I will have six months' freedom every year and the time will belong to you. Oh, what's wrong?" I asked the countess, reaching out to hold her around her waist and support her, in the presence of all her family.

"No, let me be," she said, retreating, "I am fine."

I read her mind and answered her secret thoughts: "Don't you recognize your faithful slave anymore?"

She took my arm, left the count, her children, the abbot, and the people who'd gathered there and led me towards the lawn; when she could assume nobody could hear, she said: "Félix, my friend, forgive the fears of someone who worries there is only one thread to guide her through an underground labyrinth and trembles at the thought it might be broken. Tell me again that I am more than ever *your* Henriette, that you will never forsake me, that nothing will prevail over me, that you will always be a devoted friend? I suddenly saw into the future, and you weren't there, as you always are, with your face beaming at me: you were turning your back on me."

"Henriette, you are the idol I worship more than God, the lily, the flower of my life, how can you not know, you who are my conscience, that I am so embedded in your heart that my soul resides here when my person is in Paris? Must I tell you I came here in seventeen hours, that each turn of the wheel carried a world of thoughts and desires that exploded like a storm the second I saw you . . . ?"

"Tell me, tell me, so I can be secure in myself, so I can hear you and not commit a crime. God doesn't want me to die: He sends you to me as He breathes life into His creations, as He scatters rain from His clouds over barren land; tell me, tell me! Is yours a saintly love?"

"It is."

"Forever."

"Forever."

"Like a Virgin Mary, who must stay veiled beneath her white crown?"

"Like a Virgin Mary I can see."

"Like a sister?"

"Like a sister I dote on."

"Like a mother?"

"Like a mother I long for."

"Chivalrously, hoping for nothing?"

"Chivalrously, hoping for something."

"You mean, as if you were still twenty and wearing that mischievous little blue suit you wore at the ball?"

"Oh, much more than that! I love you like that, and still love you as..."

She looked at me apprehensively.

"As your aunt loved you."

"I am so happy: you have rid me of all my fears," she said, walking back towards her family, who were all astonished by our secret confabulation. "But stay a child here, because that's what you still are! If it is your position to be a man with the king, here, monsieur, it must be to stay a child. As a child, you will be loved. I will always resist manly strength, but I could never refuse a child, who can never aspire to anything I cannot grant. All secrets are now declared," she concluded, giving the count an almost malicious, girlish glance that revealed her old spirit. "I must leave you and get dressed."

In three years I'd never heard her voice sound so happy. I recognized a swallow's cheerful mewling, the childish tones I mentioned. I'd brought hunting equipment for Jacques and for Madeleine, a sewing basket her mother still uses. I could finally make up for the meanness my mother's parsimony had reduced me to. The glee displayed by the children who were delighted to show off their presents to each other seemed to upset the count, who always sulked when nobody paid him any attention. I gave Madeleine a knowing nod and followed the count, who wanted to converse with me. He led me out to the terrace, though we stopped on the stone steps with each piece of news he solemnly announced.

"My poor Félix," he said, "you see them looking so happy and in fine fettle: I am the shadow on this stage; I've taken on their ills and, bless God, he has given them to me. I didn't know what was wrong with me, now I do: my pylorus is diseased, I can digest nothing."

"How have you suddenly become as learned as a professor in medical school?" I asked with a smile. "Is your doctor so indiscreet that he tells you this?

"God forbid I should ever consult a doctor," he exclaimed, espousing the repulsion most hypochondriacs feel towards medicine.

Then I was subjected to a lunatic exchange, during which he confided the most ludicrous things to me, and complained about his wife, his domestic staff, his children, and his life, evidently relishing the chance to rehearse his daily gripes with a friend who hadn't heard them, who might be surprised by them, and whom courtesy obliged to listen attentively. He must have been delighted by my attitude; I listened so intently, trying to see into that outrageous fellow and intuit the fresh tortures he was inflicting on his wife, who said nothing. Henriette brought his monologue to a conclusion when she appeared on the steps: the count noticed her, shook his head, and said: "You, my dear Félix, must listen to me, because nobody here shows me any sympathy!"

He walked off, as if he knew he would have muddied my conversation with Henriette, or else, in a gentlemanly gesture, he realized she would be pleased if he left us alone. His character was full of inexplicable contradictions, because he was jealous, as weak people are, though at the same time his trust in his wife's saintliness was boundless. Perhaps the way her superior insights offended his ego was the root cause of his constant opposition to her wishes, and the way he contradicted her mirrored a child's defiance of his teachers or his mother. Jacques now was having a lesson and Madeleine was dressing, so I had an hour to walk alone with the countess on the terrace.

"So, dear angel," I asked, "is the chain heavier, are the swords sharper, the thorns more plentiful?"

"Shush," she said, intuiting thoughts no doubt prompted by my conversation with the count, "you are here, everything is forgotten! I didn't suffer and am not suffering now!"

She took a few light steps as if to air her white garments, surrendering her snowy tulle ruffs, her ample sleeves, her streaming ribbons, her shawl, and her Sévigné flowing curls to the balmy breeze:[20] for the first time I saw her as a young girl, naturally cheerful and ready to play, like a child. That was when I shed the tears of joy of a man who gives pleasure.

"Beautiful human flower, caressed by my thoughts and kissed by my soul! My lily!" I rhapsodized, "ever pure and straight on its stem, ever white, proud, scented, and solitary!"

"Enough of that, monsieur," she replied with a smile. "Tell me about yourself, tell me everything."

We pursued a long conversation under a vault of rustling foliage; it was full of endless parentheses, begun, dropped, and resumed, in which I brought her up to date with my life and duties; I described my Paris apartment, because she wanted to know every detail, and I was happy in a novel way and had nothing to hide. She heard about my state of mind and every moment of an existence crammed with onerous tasks, and learned about the scope of my remit, where, if one were not truly honest, one could so easily defraud others and become wealthy, but over which I exercised due rigor. When I told her the king called me Mademoiselle de Vandenesse, she seized my hand and kissed it, shedding a blissful tear. Then roles were suddenly reversed, she voiced the highest praise, expressed her thoughts quickly, and gasped even more readily: "There's the master I have always craved! There is my dream!" Everything she confessed in that gesture, where her humble demeanor bore witness to her noble spirit, and love was revealed in a region forbidden to the senses, a heavenly onslaught that went straight to my heart and crushed me. I felt so petty and wanted to die there and then.

"Oh!" I exclaimed, "you always outdo us in every way. How can you doubt me, because you *did* just express doubts, Henriette."

"Not now," she responded, with an ineffably tender look that veiled the light in her eyes, "but when I saw that you are so handsome, I thought: 'Our plans for Madeleine will be disrupted by a woman who intuits the treasure hidden in your heart, who will adore you, who will steal our Félix, and ruin everything.'"

"Is it still all about Madeleine!" I expressed with a surprise that only faintly upset her. "Must I be faithful to Madeleine?"

We descended into a silence M. de Mortsauf interrupted inopportunely. My heart was elsewhere, but I was forced to engage in a conversation hedged with difficulties when my frank comments on the policies pursued by the king clashed with the ideas of the count, who had forced me to spell out His Majesty's intentions. Despite all my inquiries about his horses, the state of his agricultural business, whether he was satisfied with his five farms, if he would cut the trees down on the old avenue, he kept bringing our exchanges back to politics with a spinster's spite and a child's insistence; his sort of mind likes to cause nuisance in places where the light shines brightly, constantly harping on, understanding nothing, exhausting your patience as fat flies tire your ears when they buzz against the windows. Henriette said nothing. To curtail a conversation the quick temper of youth could easily inflame, I responded in positive monosyllables, avoiding futile arguments, but M. de Mortsauf was too clever not to see how rude my courtesy actually was. Angry that he was always right, he reared, his eyebrows and wrinkled forehead danced, his yellow eyes flashed, his blood-red nose reddened, all as it had been that day I witnessed one of his demented outbursts for the first time. Henriette cast imploring glances in my direction, implying she could intervene with the authority she used to defend or justify her children, on my behalf. I responded to the count by taking him seriously and skillfully deflecting his gloomy perspectives.

"Poor dear, poor dear!" said Henriette, repeatedly muttering those two words that wafted towards my ear like a breath of fresh air.

When she decided she could interrupt to some purpose, she stopped us in our tracks: "Gentlemen, do you realize you are being quite boring?"

That question reminded the count of his chivalric duty to obey women, and he stopped talking politics; we soon wearied of small talk, and he left us free to stroll, alleging that his head started to spin when he was forced to walk in circles.

My sad conjectures turned out to be true. The charming landscapes, the warm atmosphere, the beautiful sky, the intoxicating poetry of that valley, which for fifteen years had calmed that sick man's strident fantasies, were now powerless. At a time in life when the asperity of other men softens and their sharp corners are blunted, that old gentleman had become more aggressive than ever. For several months he'd been the spirit of contradiction for its own sake, with no logic, making no attempt to justify his opinions; he demanded to know the reason behind everything, was upset by anyone tardy or forgetful, meddled in every household matter, and insisted on being consulted about the tiniest domestic detail, wearying his wife and staff by not allowing them any freedom to make decisions. Previously, he'd been annoyed by the odd specious issue, but now his annoyance was constant. Perhaps the need to manage his wealth, the speculation involved in agriculture, or the hectic nature of life had refueled his anger, feeding his anxiety and activating his mind; or perhaps the lack of actual tasks to perform now made his sickness turn in upon itself; as if it no longer exercised itself in the outside world, and found expression instead in obsessive ideas; as if his moral self now ruled his physical self. He'd become his own doctor; he devoured medical tomes, thought he had the illnesses he saw described, and then embarked on peculiar, deluded courses of treatment for his health, attempted cures that nobody could predict, let alone satisfy. He'd decide he wanted there to be no noise, and, when the countess established complete silence around him, he'd immediately complain he'd been entombed; he'd say there was a happy medium between no noise and a Trappist void. Then he seemed totally indifferent to earthly things, the whole house breathed, his children played, household chores were done without carping, and, amid the cheerful bustle, he'd suddenly moan: "Somebody wants to kill me!" Or "My dear, they're your children, you ought to be able to work out what's wrong with them," he'd tell his wife, underlining his unfairness with a cold, complaining whine.

He was always dressing and undressing, studying the slightest variations in the atmosphere, and he did nothing without consulting the barometer. Despite his wife's motherly care, no food was ever to his taste: he claimed his stomach was impaired, the digestion was painful and caused him sleepless nights, yet he ate, drank, digested, and slept so soundly the most learned doctor would have been amazed. His constant changes of mind exhausted the household staff, who liked routine, as all servants do, and they were unable to adapt to the requirements of a system that was always at odds with itself. He might order the windows to be thrown wide open on the pretext that fresh air was necessary for his health; a few days later, the fresh air would prove either too damp or too warm and quite unbearable; then he griped, triggered an argument, and, to be in the right, often denied having made his previous request. His lapses of memory or his acting in bad faith gave him the upper hand in every quarrel when his wife tried to point to his own contradictory statements. Life at Cloche-ourde had become so intolerable that Abbé de Dominis, a deeply knowledgeable man, had opted for what is one solution to some of life's intractable problems: he retreated into an affected introspection. The countess no longer hoped to contain the outbreaks of rage and fury within the family circle, as in the past; the domestic staff had already witnessed scenes when the prematurely senile fellow's irrational exasperation crossed every boundary; because they were so devoted to the countess, nothing was ever said outside the house, but every day she feared an explosion of madness that basic courtesy or a desire to command respect could no longer curb. I later learned dire details of the count's behavior toward his wife; rather than soothe her, he liked to oppress her with terrible predictions and hold her responsible for every imminent disaster, because she rejected all the stupid medications he wanted to administer to his children. If the countess took Jacques and Madeleine for a walk, the count predicted a storm, however cloudless the sky; if by chance the weather justified his forecast, satisfying his own self-esteem made him insensitive to his children's illnesses; if one child were unwell, the count would channel all his mental energies into identifying the source of their plight in the system of care adopted by his wife, caviling at the tiniest detail, and always ending on this vicious note: "If your children have a relapse, it will be because that is what you wanted." He acted similarly regarding the minutiae of household management, always seeing the worst side of things, at every moment assuming the role of "devil's advocate," an expression favored by his old coachman.

The countess had set different mealtimes for Jacques and Madeleine, thus sparing them the terrible outbursts caused by the count's illness, which were all directed at her. The children rarely saw their father.

As a result of the self-deception so common among the selfish, the count hadn't the slightest idea of the hurt he was causing. In our private conversations, he'd always complain he was too generous towards his family. He flaunted his pain, threw down and broke everything around him, like a monkey; when he injured his victim, he denied ever having touched her.

That was when I understood what had etched the lines on the countess's forehead, as if with the edge of a razor, the ones that had struck me when I'd met her after such a long time apart. Noble souls possess a modesty that stops them from expressing their pain; they hide its reach from the ones they love with deeply felt exclamations of forgiveness. I asked her about it repeatedly, but failed to extract any clarity. She was afraid of upsetting me, and made confessions interrupted by sudden blushes. I soon guessed how much the count's flailing had increased the household staff's burden.

"Henriette," I said a few days later, showing I had a good sense of the depths of her new misery, "weren't you perhaps wrong to manage your land so well, now that the count finds nothing to occupy his mind?"

"My dear," she replied, "the situation is so critical it merits my every attention. Believe me, I have studied every possible solution and exhausted them all. Indeed, his taunts have steadily increased. As M. de Mortsauf and I are always confronting each other, I can no longer weaken his rage by trying to divert his focus; everything would always work out to be equally trying for me. I thought of distracting M. de Mortsauf, by advising him to establish a silkworm-breeding house at Clochegourde, where there are still mulberry trees, remnants of that ancient Touraine industry, but I realized he would be as tyrannical there as he was at home, and that such an enterprise would only bring me a thousand extra worries. You should learn, my observant friend, that a man's bad qualities are kept in check in his younger years by social convention, are stopped in flight by the interplay of passions or reined in by a respect for others; later, the little faults of a lonely, elderly man become all the more horrendous because they have been so long repressed. At its root human frailties are cowardly and brook neither peace nor truce; what you granted yesterday, they demand today, tomorrow, and always; they cling to concessions and extend them. Power is merciful, yields to the facts, is fair and calm; passion spawned by weakness is pitiless; the weak are happy to act like children who prefer fruit they have furtively stolen to the fruit they can eat from the table; thus M. de Mortsauf takes a delight in catching me out, and a man, who would never trick anyone, delights in tricking me, provided his guile stays well hidden."

About a month after I arrived, as we were leaving the breakfast table one morning, the countess took my arm, led me through a gate to the orchard, and pulled me briskly among the vines.

"He will be the death of me!" she cried. "But I want to live, if only for my children! Will I never enjoy a single day of respite! Must I always walk in bracken, practically stumbling at every step, using my strength to keep my balance? No creature could handle such an expenditure of energy. If I knew the terrain, I could deploy my efforts; if I could measure the resistance needed, my mind could prepare and adapt, but it's not so, every day he attacks differently, he surprises me; my misery isn't single, it comes in manifold forms. My dear Félix, you cannot imagine the odious character his tyranny has assumed, or the barbaric requirements his medical tomes dictate. My dear friend . . . !" she said, resting her head on my shoulders, before concluding her revelations. "What can I expect? What can I do?" she asked, continuing to debate thoughts she'd never previously expressed. "How can I resist? He will kill me. No, I will kill myself, even if that is a crime! Should I flee? Then what would happen to my children? Or separate from him? After fifteen years of marriage, how can I possibly tell my father I am leaving M. de Mortsauf, when, if my mother or father comes, he is always wise, polite, witty, and poised? In any case, do married women have mothers and fathers anymore? They belong, body and wealth, to their husbands. I was living serenely, if not happily, I found some strength in my chaste solitude, I confess, but now I am deprived even of that negative happiness, I too will go mad. My resistance is based on powerful arguments that aren't personal to me. Is it a crime to want to give life to poor children who have been sentenced in advance to perpetual sorrow? My behavior raises such serious questions I cannot answer them by myself; I am judge and plaintiff. Tomorrow I go to Tours to consult Abbé Birotteau, my new spiritual director, because my old, virtuous Abbé de la Berge has died," she said, interrupting herself. "Although he was severe, I will always miss his apostolic strength; his successor is a gentle angel who is loving rather than reprimanding; in any case, what valiant soul wouldn't be reinvigorated by the bliss of religion? What mind wouldn't be strengthened by the voice of the Holy Spirit? My God," she continued, drying her tears and looking up to the heavens, "why do You punish me? Yet we must believe," she said, resting her fingers on my arm, "Yes, Félix, let us believe that we must pass through a red-hot crucible before we enter the highest spheres, hallowed and perfect. Must I be silent? My God, will You allow me to weep in a friend's bosom? Did I love him too much?"

She pressed me to her heart, as if afraid of losing me.

"Who will resolve all my doubts? My conscience is clean. The stars shine down on humans from on high; why doesn't the soul, that human star, illuminate a friend when one wishes only to convey pure thoughts?"

I listened silently to that horrific plea, held her moist hand in mine, which was even moister; I squeezed it as tightly as Henriette did mine.

"So that's where you are?" shouted the count, advancing bareheaded in our direction.

Ever since I'd returned, he stubbornly involved himself in all of our exchanges, whether it was because he hoped to find them entertaining, or because he thought the countess was confiding her sorrows and complaining to me, or because he was jealous of a pleasure he did not share.

"He is always following me!" she said despairingly. "We should go to see the new fields; that way, we can avoid him. If we go down along the hedges, he won't see us."

Using a bushy hedge as cover, we ran to the enclosed fields and were soon far from the count, on a path lined with almond trees.

"Dear Henriette," I said, pressing her hand against my heart and pausing to look at her lined face, "you've guided me wisely through the perilous paths of high society; now let me give you advice to help you end this duel, in which there are no witnesses, and the weapons are unequal. You are bound to fail. Give up this struggle against a madman..."

"Shush!" she said, holding back the tears welling in her eyes.

"Listen, my dear! After an hour of these conversations that I am forced to endure out of love for you, my thoughts are often distorted, and my head feels heavy; the count makes me doubt my own mind; the same reiterated ideas etch themselves upon my brain despite myself. Monomanias that are easily characterized aren't contagious, but when madness lies in the way the world is envisaged and is concealed behind constant squabbling, it can destroy those who must live so close to it. Your patience is sublime, but won't it cause you to fall apart? Change the way you handle the count for your own sake and for the sake of your children. Your admirable compassion has bolstered his selfishness, you've treated him as a mother treats a child she spoils, but today, if you want to live," I continued, looking into her eyes, "and you *do* want to, so use the power you have over him. You know he loves and fears you; make him more afraid of you, set your single-minded will against his chameleon will. Extend your power, because he has learned to take advantage of the concessions you have granted him; you must shackle his malady morally, as lunatics are shackled in an asylum."

"Dear child," she replied, smiling bitterly, "only a heartless wife could play such a role. I am a mother and would make a poor executioner. Yes, I know how to suffer, but not how to make others suffer! Never, not even to achieve an honorable or noble end. Besides, wouldn't I have to tell my heart to deceive, to disguise my voice, to steel my brow, and to fake my every gesture? Don't ask me to lie like that. I can place myself between M. de Mortsauf and his children. He will lash out at me and won't have any energy to lash out at anyone else, and that's all that I can do to reconcile so many conflicting interests."

"Let me worship you. You're a saint, three times so!" I said, as I kneeled on the ground, kissed her dress, and wiped away the tears that came to my eyes. "But what if he kills you?"

She blanched and, in response, raised her eyes to the heavens: "God's will shall be done!"

"Do you know what the king asked your father, with respect to you: 'Is that Mortsauf devil still with us?'"

"A joke from the king's lips," she retorted, "is a crime when spoken here."

Despite our precautions, the count had pursued us. He was streaming with sweat when he caught us up under the walnut tree where the countess had stopped to address me so sternly. The second I saw him, I started talking about the grape harvest. Did he harbor unfair suspicions? I don't know, but he stood there silently scrutinizing us, and ignoring the cool air distilled by the walnut trees. After a brief interlude of trifling exchanges punctuated by meaningful pauses, the count announced he was suffering from heart pains and a migraine; he complained gently, neither seeking our pity nor depicting his grief in lurid images. We ignored him. As we walked back, he began to feel worse, talked about going to bed, and then did so unceremoniously, straightforwardly, which wasn't his style. We made the most of the truce afforded by his hypochondria, and decided to go down to our beloved terrace with Madeleine.

"We should take a ride over the water," suggested the countess after we'd walked round several times; "we can watch our gamekeeper land the fish that will grace our table tonight."

We left through the small gate, reached the toue, jumped in, and slowly rowed up the Indre. Like three children amused by little things, we gazed at the wild herbs on the banks and the green or blue dragonflies; the countess was astonished she could enjoy such quiet pleasures amid harrowing misery, but doesn't nature's tranquility flourish untroubled by human strife, and always subtly console us? The turmoil of love and repressed desire flow with the water; the flowers our hands have yet to spoil express our most hidden dreams; the boat's sensuous swaying vaguely imitates thoughts adrift in the soul. We felt the expansive energy of that double poetry. Our words adapted to nature's rhythm, and unfurled with mysterious ease; our gazes sparkled ever more brightly, drew on the light so generously illuminating the flaming meadow. The river was like a track we raced along alone. Undistracted by the footsteps required for walking, our minds focused and took on the power to create. Wasn't a young girl's gleeful joy at being free, at moving gracefully and being able to tease, also the live expression of two free souls taking pleasure in shaping that wonderful creature dreamed of by Plato, known to all who have experienced love's bliss in their youth? To describe that hour, not its ineffable detail but as a whole, I must tell you that we loved one another in every being and object around us; we felt the happiness we craved: it penetrated so deeply that the countess removed her gloves and dipped her hands into the water as if to cool her secret ardor. Her eyes spoke, but her mouth, which opened like a rose, was closed to desire. You are familiar with the harmony of grave tonalities, suited to higher keys, that has always reminded me of our two souls' union at that unique, unrepeatable moment.

"Where do you fish," I asked, "if you cannot fish in the streams belonging to you?"

"Near Pont-de-Ruan," she replied. "In any case, the river now belongs to us from Pont-de-Ruan to Clochegourde. M. de Mortsauf has just purchased forty acres of meadow using the money we have saved over these last two years and his pension arrears. Isn't that astonishing?"

"I wish the whole of the valley were yours!" I exclaimed.

She smiled. We reached the spot beneath Pont-de-Ruan where the Indre broadens out, finding the place where they were fishing.

"Well, Martineau?" she asked.

"Countess, we're out of luck. We've been here three hours, coming up from the mill, and caught nothing."

We made land to see the final casting of the nets. The three of us sat in the shade of a *bouillard*, a kind of white-barked poplar, which grows along the Danube, the Loire, and perhaps along all big rivers, and which in springtime releases its silky white cotton seeds from its blossoming catkins. The countess was serene and aloof again; she almost regretted unveiling her sorrows to me and crying out like Job, rather than sobbing like Magdalen, a Magdalen without loves, parties, or frivolity, though not without her scents and beauty. The dragnet pulled in at her feet was brimming with fish: tench, barbel, pike, perch, and a huge carp that leaped onto the grass.

"That's more like it!" shouted the gamekeeper.

The laborers gawped, admiring that woman who seemed like a fairy whose wand must have touched the nets. With that, the groom galloped into sight across the meadow, making her shake violently. Jacques wasn't with us, and the first thought of a mother, as Virgil poetically put it, is to grip her children to her bosom at the slightest worry.

"Jacques!" she shouted. "Where is Jacques? What has happened to my son?"

She wasn't in love with me! If she had been, she would have reacted to my suffering in this way, like a desperate lioness.

"Madame la Comtesse, M. le Comte has taken a turn for the worse."

She took a deep breath, and began to run with me, followed by Madeleine.

"Take it slowly," she bid me, "don't let my daughter get overheated. Do you see, M. de Mortsauf's haste in such hot weather brought him out in a sweat, and standing under the cool walnut tree may have precipitated disaster."

Spoken while inwardly she was so anguished, that word revealed the purity of her soul. The count's death, a disaster! She quickly reached Clochegourde, entered through a gap in the wall, and crossed the enclosed land. I did return slowly. Henriette's expression had dazzled me, but as lightning can dazzle though its strike ruins the harvest. I'd thought I was her favorite when we drifted over the water; I bitterly recalled my good faith in what she had said. A lover who isn't everything is nothing. I was alone in my love, with the desire of a love that knows what it wants, is nourished by the caresses it anticipates, and happy with the pleasures of the soul that come entwined with others reserved for the future. If Henriette loved, she knew nothing of love's pleasures or tempests. She lived on pure sentiment, like a saint with God. I was the object that her thoughts and unexplored feelings had clung to like a swarm of bees settling on the branch of a tree in full blossom, but I wasn't her mainstay, I was a mere episode in her life, I wasn't her whole life. Like a dethroned king, I kept wondering who might restore my kingdom to me. Torn by jealousy, I reproached myself for not being bolder and tightening the bonds of tenderness, apparently more tenuous than true, the chains of the de facto right granted by possession.

The count's indisposition, perhaps induced by the walnut tree's cool shade, grew more serious by the hour. I went to fetch a reputable doctor from Tours, M. Origet, whom I could bring back only in the evening, though he spent the following night and day at Clochegourde. He'd sent the groom to collect a large number of leeches, then decided a bloodletting was urgent, but hadn't brought a lancet with him. I immediately hastened to Azay in hideous weather and woke up the surgeon, M. Deslandes, and persuaded him to fly there swiftly as a bird. Ten minutes later and the count would have died; the bleeding saved him. Despite that initial success, the doctor diagnosed a most pernicious high fever, the kind of illness caught by people who've lived healthily for twenty years. The countess was horrified and thought she was the cause of this lethal attack. Too weak to thank me for my helping care, she had to be content with a few smiles she directed at me that felt like her kiss on my hand; I'd have liked to read the remorse of illicit love in them, but it was more an act of contrition that was unsightly in a soul so pure, and an expression of warm admiration for an individual she thought of as noble, while she accused herself alone of some imaginary crime. I was sure she loved as Laura de Noves loved Petrarch, not as Francesca da Rimini loved Paolo: an appalling discovery for someone who had dreamed of combining those two kinds of love!

The countess lay slumped and exhausted in a filthy armchair, her arms dangling, in a bedroom that looked like a wild boar's den. The following evening, before leaving, the doctor told the countess, who'd spent the night there, that she must hire a nurse. The illness could be a lengthy affair.

"No," she replied, "we will never employ a nurse. *We* will look care for him," she exclaimed, looking at me, "we are duty bound to save him!"

The doctor glanced at us askance, quite shocked: the way she'd spoken suggested there was a debt to be repaid.

He promised to return twice a week, told M. Deslandes the measures he must take, and outlined the threatening symptoms that might necessitate fetching someone from Tours. To give the countess at least one night's sleep out of two, I asked her to allow me to take turns watching over the count, and that was how I managed to convince her to go to bed on the third night, albeit with a struggle. When everything was quiet, when the count had fallen asleep, I heard Henriette moaning grievously. I was so anxious I rushed to her; she was a sobbing mass, kneeling in front of her prayer stool, berating herself: "My God, if this is the price to be paid for grumbling, let me never complain again."

"You've left his side!" she exclaimed, the moment she saw me.

"I heard you sobbing and moaning and was frightened for your sake."

"Oh!" she replied, "I am well."

She insisted on being assured that M. de Mortsauf was asleep; we both went downstairs and looked at him by the light of a lamp: the count had been so weakened by his large loss of blood that he'd fallen asleep; her tremulous hands pulled his blanket back over him.

"They say his are the gestures of a dying man," she said. "You know, if he dies from an illness we brought upon him, I swear I will never remarry," she added, solemnly spreading her hand across the count's head.

"I've done everything possible to save him," I replied.

"Yes, you are kind, so kind," she said. "But I'm the one who deserves all the blame."

She leaned over his convulsed forehead, wiped away the sweat with her hair, and anointed his brow with a saintly kiss, though I was secretly elated to see her administering that caress as if in atonement.

"Blanche, a drink!" muttered the count faintly.

"You see, he only recognizes me," she said, bringing him a glass.

And she sought to injure the feelings binding us together through her tone of voice and the affectionate way she attended to the sick man.

"Henriette," I implored, "go and rest, I beg you."

"No more *Henriette*," she interjected imperiously.

"Go to bed, so you don't fall ill. Your children, and he himself, bid you to look after yourself; there are instances when selfishness can be a sublime virtue."

"I agree," she replied.

She walked out, commending her husband to me with gestures that might have signaled the onset of madness, if they hadn't combined the grace of childhood with the force of repentance. I was terrified by that flurry, which I found disturbing when I compared it with the usual tranquility of her pure soul; I was afraid her mind might become unbalanced. When the doctor returned, I explained the source of the pangs of conscience that were afflicting Henriette, like the white ermine that will die rather than sully its fur. Although it was only a hint, that remark did away with any lingering suspicions M. Origet still harbored, and he soothed her beautiful but agitated soul, by declaring that the count had always been on course to succumb to this illness and that his sojourn under the walnut tree had been helpful rather than harmful in keeping the disease at bay.

The count hovered between life and death for fifty-two days: Henriette and I took it in turns, twenty-six nights each. It was true that M. de Mortsauf owed his health to our care, and to the scrupulous way we carried out M. Origet's orders. Like those philosophical doctors whose wise scrutiny could provoke doubt about noble acts that are only a secret fulfillment of duty, that man was aware of the heroic struggle between the countess and me, and he couldn't stop himself from spying on us with searching looks out of the fear that his admiration for us was misplaced.

"With this kind of illness," he said on his third visit, "death finds a sudden helpmate in morale, when it ebbs as seriously as the count's. Doctor, nurse, the people around the sick man hold his life in their hands, because a single word, a fear expressed in a gesture, can be as powerful as poison."

As he spoke, Origet scrutinized my face and demeanor and saw in my eyes the limpid expression of a pure soul. To be honest, in the course of that cruel illness, I didn't conceive any of the evil ideas that can sometimes willfully stain the most innocent conscience. Anyone who contemplates nature at large recognizes that everything tends to unity through assimilation. The moral world is surely ruled by an analogous principle. All is pure in a pure sphere. Next to Henriette, you inhaled a scent from heaven, and you thought a desire worthy of reproach would distance you from her forever. She symbolized happiness as much as she did virtue. The doctor always found us equally caring and attentive, and adopted a quite pious, affable tone and manner, as if he were telling himself: "Here are the true invalids, hiding and forgetting their wounds!" In a contrast that, according to that excellent doctor, was very common in men who were stricken like that, M. de Mortsauf was patient and accepting, never complained and displayed astonishing docility; when he was a man in good health, he never did the slightest thing without carping a thousand times. The secret behind his submission to medical science that he'd rejected so strenuously hitherto was his secret fear of death, another contrast in a man who was such a braggart! That fear might also explain several other strange features in the new character shaped by his misfortune.

Natalie, will you believe what I'm about to confess? Those fifty days and four weeks that followed were the most beautiful moments in my life. Doesn't love exist in the infinite spaces of the soul like a great river in a beautiful valley where torrents, brooks, and streams flow, trees and flowers fall, gravel from riverbanks and rocks from the highest crags tumble down? It is swollen as much by storms as by slow offerings from springs. Yes, when one loves, everything loves. After the first, most dangerous moments passed, the countess and I became accustomed to that illness. Despite the perpetual disorder produced by the count's constant attention-seeking, the bedroom we'd found in such a mess was soon clean and attractive. We sat there like two beings marooned on a desert island: misfortune may bring isolation, but it also dispenses with the most tiresome social conventions. In the interests of the sick man we were obliged to enjoy points of contact no other event could have sanctioned. Our hands, once so shy, now met so often, and in the service of the count! Wasn't it my duty to sustain and help Henriette? Often distracted by tasks comparable to those of a soldier on sentry duty, she would forget to eat; I then served her, sometimes on her knees, a meal she'd quickly consume, that required a thousand little attentions. It was a childhood tableau next to a half-open tomb. She brusquely bid me to prepare potions to alleviate the count's pain and allotted me endless small jobs. In the first phase, when imminent danger, as in battle, overrode the subtle distinctions that characterize everyday life, she was forced to pare down the decorum any woman, even the most spontaneous kind, clings to in their words, looks, and attitude, whether with other people or family, and she would no longer see that as self-demeaning. She now came to relieve me with the first morning chorus of birds, in her early-morning dress that allowed me occasional glimpses of dazzling treasures that, in my maddest moments of hope, I thought were mine! While she remained distant and proud, why shouldn't she now also be familiar in that way? Besides, in those early days, danger stripped the intimacy of our new togetherness of any resonances of passion, so she detected nothing wrong; later, when she'd had time to reflect, she may have imagined it would be insulting to herself and to me to change her ways. We discovered we had gradually been domesticated—half-married. She was nobly trusting, as sure of me as she was of herself. I further entered her heart. The countess was my Henriette again, a Henriette constrained to show more love towards the man striving to be her second soul. Soon I didn't have to wait for her hand, which would be surrendered to me without resistance at the flicker of an eyelid; she wouldn't vanish from sight if I longingly contemplated the lines of her beautiful body in

the hours we spent listening to the invalid snoring. The timid, sensuous reactions we allowed ourselves, the affectionate glances, the words
whispered quietly so as not to wake the count, the fears and hopes
voiced time and again, in brief the thousand acts in the total fusion
of two hearts long separated, stood out brightly against the painful
shadows of that present scene. We explored the depths of our souls
in that test often suffered by the most ardent and tender who can't
resist seeing each other at every moment, who become detached when
they experience a constant convergence that reveals whether life is a
light or heavy burden to bear.

You know how a master's illness can undermine everything, interrupt the flow of business, how there's never enough time; the energy
he consumes disrupts the household's days and family's life. Though
everything now fell on Mme de Mortsauf's shoulders, the count was
still useful externally; he went and spoke to the farmers, visited
businessmen, collected payments; if she was the soul, he was the body.
I acted as her administrator so she could care for the count while
nothing in the wider world would suffer from inattention. She agreed
to everything simply, without thanks. There was still a charming
togetherness beyond the sharing of household tasks, and carrying out
the orders given in her name. I often spent the evening with her, in
her bedroom, discussing her interests and the children's. Those conversations gave another aspect to our ephemeral marriage. Henriette
was thrilled to let me play the role of her husband, to let me sit in his
chair at mealtimes, and to send me to talk to his nurse; all that was
communicated so innocently but with that inner pleasure the most
virtuous woman in the world experiences when she finds an expedi-
ent to combine strict observation of the law with the satisfying of her
unconfessed desires. Rendered ineffectual by his illness, the count
was no longer a burden to his wife or household, and the countess
could be herself, had the right to devote time to me and make me the
object of myriad attentions. And I was thrilled too when I discovered
her intention, which she was perhaps vaguely aware of, that was communicated so delightfully, to reveal to me the deep worth of her
character and qualities and allow me perceive the change that would

take place in her once she was understood! The flower, trapped in the chill atmosphere of her marriage, now opened before my eyes alone; she was as happy to blossom as I was when love's inquiring gaze looked upon her. In every routine aspect of life she showed how present I was in her thoughts. The day when, after having spent the night by the side of the invalid's bed, I slept late, Henriette would rise before everyone else to ensure total silence reigned around me; without having to be told, Jacques and Madeline played far away; she used a thousand ploys to ensure she had the right to pull up my blanket; in short, she cared for me, with such a gleeful spring in her movements, swooping gently like a swallow, cheeks flushed, voice trembling, sharp-eyed like a lynx!

Can one possibly describe such expansions of the soul? She was quite exhausted, but, if by chance, in those tired moments, I was involved, she found fresh sources of energy and acted in a bright, lively manner for me and her children. She liked to cast her loving affection on the air like a sunbeam! Truly, Natalie, some women here below enjoy the privileges of angelic spirits, and, like them, spread that light which Saint-Martin, the Unknown Philosopher, described as intelligent, melodious, and perfumed. Convinced of my discretion, Henriette loved to raise that heavy curtain that hid the future and allow me a glimpse of the two women she carried within: the fettered woman who had seduced me despite her prickliness, and the free woman whose sweetness would make my love eternal. What a contrast! Mme de Mortsauf was the bird from Bengal transported to cold Europe, sadly placed on its perch, mute and dying in the cage where a naturalist kept it; Henriette was the bird singing her oriental poems in her grove on the banks of the Ganges, and was like a living jewel, flying from branch to branch among the roses of a huge volkameria that was still blooming. Her beauty was enhanced; her spirits revived. That continual radiant flame was a secret between the two of us, because the eye of Abbé de Dominis, that representative of society, was more daunting for Henriette than that of M. de Mortsauf, though, like me, she found great pleasure in couching her thoughts in ingenious turns of phrase; she hid her happiness beneath amusing words and cloaked her avowals of affection in exhilarating displays of appreciation.

"We have sorely tested your friendship, Félix! Monsieur l'Abbé, can we allow him the little freedoms we grant Jacques?" she asked at the table.

The stern abbot responded with the kind smile of a pious man who reads hearts and finds them pure; moreover, he expressed towards the countess the mixture of respect and adoration that angels inspire.

Just twice in those fifty days, the countess perhaps went beyond the boundaries that framed our affection, but even those two occasions were wrapped in a veil that was raised only on the day of ultimate confessions. I was waiting for her, she was to take my place one morning in the early days of the count's sickness, at the time when she was regretting treating me so harshly and withdrawing the innocent privileges she'd granted my chaste affection. I was so tired I'd fallen asleep leaning my head against the wall. I suddenly woke up when I felt my head touched by something refreshing, as if it had brushed against a rose. I saw the countess three feet from me, saying: "It's only me."

I left, but only after greeting her and gripping her moist, trembling hand.

"Are you in pain?"

"Why do you ask?" she retorted.

I looked at her, blushing and flustered.

"I had a dream," I replied.

One evening, on one of M. Origet's last visits, when he announced that the count's convalescence was going well, I was with Jacques and Madeleine under the terrace steps; the three of us had lain there, deeply absorbed in a game of tipcat we were playing with cornstalks and pins on hooks. M. de Mortsauf was asleep. While they waited for the doctor's horse to be saddled, he and the countess conversed quietly in the drawing room. M. Origet left without my noticing. After she had showed him out, Henriette leaned on the window and observed us for quite a time, though we were oblivious. It was one of those warm evenings with a coppery sky and a countryside that resonated with an infinite variety of sounds. A last ray of sun was dying on the rooftops, garden flowers perfumed the breeze, and the tinkling bells of livestock being led back to their stables echoed in the distance. We adapted to that tepid, silent hour by stifling our cries for fear of waking the count. Suddenly, despite the rustling of her dress, I heard the sounds triggered by the violent repression of a sigh. I rushed into the drawing room and saw the countess sitting in the window recess, a handkerchief over her face; she recognized my footsteps and waved imperiously, ordering me to leave her alone. I walked towards her, fear gripping my heart, and tried to remove the handkerchief by force; she fled to her bedroom, and emerged only for prayers. For the first time in fifty days, I led her to the terrace and asked her to account for her emotional state, but she simply pretended to be blissfully happy, and explained it away by referring to the good news Origet had given her.

"Henriette, Henriette," I said, "you knew as much when I saw you in tears. It would be horrible if a lie came between us. Why did you stop me from wiping away your tears? Were they for me?"

"I believed," she replied, "this illness had put a brake on my sorrowing. Now I no longer tremble for M. de Mortsauf, I do so for myself."

She was right. The count's good health was heralded by the return of his moodiness and his madness: he started to say that neither his wife, nor I, nor the doctor knew how to look after him; none of us knew anything about his sickly state, or his pain, or any suitable remedies. Origet was obsessed by some theory or other, and he had identified a disruption of the humors when he should simply have concentrated on the entrance to his stomach. One day, he looked at us maliciously, as though he been spying on us or had intuited something; he smiled at his wife and said: "Well, my dear, if I'd died, you would have been sorry, naturally, but, you must confess, you'd soon have come to terms..."

"I would have mourned you as they do at court, in pink and black," she said, laughing, to shut her husband up.

But it was mainly in the matter of the diet the doctor had wisely recommended, warning against catering to the convalescent's hunger, which led to violent scenes and bawling that couldn't be compared to anything in the past; the count's character seemed to have become all the more horrendous for having slumbered so long. Sustained by the doctor's instructions and her staff's obedience, and encouraged by me, who saw that struggle as a way she could learn how to wield her power over her husband, the countess was emboldened in her resistance; she managed to keep calm when confronted by his lunacy and screams; accepting him for what he was, a child, and that inured her to his insulting epithets. I was so pleased to see her finally take control of his sick mind. The count screamed, but he obeyed, and his obedience came especially after he had screamed a lot. Despite evidence of the successful outcome, Henriette sometimes wept to see that weak, emaciated old man, his forehead yellower than an autumn leaf, his pale eyes and shaking hands; she reproached herself for being so hard on him, and rarely resisted the glee she saw in the count's eyes when she exceeded the portions of food the doctor recommended. What's more, she was much warmer and more gracious towards him than she'd ever been towards me, though there were some differences that heartened me. She wasn't inexhaustible, and was sensible in calling on her staff to serve the count when his whims grew too demanding too quickly, and he complained that nobody understood his needs.

The countess decided to give thanks to God for M. de Mortsauf's return to good health, had a Mass sung, and asked for my arm to go to church: I took her, but went to see the Chessels during the actual service. On the way back, she started scolding me.

"Henriette," I said. "I can't lie. I will plunge into the water to save my drowning enemy, and I will give him my cape so he can warm up, and even forgive him, but I can never forget the slights."

She said nothing and pressed my hand to her heart.

"You are an angel, you must have given your thanks sincerely," I continued. "The Prince of the Peace's mother was rescued from the raging rabble that wanted to kill her and when the queen asked:

'What were you doing?' she replied: 'I was praying for them!' She was like that. I'm a man and necessarily imperfect."[21]

"Don't slander yourself," she said, shaking my arm violently, "I suspect you are worth more than I."

"Yes," I retorted, "because I'd surrender eternity for a single day of happiness, and you!"

"What about me?" she asked, looking at me haughtily.

I shut up and lowered my eyes to avoid her thunderous gaze.

"Me!" she continued, "which *me* do you refer to? I feel there are lots of different *mes* in me! Those two," she added, pointing to Madeleine and Jacques, are *me*. Félix," she said in a heartrending tone, "do you believe I am selfish? Do you think I could sacrifice eternity to reward the man who gives his life for me? That's a horrible thought, and it offends religious sentiment. Can a woman who falls like that ever pick herself up again? You are soon going to force me to answer those questions! And I will in the end reveal a secret that's been on my conscience: an idea that has transfixed my heart, which I've often sought to atone for with harsh penitence, and which brought the tears you asked me to account for yesterday."

"Don't you think you grant too much importance to things ordinary women value highly, and that you should—"

"Well," she interjected, "do *you* think they are less important?"

Her logic ended any argument.

"I must confess!" she resumed. "I could be cowardly enough to abandon that wretched old man whose life I am! But, my dear friend, wouldn't these two weak children we see before us, Madeleine and Jacques, then stay with their father? Do you really believe, I must ask, do you really believe they would survive three months under that man's demented bidding? If failing my duty only concerned myself..." A broad smile crossed her face. "But that would be the death of my two children, wouldn't it? There would be no stopping that. My God," she exclaimed, "why are we talking about such things? Marry, and let me die!"

She spoke those words so bitterly and so pointedly she stifled the rebellion in my heart.

"You cried out, up there, under the walnut tree and I've just cried out, under these alders, and that's an end to it. I shall keep my peace forevermore."

"Your generosity shames me," she said, looking up to the heavens.

We'd reached the terrace; we found the count sunning himself in an armchair. The sight of his sunken face, barely lit by a feeble smile, extinguished the flames that had flared from the ashes. I leaned on the balustrade and gazed at the scene of that dying man, between his two sickly children and his wife, pallid after the vigils, worn down by overwork, and the alarms and possible joys of those horrific two months, rendered all the more lurid by present emotions. I felt the bonds linking body and spirit loosen and fall away at the sight of that family's plight, surrounded by rustling foliage lit by the gray light from a cloudy, autumnal sky. For the first time, I experienced that moral spleen that, people say, is experienced by the sturdiest wrestlers in their struggles, a kind of icy madness that makes a coward of the bravest, a devout man of a nonbeliever, and that makes one indifferent to everything, even to the most vital feelings of honor and love, because doubt strips away self-knowledge and makes us loathe life. Poor, wavering souls that the wealth of your estates surrenders defenseless up to some kind of lethal spirit, where are your peers and judges? Now I understood how the valiant youth who would soon grip the baton of a French field marshal, as skillful a negotiator as he was an intrepid captain, had become the innocent assassin I now saw! Would my desires, today garlanded with roses, meet such a future? Appalled by cause and effect, wondering, like a godless man, where the hand of Providence lay, I couldn't stop two tears from rolling down my cheeks.

"What's the matter, my dear Félix?" asked Madeleine in that childish voice of hers.

Then Henriette dispersed that dark, gloomy haze with anxious eyes that shone like the sun into my soul. The old groom rushed in with a letter from Tours, a letter that brought a shocked cry from me, and made Mme de Mortsauf shake and shudder. I saw the king's private seal; he was summoning me back. I gave her the letter, which she read at a glance.

"He is leaving!" said the count.

"What will become of me now?" she asked, for the first time anticipating her desert without its sun.

We all remained in a state of shock and were equally depressed, because we had never felt we needed each other so keenly. When she spoke to me of anything at all, the countess's voice sounded differently, as if that instrument had lost some of its chords, while others had loosened. She became listless; her gaze dulled. I begged her to confide her thoughts.

"Do I have any?" she asked.

She pulled me into her bedroom, made me sit on her couch, rummaged in her dressing-table drawer, kneeled before me, and said: "This is the hair I have shed over this year, take it, it belongs to you; one day you will find out why and how."

I stooped gently over her forehead, she looked down to avoid my lips: I pressed them down devoutly, with no guilty fervor or voluptuous frissons: gravely and tenderly. Did she want to sacrifice everything? Or, like me, would she merely go to the brink of the abyss? If love had led her to surrender herself, she wouldn't have been so calm, or preserved that religious demeanor, or asked in a voice so pure: "So you no longer bear me a grudge?"

I left at nightfall, she insisted on accompanying me along the road to Frapesle, and we stopped by the walnut tree; I pointed her towards it, and told her how four years before I'd seen her from that very spot: "The valley was so beautiful!" I exclaimed.

"And now?" she responded brightly.

"You are under the walnut tree," I told her, "and the valley is ours."

She looked down and we said our farewells. She climbed back into her carriage with Madeleine, and I, into mine, alone. Back in Paris, I was happily absorbed in urgent tasks that provided a vital distraction and made me stay away from the social world, which had forgotten all about me. I corresponded with Mme de Mortsauf, sent her my diary every week, and she replied twice a month. A full life in the shade, like those fertile, flowery, out-of-the way places I'd recently admired when gathering fresh poetic bouquets deep in the woods during those final two weeks.

Those of you who are in love, impose such beautiful duties on each other! Give yourselves rules to abide by, like the ones the Church gives to Christians for everyday life. The observances created by the religion of Rome are splendid ideas and etch the lines of duty deeper in the soul through a repetition of acts that sustain hope and fear. Feelings always run high in those deep streams that retain the water, purify it, refresh the heart, and enrich life with the treasure trove of a hidden faith, a divine spring where the unique concept of a unique love grows and multiplies.

TWO WOMEN

MY PASSION, which harked back to the medieval age of chivalry, became known somehow or other; perhaps the king or the Duc de Lenoncourt had gossiped. How did that simple, romantic story of a young man who piously adored a beautiful woman not at court, grandiose in her solitude, loyal to her family duties, spread so quickly from that august sphere to the heart of the Faubourg Saint-Germain? I found I was the object of embarrassing questions in salons, since a modest life, out the public eye, has a disadvantage: once it has been experienced, it makes being the center of attention quite intolerable. Just as eyes used to seeing only soft colors are hurt by the brightness of day, so some minds cannot stand violent contrasts. Then I belonged to that category; it will astonish you today, but don't worry, I shall explain the peculiar behavior of the present-day Vandenesse. I found women engaging and the social round perfect. After the Duc de Berri's marriage, the court revived and the French liking for festivities surged again! The foreign occupation ended, prosperity resumed, and pleasure was possible. People renowned by rank or celebrated for their wealth rushed in huge numbers from all ends of Europe to its intellectual capital, where the benefits and vices of other countries existed, but were magnified and sharpened by French wit. Five months after I had left Clochegourde in the midwinter, my good angel wrote me a despairing letter in which she recounted her son's grave illness, which he had survived, though it augured badly for the future; the doctor had spoken of the necessary precautions to take to protect his chest and lungs, a horrible prognosis that, when backed by scientific evidence, blackens a mother's every moment. Hardly had Henriette caught her breath, hardly had Jacques begun his convalescence, when his sister became cause for concern. Madeleine, that pretty flower who responded so well to her mother's care, suffered an attack that had been anticipated and fought off, but which threatened her frail constitution. Already laid low by the exhaustion brought on by Jacques's long illness, the countess couldn't find the courage to face another setback, and the spectacle presented by those two dear creatures inured her to the double torture inflicted by her husband's character. Ever more devastating, gravel-laden storms, in a succession of howling gusts, wrenched out the hopes planted so deeply in her heart. She was at the mercy of the count's tyranny, who, ever since she had grown weary of war, had regained his lost terrain.

When I was funneling all my strength into my children, she wrote to me, how could I deploy it against M. de Mortsauf and defend myself from his attacks by defending myself against death? Today as I walk between the two young melancholy souls at my sides, an irrepressible hatred of life descends upon me. What hurt can I feel, what affection can I return, when I see Jacques standing motionless on the terrace, the only sign of life his two beautiful eyes, magnified by his skinniness, sunken like an old man's, darkened by that fatal prediction: profound intelligence matched by physical frailty? When I see next to me pretty Madeleine, who was so lively, so loving, so pink cheeked, now a deathly white, her eyes and hair blanched, giving me such languishing looks, as if she wanted to say her final farewells; no dish tempts her, or, if she does decide to eat, her strange tastes frighten me; though I cherish her in my heart, that dear, ingenuous child blushes when she tells me what they are. Whatever efforts I make, I cannot amuse my children; both smile at me, but their smiles come in response to my cajoling and are never spontaneous: they sob because they cannot respond to my caresses. Suffering has sundered their souls, and even the ties that bind us. You will understand how dismal Clochegourde is: M. de Mortsauf reigns unhindered. Oh, my friend, you, my heart and glory!, she wrote later, you must really love me if you do still love me, and love me when I am so limp, ungracious, and petrified by sorrow!

At this moment, feelings stirred within me as never before, and living only for that soul to whom I tried to send the luminous light of morning to gild the expectations of purple-streaked evenings, I met in the Elysée-Bourbon salons one of those illustrious ladies who seem almost regal. Immensely rich, born into a family which had avoided all improper alliances since the conquest, she was married to a most distinguished old English lord, and these were only trifles enhancing that woman's beauty, grace, manner, wit, and vivacious brilliance. She was the idol of the day, and conquered Parisian society all the more because she possessed the qualities essential for success, the iron hand in the velvet glove of which Bernadotte spoke.[22] You are familiar with the singular character of the English, the proud, impassable English Channel and the cold St. George's Channel placed between themselves and people they haven't met: humanity seems a mere anthill over which they roam; they only recognize as members of their species those they want to admit; as for anyone else, they don't understand their language; theirs are lips that move and eyes that see, but neither the sound nor the gaze reaches them: as far as they are concerned, those people do not exist. The English reflect that image of their island, where the law rules all, where everything, in every sphere, is uniform, where the exercise of virtue seems to relate to a preset movement of cogs. The polished steel barriers erected around an Englishwoman, caged in her household by threads of gold, where her trough or watering place, pedestals, and pastures are quite wondrous, imbue her nonetheless with an irresistible allure. A nation has never nurtured a married woman's hypocrisy more cleverly by placing her between death or the social round in every situation; she knows no middle ground between shame and reputation: either waywardness is total or nonexistent; it is all or nothing, Hamlet's to be or not to be. Combined with the constant disdain to which she is accustomed, that dilemma makes an Englishwoman stand out in the social whirl. She is a poor thing, forced to be virtuous yet raring to be depraved, sentenced to the continual deceit buried deep in her heart, yet delightful in her form because the English have invested everything in form. That's why that country's women are extraordinarily beautiful: the brooding fervor that is the essence of their life, the exaggerated way they deport themselves, and their delicacy in love so wittily depicted in the famous scene in *Romeo and Juliet* in which Shakespeare's genius gave expression to English women at a stroke. You envy them in so many ways, so what can I tell you that you don't already know about those white sirens, impenetrable on the surface but readily explored, who believe love suffices unto itself, and bring melancholy to ecstasy by never varying, whose soul plays a single note, whose voice utters a single syllable, an ocean of love where the man who never took a dip there has missed out on an aspect of a poetry of the senses, just as he who has never seen the sea has fewer strings to his lyre? You know why I speak like this. My affair with Lady Dudley became notorious. At an age when the senses greatly shape our decisions, a young man whose ardor had been so violently repressed, I experienced the fierce rays from the image of the long-suffering saintly martyr in Clochegourde and felt I could resist every attempt to seduce me. My fidelity was the gloss that attracted Lady Arabella. My resistance sharpened her passion. What she desired was what so many Englishwomen desire—the extraordinary, a flash of lightning. She wanted pepper and spice to season the food in her heart, just like the English crave piquant condiments to stir their taste buds. The atony introduced into these women's existence by the constant perfection of their possessions and the methodical routine of habit leads them to yearn for the romantic, for whatever is plagued with difficulty. I misread her character. The more I hid behind icy disdain, the more passionate Lady Dudley became. This struggle, on which she staked her reputation, sparked interest in a few salons, which represented in her view the first breakthrough that signaled her inevitable victory. By the way, I would have been spared if a friend had repeated to me her horrible comment about Madame de Mortsauf and myself: "I am," she said, "so bored by those doves' billing and cooing!"

I'm not trying to justify my crime, but, Natalie, I must tell you that a man has fewer resources when it comes to resisting a woman than you are able to deploy when you want to escape our charms. Our customs forbid our sex from exercising brutal repression that, with you, is only bait for a lover, that, moreover, is dictated by convention. In the case of men, I can't think what fatuous male regulations heap ridicule on our reserve; we allow you the monopoly of modesty which favors and privileges you, but if the roles are reversed, men are mocked to death. Though my passion protected me, I wasn't mature enough to stay unmoved by the triple seductive charms of pride, adoration, and beauty. In the middle of a ball where she was the star, Lady Arabella exhibited all the homages she'd received from other men there and stared hard to see if I liked her attire and toilette, then shuddered voluptuously when it was obvious I did, and it was that display of emotion that stirred me. Besides, she occupied terrain where I couldn't avoid her; it was difficult for me to turn down certain invitations from diplomatic circles; her status guaranteed her entrance to every salon, where she used a woman's wiles to get whatever she wanted, and always convinced the hostess to seat me next to her at the table, so she could whisper in my ear: "If I were as loved as Madame de Mortsauf, I would sacrifice everything for you."

She laughed and suggested a most modest liaison; she promised to be unerringly discreet, or merely asked me to allow her to love me. Another day she came out with the following words to satisfy the cowardly conscience every young man's capitulation and frenzied desires produces: "I will always be your friend, and I will be your mistress only when it suits you!"

In the end, she conspired to engineer my downfall by exploiting my fidelity. She won over my valet and, after an evening when she'd flaunted her beauty and was sure she'd aroused my desire, I found her waiting for me at home. The scandal resonated the length and breadth of England; the English aristocracy was shocked to high heaven when its most beautiful angel fell. Lady Dudley abandoned her cloud in the British empyrean, was reduced to her fortune, and decided her sacrifices would eclipse those of *she* whose virtue had caused that infamous catastrophe. Like the devil on the summit of Temple Mount, Lady Arabella found pleasure in revealing to me the richest landscapes in her ardent realm.

Read this with indulgence, I beg you. We here confront a crucial problem in human life, a crisis most men have faced, and one I'd like to elucidate, if only to be a beacon directing others away from that razor-edged reef.

This beautiful lady is built of iron, however slender and fragile she seems, a milk-white woman, broken, breakable, and sweet, with a winning forehead crowned by fine, fawn hair, a creature with a transient, phosphorescent glow. No horse, however spirited, can resist her sinewy bridle wrist, or disobey the hand that appears limp but is tireless. She has the feet of a doe, small, thin, muscular, and ineffably graceful. She is so strong she is never afraid to race; no man can match her on horseback; she could beat any centaur for the steeplechase prize; she can take down bucks or stags without ever stopping her horse. Her body doesn't know what sweat is; it absorbs the fire in the air and can endure underwater, or else she wouldn't be alive. Her passion is entirely African; her desire whips like a desert whirlwind, a vast desert reflected in her eyes: dunes of azure and amour under an unchanging sky on a cool, starry night. What a contrast to Clochegourde! The east and the west: one wicking up the least particles of moisture from the air to sustain herself; the other flowing forth with her soul, enveloping her loyal suitors in a luminous haze; the latter is svelte and energetic; the former, refined and rounded.

By the way, have you ever reflected on the general thrust of the English tradition? Does it not deify matter, in an epicureanism that is well defined, thought through, and wisely practiced? Whatever England does or says, it is materialistic, perhaps unconsciously so. It espouses religious and moral pretensions, which lack the divine spirituality and Catholic soul whose enriching grace can never be replaced by hypocrisy, however well hidden. It possesses in the highest degree a knowledge of existence that takes advantage of the smallest niceties of material things, that makes your slipper the most wonderful slipper in the world, deliciously scents your linen and perfumes the furniture with a hint of cedar, that pours an exquisite cup of tea at exactly the right time, banishes dust, nails down carpets from a house's doorstep to its remotest crannies, that brushes cellar walls, polishes door knockers, oils carriage springs, and turns matter into a lush, cottony pulp that is all spick-and-span, in the midst of which the soul meets an ecstatic death, that creates the dreadful monotony that comes with well-being, a life without contradictions, stripped of spontaneity, in a word, a life that *mechanizes* one. In this way, luxuriating in the full English manner, I suddenly experienced a woman, perhaps unique to her sex, who enmeshed me in nets of a love, reborn from its death agony, whose excesses I met with intense restraint, a love possessed by stunning beauty and a unique electricity that flies you to the heavens through the ivory doors of drowsy slumber, or hurtles you upwards astride its wingèd back. A cruelly ungrateful love, that likes to mock the corpses of those it slaughters; a love without memory, a love as vicious as English politics, one to which almost all men inevitably succumb. You must already see the problem. Man is made of matter and spirit; the beast ends in him and the angel begins in him. Here lies the source of the conflict we all experience between a fate we foresee and memories of previous instincts from which we haven't completely detached ourselves: carnal love and divine love. One man resolves them into a single love; another abstains; one explores the whole sex, seeking to satisfy his previous appetites; another idealizes them in a single woman who sums up the entire universe; some drift indecisively between the sensuality of matter and the sensuality of spirit; others spiritualize the flesh and ask of it something it could never deliver. Yes, when one thinks of love's general features, one considers the repugnances and the affinities that arise from the diversity of our compositions and can tear apart pacts entered into by those who have little experience of each other; if you add in the errors created by the expectations of people who live mostly through the spirit, the heart, or by action, who think, feel, or act, and whose vocations are betrayed and ignored in alliances in which two beings are equally ambivalent, you will show greater indulgence toward those misfortunes that society judges pitilessly. So then! Lady Arabella satisfies instincts, organs, and appetites, the vices, and the virtues of the subtle stuff of which we are made. She was mistress of my body. Mme de Mortsauf was wife of my soul. The love that satisfies a mistress has its frontiers, matter is finite, its properties have limited strength, and it is subject to inevitable satiation; next to Lady Dudley, I often felt a kind of void in Paris. The infinite is the heart's domain; boundless love was located in Clochegourde. I passionately loved Lady Arabella, and indeed, she was a sublime specimen and a superior mind; her mocking utterances spared nothing. But I worshipped Henriette. At night I wept tears of happiness; in the morning, I wept tears of remorse.

Some women have sense enough to conceal their jealousy beneath the most angelic goodness: those who are at least thirty, like Lady Dudley. These women know how to feel and to calculate, and can squeeze all the juice from the present while they think of the future; they can suppress their often legitimate complaints with the energy of a hunter who doesn't notice he's been injured as he hotheadedly pursues his prey. Without mentioning Mme de Mortsauf, Arabella tried to kill her in my soul, where she kept finding her, her passion revived by a breath from that invincible love. In order to vanquish the other by inviting comparisons that would be to her advantage, she was never suspicious, sly, or prying, as young women tend to be, but instead acted like a lioness who has seized her victim in her jaws, taken him back to her den, and remains vigilant to ensure nothing spoiled her happiness, keeping me as her trophy, but alert for signs of rebellion. I wrote to Henriette under her gaze, and she never read a single line, and never tried to find out the address written on the envelopes. I had my freedom. She seemed to have decided: "If I lose him, I will only have myself to blame." And she proudly embarked on a love so devoted she'd have surrendered her life if I had asked her to. In the end, she persuaded me that if I stopped loving her, she would kill herself. In that respect, I heard her celebrate the custom by which Indian widows are burned on the pyres of their husbands.

"Although that Indian tradition is a distinction reserved for the nobility, and, as such, is little understood by Europeans, who are incapable of recognizing the disdainful grandeur of that privilege, you must agree," she asked, "that the aristocracy in our dull modern times will only make a resurgence if there is a display of an extraordinary vitality of feeling? How can I teach the bourgeois that the blood running through my veins is not like theirs, if not by dying in a way they never die? Women of low extraction may own diamonds, horses, even coats of arms that ought to be reserved for us, though names can now be bought! But to die, head held high, in defiance of the law, dying for an idol one chose by cutting a shroud from his bed linen, subjecting earth and heaven to a man, and thus robbing the Almighty of the right to create a god, not betraying him for any reason, not even for virtue's sake, because to refuse him in the name of duty, wouldn't that be to surrender to something that wasn't *him*? Whether it be to a man or an idea, it is always a betrayal! That is the greatness ordinary women can never attain; they only know the two common roads: the high way of virtue and the muddy path of the courtesan!"

She was driven, you see, by pride; she flattered every vain instinct by challenging it; she raised me to such a height she could live only by my knee, and she expressed all the seductiveness she could muster by acting as a slavish, wholly submissive being. She would spend an entire day, stretched out at my feet, silent, gazing intently at me, ready to seize the moment for my pleasure, like a sultan's harem favorite, provoking it with flirtatious gestures, while seeming to wait patiently. Where could I ever find the words to describe my first six months, when I was constantly prey to enervating ecstasies of a love so packed with pleasure, varied by knowledge that comes with experience, and which conceals its expertise beneath the violence of passion? That bliss, that sudden revelation of sensuous poetry, constitute the vibrant bond by which young men attach themselves to older women, but it is a convict's shackle, indelibly branding the soul, instilling hatred of pristine, sincere, flower-bedecked loves that don't serve up alcohol in bizarrely carved golden goblets inset with jewels that shine with eternal fire. Savoring the voluptuous pleasures from my dreams that I had never before experienced, that I had expressed in my salaams, that a union of souls renders a thousand times more ardent, I was never short of paradoxes to justify to myself the relish with which I drank from those cups. Often, when languishing in an endless swoon, my soul hovered far above this earth, separated from my body, and I felt those pleasures were a way to cast off matter and surrender my spirit to that sublime flight. Often Lady Dudley, like so many women, used that exultation infused with a surfeit of happiness to bind me to her with promises, and the goad of desire to incite me to curse my angel in Clochegourde. Once I'd betrayed her, I became devious. I continued writing to Mme de Mortsauf as if I were still the child in that mischievous blue outfit she liked so much, though, I confess, her gift of second sight terrified me whenever I thought how a single indiscretion could destroy the pretty castle of my hopes. Often, as I thrilled, my blood was chilled by a sudden wave of sorrow, and I heard Henriette's words proclaimed from on high, like the "Cain, where is Abel?" of the Scriptures.

My letters went unanswered. I became deeply distressed, and I decided to leave for Clochegourde. Arabella didn't object, but naturally said that she would accompany me to the Touraine. Caprice intensified by hurdles, patience warranted by unexpected happiness, had shaped a real love she wanted to make unique. Female insight led her to see that journey as a way to detach me completely from Mme de Mortsauf; though I was blinded by fear, and, transported by the naiveté of true passion, I didn't foresee the trap that would snare me. Lady Dudley came up with the most modest compromises and anticipated all my objections. She agreed to stay near Tours, in the countryside, undeclared, disguised, never going out during the day, and agreeing to nighttime rendezvous when nobody would see us.

I left Tours for Clochegourde on horseback. I had my reasons to travel that way, because I needed a horse for my nighttime excursions and mine was an Arab horse Lady Esther Stanhope had sent to the marquise, and that she'd traded me for the famous Rembrandt she exhibited in her London drawing room, which I had come by in such a peculiar way. I took the route I'd walked six years earlier, and stopped under the walnut tree. From there I could see Mme de Mortsauf in a white dress on the terrace. I rushed to her as quick as lightning, and in a few minutes was past the wall, covering that distance in a straight line as if racing to the belfry. She heard the desert swallow swoop, and when I halted by the corner of the terrace, she said: "Oh, so there you are!"

I was struck dumb by those five words. She knew of my affair. Who had told her? Her mother, whose odious letter she showed me later! The blank indifference of her voice, once so animated, its limp tone, betrayed a sorrow that had been ripening and now gave off the scent of ruthlessly cropped flowers. The hurricane of infidelity, like the Loire flooding its banks and sanding the fields forever, had swept through her and left a desert where verdant meadows once flourished. I led my horse through the small gate, and the countess, who'd tiptoed forward, exclaimed: "What a handsome animal!"

She stood there, her arms crossed so I couldn't take her hand: I'd seen her intention.

"I must tell M. de Mortsauf," she said, walking away.

I stood there, bewildered, letting her leave, observing her, as noble as always, unhurried, haughty, paler than I'd ever seen her: her forehead wore the yellow badge of bitter melancholy and her head bowed like a lily heavy with rain.

"Henriette!" I shouted, with the fury of a man who feels himself on the verge of death.

She didn't turn around, didn't stop, deigned only to say she was vetoing my use of a name she no longer answered to, and kept on walking. In that terrible vale where the dust of millions must linger, their souls animating the globe's surface, I would feel how minute I was, at the core of that multitude, packed beneath the immense luminous spaces shining down so gloriously, but I'd feel less flattened by that than I did before that figure in white, walking steadily, like a flood implacably surging up a town's streets, towards her Clochegourde château, the glory and torment of that Christian Dido. I cursed Arabella with a single oath that would have killed her, had she ever heard it, she, a woman who'd abandoned everything for me, as one renounces everything for God! I was deep in thought and saw endless pain everywhere. Then I spotted them all coming. Jacques ran impetuously, like the ingenuous youngster he was. A gazelle with mournful eyes, Madeleine accompanied her mother. I hugged Jacques to my chest, poured out the anguish in my soul and the tears his mother rejected. M. de Mortsauf walked towards me, arms outstretched; he gripped me tight, kissed me on the cheeks, and said: "Félix, I now realize I owe my life to you!"

Mme de Mortsauf turned her back to us during that whole scene, on the excuse she was showing my horse to an astonished Madeleine.

"What in hell, isn't that women for you!" shouted the furious count, "they have eyes only for your horse."

Madeleine turned around and came over; I kissed her hand while I gazed at the blushing countess.

"Madeleine is much better," I said.

"Poor little dear!" retorted the countess, kissing her forehead.

"Yes, for the moment, they are all in the pink of health," replied the count. "I'm the odd one out, as dilapidated as a tower that's about to collapse."

"So the General still has his black demons?" I asked, staring at Mme de Mortsauf.

"We all have our blue devils," she replied. "Isn't that what the English say?"

We walked back towards their enclosed land together, sensing that something serious had taken place. She showed no wish to be alone with me. What it meant was that I was no more than her guest.

"By the way, what about your horse?" said the count, when we'd started walking.

"You see," retorted the countess, "it would be wrong for me to think about it, and wrong not to."

"Indeed," he remarked, "one must do everything when the time is right."

"I'll go," I countered, finding that frosty welcome quite intolerable. "I'm the only one who can lead him and settle him down properly. My groom is coming in the post chaise from Chinon, and he will rub him down."

"Is the groom from England too?" asked the countess.

"They only make them there," replied the count, cheered to see his wife so sad.

His wife's frostiness gave him the chance to go against her and be effusive in his friendliness towards me. I recognized the deadweight of a husband's attachment. Don't think for one moment they act to murder a noble soul when their wives lavish affection apparently stolen from them; on the contrary, they become loathsome and unbearable once love has flown the nest. Cunning, a vital aspect of that kind of bond, then makes its appearance, as a means: it is onerous and hateful, like all means that the ends no longer justify.

"My dear Félix," said the count, taking my hands and squeezing them affably, "please forgive Mme de Mortsauf: women need to be querulous, their frailty is their excuse, and they are incapable of equanimity, the gift affording us strength of character. She loves you dearly, I know, but..."

While the count spoke, Mme de Mortsauf gradually moved away, until we were left alone.

"Félix," he whispered as he gazed at his wife walking back to the château, accompanied by her children, "I can't think what's wrong with Mme de Mortsauf. Her character has completely changed over the last six weeks. She'd been so sweet and charming, and suddenly she became incredibly sullen!"

Manette later told me the countess had become so despondent she was deaf to the count's jibes. As he could no longer find soft ground where he could sink his barbs, he was restless, like a child who has been torturing a poor insect and no longer sees it twitch. He required a confidant, as an executioner needs an assistant.

He paused, then went on, "Do try to ask Mme de Mortsauf. A wife always keeps secrets from her husband, but she may confide in you the reason for her grief. Even if it cost me half the days left to me and half my fortune, I'd willingly sacrifice everything to make her happy. I need her so much! If I didn't feel that angel always at my side in my old age, I'd be the most wretched of men! I would prefer to die peacefully. Tell her she won't have to put up with me for long. Félix, my poor friend, I know I am on my way out. I've been hiding the fatal truth from everyone. Why afflict them in advance? It's my pylora, my friend, as usual! I have finally discovered the cause of my illness, it is sensitivity that has been the death of me. In effect, all our affections strike at the center of our gastric..."

"You are implying," I said, and smiled, "that the emotionally sensitive perish because of their stomachs."

"Don't mock, Félix, nothing could be truer. Sorrow that's too painful overactivates the generation of emotion. Overexcitement of the sensibility keeps stomach mucous in a constant state of irritation. If that persists, it leads to a disruption that initially goes unnoticed by the digestive system: secretions change, appetites are disturbed, and the digestive system reacts capriciously; soon, more searing pain comes, worsens, and becomes increasingly frequent; the disarray then peaks, as if a slow poison had entered the alimentary canal; mucous thickens, the pylora valve hardens, and a tumor is formed that will cause death. Well, my friend, that's the point where I am at now! The hardening proceeds and nothing can stop it. You see my straw-yellow complexion, my dry, shiny eyes and skinny body! I am desiccating. What could one expect! I carried the germ of this affliction from exile: I suffered so much there! My marriage, which should have righted the wrongs of emigration, far from soothing the ulcers in my soul, has reopened the sores. What did I find here? Eternal alarums caused by the children, household penury, a fortune to rebuild, the need for economies that required a thousand privations I imposed on my wife and from which I was the first to suffer. And then a secret I can only confide in you, that is my deepest chagrin: though Blanche is an angel, she doesn't understand me; she knows nothing of my sorrow, she exacerbates it; I forgive her! You know, it's terrible to say this, my friend, but a less virtuous woman would have made me happier, by lending herself to acts of pleasure Blanche cannot imagine, because she is ignorant as a child! On top of that, my staff torture me, and are blockheads who hear Greek when I speak French. While our fortune was being rebuilt, it was touch and go, but by the time I faced less hardship on that front, the deed was done, I had reached the phase when my appetites went awry; then came my awful deterioration that Origet's treatments worked so poorly for. In short, I today have only six months to live…"

I listened to the count and felt terror in my soul. Seeing Henriette again, I'd been struck by *her* dry, shiny eyes and *her* straw-yellow forehead; I dragged the count towards the house, pretending to listen to his mixture of moans and medical treatise, but I could think only of Henriette and I wanted to observe her.

I found the countess in the drawing room, where she was sitting in on a math lesson being given to Jacques by Abbé de Dominis, while she taught Madeleine an upholstery stitch. At other times, when I had arrived, she'd have arranged to defer all tasks so she could devote herself to me, but my love was deep and true and I warded off the misery caused by the contrast between present and past, because I saw her lethal, straw-yellow complexion and it recalled the reflection of divine light Italian painters gave to the faces of saints. Then I felt death's icy blast. I shuddered when, stripped of the limpid waters where her gaze once swam, the fire in her eyes fell on me; I noticed more changes wrought by sorrow that I hadn't seen outside: the tiny lines lightly etched on her forehead on my last visit were now pronounced; her bluish temples seemed hollow and burning; her eyes had retreated under drooping arches, and her skin had turned brown; she was damaged like a bruised fruit a maggot is slowly consuming from the inside. Wasn't I the one, the man who wanted only to pour bliss into her soul, to have cast bitterness into the spring where her life had found succor, where her bold spirit revived? I walked over, sat by her side, and asked mournfully: "Are you happy with your state of health?"

"Yes," she replied, staring deep into my eyes. "That is my health, over there," she continued, pointing to Jacques and Madeleine.

At fifteen, Madeleine had won her battle against nature, and she was a woman; she had grown up, the colors of a Bengal rose had returned to her pallid cheeks; she had lost the insouciance of a child who looks at everything head-on, and was starting to lower her gaze;

her movements had become spare and serene, like her mother's; her slender waist and graceful bosom were already blossoming; her magnificent black hair, parted down the middle over her Spanish forehead, glinted coquettishly. She was like a medieval statuette so delicate in form and so fragile in substance that you fear your gaze will break it, but her health, a fruit now blooming after a long struggle, had given her cheeks a peachy velvet and her neck silky down where the light played, as it did on her mother's. She was going to live! God had traced the bud of the most beautiful human flower on her long eyelashes, on her curvaceous shoulders, which promised to mature as sumptuously as her mother's! That young brunette, straight-backed as a poplar, was such a contrast to Jacques, a frail seventeen-year-old, whose head had expanded and whose forehead had extended so quickly, so worryingly, and whose feverish, weary eyes were in step with his deeply resonant voice. The latter sounded too loud, while the former expressed too many thoughts. Henriette's heart, soul, and intellect were burning within that insubstantial body, in rapidly spreading flames, because Jacques's complexion was milk white, dashed with a feverish hue, like a young Englishwoman marked out by the plague to be killed at the assigned hour; *his* health wasn't all it seemed! Reacting to a gesture from Henriette, who pointed me to Madeleine, and then to Jacques, drawing geometrical figures and algebraic equations on a blackboard in front of Abbé de Dominis, I was startled by the spectacle of death concealed by flowers, and respected an unhappy mother's self-deception.

"When I see them like that, joy silences my sorrow; it goes silent and vanishes when I see them looking sickly. My friend," she continued, her eyes glowing with maternal pleasure, "if other affections betray us, the feelings rewarded here, the duty done and crowned with success amply compensate for defeat suffered elsewhere. Like you, Jacques will be a man of learning, full of virtuous knowledge; like you, he will honor his country, that he may perhaps govern with your help, a man of such high rank, but I will try to convince him to remain loyal to his first loves. Madeleine, dearest child, is already showing sublime sentiments, as pure as snow on the highest Alpine peak, that will embody a woman's devotion and her wit, grace and pride will make her a worthy Lenoncourt! Their mother, once so full of anguish, is now extremely happy, with infinite, unblemished bliss; yes, my life is full, my life is rich. Do you see, God is allowing my joy to flourish with legitimate feelings and sours those affections that were steering me to dangerous inclinations."

"Very good," exclaimed the abbot excitedly. "M. le Vicomte knows as much as I do."

As he finished his diagrams, Jacques gave a little cough.

"That will be enough for today, dear abbot," said the countess, deeply moved, "and, above all, no chemistry lessons."

"Ride your horse, Jacques," she continued, letting her son hug her with a mother's loving tenderness, while her eyes stared at me as if to decry her memories of me. "Off you go, dear, and take care."

"But," I asked, as she looked lingeringly after Jacques, "you didn't answer my question. Do you still feel pain?"

"Yes, sometimes in my stomach. If I were in Paris, I'd be blessed with gastroenteritis, an illness that seems so fashionable."

"My mother is often in a lot of pain," said Madeleine.

"Oh!" she went on, "are you really interested in my health?"

Shocked by her mother's ironic tone, Madeleine looked at us in turn; my gaze counted the pink flowers on the seat of the green-gray couch adorning the drawing room.

"This situation is unbearable," I whispered in her ear.

"And did I create it?" she asked.

"Dear child," she added, loudly affecting that cruel playfulness with which women like to embellish their revenge, "do you know nothing about modern history? Aren't England and France always enemies? Madeleine knows that much; she knows a huge sea separates it from us, and that it is a cold, stormy sea."

Candelabra had replaced the vases on the mantelpiece, no doubt to deprive me the pleasure of filling them with flowers. When my servant arrived, I went out to give him his orders; he'd brought a few items I'd decided to put in my bedroom.

"Félix," said the countess, "don't get it wrong. My aunt's old bedroom is now Madeleine's. Yours is above the count's."

Though guilty, I had my feelings, and her words were dagger thrusts stabbing my sorest places. Moral pain isn't absolute, it is in proportion to a soul's fragility, and the countess had cruelly run that gamut of grief, but, following that same logic, the finest woman will always be all the more cruel for having been benign once; I glanced at her, but she lowered her gaze. I entered my new bedroom, which was pretty, appointed in white and green. I dissolved into tears. Henriette heard me and came in with a bunch of flowers.

"Henriette," I said, "can't you bring yourself to forgive what is the most forgivable of faults?"

"Don't call me Henriette ever again," she replied, "that poor woman no longer exists, though your devoted friend Mme de Mortsauf will always be here to listen to you and to love you. Let's speak later, Félix. If you still feel anything towards me, let me become used to the sight of you again, and when words make me less distraught, when I've recovered some of my courage, then, and only then . . . Do you see this valley?" she continued, indicating the Indre. "I find it depressing, but I still love it."

"Oh, may England and every woman who lives there perish! I shall hand the king my resignation and die here, with your forgiveness."

"No, love *her*! Henriette is no more, and this is no game, as you will soon discover."

She withdrew, revealing her anguish in the way she intoned that final word. I ran after her, held her back, asked: "Don't *you* still love me?"

"You've hurt me more than all the rest put together. Now I suffer less, and love you less, but it's only in England that they say: 'Neither forever, nor always!' Here we say: 'Always!' Be good, don't make me sorrow any more, and if you grieve, remember—I *am* still alive!"

She withdrew from me her hand, which was cold and still, but moist, then she shot like an arrow across the passageway where that truly tragic scene had taken place. During lunch, the count had a torment in store that I hadn't foreseen.

"So, isn't Lady Dudley in Paris?"

I blushed far too red as I replied: "No."

"And is she not in Tours?" continued the count.

"She isn't divorced, so she may go to England. Her husband would be very happy if she decided to return," I quipped.

"Does she have children?" asked Mme de Mortsauf, her voice shaking.

"Two sons," I answered.

"Where are they?"

"In England, with their father."

"Come on, Félix, be frank. Is she as beautiful as they say?"

"What a question to ask! Isn't the woman one loves always the most beautiful?" exclaimed the countess.

"Yes, always," I said, proudly glancing in her direction, though her eyes didn't meet mine.

"You're lucky," resumed the count, "yes, you are a lucky devil. You know, in my youth I would have gone insane if I had made such a conquest."

"Shush," said Mme de Mortsauf, indicating that Madeleine was in the room.

"I am no child," said the count, who liked to feel young again.

When we left the table, the countess pointed me to the terrace, and, the second we were outside, she cried: "Do women really exist who sacrifice their children for a man? I might understand wealth, society, eternity! But to give up your children!"

"Yes, and women willing to do that would have liked to sacrifice even more, they give everything..."

In the countess's mind, the world had been turned upside down, and her ideas confounded. Shocked by such an extraordinary act, imagining that bliss must justify the self-sacrifice, feeling her own flesh rebel, she was struck dumb for a moment by her own failure in life. Yes, it was a moment of horrible doubt, but she soon recovered, proudly, saintly, and carrying her head high.

"Well, then, Félix, love this woman dearly," she said tearfully, "she can be my lucky sister. I forgive her the wrongs she has done me, if she can give you what you never found here, what you can no longer expect from me. You were right: I never told you I loved you, and never loved you, as women love in this world. But, if she isn't a mother, how can she give you love?"

"My saintly love," I replied, "I'd have to be less elated than I am to tell you how triumphantly you soar above her: she is a woman tied to this earth, a daughter of races on the wane, and you are a daughter of the heavens, an adored angel. All my heart is yours, she has only my flesh; she knows that and despairs, and would change places with you, even if the price to pay was the cruelest torture. But everything is set now. You have my feelings and my thoughts, pure love, my youth and my old age; she has the desires and pleasures of a fleeting passion; you, my memory in its entirety, and she, deepest oblivion."

"Please tell me that is true, dearest friend!"

She walked away, sat on a bench, and melted into tears.

"Virtue, Félix, the sanctity of life, and motherly love cannot be mistakes! Apply this balm to my wound! Repeat a word and return me to the heavens where I want to fly with you! Bless me with a glance, a hallowed word, and I will forgive you all the wrongs I have suffered over the last two months."

"Henriette, there are mysteries in our life that you still don't know. I met you at an age when sentiment can silence the desires nature stirs, but several scenes, the memory of which will console me when death comes, must have shown you that that phase was nearing its end and your continued victory depended on extending those silenced delights. Love without possession is sustained by frustrated desire, but a time comes when we only sorrow, when we aren't at all like you. We are driven by impulses we cannot reject, on pain of ceasing to be men. Deprived of the food that should nourish it, the heart consumes itself, and feels a peace that isn't death, but that is a predecessor to it. We cannot dupe our nature for long; at the least turn, it wakens with an energy that verges on madness. No, I haven't loved, I have thirsted in the middle of the desert!"

"The desert!" she exclaimed bitterly, pointing to the valley. "Oh," she added, "you are so skilled in logic, and make such fine distinctions! The faithful aren't endowed with such subtlety."

"Henriette," I replied, "let's not quarrel over a few chance phrases. My soul has never doubted, but I haven't been in control of my senses. That woman knows full well you are the only one I love. She occupies a secondary place in my life, she's aware of that, and resigned to it; I have the right to leave her, as one leaves a courtesan."

"And ... ?"

"She said she would kill herself," I replied, thinking the very idea would shock Henriette.

But, as she listened, she smiled contemptuously, a smile more dramatic than any thought it translated.

"My dear conscience," I went on, "if you only knew how I resisted and the seductive ruses she used to plot my downfall, you would understand that lethal ..."

"Yes, I know, it was so very 'lethal'!" she retorted. "I believed too wholeheartedly in you! I believed you wouldn't lack the virtue the priest practices and ... M. de Mortsauf possesses," she added, giving her words an epigrammatic twist. "It's all over," she continued after a pause. "I owe you so much, my friend: you have extinguished the bodily life that flamed within me. I have traveled the most difficult path, now old age approaches, I am in pain and will soon be sick; I could never be that shining angel who rains favors on you. Be faithful to Lady Arabella. And Madeleine, whom I raised so fondly for you, whose will she be now? My poor Madeleine! My poor Madeleine!" she repeated mournfully. "If only you had heard her say: 'Mother, you're too hard on Félix!' My dear child!"

She looked at me as the setting sun's lukewarm rays slipped through the leaves and branches, and, feeling some sort of pity for the shards of our love, she revisited our past that was so pure, and launched into observations that we shared. We recalled memories, our eyes went from the valley to the land she had enclosed, from the windows of Clochegourde to Frapesle, peopling our reveries with fragrant bouquets, the fictions of our desires. It was her last pleasure, savored with the innocence of a Christian soul. The panorama we felt so profoundly had plunged both of us into the same melancholy. She believed what I said and saw herself where I had placed her, in the heavens.

"My friend, I obey God, because His finger is behind all of this."

It was only later that I realized the significance of those words. We walked slowly back up the terraces. She took my arm, leaned on it, resigned, her heart still bleeding, but she was tending her wounds.

"Human life was ever thus," she said. "What did M. de Mortsauf do to deserve his fate? It all shows that a better world exists. Woe betide anyone who complains about keeping to the path of righteousness!"

She started to scrutinize her life minutely, examining it so thoroughly, from every angle, that her ice-cold analysis revealed how much everything on this earth repelled her. When we reached the terrace steps, she let go of my arm and spoke these final words: "If God has given us a feeling and taste for happiness, he must surely care for the innocent souls who encountered only affliction here below. That must be so, or God doesn't exist, or our life would be but a joke in poor taste."

With that, she rushed indoors where I found her stretched out on her couch, as if she'd been struck by the same voice that knocked Saint Paul to the ground.

"What's the matter?" I asked.

"I no longer know what virtue is," she replied, "and have no sense of my own!"

We were both stunned, as we listened to that word echo like a stone thrown down an abyss.

"If I've been wrong in my life, *she* is right, *she* is!" concluded Mme de Mortsauf.

Her final struggle followed her final pleasure. When the count reappeared, she, who never complained, complained; I begged her to spell out the source of her pain, but she refused, and went off to lie down, leaving me prey to remorse that fed on remorse. Madeleine accompanied her mother, and the next morning she told me the countess had been vomiting all night, as a consequence of the previous day's turbulent emotions. So I was killing her, I, the man who wanted to give my life for her.

"Dear count," I said to M. de Mortsauf, who obliged me to play backgammon, "I think the countess is seriously ill; there is still time to save her; summon Origet, and beg her to follow his advice—"

"Origet, the man who murdered me?" he interjected. "Never, I shall consult Carbonneau."

That whole week, especially the first few days, I was a grieving mass, my heart was paralyzed, my pride wounded, my soul too. You need to have been the center of everything, the center of glances and sighs, the mainstay of a life, the hearth where everyone found light, to recognize the horror of the abyss. The same objects were there, but the spirit giving them life had been snuffed out like a flame. I understood why lovers are loath to meet again when love has gone. It is devastating to find a void where you once reigned, to find death's mute chill where life's bright rays once sparkled! Comparisons are onerous. I soon began to regret the dearth of happiness that had blighted my youth. My despair became so intense I think it moved the countess. One day, after dinner, when we were all taking a stroll along the water's edge, I made one last attempt to find forgiveness. I asked Jacques to walk in front with his sister, I let the count proceed alone, and I led Mme de Mortsauf towards the toue: "Henriette," I pleaded, "a word of forgiveness, or I will throw myself into the Indre! It's true, I have let you down, but haven't I displayed the devoted loyalty of a dog? I have returned like one, full of shame; if a dog behaves badly, it receives its punishment but will continue to adore the hand that beats it; break me asunder, but give me your love once more."

"My poor child!" she replied, "you are still my son, aren't you?"

She took my arm and we silently caught up with Jacques and Madeleine, whom she accompanied back to Clochegourde through the meadows, leaving me with the count, who began to talk about his neighbors' politics.

"Let's go back," I said, "your head's bare and the evening dew might give you a chill."

"You feel sorry for me, my dear Félix!" he retorted, misunderstanding what I was suggesting. "My wife has never tried to console me, perhaps deliberately."

Previously she would never have left me alone with her husband; now I needed an excuse to go back to her. She was with her children, busy explaining the rules of backgammon to Jacques.

"There you are," said the count, always jealous of the love she showed her children, "that's why I'm always forgotten. Husbands, my dear Félix, are always the last to be considered; the most virtuous wife finds the means to satisfy her own need, to steal from conjugal love."

She continued to caress them and made no response.

"Jacques," he said, "come here!"

Jacques seemed reluctant.

"My son, your father wants you, so go to him," said his mother, giving him a push.

"They love me on her orders," retorted the old man, who did occasionally recognize his true situation.

"Monsieur," she replied, passing her hand several times through Madeleine's hair, which was in the beautiful Ferronière style,[23] "please don't be unfair to poor women; their lives aren't easy to endure, and perhaps children represent a mother's virtue!"

"My dear," replied the count, daring to be logical, "what you are implying is that women wouldn't be virtuous without their children, and would leave their husbands."

The countess hurriedly got to her feet and took Madeleine out to the steps.

"That's marriage for you, my friend," commented the count. "By rushing out like that, are you suggesting I'm not right in the head?" he shouted, grabbing his son's hand, standing next to his wife on the steps, glaring angrily.

"On the contrary, monsieur, you frightened me. Your comment was extremely hurtful," she replied blankly, giving me a livid glance. "If virtue isn't about sacrificing oneself for one's children and husband, what is it?"

"Self sa-cri-fice!" responded the count, turning each syllable into an iron blow to batter his victim's heart. "You sacrifice yourself to your children? You sacrifice yourself to me? Who? What? Answer me, will you? What's this all about? What do you mean?"

"Monsieur," she replied, "would you be happy to be loved for the love of God, or to know your wife is virtuous for virtue's sake?"

"Madame is right," I interjected heatedly, words that resonated in the two souls where I cast hopes that had been dashed forever, that I soothed by expressing the most grievous sorrow, a mute cry putting an end to their squabble, as everything else goes silent when a lion roars. "Yes, the finest privilege reason has given us is the ability to extend our virtues to beings whose happiness we have wrought, whose happiness we cause not out of dutiful calculation, but from spontaneous, undying tenderness."

A tear glinted in Henrietta's eyes.

"And, dear count, if by chance a woman were unwillingly subject to a sentiment alien to those allowed her by society, you must agree that the more irresistible that sentiment, the more virtuous she must be when she chokes it dead, by *sacrificing herself* to her children and her husband. What's more, that idea cannot be applied to me, an unfortunate example of the opposite, nor to you, whom it will never encompass."

A moist, burning hand settled on my hand and squeezed it silently.

"You are quite sublime, Félix," said the count, graciously putting his hand around his wife's waist and drawing her towards him: "My dear, forgive this wretched, sickly man who no doubt seeks to be loved more than he deserves."

"There are hearts made of generosity," she replied, leaning her head on the shoulder of the count, who thought she was referring to him.

That misconception led the countess to shake in the strangest way; her clasp fell, her hair loosened, she turned pale; her husband, who was supporting her, howled as he felt her going faint; he grasped her as if she were his daughter and carried her to the drawing-room couch where we all surrounded her. Henriette kept my hand in hers, as if to say that we alone knew the secret behind a scene that seemed so simple, though it had torn her soul apart.

"I was wrong," she whispered the moment the count left us alone and went to fetch a glass of orange blossom–scented water, "I've wronged you a thousand times, I acted despairingly, when I ought to have welcomed you with my forgiveness; your goodness is such that I alone can appreciate it. Yes, I know, passion inspires some goodness. Men find various ways to be good: they are good out of disdain, temptation, self-interest, natural indolence, but, my friend, you are blessed with a goodness that is absolute."

"If that's true," I said, "you should know that you have inspired everything noble within me. Can't you see you have made me what I am?"

"Those words are enough to make a woman happy," she responded as the count returned. "I'm feeling better already," she said, getting to her feet. "I need some fresh air."

We all went down to the terrace, still scented by acacia blossom. She'd taken my right arm and pressed it against her heart, squeezing out sorrowful thoughts, which were, to keep to her words, sorrows she loved. Of course, she wanted to be alone with me, but her imagination, unskilled in womanly wiles, wouldn't give her an excuse to send her husband and children away; so we spoke of inconsequential matters, as she racked her brain trying to create a moment when she could finally unburden her feelings to me.

"It is a long time since we went for a drive in our carriage," she eventually declared, when she saw it was such a beautiful evening. "Monsieur, please give the order so I can go for a drive."

She knew it would be impossible to say anything before prayers, and she was afraid the count would insist on a game of backgammon. She could always meet me on the warm, scented terrace when her husband was in bed, but perhaps she was afraid of finding herself in shadowy places dotted with voluptuous glimmers of light, of walking along the balustrade from which our gazes could watch the Indre flow through the meadow. Just as a cathedral's dark, silent vaults encourage prayer, moonlit arbors, perfumed by strong scents and animated by the silent sounds of spring, arouse the flesh and weaken the will. Countryside that quietens the ardor of old men, stirs the young at heart; we both knew all about that! Two chimes of the bell announced it was time for prayers, the countess gave a start.

"What's the matter, dear Henriette?"

"Henriette no longer exists," she replied. "Don't bring her back to life, she was too demanding and capricious; you now have a tranquil friend whose righteousness was reaffirmed by the words dictated to you by heaven. We can discuss this later. Let's get to prayers on time. It's my turn to say them."

When the countess spoke those words with which she asked God for His help to face the adversities of life, she struck a tone I wasn't the only one to notice; she had apparently used her gift of second sight to glimpse the strength of emotion she would feel as a result of a contretemps caused by the fact that I had forgotten what I'd agreed to with Arabella.

"There's time for three rounds before the horses are harnessed," said the count, dragging me into the drawing room. "Then you can go for a drive with my wife; I must go to bed."

It was stormy, like all our games. The countess could hear her husband's voice from her bedroom or Madeleine's: "You have a most peculiar way of playing the host," she told the count when she returned to the drawing room.

I looked at her, taken aback; I wasn't used to her being so harsh; once she'd have been wary of rescuing me from the count's tyranny; she used to like to see me share in her suffering and endure him patiently, out of love for her.

"I'd give my life," I murmured in her ear, "to hear you whisper again: 'My poor dear! My poor dear!'"

She looked down as she remembered that moment; her eyes sought me out furtively, expressing the joy of a woman who sees her heart's most fleeting caresses preferred to the ecstatic delights of another love. Then, as always when I suffered such a slight, I forgave her, and felt she had understood. The count was losing, he said he was tired and we should abandon the game; we walked around the lawn while waiting for the carriage. The second he departed, pleasure so brightened my face the countess gave me a quizzical, surprised look.

"Henriette exists," I said, "she still loves me; you hurt me and clearly intended to break my heart, but I can still be happy!"

"Only a scrap of that woman remains," she replied aghast, "and you have it. May God be blessed, He who gives me courage to endure the torture I deserve. Yes, I still love you too much, I was going to die, and that Englishwoman lights up the abyss for me."

With that we climbed into the carriage and the coachman asked for his orders.

"Take the Chinon road via the approach, bring us back across the Charlemagne heaths and the Saché road," she instructed.

"What day is it?" I asked, too eagerly.

"Saturday."

"Let's not go that way, madame. On a Saturday evening, the road will be crowded with the carts of egg and poultry dealers on their way to Tours."

"Do what I told you," she repeated, looking at the coachman.

We were both too familiar with the slightest inflections in our voices to disguise the tiniest emotion. Henriette had grasped what *that* implied.

"You weren't thinking of poultry dealers when you chose tonight," she said with a hint of irony. "Lady Dudley is in Tours. Don't lie, she is waiting for you somewhere near here. *What day is it? Poultry dealers! Carts!*" she parroted. "Did you ever make that kind of comment when we rode out before?"

"It only goes to show how I forget everything else when I'm in Clochegourde," I replied.

"*Is* she waiting for you?"

"Yes, she is."

"When?"

"Between eleven and midnight."

"Where?"

"On the heath."

"Don't lie. Are you sure it's not under the walnut tree?"

"On the heath."

"We must head there," she said, "I must see her."

When I heard that, I saw that my life had reached a turning point. In a flash I decided to marry Lady Dudley and end the grievous struggle threatening to exhaust my senses, to take away, by dint of repeated clashes, sensual delights that were like the velvety touch of fruit. My stunned silence wounded the countess, whose sublime nobility I still hadn't encompassed.

"Don't be angry with me," she said in her golden voice, "this, my dear, is *my* punishment. You'll never be loved as you are here," she went on, resting her hand on her heart. "Didn't I tell you? Lady Dudley saved me. She can have the dross; I don't envy her that. I will enjoy the glorious love of angels! I have crossed vast terrains since you last came. I have made my judgment on life. Elevate your soul and you rent it asunder; the higher you go, the less sympathy you find: rather than suffer in the valley, you suffer in the air, like an eagle gliding along with an arrow transfixed in its heart that an uncouth shepherd fired. Today I have understood that heaven and earth are incompatible. Indeed, God alone is the only goal possible for those wishing to live in the celestial sphere. Our soul must be detached from all things terrestrial. One must love one's friends like one loves one's children, for their sake, not for oneself. The *ego* brings unhappiness and sorrow. My heart will soar higher than any eagle; a love does exist that will not cheat me. As for living an earthly life, that is too debasing, and means the selfish senses rule over the spirituality of the angel within us. The ecstasy passion brings is tempestuous, leaving an enervating anguish that smashes the wellsprings of the heart. I come from the seashore where those tempests blow, I have seen them too close; they often enveloped me in cloud; the waves haven't always crashed at my feet, I've felt their cruel lashes freezing my heart; I must withdraw to high places, or I would perish by the shore of that vast sea. I behold you, like all who have afflicted me, as the guardians of my virtue. My life has been filled with distress that fortunately found its match in my fortitude, and thus kept itself unsullied by evil passions, avoiding seductive snares, always remaining ready for God. Our coming together *was* the foolish effort made by two ingenuous children striving to satisfy their hearts, men, and God... Pure madness, Félix!

"By the way!" she continued after a pause, "how does that woman address you?"

"Amédée," I replied. "Félix is someone else, who will only ever belong to you."

"Henriette finds the idea of death troubling," she said, smiling radiantly. "But she will perish at the first attempt made by this humble Christian woman, this proud mother and wife whose virtue wavered yesterday only to be reaffirmed today. What can I say? Of course, my life is true to itself in the big and small picture. The heart where I should have attached my first tender roots, my mother's, was a closed door to me, despite my stubborn search for an opening where I might gain entry. I was a girl, I followed after three boys who had died, and I tried unsuccessfully to fill their place in my parents' affections; I couldn't heal my family's deeply wounded pride. After that gloomy childhood, I met my lovely aunt, but death took her away almost immediately. M. de Mortsauf, to whom I pledged myself, struck me down, relentlessly, quite unaware, the poor fellow! His love displays the naive selfishness of a child. He doesn't see the secret wrongs he does me, and I will always forgive him! My children, those dear children, are joined to my flesh by their pain, to my soul by all their qualities, and to my nature by their innocent joys. Was I granted those children to show how strong and patient we mothers are? Yes, my children truly are my virtue! You know how scourged I am by them, in them, in spite of them. As far as I was concerned, to become a mother was to purchase the right to constant suffering. When Hagar cried out in the desert, an angel ensured a pure spring spurted for a slave who was loved too much; but, in my case, when the limpid spring (do you remember?), to which you wished to guide me, flowed around Clochegourde, it only flowed with bitter waters. Yes, you caused me unheard suffering. I am sure God will forgive someone who met love only through grief. But if the worst pain I endured was all your doing, perhaps I deserved it. God isn't unjust. It's true, Félix, a kiss furtively placed on a brow may represent a crime! Perhaps one has to be cruel to atone for steps taken in front of one's children and husband, when strolling in the evening in order to be alone with memories and thoughts they didn't share, and when on such a walk one's soul espoused another! When one's inner self grows, then shrinks, so as to occupy only that space offered to a kiss, that may be the worst crime of all. When a wife lowers her head to receive her husband's kiss on her hair and looks blank, that is a crime! It is a crime to build a future that depends on death, to imagine motherhood in the future without alarums: beautiful children playing at dusk with a father adored by the whole family, contemplated by a mother's loving gaze. Yes, I have sinned, and sinned grievously! I have developed a fondness for the penitence inflicted by the Church, which doesn't adequately atone for errors the priest probably judged too leniently. I suspect God has punished harshly all my waywardness by making the man on behalf of whom they were committed the instrument of His vengeance. Wasn't giving my hair a pledge? Why did I so love to wear a white dress? It was my way of thinking I was more like your lily; didn't you see me for the first time here in a white dress? Alas, I deprived my children of love, because affection given is taken from affection owed elsewhere. Do you see, Félix, all suffering possesses a meaning. Strike, strike me harder than M. de Mortsauf and my children struck me. This Englishwoman is an instrument of God's wrath, and I will confront her without hatred, smiling at Him; I must love Him, or risk not being a Christian wife and mother. If, as you say, I could have protected your heart from the contact that despoiled it, that woman could never hate me. A woman must love the mother of the man she loves, and I am your mother. What did I ever seek from your feelings? The place Mme de Vandenesse left empty? Yes, it is true you have always complained about my coldness! Yes, I am *only* your mother. Forgive the harsh words I greeted you with, quite unaware, when you arrived, for a mother should always rejoice to know her son is loved so dearly."

She rested her head on my chest and repeated: "Forgive me, forgive me!"

Then I heard a tone I didn't recognize. It wasn't the young woman's voice, with its joyful rhythms; or the wifely voice, with its tyrannical demands; or the grief-stricken mother's sighs; it was heartbreaking, a new voice for a new sorrow.

"And you, Félix," she continued, now more energetically, "you are the friend who could never do wrong. You have lost no ground in my heart; don't reproach yourself or harbor the slightest remorse. Wasn't it the height of selfishness for me to ask you to sacrifice the greatest pleasures to an impossible future, because a woman must forsake her children, abdicate her rank, and renounce eternity to enjoy them? I have so often found you to be superior to me! You were grand and noble; I was petty and ignoble! Let us agree, it was fated: for you I can only be a cold, glittering light on high that never changes. I only ask, Félix, make sure I am not alone in loving the brother I have chosen. Cherish me! A sister's love should have no difficult moments or unwelcome tomorrows. You never need lie to this indulgent spirit, who will live off your beautiful life and never fail to be afflicted by your pain, who will delight in your bliss and curse every betrayal. I never had a brother I could love like that. Be noble enough to cast off all self-love and reaffirm our bond, that has been so fragile and storm-tossed, through that warm, saintly affection. Then I can live on, and I will begin by being the first to shake the hand of Lady Dudley."

She wasn't crying as she spoke those words full of bitter insights that she used to rent the last veil over her soul and sorrows, revealing the many bonds with which she had tied herself to me and the many sturdy chains I had fractured. We were in such a delirious state we hadn't noticed the rain streaming down.

"Would Madame la Comtesse prefer to take shelter here a while?" asked her coachman, pointing to the main inn of Ballan.

She nodded, and we stayed almost half an hour in its vaulted entrance, much to the astonishment of people in the hostelry, who must have wondered why Mme de Mortsauf was out on the road at eleven at night. Was she going to Tours? Or returning? When the storm abated, when the rain turned into what the people of Tours call *une brouée*, it didn't prevent the moon from lighting up higher mists that gusts of wind soon dispersed, the coachman drove the carriage out and retraced his steps, much to my delight.

"Follow my orders," the countess instructed him quietly.

We took the road across Charlemagne heath, where the rain began to pour down again. Halfway across, I heard Arabella's favorite dog bark; a horse suddenly hurtled out of a clump of oak trees, galloped over the road, jumped the dike dug by the owners to mark out their respective terrain on wasteland judged suitable for farming, the place where Lady Dudley now stationed herself on the heath so she would see our calash ride by.

"It's such a pleasure waiting for one's child like this, when one can do so without committing a crime!" exclaimed Henriette.

The dog's barks had informed Lady Dudley that I was in the carriage; she no doubt concluded that I had come to fetch her because of the bad weather. When we reached the place where she was standing, she flew along the roadside with the cavalier's deftness that is her mark, a feat that filled Henriette with wonder. In a dainty touch, Arabella simply uttered the final syllable of my name, pronouncing it in the English fashion, a summons that on her lips had a fairylike magic. She knew I alone must know the meaning of her shouting "My Dee!"

"He is here, madame," replied the countess, staring in the bright moonlight at that fantastic creature and her impatient face strangely framed by long, loose uncurled hair.

You can imagine how rapidly the two women looked each other up and down. The Englishwoman recognized her rival and reacted in gloriously English style; her gaze withered us with English scorn and she disappeared into the heather, swift as an arrow.

"Head to Clochegourde at once!" shouted the countess, for whom that embittered glance was a hatchet blow to the heart.

The coachman drove back, taking the Chinon road that was preferable to the one from Saché. As our calash sped alongside the heathland, we heard Arabella's horse galloping furiously and her dog padding. All three flew past the woods on the other side of the heather.

"She is leaving, and you will lose her forever," said Henriette.

"So be it," I replied, "let her leave! She will have nothing to regret."

"We women are *so* wretched!" screamed the countess in a horrible outburst. "But where will she go?"

"To Grenadière, a small house near Saint-Cyr," I replied.

"She is leaving by herself," responded Henriette in a tone that told me women feel solidarity in love and never abandon one another.

As we turned into the approach to Clochegourde, Arabella's dog yapped cheerfully, running to meet the calash.

"She got here before us!" exclaimed the countess.

She paused, then continued: "I have never seen a more beautiful woman. What hands! What a waist! Her complexion outdoes any lily and her eyes sparkle like diamonds! And she is a fine horse rider too, and evidently likes expressing her bodily vigor. I think she must be active and headstrong; she defies convention too audaciously: a woman who respects no laws is close to obeying only her own caprices. Women who like to be stars and promote themselves are never granted the gift of constancy. In my book, love requires greater serenity: I've always imagined it to be a vast lake whose bottom can never be sounded, where storms may be violent, but are rare, and contained within insuperable boundaries, where two humans inhabit a flower-bedecked island, far from a society whose outrageous luxury would offend them. But love must adapt to character, if I'm not wrong. If natural features adapt to forms desired by climate, why shouldn't that be the case with individual feelings? No doubt, feelings, which conform to the general law, only vary once they are expressed. Every soul has its style. That English lady is strong, travels long distances, and acts with a man's power; she is someone who would rescue her lover from captivity, killing jailers, guards, and executioners; others can only love with all their souls; when they are in danger, they kneel, pray, and die. Which of these two women do you prefer? That is the question. Yes, of course, the lady loves you, and has sacrificed so much for you. Perhaps she is the one who will love you forever, when you no longer love her?"

"Dear angel, let me repeat what you once said to me: How can you know such things?"

"Each moment of pain teaches us something, and as I have suffered so very much, my knowledge is immense."

My servant thought he'd heard me issue an order. He'd expected we would return via the terraces, and he had my horse at the ready in the approach. Arabella's dog had scented the horse, and, its mistress, driven by a quite legitimate curiosity, had followed it through the woods, where I expect she was now hiding.

"Go and make your peace," said Henriette, with a smile, and without a hint of melancholy. "Tell her how wrong she was about my intentions; I wanted to tell her the true value of the treasure that has fallen to her; my heart holds only good feelings towards her, and certainly not anger or disdain; tell her I am her sister, not her rival."

"I won't go!" I cried.

"Have you never experienced," she asked with a martyr's glowering pride, "how respect can lead to insults? Go to her!"

I ran towards Lady Dudley to find out what state of mind she was in.

If only she would be angry and leave me! I thought, I could return to Clochegourde!

Her dog led me beneath an oak tree that she ran out from behind, shouting: "Away! Away!"

I simply had to follow her to Saint-Cyr, where we arrived at midnight.

"That lady enjoys perfect health," said Arabella, as she dismounted.

Only people who knew her could imagine the sarcasm in that remark she let fly so drily, in a tone that meant: In her situation, I would have died!

"I forbid you to fire one of your three-pointed barbs at Mme de Mortsauf."

"Does it displease Your Grace if I comment on the perfect health enjoyed by someone dear to his precious heart? French women, so they say, hate even the dogs of their lovers; in England, we love everything our sovereign masters love, we hate all they hate, because we live inside the skins of our masters. Allow me to love this lady as much as you love her. Except, dear child," she said, putting her rain-sodden arms around me, "were you to betray me, I wouldn't be stand-ing or supine, in a carriage escorted by lackeys, or walking on Charlemagne heath, or any heaths in any country in the world, or in my bed, or under my parents' roof! I would simply not *be* anymore. I was born in the county of Lancashire, where women die of love. How could I know you and surrender you? I will surrender you to no power in the land, not even to death, because, were that to happen, I would accompany you."

She pulled me into her bedroom, where she'd already languidly flaunted her attractions.

"Love her, my dear," I told her warmly, "she loves you, not in a scoffing way, but sincerely."

"Sincerely, my little lad?" she retorted, unlacing her riding habit.

A vain lover, I tried to depict Henriette's sublime character to that haughty creature. While her maid, who didn't know a word of French, was arranging her hair, I tried to portray Mme de Mortsauf by sketch-ing out her life, repeating the profound thoughts she conceived as a result of a crisis that usually makes women petty and mean. Arabella didn't seem to pay any attention, but she hadn't missed a single word I said.

"I'm delighted," she commented, when we were alone, "to learn of your liking for this kind of Christian conversation. A priest lives on one of my properties and is reputed to be a man who can write a sermon; our peasants understand him: his prose is at the level of his audience. I shall write to my father tomorrow and request he send this fine fellow on the next boat, and we shall meet him in Paris; when you've listened to him once, you will only want to hear more, especially since he too enjoys excellent health. His moral teaching won't disturb you in a way that makes you weep, it flows without tempests, like clear spring water, and induces the most soporific slumber. Every evening, if you wish, you can satisfy your passion for sermons while digesting your supper. English morality, my lad, is as superior to Touraine morality as our cutlery, silverware, and horses are to your knives and livestock. Please do listen to my priest, prom-ise me you will! I am a mere woman, my love, but I know how to love,

I can die for you, if you want, even though I didn't study in Eton, Oxford, or Edinburgh, and couldn't equip you morally. I'm completely unsuited, I'd be found most lacking if I tried. I'm not reproaching your taste; you might have found something even more depraved. I'll try to adapt, because I would like you to find everything you want at hand, the pleasures of love, the pleasures of cuisine, the pleasures of church, fine claret, and Christian virtues. Would you like me to don a hair shirt tonight? Yours truly is always ready to dish up morality! In which university do French women take their grades? Poor me! I have only myself to give, I am but your slave."

"So why did you race off when I wanted to bring you together?"

"Are you crazy, dear Dee? I'd travel from Paris to Rome disguised as a lackey, I'd do the most outlandish things for you, but how can I speak on the open road to a woman who hasn't been introduced to me and who was about to launch into a full-blooded sermon? I will speak to peasants, or if I'm hungry ask a worker to share a crust with me, I'll give him a few guineas, and everything will be as it should be, but it's not part of the rules of *my* game to stop a calash, as gentlemen of the road do in England. Poor child, is to love all you can do? Don't you know how to live too? In any case, I'm not completely like you, my angel— yet! I dislike moralizing. But I'll do my very best for you. Come on, shush, and I will make an attempt. I'll try to be a preacher. In comparison, Jerome will soon seem a buffoon. I will caress no more, without stuffing a verse from the Bible into each caress."

She drew on her every talent; she abused these talents the second she saw desire burn in my eyes as she started on her sorcery. She was all conquering, and I readily agreed that I prized, most of all, beyond Catholic casuistry, the greatness of a woman who ruins herself, renounces the future, and makes a virtue of love.

"So does she love herself more than she loves you?" she asked. "Does she prefer anything that's not you to you? How can we tie ourselves to a different standard than the one we honor you with? No woman, however great a moralist she is, can rival a man. Trample on us, kill us, never soil your existence with us. We must die; you must live, proud and strong. You show us the dagger; we show you love and forgiveness. Does the sun ever worry about the midges that live in its rays? They survive as long as they can; when the sun disappears, they die."

"Or fly away," I interrupted.

"Or fly away," she repeated with an indifference that would have stung a man determined to use the singular power she granted to his kind. "Do really think it dignifies a woman to force a man to swallow slices of toast she has buttered with virtue in an effort to convince him that religion and love are incompatible? Does that make me a heathen? You surrender yourself or refuse yourself, but refusing yourself and occupying the moral high ground is a double sentence against the law of every land. Here, you'll eat only excellent sandwiches prepared by the hand of your servant Arabella, whose moral principles will be to conjure up caresses no man has felt before, that the angels inspire in me."

I can think of nothing more disarming than humor fashioned by an Englishwoman; she lends it her studied eloquence, a veneer of high-minded conviction that the English use to hide the rank stupidity of their prejudices. French humor is a square of lace women use to embellish the bliss they impart and the squabbles they set up; it is a moral adornment as fetching as their elegant attire. But English humor is a corrosive acid that turns the individuals it splashes into skeletons stripped to the bone and washed clean. An Englishwoman's scabrous tongue is like that of a tiger: tearing flesh off the bone in what was meant to be only a game. The almighty weapon of the devil who comes to jeer: "Is that all?" Such sneering deposits fatal poison in the wounds it delights to open. That night Arabella tried to flaunt her powers like a sultan who pleasures in beheading innocents just to prove how powerful he is.

"My angel," she said, after plunging me into that lethargy when all is forgotten, except the ecstasy, "I too have been taking a moral look at myself! I have asked myself if I was committing a crime by loving you, or violating divine law, and I concluded nothing could be more religious or natural. Why would God create some beings more beautiful than others, if it wasn't to tell us to adore them? Not to love you would be a crime; after all, you are an angel, aren't you? That lady insults you when she puts you on a level with other men; morality's rules don't apply to you; God has stationed you above everything. Doesn't loving you bring one closer to Him? How can anyone begrudge a poor woman her hungering for the divine? Your immense, luminous heart is so celestial I stray like a moth flying at party candles that are burning down! Must they be punished for their waywardness? In fact, are they wayward? Aren't they simply worshipping the light? They perish due to religious excess, if to perish is to throw oneself around the neck of one's beloved. My weakness is my love for you, whereas that woman has the fortitude to stay in her Catholic chapel. Don't frown! Do you think I begrudge her? Not at all, my love! I adore her moralizing that instructed her to leave you to roam freely and thus allow me to conquer and keep you forever, because you are mine forever, aren't you?"

"Yes."

"Forever and ever?"

"Yes."

"Then will you grant me one more favor, my sultan? Only I have grasped your true worth! You say, she knows how to cultivate her land? Well, I'll leave such knowledge to farmers, as I prefer to cultivate your heart."

I am trying to recall her enervating sallies and paint an accurate picture of this woman, to illustrate what I've said about her and to enable you to intuit the way that it all will unravel. But how can I possibly describe the way she accompanied her pretty words? It was madness comparable to the most extraordinary fantasies in our dreams, artifacts like my bouquets: grace allied with strength, smoldering, languid tenderness followed by volcanic eruptions of passion; subtlest musical crescendos brought to the concert of our sensual delight; games as played by squirming, entangled snakes; climaxing in the most deliquescent utterances spiced with the finest wit, all the poetry a mind can bring to the pleasure of the senses. The thunderbolts of her impetuous love aimed to obliterate every trace in my heart of

Henriette's chaste serenity. Lady Dudley had perceived the countess as clearly as Mme de Mortsauf had observed her, and they had both judged soundly.

Arabella's inordinate onslaught showed me how much she feared and even secretly admired her rival. In the morning, I awoke to her tears; she hadn't slept.

"What's wrong?" I asked.

"I'm afraid the intensity of my love will do me harm," she replied. "I've given everything. That woman is more adept than I, and possesses an inner quality you still desire. If you'd rather, stop thinking about me; I won't bother you with my grief, remorse, or suffering, and will go to die far away, like a plant deprived of its life-giving sun."

She succeeded in coaxing declarations of love from me that filled her with bliss. I ask, what *does* one say to a woman who wakes up weeping the next morning? Harsh words would be unforgivable. If we didn't resist her the previous night, aren't we obliged to lie the morning after—the male code of gallantry makes deceit a duty.

"In any case, I'm generous," she said, wiping away her tears, "go back to her, I don't want you because of the strength of my love, but because it is your own will. If you come back, I'll believe you love me as much as I love you, something I've always thought quite impossible."

She convinced me to return to Clochegourde. Only a man gorged on passion could have grasped the dilemma I had contrived for myself. By refusing to go to Clochegourde, I'd be deciding on Lady Dudley rather than Henriette. Arabella would take me to Paris. But if I went, wouldn't I be insulting Mme de Mortsauf? In that case, I should return even more confidently to Arabella. Has a woman ever forgiven such crimes of *lèse-amour*? Unless she is an angel descended from heaven, and not a purified spirit ascending there, a woman in love would prefer to see her beloved in agony than to see him made happy by another woman: the more she loves, the more she will feel her wounds. Seen from either perspective, once I had left Clochegourde to go to La Grenadière, my position was as fatal to my chosen love as it favored my haphazard love. Milady had coldly calculated everything. She later confessed that, if Mme de Mortsauf hadn't met her on the heath, she had planned to compromise me by prowling around Cloche-gourde.

When I approached the countess—who was pale and downcast, as if she'd experienced the worst of sleepless nights—I deployed not tact but that instinct which makes hearts that are still young and generous feel the force of deeds that go unperceived by the crowd, but that are criminal according to the laws noble souls like to decree. Immediately, like a child who has slipped down into an abyss when playfully gathering flowers and can see no way out, knowing that human terrain is an impossible distance away, and feels alone at night listening to the screeching in the wild, I understood that a whole world had come between us. A dreadful clamor arose from both our souls, an echo of the lugubrious *Consummatum est!* proclaimed in churches on Good Friday, when our Savior expires, a horrendous scene that freezes young souls for whom religion is their first love. All Henriette's expectations were dashed at a stroke; her heart had suffered its passion. Respected by pleasures that had never wrapped her in their numbing folds, was she imagining the sensuous charms of blissful love, as she averted her gaze from mine? Because she'd deprived me of the light that had illuminated my life for the last six years, had she recognized that the source of the rays pouring from our eyes was to be found in our souls, where they served as the path to penetrate each other or to meld us into a single, separate being, or to enable us to play like two trusting women, prepared to tell each other everything? I felt remorseful: I had erred by bringing under this roof, one that had never known caresses, a countenance where wings of pleasure had scattered their mottled dust. If, on the previous evening, I had allowed Lady Dudley to leave by herself; if I had returned to Clochegourde, where Henriette was perhaps waiting for me; perhaps . . . in the end, perhaps Mme de Mortsauf wouldn't have suggested so cruelly that she should be my sister. She lent her dutiful ways a surfeit of visibility, she assumed her role wholeheartedly so that she could never abandon it. During breakfast, she was attentive to my wishes, to a humiliating degree, and treated me like an invalid who was to be pitied.

"You've been for an early-morning walk," said the count, "you must be starving, after all, that stomach of yours is still in one piece!"

His statement didn't arouse a knowing, sisterly smile on the countess's lips, and only confirmed how ridiculous my position was. It was impossible to be in Clochegourde by day, and Saint-Cyr by night. Arabella had counted on my susceptibilities and Mme de Mortsauf's nobility of soul. Throughout that long day, I felt how difficult it was to become the mere friend of a woman you have desired for so long. Such a transition might be straightforward if it were the fruit of years of preparation, but it's more like a malady while one is young. I was ashamed, I cursed my recourse to pleasure, I would have preferred for Mme de Mortsauf to have demanded my blood. I would have torn her rival to shreds, but she didn't even mention her; and if I had slandered Arabella, it would only have earned me Henriette's contempt, so noble was she, even in the deepest recesses of her heart. After five years of delightful intimacy, we couldn't think of anything to say now; our words masked our thoughts; we concealed our desperate pain, which we'd always seen as a faithful guide. Henriette affected to be happy in herself and with me, but she was sad. Although she kept saying she was my sister, and although she was a woman, she wasn't of a mind to brighten our conversation, and we suffered in silence for most of the time. She deepened my anguish, by pretending to vaunt herself as Lady Dudley's only victim.

"I sorrow more than you," I remarked when she let slip a very female irony.

"How can that be?" she answered in that haughty tone women adopt when you try to ruffle their feelings.

"All the wrongs were inflicted on me."

The countess had become cold and indifferent, and it broke my heart: I decided to leave. That evening I said my farewells to the family, who were gathered on the terrace. They all followed me to the lawn, where my horse was pawing the ground, and then they all withdrew. She came over when I seized the bridle.

"Let's walk alone to the approach."

I gave her my arm, and we walked slowly through the farmyards, as if savoring our every step in tandem; we reached a clump of trees at a corner of the outer enclosure.

"Farewell, my friend!" she said, stopping, and she threw her head at my heart and her arms around my neck. "Farewell, this is the last time we shall meet! God has granted me the sad power to see into the future. Don't you remember how terrified I was the day you came here, looking so young and handsome, and I saw you turn your back on me, just as you are going to leave Clochegourde today and go to La Grenadière? Well, last night I caught a glimpse of our destinies once again. My friend, this is the last time we shall speak. Even now I can find few words to say, because it is not my whole self any longer that speaks to you. Death has already killed something within me. You will have deprived my children of their mother; replace her by their side! You can! Jacques and Madeleine love you as if you had always made them suffer."

"You are dying!" I cried in horror, watching dry fire burn in gleaming eyes that you can describe only to someone who has never seen their own beloved stricken by that horrible infirmity by comparing these eyes to globes of burnished silver. "You are dying! Henriette, I insist you live. You once asked me to make a pledge, and now I'd asking you make one: swear to consult Origet and obey his every instruction."

"So you are set on defying God's mercy?" she asked, with a cry of despair, angry to be spurned.

"Isn't your love strong enough to obey me blindly in everything, like that other wretched lady?"

"Yes, whatever you ask," she replied in a fit of jealousy that led her in a second to cross distances she'd respected until then.

"I will stay," I reacted, kissing her eyes.

Frightened by my relapse, she fled from my arms and leaned against a tree; then rushed towards her house, never looking back; I followed; she wept and prayed. When we reached the lawn, I took her hand and kissed it respectfully. My unexpected gesture moved her.

"I am yours, after all!" I added, "I love you—as your aunt loved you."

She gave a start and squeezed my hand.

"A glance!" I shouted, "a glance from our past! A woman surrendering herself completely!"—and I felt my soul was illuminated by her gaze—"gives less of her life and soul than you just granted me. Henriette, you are the one I love most, the only one I love."

"I will live!" she replied, "but you too must heal yourself."

Her look had erased all traces of Arabella's sarcasm. I was the plaything of the two irreconcilable passions I have described, and whose influences I had experienced in succession. I loved an angel and a demon; two equally beautiful women, one blessed with all the virtues we cast down because we hate our own imperfections, the other blessed with all the vices we venerate out of selfishness. As I walked down the approach, I occasionally turned my head to catch another sight of Mme de Mortsauf leaning against a tree, surrounded by her children, who waved their handkerchiefs; I was filled with pride to know I was the arbiter of two such beautiful fates and had been the glory, for very different reasons, of such exalted women, inspiring such great passions that death would come to either one if I were to fail her. My moment of fatuousness was punished twice, as you can imagine! I don't know what devil told me to wait by Arabella's side until either despair or the count's death released Henriette to me, because Henriette still loved me: her strictures, tears, remorse, and Christian resignation were eloquent traces of a feeling that could no longer be erased from her heart or mine. As I walked along that pretty avenue, I reflected that I no longer felt twenty-five years old, but fifty. Isn't it really young men, rather than women, who go from thirty to sixty at a stroke? Although I resisted those morose thoughts, they obsessed me, I have to admit! Perhaps they'd begun in the Tuileries under the paneled ceiling of the royal chambers. Who could deny Louis XVIII's withering ways, the man who said that one experiences real passion in one's mature years, because passion can rage and be beautiful only when it is mingled with impotence, and one faces each new pleasure like a gambler staking his final wager? When I was at the end of the approach, I looked around, blinked, and walked back to Henriette, who was still lingering there alone. I went to say a last goodbye, dampened by tears of atonement whose reason I hid from her. Sincere tears, granted unknowingly to a beautiful love that was lost forever, to innocent emotion, to flowers of life that would never bloom again, because later in life, a man doesn't give more of himself, he receives; he loves himself in his mistress; when young, he loves his mistress within himself: later, we may perhaps introduce the woman we love to our likes and vices; although initially, we like the one we love to impose her virtues and subtlety on us: her smile invites us to explore beauty; her example teaches us devotion. Unhappy the man who hasn't met his Henriette! Unhappy the man who hasn't encountered his Lady Dudley! If he marries, one won't keep his wife, another may be abandoned by his mistress, but blessed be the man who finds both in one; Natalie, blessed is the man who loves you!

On our return to Paris, Arabella and I became much closer. We soon abolished the laws of convenience I'd imposed on myself, the strict observation of which usually led high society to forgive the artificial situation Lady Dudley found herself in. Society, that so loves to penetrate behind appearances, gives its stamp of approval as soon as it knows the secrets they hide. Lovers forced to live in the bosom of high society will always err if they overthrow the barriers required by drawing-room legislators, and they will err if they don't scrupulously obey the conventions custom enforces; this is less for the sake of others than it is for the lovers themselves. The distances to negotiate, the external respect to maintain, the roles to play, the mysteries to shroud, that whole tragedy of blissful love occupies life, refreshes desire, and protects hearts against loosening habits. Nevertheless, first passions, like young people, are essentially profligate, and will raze their forests rather than steward the land. Arabella didn't adopt these bourgeois ideas, she *adapted* to them to please me; like an executioner selecting his victim in advance in order to appropriate him, she wanted to compromise me before all of Paris and make me her *sposo*. And she used all her flirtatious wiles to bind me to her household, because she delighted in an elegant scandal that, in the absence of evidence, only encourages gossip whispered behind fans. When I saw her so ready to be rash and openly flaunt her state, how could I not have believed in her love?

Once immersed in the sweet pleasures of an illicit union, I despaired to see my life set on a course contrary to Henriette's ideas and advice. I raged like a consumptive who anticipates his demise and refuses to let anyone check his lungs. There was a corner of my heart I could withdraw to without suffering, but a vengeful spirit kept hurtling ideas in my direction I dared not contemplate. My letters to Henriette described my sickly moral dilemma, and caused her unimaginable pain. "In exchange for so much treasure lost, at the very least I want you to be happy!" But I wasn't! Natalie, happiness is absolute and brooks no comparisons. After the first ardors had passed, I inevitably compared the two women, something I hadn't been able to contemplate before. To be frank, every grand passion influences our character so much, at first by concealing rough edges and submerging the traces of habits that constitute our faults and our good qualities, but, later, when the two lovers have grown accustomed to each other, the components of their moral makeup rise to the surface; both pass judgment on the other, and often, when character dissects passion, divergences stand out and become the impasses the frivolous use to accuse the heart of fickleness. That phase began. Less spellbound by her seductive ploys, and, as it were, itemizing my pleasures, albeit reluctantly, I now embarked on an analysis that was to the detriment of Lady Dudley.

First I found she lacked the spirit that distinguishes French women from all others and makes them more delightful to love, according to the views of people whose lives have happened to give them the opportunity to experience the ways of love in different countries. When a Frenchwoman loves, she undergoes a metamorphosis; she devotes her famed flirtatiousness to gilding her love; she sacrifices her dangerous vanity and concentrates on refining her beloved. She espouses her lover's interests, hates, and friendships; in a day she acquires the insights of an experienced businessman, studies the law, understands credit and rivals a banker in her financial knowledge;

inspired and prodigal, she won't take a single wrong step, or waste a single louis; she becomes mother, governess, and doctor, endows all her changes with utmost grace, revealing her infinite love in the tiniest detail; she combines the special qualities upheld by women from each country and gives to that mix a unity of purpose, that French spark that drives, ratifies, justifies, and varies everything, eliminating the monotony of feeling that depends on the first tense of a single verb. A Frenchwoman loves always, never relents, never wearies at any time, whether it be alone or in public; in public, she finds an accent that resonates in one ear alone, her silence is eloquent, and she knows how to see you with lowered eyes; if the occasion prevents her from speaking or looking, her foot leaves its mark and writes a thought in the sand; only she can communicate passion even when she is sleeping; in a word, she bends the world to her love.

Quite to the contrary, an Englishwoman bends her love to the world. Trained by her upbringing to maintain a frosty attitude, the egotistical British self-control I mentioned before, she opens and shuts her heart with the facility of an English flush toilet. She possesses an impenetrable mask that she dons and removes phlegmatically; passionate as any Italian woman when nobody is looking, she becomes coldly dignified the moment company is at hand. A very loved man will begin to doubt his powers when he perceives the blank expression, modulated tone, and immaculate self-control that distinguishes an Englishwoman who has just walked out of her boudoir. At that point, hypocrisy verges on indifference; the Englishwoman has forgotten everything. Obviously, a woman who casts love off as easily as a dress gives one the impression that she could change altogether. What storms then stir waves in a heart whose self-esteem has been wounded by the sight of a woman who takes her love, puts it down, and picks it back up, as if it were a tapestry she were sewing! Such a woman is too much her own mistress to really belong to you; she grants society too much power for your own rule to compete. While a Frenchwoman's glance consoles a love-stricken man, and she inflicts her anger on visitors with a few sarcastic barbs, an Englishwoman's silence is absolute; it rocks the soul and offends the mind. Those women are imperious all the time, and most of them believe all-conquering fashion should extend to their pleasures. Whoever exaggerates tact must exaggerate love, and that sums up Englishwomen, who subject everything to form, but whose love of form never creates a feeling for art: whatever beliefs they profess, Protestantism and Catholicism are behind the differences that make a Frenchwoman's soul so superior to the calculated, premeditated love of an Englishwoman. Protestantism doubts, scrutinizes, and kills belief: it is the death of art and of love.

When society dictates, the inhabitants of that world must obey, but passionate individuals flee there as soon as they can; they find it intolerable. You will now understand why my self-esteem sank so low when I saw how Lady Dudley couldn't exist without society, and that she was so accustomed to the British way of moving on: it was no sacrifice imposed on her by society. That was not the case at all, she naturally embraced both contrary forms; when she loved, she loved to the point of inebriation; no woman from any country could compete, she was a match for any harem, but when the curtain fell on that fairylike scenario, it banished even the memory of it. She reacted to neither a smile nor a glance; she was neither mistress nor slave; she was like an ambassador compelled to soften her words and her gestures; her serenity was annoying, her decorum outraged your feelings; she swallowed her love to suit her needs, rather than raise it enthusiastically to the level of an ideal. She expressed no fear, no regrets, no desire, but when the time came, her tenderness flamed like a fire that had been suddenly lit and seemed to mock her previous restraint. Which of these two women was I to believe?

I felt the infinite differences that separated Henriette from Arabella in a thousand pinpricks. When Mme de Mortsauf departed for a moment, she left me with a need to talk to myself about her; as she did so, the folds of her dress appealed to my eyes, then they sweetly rustled and fluttered in my ears when she returned; she lowered her eyelids with infinite tenderness when she looked down; her voice, its musicality, was a constant caress; the words flowing to her lips were evidence of steadfast thought; she was always her same self; she didn't split her soul into two zones, one fiery, the other icy; in short, Mme de Mortsauf reserved her mind, with its wealth of thought, for expressing her feelings and she playfully tried out her ideas on her children and me. But Arabella's purpose wasn't to make life pleasant, and she never exercised her wit to my advantage; it only existed through and on behalf of society, she was pure, destructive mockery; she liked to rip and tear, not to amuse herself, but to satisfy a taste for it. Mme de Mortsauf worked to spare her happiness the scrutiny of all and sundry, while Lady Arabella wanted to show hers to all of Paris, and with ghastly artifice, she kept to all strictures of decorum while parading around with me in the Bois de Boulogne. Her blend of ostentation and worthiness, of love and iciness, continuously wounded my feelings that were at once pristine and passionate, and as I couldn't shift from one zone to another, my mood was affected; I would be aflame with passion and she would relapse into prurient restraint.

When I tried to complain, using the utmost circumspection, she turned her three-pronged darts against me, boasting about her passionate lovemaking and using the English style of humor I've tried to describe. The moment she engaged in argument, she toyed with my feelings and humiliated my intellect, kneading me like a piece of dough. When I remarked on the golden mean that one should observe in everything, she caricatured my ideas by exaggerating them. When I criticized her attitude, she asked me if I wanted her to kiss me in the presence of all of Paris, at the Italiens; she suggested it so earnestly that, knowing how she liked to be the center of attention, I cringed at the thought she might carry out her promise. Despite her very real passion, I never found any of Henriette's serenity, saintliness, and depth: she was always as insatiable as sandy soil. Mme de Mortsauf was always self-assured and sensed my feeling in an inflection or glance, while the English lady was never overwhelmed by a gaze, a hand squeezing hers, or a word of love. And that's the least of it! Last night's ecstasy would be gone by the morning; no proof of love took her by surprise; she felt such a need for turmoil, for the outlandish and the excessive, that nothing could rival her beautiful ideal in that vein, and one could only fan her furious striving after love; she, not

I, was always the epicenter of her wild fantasies. That letter from Mme de Mortsauf, a light that still shone in my life, revealed how even the most virtuous wife could obey the nature of French women, by exercising perpetual oversight and insight in respect to every twist of my fate; that letter must surely have given you a sense of how carefully Henriette cultivated my material interests, political contacts, and moral progress, the enthusiasm with which she embraced my life in every legitimate sphere. In all these matters, Lady Dudley adopted the aloofness of a mere acquaintance. She never inquired after my business affairs, my success, my work, my difficulties in life, my male hatreds or friendships. Lavish toward herself, she was never generous, she liked to demarcate too sharply between her own self-interest and her love; conversely, though I never tested this out, I knew Henriette would have sought for me what she would never have sought for herself, if it would spare me an upset. If I had ever been trapped in a plight that affected the richest and highest-ranking individual—and history is full of such plights—I would have appealed to Henriette, but it would be better to be locked in jail than to say a word to Lady Dudley.

Thus far, this contrast relates to feelings, but it was no different in the realm of material things. In France, luxury is the man, the embodiment of his ideas and a special poetry; it expresses character and, where lovers are concerned, values the tiniest feature by making the central focus whatever love shines on within us, but English luxuriousness and its exquisite refinements that had seduced me were solely mechanical! Lady Dudley put nothing of herself there; it was all the work of others, it was bought in. In Arabella's eyes Clochegourde's delightful attentiveness was down to the servants; each had their area of duty and expertise. Choosing the best domestic staff was the butler's responsibility, as if the servants were horses. She felt nothing for her staff, and the death of the most precious one of them wouldn't have moved her a jot; the servant would have been replaced at market cost by someone else equally adept. As for her neighbors, I never caught her shedding a tear over their misfortunes; she possessed a naive selfishness that was absolutely laughable. The red drapes of the grand lady covered a hard metallic interior. The desirable dancer cavorting on her rugs in the evening, tinkling all the bells of amorous folly, soon won a young man over to that hard, insensitive English-woman, and I realized only gradually that the volcanic terrain where I scattered my seed was never going to produce a harvest. Mme de Mortsauf plumbed her character at a glance; I recall her prophetic words. Henriette was correct on every front; Arabella's love would become unbearable. I've since noticed that most women equestrians lack feeling. Like Amazons, they are short of a breast, and have hardened a place somewhere in their hearts.

When I began to feel the weight of those chains, when fatigue overcame my body and soul, when I understood the saintliness true sentiment brings to love, and when I was overwhelmed by memories of Clochegourde and inhaled, despite the distance, the scent of its roses, the warmth of its terrace, even heard the song of its nightingales, at that horrible moment when I had seen the stony bed of the stream once its flow had diminished, it was then that I was struck by a blow that still resonates: It echoes with every hour that passes. I was working in the office of the king, who was to leave at four o'clock; the Duc de Lenoncourt was out on duty; when the king saw him return, he asked after the countess; I looked up too purposefully; shocked by my reaction, the king glanced at me the way he does to precede the harsh words he was adept at voicing.

"Sire, my poor daughter is dying," replied the duke.

"Would the king deign to give me leave?" I asked, tears welling, defying the anger that was about to explode.

"Run, *my lord*!" he replied, striving to turn each word into a witty epigram and spare me his reprimand.

More courtier than father, the duke didn't ask for leave and he climbed into the king's carriage to provide him with company. I left without saying goodbye to Lady Dudley, who luckily had gone out, and I left her a note to the effect that I was away on a mission for the king. In Croix-de-Berny I met His Majesty returning from Verrières. While accepting a bouquet of flowers that he then dropped at his feet, the king gave me one of his regally ironic, deeply meaningful looks, as if to say: "If you want a future in politics, come back now! Don't waste time chatting with the dead!" The duke waved gloomily. Both pompous eight-horse calashes, along with the gilded colonels, the retinue's escort, and their clouds of dust, rushed by, to cries of "Vive le roi!" I felt the court had ridden roughshod over Mme de Mortsauf's body, as ruthlessly as nature ignores our disasters. Although a fine man, the duke would no doubt play a round of long whist, after the king had retired to bed. As for the duchess, she had long since dealt her daughter the initial blow when she had told her about Lady Dudley.

My journey went quickly enough, like a dream, but it was the dream of a bankrupted gambler. I despaired that I had received no news from Clochegourde. Had her confessor been so strict as to forbid my entry to Clochegourde? I blamed Madeleine, Jacques, Abbé de Dominis, everyone, even M. de Mortsauf. Past Tours, crossing the Saint-Sauveur bridges and turning down the poplar-lined road to Poncher that I'd so admired when I'd run in search of my unknown love, I bumped into M. Origet; he guessed I was on my way to Clochegourde, I guessed he was returning from there; we both halted our carriages and alighted: I wanted his news and he wanted to give me his latest prognosis.

"So then, how is Mme de Mortsauf?" I asked.

"I doubt you'll find her alive," he replied. "She's dying a horrible death: she is starving to death. When she summoned me last June, no medical knowledge could fight her illness; she showed the gruesome symptoms I'm sure M. de Mortsauf will have described to you, because he believed he himself was suffering from them. Madame la Comtesse wasn't the victim of some passing upset prompted by inner turmoil, one that medicine can control and allow for an improved state of health, nor had she been felled by a sudden disease, with damage that can be repaired; no, her illness had reached that stage where medical art is futile: it was the incurable consequence of her anguish, as lethal as injuries from a dagger's thrust. This affliction is created by the inertia of an organ that is as vital to the body as it is to the heart. Sadness has done the dagger's job. Don't deceive yourself! Mme de Mortsauf is dying from some mysterious malady."

"'Mysterious?'" I repeated. "Have her children been ill?"

"No," he replied, looking at me meaningfully, "and, from the moment she became seriously ill, M. de Mortsauf stopped tormenting her. I can do no more. M. Delandes, from Azay, will suffice; there's no remedy, and she is in horrendous pain. Rich, young, and beautiful, she will die emaciated, aged by hunger, for she is going to starve to death! For forty days her stomach has apparently closed up and rejected any food, in whatever shape or form it is offered."

M. Origet shook the hand I held out, which he'd almost asked for, in a show of respect.

"Steel yourself, monsieur!" he exclaimed, raising his eyes to the heavens.

His words expressed compassion for a pain he thought we shared equally; he couldn't imagine they were poisoned darts that pierced my heart. I climbed brusquely back into my carriage and promised the coachman a handsome reward if we arrived in good time.

Although I was feeling desperately impatient, we seemed to cover the ground in a few minutes because I was so absorbed by the bitter reflections pounding my brain. She is dying of sorrow, and her children are well! So she must be dying because of *me*! My glowering conscience issued an ominous indictment that would echo throughout my life and probably beyond. Human justice is so weak and impotent! It avenges only acts that are there for all to see. Why are death and shame reserved for a murderer who kills with one blow, who generously catches you asleep and puts you eternally to rest, or strikes out of the blue and spares you a death agony? Why are a life of happiness and esteem granted to a murderer who pours his bile drop by drop into another's soul and undermines her body to the point of destruction? So many murders unpunished! So much leniency for such an elegant vice! So many acquittals for homicides wrought by moral persecution!

I don't know what vengeful hand suddenly raised the painted

curtain that cloaks society. I saw several victims of that kind, ones you are as familiar with as I am: the dying Mme de Beauséant, who departed for Normandy a few days before I did, the compromising of the Duchesse de Langeais; Lady Brandon, who came to the Touraine to die in that humble abode where Lady Dudley stayed for two weeks, where she met such a horrible death, killed in the manner you know! Our era is awash in that kind of incident. Who didn't know about that wretched young woman who poisoned herself, distraught by the jealousy that was perhaps killing Mme de Mortsauf? Who didn't shudder at the fate of that delightful young woman who, like a flower eaten away by a horsefly, withered over two years of marriage, victim of the hateful Ronquerolles, with Montriveau and de Marsay lending a hand because it suited their political agenda? Who didn't shiver when they heard the tale of the final moments of that woman no prayer could destroy, who refused to see her husband after so nobly paying off his debts? Wasn't Mme d'Aiglement within an inch of the grave, and would she have survived without my brother's loving care?

Society and science are complicit in these crimes for which there are no courts of law. Apparently nobody dies of sorrow, of despair, of love, of hidden misery, or of expectations that are nurtured in vain, then continuously resown and uprooted. The new nomenclature finds clever words to explain everything: gastritis, pericarditis, a thousand female maladies, their labels whispered in the ear, passports to coffins attended by hypocritical tears the hand of a notary soon wipes away. Is there a law unknown to us at the heart of all this misfortune? Must a person who lives to be one hundred years old pitilessly strew the terrain with corpses and thus refertilize it around himself so he might rise up again, as a millionaire takes over the enterprise of a multitude of small industries? Does a potent, poisonous organism exist that feasts on tender, loving souls? My God, do I belong to a race of tigers?

The corrosive fingers of remorse gripped my heart, tears streaming down my cheeks when I entered the approach to Clochegourde on a damp October morning that was taking the dead autumn leaves from the poplars Henriette had planted along this avenue, where not too long ago she had waved her handkerchief as if wanting to summon me back. Was she still alive? Would I feel her two white hands on my bowed head? In a single moment I paid for all the pleasure Arabella ever gave me, and found the purchase price extortionate! I swore never to see her again, and hated England. Though Lady Dudley is only one variety of the species, I swathed all English women in the mourning bands of my curses.

When I entered Clochegourde, I received another brutal blow. I saw Jacques, Madeleine, and Abbé de Dominis kneeling at the foot of a wooden cross on a piece of fenced-off land within the enclosure. Neither the count nor the countess had ever wanted to remove it. I jumped down from my carriage and raced toward them, tears flowing down my cheeks: the sight of the two children and that solemn figure imploring God broke my heart. The old groom was there too, standing a few feet away, head bared.

"Well, monsieur?" I asked Abbé de Dominis as I kissed the foreheads of Jacques and Madeleine, who gave me frosty looks and didn't break off their prayers.

The abbot stood up, and I leaned on his arm as I asked: "Is she still alive?"

He nodded his head, gently, sadly.

"Say something, I beg you, in the name of the suffering of our Lord! Why are you praying at the foot of this cross? Why are you here and not by her bedside? Why are the children outside on such a cold morning? Tell me, before I do something hurtful out of ignorance."

"Over the last few days Mme la Comtesse has stipulated she only wanted to see her children at certain agreed times."

"Monsieur," he continued after a pause, "perhaps you ought to wait for several hours before seeing Mme de Mortsauf again; she is greatly changed! It would only be right to prepare such a meeting properly, you might cause her pain to deepen ... And death would be a blessed relief."

I gripped the hand of a holy man whose gaze and voice always soothed, never exacerbated the grief of others.

"We all pray for her here," he continued, "because she is so saintly, so resigned, and so ready to die, although more recently she has shown a secret horror of death. For the first time, she glances at people enjoying life to the full in a manner that bristles with somber, envious sentiment. I believe her dizzy spells are caused less by her fear of death than they are by some inner intoxication, by faded flowers of youth fermenting as they wither. Yes, the angel of evil is fighting heaven over this beautiful soul. Madame is engaged in the conflict of the Mount of Olives, her tears accompany the white roses that wreathed married Jephthah's head as they fall one by one.[24] Please wait, don't go to her yet. You would bring to her the bright lights of court and she would see the social whirl reflected on your face and that would only reinforce her rancor. Show pity towards a weakness God Himself forgave in His son who had become a man. Besides, what merit would victory have if there were no adversary? Allow her confessor or me, two old men whose decrepitude does not offend her eyes, to prepare the way for this unforeseen encounter and emotions Abbé Birotteau has asked her to renounce. In my case, the things of this world are invisibly threaded by celestial causation only a religious eye can perceive, and, if you have come, perhaps you were summoned by one of those heavenly stars that shine in the moral sphere and can lead to the tomb and to the cradle."

He then informed me, employing mellifluous eloquence that descends like the dew on one's feelings, that the countess had been in steadily worsening pain over the last six months, despite all the attentions of M. Origet. The doctor had visited Clochegourde every evening for two months, striving to rescue that prey from death, because the countess had said, "Save me!"

"But to cure the body, the heart must first find a cure!" the old doctor had exclaimed one day.

"As her health deteriorated, that sweet woman's words became more embittered," Abbé de Dominis went on. "She implores the earth to hold on to her rather than beseeching God to take her; then repents for speaking against decrees from above. The twists and turns tearing her heart unleash a horrendous struggle between body and soul. And often the body triumphs! 'You cost me so dearly!' she told Madeleine and Jacques one day, pushing them away from her bedside. But, immediately, restored to God by sight of me, she whispered angelically to Mlle Madeleine: 'The happiness of others becomes the happiness of those who no longer hope to be happy.' Her tone was so anguished I felt my eyelids moisten. Truly, she is prone to falter, but with each false step, she climbs back closer to heaven."

Struck hard by a series of messages that I'd received by chance, whose painful harmonies prepared the entry of a funeral theme in that great concerto of misfortune, a dying love's last cry, I exclaimed: "Do you believe this beautiful severed lily will flower anew in heaven?"

"When you left her, she was still a flower," he replied; "now you will find she is diminished, purified by pain's fires, a pure diamond still glinting in the ash. Yes, this beautiful spirit, this angelic star, will emerge resplendent from these clouds and enter the kingdom of light."

I gripped the saintly man's hand, my apprehension dimmed by gratitude, as the count stuck his gray head out of the house, and rushed towards me at a pace that denoted his surprise.

"She was right! He *is* here. 'Félix, Félix is on his way!' Mme de Mortsauf had exclaimed. "My friend," he went on, glaring at me, "Death is with us. Why didn't he take an old fool like me, whom he'd already paid a visit . . . ?"

I walked towards their mansion, summoning my courage, but was then halted by Abbé Birotteau on the threshold of the long gallery that crossed the house from the lawn to the terrace steps.

"Mme la Comtesse begs you not go in yet," he warned me.

I glanced inside and saw the servants coming and going, all very busy, grief-stricken, and no doubt shocked by the orders Manette was issuing.

"What *is* the matter?" asked the count, startled by the hectic bustle, as much from fear of their potentially horrible cause as from his natural tendency to worry.

"The whims of the sick," replied the abbot. "Mme la Comtesse doesn't want to see M. le Vicomte in her present state; she wants to dress, and who are we to say she shouldn't?"

Manette fetched Madeleine, and a few moments later we saw

Madeleine leave after having gone in to her mother. The five of us—
Jacques and his father, the two abbots, and I—silently walked on the
lawn along the front of the mansion and beyond. I gazed in turn at
Montbazon and Azay, and the yellowing valley whose mourning tints
responded as ever to the emotions I was struggling to control. I suddenly spotted the young child running to find autumn flowers and
picking some, I assumed, to make bouquets. As I thought of things
that reiteration of my loving care evoked, I felt a strange turn in my
belly, I staggered, my vision clouded, and the two abbots, walking on
either side, carried me to the edge of a terrace, where I rested a moment as if I'd fainted, though I never completely lost consciousness.

"Poor Félix," said the count, "she vigorously forbade us to write,
she knows how much you love her!"

Although I was prepared to suffer, I couldn't find the strength to
confront a landscape that held all my memories of happiness.

There it is, I reflected, that heath, dry and bare like a skeleton in
the gray light of day, in the center of which stood a single flowering
bush, that on previous promenades I had never admired without
shuddering ominously: It was the image for this hour of gloom!

Everything was lugubrious in a mansion that was once so lively!
Everything wept, everything spoke of despair and neglect. There were
half-raked paths, work begun and abandoned, laborers standing and
staring at the house. Though the vineyards had been tended, there
was no noise or chatter. The fields seemed uninhabited, the silence
was so profound. We walked like people whose grief rejects commonplace words, and we listened to the count, the only one of us who
talked. After sentences dictated by the mechanical love he felt towards
his wife, the count was again driven by his inclination to gripe about
the countess. She had always refused to look after herself or to listen
to him when he gave good advice; he'd spotted the first symptoms of
the illness, because he'd studied them in himself, fought them, and
cured himself, helped by only diet and the avoidance of strong emotions. He could have cured the countess in the same way, but a husband
couldn't take that responsibility on his shoulders, especially when he
was unfortunate enough to see his experience scorned at every stage

as the illness advanced. Despite his objections, the countess had engaged Origet as her physician. Origet, who'd cared for him so poorly, was now killing his wife. If one cause of that illness was a surfeit of sorrow, he'd have been in a better position to be struck down by it, but what sorrow could his wife have ever suffered? The countess was happy; she had no troubles or grave concerns. Thanks to his diligence and clear thinking, their finances were in a satisfactory state; he let Mme de Mortsauf rule over Clochegourde; his well-reared children behaved and were no cause for concern; what could ever have given her harm? And he rattled on, mixing expressions of his own despair with foolish accusations. Then, when a memory suddenly reminded him of the admiration that noble soul inspired, a few tears escaped his eyes, which had been dry so long.

Madeleine came to inform me that her mother was expecting me. Abbé Birotteau followed me. The stern daughter stayed with her father, saying the countess wanted to be alone with me, using as her excuse that she would find the presence of several people exhausting. The gravity of the moment created that feeling of inner warmth and outer chill within me that can be crushing at pivotal times in life. Abbé Birotteau, a man God has marked as His own by investing him with charm and simplicity, and granting him patience and charity, took me to one side.

"Monsieur," he said, "you ought to know I have done all that was humanly possible to prevent this meeting from taking place. That was what the health of this saint truly required. I considered only her, never you. Now you are going to see this woman, access to whom the angels should have denied you, I should tell you that I shall remain between the two of you, to defend her against you, and even against herself! Respect her fragility. It is not as a priest that I ask you to show her understanding, but as a humble friend you were not aware of, one who would like to spare you remorse. Our beloved patient is dying of hunger and thirst. This morning she has been visited by the waves of fever that precede a horrible death, and I cannot hide from you how much she regrets her life. The cries from her rebel flesh fade to silence in my heart, though they still hurt with echoes that are too tender. However, M. de Dominis and I accepted this religious task in order to conceal the spectacle of her moral agony from a noble family that no longer recognizes their beautiful morning and evening star, because husband, children, and servants all ask: 'Where is she?' the changes in her are so great. When you appear, she will start complaining again. Abandon any thoughts as a man of society, forget the vanities of the heart, be at her side as a helper from heaven, not one from earth. Don't let this saint die doubting and uttering words of despair."

I said nothing. My silence worried the poor confessor. I could see, hear, and walk, but was no longer of this earth.

I thought, Whatever has happened? What state am I going to find her in, if everyone is taking such precautions?, and this led me to cruel apprehensions, all the more cruel for being vague; they comprised all possible grief.

We reached her bedroom door, which the anxious confessor opened. Then I saw Henriette in a white dress, sitting on her small couch that had been placed in front of the fireplace adorned by two vases of flowers; there were more flowers on the pedestal table by the casement window. Abbé Birotteau's face, shocked by the improvised cheerfulness of a room suddenly restored to its former state, made me suspect the dying woman had also banished those repulsive medical implements that often surround the beds of the sickly. She had expended her feverish, dying body's last energy on arranging her untidy room to be able to give a dignified welcome to the individual she loved more than anyone at that time. Beneath layers of lace, tinged by the greenish pallor of magnolia flowers newly blossoming, her emaciated features stood out like a first chalk sketch of a beloved face on an unbleached portrait canvas, but if you want to feel how deeply the vulture's claws sank into my heart, you must imagine the eyes in the final sketch brimming with life, hollow eyes shining with unlikely brilliance from a drawn, pallid face. Her face was no longer home to the calm majesty granted by her constant victories over suffering. Her forehead, the only feature to retain its beautiful proportions, expressed the aggressive audacity of desire, its repressed threat. Despite her elongated face's waxen sheen, inner fire poured out like the haze that simmers over fields on a hot day. Her hollowed temples and sunken cheeks exposed her face's inner structure and the white smile on her lips vaguely suggested death's sneering grin. The dress, gathered across her bosom, revealed how shrunken her beautiful form had become. The way she held her head declared she knew she had changed and that it was making her despair. She was no longer my lovely Henriette, or the sublime, saintly Mme de Mortsauf; she was Bossuet's thing without a name, defying the void, and hunger and wayward desire were pulling her into life's final selfish struggle against death.

I walked over, sat next to her, and took her hand to kiss; it felt feverish and desiccated. She could imagine my grievous shock from the way I strove to disguise it. Her discolored lips flattened over her starving teeth in an attempt to force a smile that served to hide the irony of revenge, the anticipation of pleasure, the rapture in her soul, and her fury at all the disappointments.

"My poor Félix, death is here," she said, "and you don't like death— hateful death, which horrifies all living creatures, even the boldest lover! Love stops here, as I know only too well. Lady Dudley will never see you looking appalled by such a transformation. Félix, why did I want you so? At last you have come, and I reward your devotion with a spectacle that made a Trappist of the Comte de Rancé.[25] I wanted to stay beautiful and noble in your memory and live there like an eternal lily, but I am depriving you of any such hope. True love is never calculated. But don't run from me, please stay. M. Origet thought I was much better this morning, I shall return to the land of the living and be reborn under your gaze. When I have regained my strength and start eating, my beauty will return. I am only just thirty-five, and glorious years can lay ahead. Happiness is rejuvenating, and I want to know what happiness is like. I have made the finest of plans: we will leave *them* in Clochegourde and go to Italy together."

Tears moistened my eyes, I turned to the window as if to look at the flowers; Abbé Birotteau rushed over and stooped over the bouquet: "No tears!" he muttered.

"Henriette, don't you still love our dear valley?" I replied, to justify my brusque movement.

"Yes," she answered, bowing her forehead beneath my lips in a cajoling fashion, "but, without you, I find it funereal ... *Without you*," she repeated, brushing her warm lips against my ear and whispering those three syllables like three sighs.

I was shocked by a wild caress that only underlined the terrible things the two abbots had said. Immediately, my first sense of shock vanished, and, though I appealed to my reason, my will was too weak to suppress my nervous trembling during our conversation. I listened without responding or, rather, replied with blank smiles and nods, so as not to upset her, behaving like a mother with her child. After being taken aback by her physical transformation, I saw how a woman who'd been so sublime and imposing now possessed in her attitude, voice, manner, gaze, and ideas the naive ignorance, ingenuous charm, and spontaneous gestures of children, together with their complete lack of concern for whatever doesn't suit their desires or selves; in a word, every frailty from which one must protect children. Is that the way of the dying? Do they all throw off social restraint to be like a child, who has yet to develop any? Or, finding herself on the brink of eternity, could the countess only accept love from the whole range of human emotion, was she expressing its gentle innocence, like Chloe?

"Once again, Félix, you will restore me to good health," she said, "and my valley will be a source of bounty. How could I ever refuse to eat what you bring? You are such a good nurse! You are so strong and healthy, life becomes infectious by your side. My friend, show me I cannot die, and die wronged! They believe my most grievous pain is thirst. Yes, my friend, I do thirst. I long to see the waters of the Indre, but I have a more burning thirst. I thirst for you," she said, her voice more subdued, holding my hands between her feverish palms and pulling me towards her to whisper in my ear: "My agony was not being able to see you! Didn't you say I should live! That is what I want. And I too want to ride a horse, I too want to explore everything, Paris, parties, and pleasures!"

Natalie, her ghastly exclamations, remotely tempered by the material causes of her errant logic, rang in my ears and the priest's: her magnificent voice resonated with a lifetime of struggle and the anguish of real love that has been disappointed. The countess lifted herself up impatiently, like a child who wants a toy. When the confessor saw his penitent in such a state, he fell to his knees, joined his hands together, and recited some prayers.

"Yes, I want to live!" she said, forcing me up so she could lean on me, "to live realities, not lies. Everything has been a lie in my life. I have been counting those lies, that deceit, over the last few days! How can I die, when I have never lived, when I have never gone in search of someone on the heath?"

She stopped, appeared to hear or smell something through the walls.

"Félix, the grape pickers are about to eat, and I," she said childishly, "the mistress of this house, go hungry. And the same goes for love; *those* women are happy!"

"Kyrie eleison!" sang the poor abbot, who chanted the litanies, hands clasped and eyes raised heavenwards.

She threw her arms around my neck, embraced me violently, and said: "I won't let you escape me again! I want to be loved, and will commit as many follies as Lady Dudley. I will even learn English so I can say 'My Dee' correctly."

She nodded as she used to do when she was about to leave me, indicating she'd be back right away.

"We will have lunch together," she said, "I must warn Manette..."

She suddenly weakened, and I laid her on her bed fully dressed.

"And that's not the first time you've done that," she said, opening her eyes.

She weighed nothing, but was burning hot; when I lifted her, I felt her whole body was on fire. M. Deslandes walked in and was astonished to see the room looking so tidy, but, the moment he saw me, he knew why.

"One suffers horribly on the path to death, monsieur," he said, his voice faltering.

He sat down, felt his patient's pulse, stood up abruptly, went to whisper to the priest, and left the room; I followed.

"What are you intending to do now?"

"Spare her a horrible death agony," he replied. "Who would believe she could be so vigorous? We can only understand why she is still alive if we remember the way she lived. This is the forty-second day that Madame la Comtesse has not drunk, eaten, or slept."

M. Deslandes summoned Manette. Abbé Birotteau led me into the gardens.

"Let the doctor do what he must," he told me. "With Manette's help, he will cover her in a gauze of opium. You heard her," he continued, "if she is at all aware of her mad outpourings...!"

"No!" I said, "she is not herself anymore."

I was numb with pain. The more I thought about it, the more poignant each detail of that scene became. I left quickly through the small gate at the bottom of the terrace, and walked down and sat in the toue, where I hid to be alone and examine my thoughts. I tried to detach myself from the strength that gave me life, a torture similar to the one the Tartars used to inflict on an adulterer by trapping a guilty man's member within a piece of wood and giving him a knife with which to sever it, if he didn't want to starve to death: my soul had been taught a horrendous lesson, and was about to lose its most beautiful half. My life too was a failure! Despair triggered the strangest ideas. First I wanted to die with her, then to shut myself in the Meilleraye, where the Trappists had just established themselves. My listless eyes no longer registered external objects. I gazed at the windows of the bedroom where Henriette was suffering and thought I saw the light from that night when I pledged myself to her. Shouldn't I have pursued the simple life she'd created for me, and kept myself for her by managing the business of the estate? Hadn't she bid me be a great man of state, to save me from the base, shameful passions that I, like all men, felt? Wasn't chastity a sublime goal I had failed to achieve? Suddenly, love, as represented by Arabella, disgusted me.

When I looked up, wondering from what place I could now salvage light and hope, or the will to live, the air was stirred by a tiny sound. I looked back towards the terrace and saw Madeleine walking there slowly, alone. As I returned to the terrace to ask her to explain her frosty attitude when I saw her at the foot of the cross, she sat down on the bench; when she saw me on my way, she stood up, pretending she hadn't seen me, so as not to have to be alone with me. Her departure was rushed, and it told me all I needed to know.

She hated me, and fled from her mother's murderer. When I walked back up the terrace steps to Clochegourde, I spotted Madeleine, as still as a statue, listening to my footsteps. Jacques was sitting on a step, and his affect was as blank and unresponsive as when we'd all last strolled together, when it had stirred ideas in me that we stash in a corner of our hearts to revisit and analyze later, at our leisure. I concluded that all young people who harbor death within themselves must be unresponsive to funerals. I resolved to question that gloomy young man. Had Madeleine kept her thoughts to herself, or had she also inspired hatred in Jacques?

"You know," I said, to begin the conversation, " that you will find me a most devoted brother."

"Your friendship is of no use, I will follow my mother!" he replied, his eyes wracked by pain.

"Jacques," I shouted, "you too?"

He coughed and distanced himself from me; when he walked back, he showed me his bloody handkerchief.

"Now do you understand?" he asked.

So each of them kept a lethal secret. As I was to see, sister and brother were avoiding each other. Henriette had fallen, and the whole of Clochegourde had fallen apart.

"Madame is sleeping," Manette came out to tell us, happy in the knowledge that the countess was no longer suffering.

At such terrible moments, though everyone can see the inevitable end, true love goes crazy and clings to the least straws of happiness. Minutes turn into centuries that one desperately hopes will be benign. You wish the sick one could rest on roses, that you could take on her pain, that the last sigh would catch her by surprise.

"M. Deslandes had the flowers removed, their scent was too strong for her nerves," Manette told me.

So it was the that flowers had prompted her ravings; she wasn't complicit. Love of that land, rites of fertility, and the plants' caresses had intoxicated her with their scents and surely aroused thoughts of happy love that had slumbered within her since her youth.

"Come, Monsieur Félix," she said, "come and see her, she is beautiful, like an angel."

I returned to the dying woman's bedside as the sun sank and gilded the lace tracery of the roofs of the Azay château. Everything was tranquil and pure. Soft light lit the bed where Henriette rested, bathed in opium. At that moment her body was, as it were, nullified; her soul alone reigned on her face, serene as a beautiful sky after the storm. Blanche and Henriette, the two sublime faces of the same woman, reappeared, all the more beautiful because my memory, my thoughts, and my imagination helped nature set aright the changes to each feature, where an all-conquering soul glowed in surges in step with her breathing. The two abbots were sitting next to the bed. The count stood there, dumbstruck, recognizing death's standards flapping above that soul he adored. I sat where she always liked to sit on her couch. The four of us exchanged glances where our admiration of her heavenly beauty mingled with tears of sorrow. The light in our thoughts heralded the return of God to one of His most beautiful tabernacles. Abbé de Dominis and I spoke through signs that communicated similar ideas. Yes, the angels were watching over Henriette! Yes, their swords were glinting above that noble brow where exalted expressions of virtue were now returning, expressions that once acted as the visible sign of a soul engaged by the spirits in her sphere. Her lined face was made pure, everything about her grew majestically beneath the invisible censers of the seraphim watching over her. The green hues of physical pain gave way to the whitest tones, to the matte marble pallor of approaching death. Jacques and Madeleine walked in; Madeleine made us all tremble with the adoring way she rushed to the bedside, joined her hands, and, inspired, made a sublime exclamation: "Finally, my mother is here!"

Jacques smiled, certain he was about to follow his mother where she was going.

"She is arriving in a safe harbor," declared Abbé Birotteau.

Abbé de Dominis looked at me as if to say: Didn't I tell you the star would rise as brilliant as ever?

Madeleine kept her eyes fixed on her mother, breathed when she breathed, imitated her faint wheeze, the last thread by which she clung to life, which we followed in terror, afraid it would break with each effort she made. Like an angel at the gates to the sanctuary, the young woman was eager and serene, strong and supine. The Angelus rang from the village belfry. Waves of sweetly scented air wafted in, driven by chimes proclaiming that the whole of Christianity was now repeating the words spoken by the angel to the woman who was redeeming the waywardness of her sex. That evening, the Ave Maria seemed like a greeting from heaven. The prophecy was so clear and the event so nigh we dissolved into tears. Evening sounds, the melodious breeze in the leaves, the birds' last cheeps, the chorus and buzz of insects, the splashing of streams, and the mournful cry of the tree frog: the whole countryside was bidding farewell to the valley's most beautiful lily and to her simple, rural existence. That religious poetry, together with all nature's poetry, sang the song of departure so beautifully we immediately began to sob again. Although the bedroom door was open, we had sunk so deep into melancholy contemplation, as if we wanted to etch all of that on our souls forever, that we hadn't noticed the servants kneeling in a group and praying fervently. Those poor people were accustomed to hope and still believed they could hold on to their mistress, but that clear premonition was too much for them.

At a sign from Abbé Birotteau, the old groom left to fetch the priest from Saché. The doctor, standing by the bed, with the calm that science brings, held his sleeping patient's hand, after indicating to her confessor that this sleep was the last hour without suffering left to an angel who was being summoned back. It was time to administer the last rites of the Church. At nine o'clock she woke up gently, gave us all a surprised but gentle look, and we saw our idol as beautiful as she ever was on her finest days.

"Mother, you are too radiant to die, your health and life are coming back!" exclaimed Madeleine.

"Dear daughter, I shall live on, through you!" she said, smiling.

Then came the mother's anguished embrace of her children and the children's of their mother. M. de Mortsauf kissed his wife piously on her forehead. The countess blushed when she saw me.

"My dear Félix," she said, "I believe this is the only sorrow I have brought you, but please forget all I said in that wretched, delirious state."

She held out her hand, which I took and kissed, then she added with that gracious, virtuous smile: "Just like old times, Félix . . . ?"

We all entered the drawing room for as long as her last confession would last. I stood next to Madeleine. In the presence of everyone, she could avoid me without seeming discourteous, but now she imitated her mother, looked at nobody, remained silent, and never once glanced in my direction.

"Dear Madeleine," I whispered, "what grudge do you hold against me? Why be so cold, when everyone should be reconciled in the presence of death?"

"I think I understand what my mother just said," she replied, assuming the air Ingres found for the face of his *Mother of God*, that virgin who is already grieving and preparing to protect the world where her son is about to perish.

"Will you condemn me at the very moment your mother absolves me, if I was ever guilty?"

"*You*, it's always *you*!"

Her emphatic tone imitated the hatred a Corsican feels and has long harbored, the implacable judgment of someone who has never studied life, and shows no leniency towards errors committed against the laws of the heart. An hour of profound silence followed. Abbé Birotteau emerged after hearing the Comtesse de Mortsauf's general confession, and we all went back into the bedroom, after Henriette had had herself dressed in a long garment that would serve as her shroud, in keeping with an idea suffusing the sisterly purposes of an august soul. We found her on her couch, resplendent in her atonement and her expectations; in the fireplace I saw the black ash of my letters, which had just been burned, a sacrifice she had only wished to make, her confessor told me, in the hour of her death. She regaled us all with a smile from the past. Her tearful eyes heralded the supreme removal of scales: she could already perceive the heavenly bliss of the Promised Land.

"Dear Félix," she said, offering me her hand and squeezing mine, "stay. You should be present at one of the last scenes in my life, and it won't be the least painful scene, but it has a great deal to do with you."

At a wave of her hand, the door was closed. At her invitation, the count sat down; Abbé Birotteau and I remained standing. Helped by Manette, the countess stood up, kneeled before the count, and insisted on remaining in that position. When Manette withdrew, she raised her head and rested it on the knees of an astonished count.

"Although I have behaved like a faithful wife," she said, her voice shaking, "I may sometimes, monsieur, have failed in my duties; I have just begged God to grant me strength to ask you to forgive my errant ways. I have brought to the cultivation of a friendship outside our family more loving care than I owed to you. I may have aroused your anger when you contrasted such care and thoughtfulness with what I offered you. I felt," she whispered, "a keen friendship that nobody, not even the person concerned, entirely appreciated. Although I remained virtuous in the eyes of human law, and have been a wife beyond reproach, reflections, wanted and unwanted, often visited my heart, and I fear I welcomed them too benevolently. But, as I loved you dearly and stayed your submissive wife, as the clouds crossing the sky never sullied my purity, you now see me seeking your blessing with a pure spirit. I shall die without a single bitter thought if I hear from your lips a sweet word for your Blanche, for the mother of your children, and if you forgive her things she herself has only forgiven herself after receiving assurances from that tribunal we must all appear before."

"Blanche, Blanche," exclaimed the old man, suddenly bursting into tears over his wife's head, "do you want to be the cause of my death?"

He lifted her up with an unexpected display of strength, gave her forehead a saintly kiss, and held her there: "Shouldn't I be the one asking for your forgiveness?" he continued. "Haven't I often been harsh? Didn't you often have to tiptoe like a wary child?"

"Perhaps," she replied, "but, my friend, show indulgence to the weaknesses of the dying, console me. When you reach this moment, you will reflect that I left you with a blessing. Will you allow me to leave our friend this token of deep feeling?" she said, pointing to a letter on the mantelpiece. "He is now my adopted son, nothing more. The heart, dear count, has a will of its own; my last wishes demand of dearest Félix a few saintly acts he must carry out. I don't think I request too much of you if I let myself bequeath him a few thoughts. I am still a woman, after all," she said, with a gentle, melancholy bow of the head: "Apart from your forgiveness, I ask only one other favor. Read this after my death," she said, handing me the mysterious epistle.

The count saw his wife turn pale, took her in his arms, and carried her to her bed. We all stood around her.

"Félix," she said, "I may have wronged you. I may often have caused you sorrow when I let you imagine pleasures that I then fled from: but shouldn't I die reconciled to you as a courageous wife and mother? Will you too forgive me, you who have reproached me so often, an injustice I found so delightful!"

Abbé Birotteau put a finger to his lips. At that gesture, the dying woman lowered her head, relapsed, and waved her hands to order the clergy, her children, and the servants to be allowed in; then she imperiously pointed me towards the dumbstruck count and the children rushing to her. The sight of a father whose secret lunacy we alone appreciated, now the guardian of those fragile beings, gave rise to silent supplications that enfolded my soul in holy fire. Before receiving extreme unction, she asked her servants to forgive her if she had sometimes been brusque; she begged them to pray for her and recommended them all individually to the count; she nobly confessed that over the last month she had complained in a way that was far from Christian, that some might have found shocking; she had spurned

her children, she had felt unseemly feelings, but blamed her excruci-
ating pain on her lack of subjection to God's will. Finally, with a
touching show of feeling, she publicly thanked Abbé Birotteau for
convincing her of the emptiness of all things human.

When she stopped speaking, prayers began: the priest from Saché
gave her the last sacrament. A few seconds later her breathing faltered,
her eyes clouded, reopened, and then she gave me one last glance and
died in sight of everyone, perhaps hearing the concert of our sobs. As
she sighed her last, at the end of a long life of suffering, I felt something
inside me snap. The count and I stayed by the funeral bed the whole
night, with the two abbots and the priest, in a candlelit vigil for the
dead woman lying on the mattress of her bed, tranquil now, where
she had suffered so much.

It was my first encounter with death. The entire night I kept my
eyes trained on Henriette, fascinated by the pure expression left after
the storms had all subsided, and by the pallid face I saw still suffused
with her infinite affection, which no longer responded to my love.
So majestic in that icy silence! Suggesting so many ideas! So beautiful
in that absolute repose, so tyrannical in her stillness! The whole past
lingered where the future now began. I loved her dead as much as I
loved her alive.

The following morning, the count took to his bed, the three weary
priests fell asleep at that onerous hour familiar to all who have endured
a vigil. Then, without witnesses, I could kiss her forehead, with all
the love she had never allowed me to express.

The fresh, autumnal morning after, we accompanied the countess
to her last resting place. She was carried by the old groom, the two
Martineaus, and Manette's husband. We walked down the path I
had so gleefully climbed the day when I was reunited with her; we
crossed the valley of the Indre to reach the small cemetery in Saché;
a modest village cemetery, behind the church, on the brow of a hill,
where, out of Christian humility, she had elected to be buried with
a simple cross of black wood, like a poor country woman, she had
said. From the middle of the valley, I saw the village church and the
cemetery and began to shake and convulse. Alas, we all carry a Gol-

gotha in our lives where we leave behind our first thirty-three years when a spear is thrust into our heart, when we feel a crown of thorns replace the crown of roses on our head, and that hill should be my mount of atonement. We were followed by a huge crowd, come to voice the sorrow of a valley where she had silently performed a mass of beautiful deeds. Manette, her confidante, told us how, to help the poor, she used to scrimp on her own wardrobe, when her savings didn't suffice. She clothed naked children, provided baby necessities, helped mothers, in winter paid millers for sacks of corn for destitute old men, gave the odd cow to a poor household, in a word, the good works of a Christian, as a mother and a chatelaine; then the dowries offered expressly to join loving couples, and the sums paid to young folk struck down by bad luck, moving offerings from a loving woman who had said: "The happiness of others brings consolation to those who can no longer be happy." Those acts, recounted at every vigil over three days, had attracted that multitude. I walked with Jacques and the two abbots behind the coffin. Following custom, neither Madeleine nor the count were with us, they stayed by themselves in Clochegourde. Manette had insisted on coming.

"Poor Madame! Poor Madame! She is happy now," I heard her say repeatedly through her sobbing.

When the cortege left the road to the mills, a unanimous, lachrymose moan exploded as if the valley's soul had cried out. The church was packed. After the service we went to the cemetery, where she was to be buried near the cross. When I heard the pebbles and gravelly soil clatter on the coffin, my courage deserted me. I staggered and begged the two Martineaus to support me, and they took me in that moribund state to the château in Saché: the masters politely offered me a haven, and I accepted. I must confess to you that I had no desire to return to Clochegourde, and I was repulsed by the idea of returning to Frapesle, from which I would be able to see Henriette's mansion. I would be nearer to her there. For a few days I stayed in a bedroom whose windows looked out across the quiet, solitary dale I have described. It is a huge fold of land bordered by two-hundred-year-old oaks, where torrents race when storms break. That scenario was ideal for the stern, solemn meditation I wished to undertake. The day after that fatal night, I understood that my presence would be inopportune in Clochegourde. The count had reacted violently to Henriette's death, but he had been expecting that terrible moment, and the attitude residing deep in his mind verged on indifference. I had noticed that more than once, and when the prostrate countess had given me the letter I dared not open, and spoke of her affection for me, that grumpy fellow hadn't directed the thunderous look my way that I was expecting. He'd attributed Henriette's words to the excessive susceptibility of a conscience he knew to be so pure. That egotist's insensitivity was natural. Their two souls had only ever been married physically and they had never enjoyed the constant exchanges that reinvigorate feelings; they had never shared pain or pleasure, or the strong bonds that shatter us to smithereens when they break, because they touch our every fiber, because they are woven into the folds of our heart, as they have also touched the soul that sanctioned every single one of those ties. Madeleine's hostility put Clochegourde off-limits. That harsh young woman hadn't been prepared to reconcile her hatred, not over her mother's coffin, and I would have been miserably out of sorts between the count, who'd have only talked about himself, and the mistress of the house, who'd have shown me intolerable repugnance. To be there, where even the flowers once caressed me, where the terrace steps were eloquent, where my memories were bedecked in the poetry of balconies, borders, balustrades, terraces, trees, and every perspective; to be hated where everything had loved me: the very idea was unbearable. And so, my mind was made up from the start. That, alas, was the outcome of the finest love ever to enter a man's heart. My behavior would be seen as unworthy by strangers, but my conscience endorsed it. It is the way the most beautiful feelings and greatest dramas of youth must conclude. Almost all of us depart in the morning, as I did from Tours to Clochegourde, seeking strength in society, our hearts hungering for love; when our riches have passed the test of adversity, and we have experienced social life and the events of the day, then everything suddenly shrinks, and we find little gold among the ashes. Such is life! Life as it really is:

great on pretension, small on reality. I reflected at length on my situation, wondering what I would do after that blow that had scythed down all my flowers. I decided to throw myself into politics and the spheres of power, follow the tortuous paths of ambition, exclude women from my life, and be a cold, aloof man of state, staying faithful to the saint I had loved. My reflections vanished out of sight, as my eyes clung to the magnificent tapestry of golden oaks, to the austere peaks, to their feet of bronze: I wondered if Henriette's virtue hadn't stemmed from lack of knowledge, and if I really was to blame for her death. In my remorse I debated with myself. Finally, one warm midday in autumn, under one of the last sunny, smiling skies, which are so beautiful in the Touraine, I read her letter, that, according to her instructions, I shouldn't open until after her death. Imagine my reactions as I read it!:

MADAME DE MORTSAUF'S LETTER TO LE VICOMTE FÉLIX DE VANDENESSE

Félix, my friend whom I loved too much, I must now open my heart to you, less to show how much I love you than to inform you of the extent of your obligations by revealing the truly serious wounds you inflicted there. At a time when I fall wearied by my journey and exhausted by the wounds received in battle, fortunately the woman in me is dead, and only the mother survives. You will see, my dear, how you were the first cause of my sorrows. If I later offered myself up willingly to your onslaught, today I am dying from the last injury you dealt, although it is true one feels too much pleasure at being broken by the man one loves. I am sure pain will soon make my strength ebb, so I must put every last glimmer of intelligence into begging you, on my children's behalf, to replace the heart you have taken from them. I would charge you with this burden more emphatically if I loved you less, but I would prefer to let you assume it yourself, by way of saintly repentance and the continuation of your love: Wasn't our love a constant mingling of sudden insights and atoning fears? And, yes, I know, we do still love each other. Your waywardness isn't so dire because of you yourself, but rather it is the manner in which you made it resonate within me. Didn't I say I was jealous, and jealous enough to die? Here you have it: I am dying. However, be consoled: we transgressed no human laws. One of the Church's purest voices told me God showed indulgence towards those who sacrifice their natural leanings in order to obey his commandments. My beloved, be apprised of all this, because I want you to be aware of every single one of my thoughts. What I will confide to God in my last moments must also be known to you, the king of my heart, as He is the King of Heaven.

Until that ball given for the Duc d'Angoulême, the only one I have ever been to, marriage had left me in that state of ignorance that endows young girls with angelic beauty. True, I was a mother, but love had never enveloped me in its licit pleasures. How had I stayed like that? I have no idea; any more than I know what laws caused everything about me to change in an instant. Do you remember your kisses? They have dominated my life and furrowed my soul; the ardor in your blood aroused mine; your youth penetrated mine, your desires entered my heart. When I stood up so haughtily, I experienced a sensation for which I know no word in any language, because children have yet to discover the word to express the marriage of light with their eyes, or the kiss of life on their lips. Yes, it really was the sound that thundered, the light that illuminated the darkness, the movement that was injected into the universe; it was as rapid as all those things, but much more beautiful, because it was life infusing the soul! I then realized something existed in this world I hadn't experienced, an impulse more beautiful than thought, that was all thought and all impulse, a whole future of shared emotion. I felt I was but half a mother. That thunderbolt struck my heart and fired desires that had been slumbering in unknown places; suddenly I intuited everything my aunt had been hinting when she kissed my forehead and cried out: "Poor Henriette!" Returning to Clochegourde, to spring, the first leaves, the scent of flowers, the pretty white clouds, the Indre, the sky, everything spoke a language I hadn't understood till then, and that restored to my soul some of the elation you had brought to my senses. Perhaps you have forgotten those terrible kisses; I could never erase them from my memory: they are my death! Yes, whenever I saw you after that, you revived their traces; I was moved from head to foot by every sight of you, by the mere anticipation of your arrival. Neither time nor the farm could tame that imperious, voluptuous sensation. Quite spontaneously I asked myself: "What can those pleasures be?" The looks we exchanged, the respectful way you kissed my hands, the arm I rested on yours, the tender inflections of your voice, the least thing, in fact, stirred me so furiously my eyes almost always misted: the sound of rebellious senses filled my ears. At such moments when I racked up the coldness of my responses, if you had only taken me in your arms, I would have died of happiness. I sometimes wished you would react physically, but prayer quickly dismissed that evil thought. Your name on my children's lips warmed the blood in my heart and reddened my cheeks, and I set traps for poor Madeleine so she would be forced to say it, and I so adored that tingling feeling. What can I say? Your handwriting was a delight; I looked at your letters as one gazes at a portrait.

If from that very first day you had won me over through some fatal force, it became infinite, my friend, when I read into your soul. I was filled with wonder to find you so pure, so completely true, blessed with such beautiful qualities, capable of such great things, and already so experienced! Man and child; shy and valiant! What bliss to find we both shared common suffering in the past! After the evening when we confided in each other, losing you was tantamount to death, so I allowed you to be near me out of selfishness. M. de la Berge was convinced I would court death if you moved away and he was deeply affected, for he could read into my soul. He said my children and the count needed me: he didn't order me to shut the door of my house to you, because I promised I would remain pure in my acts and in my thoughts. "Thought cannot be controlled," he told me, "but a circle of thorns can keep it in check." "If I think," I replied, "all will be lost; save me from myself. Make it possible for him to stay close to me and for me to remain pure!" Although he was severe, that fine old man indulged me for having such good faith: "Love him as one loves a son, by giving him your daughter." I bravely accepted a life of suffering so as not to lose you, and I suffered lovingly to see us both yoked to the same harness. My God, I stayed so passive, so loyal to my husband, I didn't allow you to take a single step, Félix, in your own realm. My strength of feeling affected my attitudes. I saw the torture inflicted on me by M. de Mortsauf as an atonement, and bore it with pride as a way to counter my guilty inclinations. Once I was prone to complain, but from the moment you stayed at my side, I became happier and M. de Mortsauf believed that was because of him. Without the fortitude you gave me, I would long since have yielded to that inner self I have described. If you were partly responsible for my waywardness, you are in good measure the reason why I fulfilled my duties. It was similar as regards my children. I thought I had deprived them of something and feared I never did enough for them. From then on my life was continually anguished, which I loved. When I felt less of a mother, less of a respectful wife, remorse swept through my heart, and, fearful I wasn't doing my duties, I constantly strove to do so in excess.

So that I didn't stray, I positioned Madeleine between you and me, and destined you to her, thus erecting barriers between us. Futile barriers! Nothing could stifle the way you made me tingle and start. Absent or present, your power reigned. I preferred Madeleine to Jacques, because Madeleine would be yours. But I didn't yield my daughter to you without a struggle. I would tell myself I was only twenty-eight when I met you and you were almost twenty-two; I kept closing distances and harboring false hopes. Oh my God, Félix, I confess these things to spare you remorse, and perhaps also to let you know I wasn't insensitive, that our amorous plight was cruelly shared, and that Arabella was in no way superior to me. I too was a daughter of that fallen race men love so much. There were times when the conflict raged so fiercely within me I wept every night; my hair fell out. I gave it to you! Do you remember M. de Mortsauf's demented behavior? Your nobility of spirit, far from reinvigorating me, cast me down. Alas, after that day I wanted to give myself to you as a reward earned by your heroic attitude, but that lunacy was short-lived. I placed it at the feet of God during that Mass you refused to attend. Jacques's illness and Madeleine's suffering seemed like threats from God, intent on dragging his stray sheep back to the fold. Then your natural love for that Englishwoman revealed secrets I had been unaware of. I loved you more than I thought. Madeleine disappeared. The emotional ebbs and flows in my stormy life, the efforts I made to curb myself, with religion as my only succor, have all prepared the path for the illness that is now killing me. That terrible shock triggered attacks which I revealed to nobody. I saw death as the only possible conclusion to my secret tragedy. I lived an irascible, jealous life in the two months that passed between the news I received from my mother of your affair with Lady Dudley and your arrival here. I wanted to go to Paris, I thirsted for murder, I wanted that woman dead, and shunned my children's caresses. Prayer's soothing consolation now made no impact on my soul. Jealousy forged a gaping hole through which death came in. Nonetheless I stayed calm on the surface. Truly, that season of battle was a secret between God and me. When I clearly saw that you loved me as much as I loved you and that I had been betrayed only by nature and not by your thoughts, I wanted to live again . . . but it was too late. God had placed me under His protection, no doubt He had taken pity on a creature who was true to herself, true to Him, whose suffering had often brought her to the gates of His sanctuary. My dear beloved Félix, God has judged me. I expect M. de Mortsauf will forgive me, but will *you* too be merciful? Will you listen to the voice now reaching you from my grave? Will you atone for the ills of which we are both guilty, you perhaps less so than I? You know what I am asking. Act towards M. Mortsauf like a Sister of Charity attending to the infirm, listen to him and love him; nobody else will. Put yourself between him and the children, as I used to. It won't be a task that will last long: Jacques will soon leave to be with his grandfather in Paris, where you promised to help him negotiate the reefs of that social whirl. As for Madeleine, she will marry; I hope one day she will take to you! She is myself all over again, she is strong and has the will I lacked and the energy necessary to be the companion of a man fated to face the storms of political life; she is insightful and quick-witted. If your fates are wedded, she will be happier than I ever was. By thus acquiring the right to continue my work in Clochegourde, you will wash away all the waywardness you haven't sufficiently atoned for, even though it has been forgiven in heaven and on earth, because *He* is generous and will forgive me. As you can see, I am as selfish as ever, but isn't that proof of the tyranny of love? I wanted to be loved by you through my children. As I can no longer be yours, I bequeath you my thoughts and duties! If you love me too much to obey, if you don't wish to marry Madeleine, at least cherish the peace of my soul by making M. de Mortsauf as happy as he can possible be.

Adieu, dear beloved child, this is a completely conscious adieu, one that is still full of life, the adieu of a soul you filled with joys too great to make me feel the least remorse for the disaster they have created; I use that word in the belief that you love me, because I am now reaching my final resting place, after sacrificing myself to duty, not without regret, and that makes me tremble! God knows better than I whether I have practiced the spirit of His holy laws. I am sure I have often stumbled, but I never fell, and the most powerful excuse for all my faults resides in the seductive splendors that surrounded me. Our Lord will also see me tremble, as if I had yielded. Adieu again, an adieu like the one I wished our beautiful valley yesterday, within whose bosom I shall soon be at rest, and which you will visit often, will you not?

Henriette

I was plunged into turmoil by the revelation of the unknown depths of a life that were now illuminated by this last flame. The clouds of my selfishness scattered. She had suffered as much as I had, no, more than I had, because she was dead. She believed others would be benevolent towards her friend; she had been so blinded by her love she hadn't foreseen her daughter's hostility. The final evidence of her affection hurt me terribly. Poor Henriette, she wanted to give me Clochegourde and her daughter!

Natalie, from that wretched day when I entered a cemetery for the first time to accompany the remains of noble Henriette, whom you now know well, the sun has seemed less warm and bright, the night darker, all movement less fluid, and all thought more lethargic. There are those we bury beneath the earth, and others we particularly cherished, whose shroud was our heart, whose memory melds daily into our every palpitation; we think of them as we breathe, they endure in us through love's sweet law of metempsychosis. Another soul exists in mine. When something good is done on my behalf, when a beautiful word is said, that soul speaks and acts; everything good I possess emanates from that grave, like the scent of a lily perfuming the air. Gossip, evil, everything you find to criticize in me originates from myself. Now, when a cloud darkens my eyes and I look skywards, after gazing at the earth, when my lips don't respond to your words or affection, never again ask: "What is on your mind?"

Dear Natalie, I was forced to stop writing for quite some time; all those memories affected me too greatly. Now I owe you an account of the events that followed that catastrophe, and that requires few words. When a life is action and movement, it is soon described, but when it has developed in more august spheres, its narrative is more diffuse.

Henriette's letter made hope shine in my eyes. In that huge shipwreck, I saw an island I could aim for. A life in Clochegourde by Madeleine's side, dedicating myself to her, was a fate that satisfied the tumult of ideas in my heart, but I needed to find out what Madeleine really thought. I had to say my farewells to the count. I went to Clochegourde and found him on the terrace. We went for a long walk. At first, he spoke of the countess like a man who recognized the extent of his loss and the harm it was doing to his inner soul. But, after his first whelp of pain, he seemed more anxious about the future than the present. He feared his daughter, whom, he declared, wasn't self-effacing like her mother. Madeleine's resolute character, a mixture of the heroic and her mother's grace, terrified an old man accustomed to Henriette's tender care, and encountering now a will nothing could bend. But the belief he would soon join his wife could console him for his irreparable loss: his sickly state had deteriorated as a result of the hectic bustle and grieving of recent days and reawakened older pains; the nascent conflict between paternal authority and that of his daughter, the new mistress of the house, would lead him to end his days in a state of bitterness, because while he could always quarrel with his wife, he always yielded to his child. Besides, his son would leave and his daughter would marry: Who would his son-in-law be? Although he spoke of his immediate death, he felt alone and had found no source of sympathy for a long time.

In the course of that hour when he only spoke about himself and asked for my friendship in his wife's name, he gave the final touches to the portrait of the grand figure of the émigré, one of the most powerful types of our era. He seemed weaker and more broken, but clung to life, precisely through his sober ways and rural tasks. As I write, he is still alive.

Although Madeleine could see us walking along the terrace, she didn't come down to meet us; she walked up the steps and into the house to show her contempt for me. I seized the moment she reached the steps to beg the count to go up to the château; I had to speak to Madeleine, and I made my excuse a last wish the countess had confided in me. It was the only way I was ever going to see her alone; the count fetched her and left us on the terrace.

"Dear Madeleine," I said, "if I must talk to you, shouldn't it be here where your mother complained less about me than she did about everything else that was happening in her life? I know what you're thinking, but don't condemn me without establishing the facts. My life and happiness are linked to these places, as you know, yet you banish me with an iciness that has replaced the brotherly friendship that once united us, that death should have strengthened through a shared bond of sorrow. Dear Madeleine, for whom I would give my

life today without hope of reward, without your even being aware—
we so love the children of those who protected us in life—you know
nothing of the plan your mother nurtured over the last seven years,
and which would surely change your feelings, but I don't want to call
on those advantages. All I beg is that you don't deprive me of the
right to come and breathe the air on this terrace, and that you wait
until the passage of time has changed your ideas about life in society;
now I will make no attempt to challenge them; I respect the grief
that makes your mind err, because that grief also strips me of the
ability to think properly about the circumstances I now face. The
saint watching over you will look down approvingly upon my restraint
when I merely ask you to stay neutral regarding your feelings towards
me. I love you too much, despite the aversion you display, to tell the
count of a plan he would joyfully embrace. Be free for the moment.
Later, reflect that you can know nobody better in this world than
myself, that no man's heart can hold feelings of greater devotion."

Up to that moment Madeleine had listened, her eyes lowered, but
now she gestured to me to stop.

"Monsieur," she said, her voice shaking with emotion, "I know
what you are thinking, but I won't change my feelings towards you
one iota, and would rather fling myself into the Indre than be married
to you. I won't speak on my behalf, but, if my mother's name still
exerts any influence over you, it is in her name that I must beg you
never to return to Clochegourde, for as long as I am living here. The
very sight of you causes me distress I could never describe, let alone
overcome."

She bid me a dignified farewell and walked back up to Clochegourde, never once looking back, as impassive as her mother had been
for a single day, but pitiless too. That young woman's perceptive eye
had intuited everything in her mother's heart, if rather late in the
day, and perhaps her hatred of the man she judged to have been lethal
was tinged with a few regrets in relation to her own innocent com-
plicity. It was a gaping chasm. Madeleine hated me and didn't want
to say if I was the cause of or a victim to those misfortunes: she would
have hated her mother and me equally if we had been happy. Thus

everything in the beautiful edifice of my bliss collapsed. I alone would know in its entirety the life of that great, uncanny woman; I alone would be privy to her secret feelings; I alone had explored the vast realm of her soul; her mother, her father, her husband, and her children had never known her. It is truly strange! I explore that mound of ashes and find pleasure in spreading them before you; we can all find something there of our own fortunes in life. So many families have their Henriette! So many noble souls leave this earth without ever finding the wise historian who plumbed their hearts and measured their depth and breadth! That is the naked truth of human life: mothers often know less of their children than their children know of them. And the same goes for married couples, lovers, and siblings! How could I anticipate that one day, over my father's coffin, I would have to plead with my brother, Charles de Vandenesse, whose advancement I helped so much. My God, one can learn so much from the simplest of stories! When Madeleine disappeared through the raised entrance, I returned with a broken heart to say farewell to my hosts, and left for Paris along the left bank of the Indre, along which I had walked to this valley for the very first time. I passed through the pretty village of Pont-de-Ruan sadly. Nevertheless, I was wealthy now. Political life was being good to me. I was no longer the weary walker I'd been in 1814. At that time, my heart had been full of desires; today my eyes were full of tears; once I had a life to fulfill; now it felt like a desert. At twenty-nine, I was young, but my heart had already withered. A few years had sufficed to strip that landscape of its initial splendor and make me loathe life. You will understand what I felt when I turned around and saw Madeleine on the terrace.

In the depths of despair, I no longer reflected on the purpose of my journey. Lady Dudley was far from my thoughts when I walked blindly into her courtyard. Once the folly had been committed, I had to see it through. I had fallen into a marital routine with her, and my distress levels surged at the mere thought of the havoc separation would spark. If you have grasped Lady Dudley's character and manner, you can imagine how mortified I felt when her butler ushered me, in my traveling garb, into a drawing room where I found her dressed in overblown frippery, surrounded by five people. One of the highest-ranking English men of state, Lord Dudley was standing in front of the fireplace, his usual arrogant, stuck-up, cold-blooded self, with that supercilious glint he must display in the Houses of Parliament; he smiled when he heard my name. De Marsay, one of the old lord's bastard sons, was there, and he sat on a small settee next to her ladyship. Arabella's own two children, who showed an amazing likeness to de Marsay, were also sitting close to their mother. The second she saw me, Arabella gave me a superior look, staring at my riding hat as if she wanted to ask me at every second what on earth I were doing there. She looked me up and down as if I were a rural yeoman she'd just been introduced to. As for our tryst, that eternal passion, that Armide's fantasy, it had faded like a dream.[26] I had never clasped her hand in mine, I was a stranger, she didn't know me. Although I was beginning to be familiar with diplomatic froideur, I was taken aback, as anyone in my position would have been. De Marsay smiled at his boots, inspecting them with the utmost affected interest. I soon reached a decision. Had it been any other woman, I would have humbly accepted defeat, but, infuriated to see that heroine who had sworn to die of love, who had ridiculed the dead woman, I was determined to match impertinence with impertinence. She was aware of Lady Brandon's disaster: to remind her would be to stab her in the heart, even if it only blunted the dagger.

"Madame," I said, "you must forgive me for entering your drawing room in such a cavalier fashion, when you must know I have just come from the Touraine, where Lady Brandon gave me a message which brooked no delay. I was afraid you would have already left for Lancashire, but, since I find you still in Paris, I await your orders and a time when you will deign to receive me."

She bowed her head, and I left. From that day on, I've only ever met her in society gatherings, where we exchange friendly greetings and the occasional epigram. I speak to her of the inconsolable women of Lancashire, she tells me about French women who honor their despair and stomach complaints. Thanks to her influence, I now have a mortal enemy in De Marsay, on whom she quite dotes. And I simply say she is wedding two generations.

So my disaster is complete. I followed the plan I drew up during my retreat in Saché. I threw myself into work, dedicated myself to learning, literature, and politics; I entered the diplomatic ranks with the advent of Charles X, who did away with the position I'd held under the late king. From then on, I resolved never to pay attention to any woman, however beautiful, witty, and loving she might be. It was a perfect decision: I acquired a glorious mental serenity, a tremendous capacity for work, and an understanding of how much those creatures dissipate our lives when we think they have rewarded us with a few gracious words. But all my fine resolutions collapsed: you know how and why.

Dear Natalie, by recounting to you my life so unreservedly and candidly, as I'd describe it to myself; by telling you of feelings that did not involve you, I may have ruffled folds in your delicate, jealous heart, but what would enrage an ordinary woman, will, I am sure, in your eyes, be fresh reason to love me. When attending to sick and suffering souls, women of high standing have a sublime role to play, as Sisters of Charity caring for the wounded, and as mothers, forgiving their children. Artists and great poets aren't the only ones who suffer: Men who live for their country, for the future of nations, when they widen their circle of passions and ideas, often create for themselves the cruelest solitude. They need to feel pure, devoted love by their side; believe me, they completely understand how noble and valuable that is. Tomorrow, I will know whether I erred in loving you.

TO MONSIEUR LE COMTE FÉLIX DE VANDENESSE

Dear Count, You are in receipt of a letter from that poor Mme de Mortsauf that, you say, has not been without its uses in opening a path for you in high society, a letter to which you owe your great good fortune. Allow me to complete your education. Please desist from what is a most hateful habit; don't imitate those widows who always talk about their first husbands, who always throw the deceased's virtues at the faces of their second. I am French, dear count; I would wish to marry the whole of the man I loved, and I could never, in truth, marry Mme de Mortsauf. After reading your tale with the attention it deserved, and you are aware of my interest in you, I have concluded that you really annoyed Lady Dudley by constantly comparing her to the perfect Mme de Mortsauf, and that you did the countess much harm by overwhelming her with wellsprings of English-style love. You've hardly shown tact towards me, dear child; my only merit seems to be that you find me attractive; you have given me to understand I didn't love you like Henriette or Arabella loved you. I admit my imperfections, I know them well, but why must you make me feel them so acutely? Do you know the woman I pity? The *fourth* woman you love. Of necessity, she will be forced to fight the three others, and thus I must forewarn you, in your interest and hers, against the perils of your memories. I renounce the glorious task of loving you: it would require too many Catholic or Anglican qualities, and I'm not of a mind to combat ghosts. The virtues of the virgin of Clochegourde would make the most self-confident woman despair, and your intrepid Amazon would discourage the most audacious quest for happiness. Whatever she might do, a woman can never give you joys equal to her ambition. Neither her heart nor her senses will ever triumph over your memories. You seem to have forgotten that we often go horseback riding. I could never warm a sun cooled by the death of your saintly Henriette: you would shiver by my side. My friend, for you will always be my friend, take care not to repeat this kind of revelation that exposes your disillusion, discourages love, and forces a woman to doubt herself. Love, dear count, only exists where there is trust. The woman who, before she says a word or mounts a horse, must wonder whether celestial Henriette would speak more eloquently, or an equestrian Arabella would be more graceful, that woman, you can be sure, will find her tongue and legs are shaking. You fired in me the wish to receive some of your enticing bouquets, but you no longer confect them. Likewise there are lots of things you no longer dare do, and ideas and ecstasies you will never relive. No woman, I warn you, will ever want to enter your heart and rub shoulders with the dead woman you keep there. You beg me to love you out of Christian charity. I must confess, I can do an infinite number of things out of charity, but not induce love.

You are at times weary and wearisome, you give your sadness the name of melancholy: A splendid name, but you are unbearable and can only make the woman who loves you cruelly anxious. I have found the saint's grave between us far too often: I have given it some thought, I know myself, and I do not wish to die like her. If you have wearied Lady Dudley, an extremely distinguished woman, I feel that I, who don't feel such fervent desires, will go cold sooner even than she did. Let's now end the love between us: you can only feel happiness with dead women. I do hope we remain friends. Dear count, how could you have had as your first love an adorable woman, a perfect mistress, who dreamed of your success, who gave you a peerage, who loved you rapturously, who only asked you to be faithful, and how could you have then made her die of sadness because of you? I can think of nothing more monstrous. Who among the most ardent, unhappy young men trailing their ambitions along the streets of Paris couldn't stay loyal for ten years to enjoy half the favors that you haven't found it within you to respect? When one is loved like that, what more can one ask for?

Poor woman! She suffered so much, and once you had uttered a few sentimental words, you thought you could disavow her coffin. No doubt a similar prize awaits my affection for you. Thank you, my dear count, but I want rivals neither beyond the grave nor here below. When such crimes are on one's conscience, at least keep quiet about them. My request was a rash one; I was playing my female role, as a daughter of Eve; yours was all about calculating the purview of your response. You should have deceived me; I would have thanked you later. Have you never understood the virtue of a Don Juan? Don't you sense his generosity when he swears he has never loved, and is in love for the first time? Yours is an impossible ideal. Being at once Mme de Mortsauf and Lady Dudley, my friend, isn't that to attempt to combine fire and water? Do you know nothing about women—what they are and how they inevitably have the faults that arise from their qualities? You encountered Lady Dudley too soon to appreciate her, and I believe your criticism of her comes from your wounded pride's need for revenge; you understood Mme de Mortsauf too late, you punished one because she wasn't the other; so what will become of me, neither one nor the other!

I love you enough to have considered your future at length, for I really do love you. I have always been fascinated by your Knight with a Sad Countenance airs: I believed in the constancy of melancholy individuals, but I wasn't aware you had killed the most beautiful and most virtuous of women when you entered high society. And so I've wondered what there's left for you to accomplish. My friend, I think you should marry a Mrs. Shandy, who knows nothing of love or passion, who won't be worried by Lady Dudley or Mme de Mortsauf, who will be indifferent to the moments of boredom you call melancholy, when you are as much fun as drizzle, and who will be that excellent Sister of Charity you so crave. As for love, trembling at a word, knowing how to wait for happiness, how to give and receive it, feeling a thousand onslaughts of passion, and espousing the small vanities of a beloved woman, my dear count, forget it. You have followed too closely the sage advice your good angel gave you about young women; you have avoided them so adroitly you don't understand them at all. Mme de Mortsauf was right to establish you early in such a high position: all women would have been against you, and you would have achieved nothing. It's too late now to start studying and learning to say what we love to hear, to be grand when appropriate, or to worship our foibles when we feel like being petty. We are not as foolish as you think: when we love, we place the man we have chosen above everything else. Whatever destroys our faith in our superiority destroys our love. By flattering us, you flatter yourselves. If you want to stay in the social whirl and enjoy the company of women, take care to hide everything you told me: women don't like to sow the flowers of their love on rocky ground, or squander their caresses on tending to a sick heart. All women would see the parched nature of your heart and you would always be unhappy. Very few will be frank enough to tell you what I'm telling you, or kind enough to leave you without rancor and offer you their friendship, as does this woman, who today thinks of herself as your devoted friend.

Natalie de Manerville

NOTES

1. In 1563 Bianca Cappello, the daughter of a wealthy family, fled from Venice to Florence with her lover, Pietro Bonaventuri, a poor clerk.
2. In his history of the Gallic Wars, Julius Caesar claimed that Druid priestesses in Gaul were responsible for gory sacrifices.
3. In January 1834 Balzac visited the Villa Diodati on the banks of Lake Geneva with Madame Eveline Hańska.
4. Henry Morgan, a Welsh pirate and plantation owner, was notorious for his bloody raids on the Spanish in the Caribbean and Panama. The "flower that sings" is the mandrake, a species of deadly nightshade that, according to legend, would scream when pulled up and kill its uprooter.
5. An émigré field army, led by Louis Joseph de Bourbon, Prince de Condé, that fought in counterrevolutionary campaigns before it was eventually of dissolved, in 1801. It was largely financed by foreign powers: Spain, England, and Russia.
6. Leaders of the Catholic army of the Vendée, involved in bloody battles against the republican army in 1793.
7. The protagonist of Samuel Richardson's epistolary novel from 1748, *Clarissa Harlow; or, The History of a Young Lady*, is a tragic heroine, whose wealthy family keep her virtually locked up in their mansion, in an effort to defend her virtue against the advances of the libertine Robert Lovelace, who had already jilted her elder sister, Arabella.
8. Louis XVIII's cavalry guard, made up of noblemen.
9. The words, according to a popular telling, of the last Aztec emperor, Cuauhtemoc, as he was tortured by the Spanish conquistadors, who applied red-hot coals to the soles of his feet.
10. Father Louis-Bertrand Castel (1688–1757) wrote treatises on physics and mathematics and developed theories proposing that colors could transmit to the eye effects similar to the effect of music on the ear.

11. Saadi of Shiraz (ca. 1213–ca. 1291), a poet writing in Arabic and Persian, author of *The Rose Garden*, one of the best-known literary works of the Muslim world, and a text translated with much enthusiasm by English Orientalists.

12. Juana de Mancini, the daughter of an Italian nobleman and a Venetian courtesan, marries a Captain Diard, whom she finally kills because he has gambled away all their money, a drama recounted by Balzac in *Les Marana* (1834). The Vicomtesse de Beauséant is abandoned by her Portuguese lover, the Marquis Miguel d'Ajuda Pinto, then by Colonel Franchessini, before she goes to seek refuge in Normandy, where she finds a new lover, Gaston de Nueil, as recounted in *Le Père Goriot* (1835) and *La Femme Abandonée* (1832). Julie de Chatillonest marries her cousin the Marquis Victor d'Aiglemont, who abandons her to a melancholy year in an isolated château, though she finally returns to Paris high society and marries Charles de Vandenesse in *La Femme de Trente Ans* (1832). Jeanne-Clémentine-Athénaïs de Blaumont-Chavry marries the Marquis d'Espard at the age of sixteen, but he leaves her because of her lavish spending, as recounted in *L'Interdiction* (1836).

13. Admiral Gaspard de Coligny (1519–72), a champion of Protestantism, was renowned for his tenacity in the wars he fought first as a Catholic and then as a Huguenot in the sixteenth century.

14. Niobe was the daughter of Tantalus in Greek mythology and went into deep mourning when her children were slaughtered.

15. The protagonists of Molière's play *Le Misanthrope*.

16. The word used by Muslims and Persians in the Middle Ages and afterward to refer to Western Europe, "the land of the Franks."

17. Jean Bart (1650–1702), born in Dunkirk, first served in the Dutch navy, then as a privateer in the French service; he became renowned for his abilities to break blockades and capture enemy ships.

18. Louis René Quentin de Richebourg, Marquis de Champcenetz (1723–1813), in charge of the Tuileries Palace at the time of the French Revolution. He escaped the Terror through the help of Grace Dalrymple Elliott.

19. The king's intimate circle.

20. A new hairstyle fashioned by Madame Martin, the hairdresser to Louis XIV, in 1671, in which a woman's hair was shaped into two mounds of curls on either side of the head. It was at first hated and ridiculed by the woman of letters Madame de Sévigné, who was eventually won over and recommended the style to her daughter.

21. Manuel de Godoy, Duke of Alcudia (1767–1851), was given the title of Prince of the Peace for his role in negotiating peace between Spain and France in 1795.

22. Jean-Baptiste Bernadotte (1763–1844), a leading French marshal in the Napoleonic armies and the author of a book of maxims, *The Art of War*, subsequently becoming Charles XIV, king of Sweden and Norway, in 1818.

23. Style named after Leonardo da Vinci's portrait *La Belle Ferronière*, a favorite in the court of François I, with the hair parted down the middle and held in place by a gold chain or diadem.

24. Jephthah was an Old Testament judge who, in order to defeat the Ammonites, promised Jehovah that he would burn whoever came out of his house first when he returned home: to his grief, it was his daughter, but he carried out the sacrifice to fulfill his vow.

25. The Comte de Rancé (1626–1700) became the founder of Trappism after the sudden, unexpected death of his lover, Marie de Montbazon, from measles or scarlet fever. He purportedly discovered her death by coming home to find her disfigured corpse. Already the abbot of la Trappe at that time, he went on to institute the monastic reforms that created the especially austere discipline the Trappist order is known for.

26. Armide, the princess of Damascus, defeats King Godefroi of Jerusalem and then wants to kill one of his knights, Renaud, but finds she can't stab him to death—her love for him stops her. She takes him to her palace in the desert, but he eventually escapes. Armide spends the rest of her life despairing in her palace. The story is recounted in Torquato Tasso's epic poem *La Gerusalemme Liberata* (Jerusalem Delivered), which was adapted into an opera, *Armide*, by Jean-Baptiste Lully (1686).

OTHER NEW YORK REVIEW CLASSICS

For a complete list of titles, visit www.nyrb.com.